Praise for ...

'Funny, often agonisingly sad – and familiar' *The Lady*

'Witty ... this is a
delightfully irreverent look at growing older' *The Spectator*

'Some great laugh out loud moments' *Woman & Home*

'Wise, funny and heart-warming' *Daily Mail*

'Ironside once again serves up a charming mix: gossip,
revelations and acerbic aperçus' *Independent*
(on *No! I Don't Need Reading Glasses!*)

'I once thought I was Bridget Jones and now I want to be
Marie Sharp: funny, sensible, poignant, life-affirming,
entertaining and oh so human' *BookBag*

'Full of humour and warmth, it also had many insights that
anyone over sixty will recognise and relate to; it's certainly
an entertaining read' *Choice*

'Amusing, unguarded and of the moment, Ironside's
observations will strike a chord with baby-boomers'
Independent (on *No! I Don't Want to Join a Bookclub!*)

'The book ripples with shrewd, comic observations of the
way we live now. Anyone even approaching Marie's age
will find this a fine guide to growing old disgracefully'
Reader's Digest

Also by Virginia Ironside

No! I Don't Need Reading Glasses!
No! I Don't Want to Join a Bookclub
The Virginia Monologues
Janey and Me
You'll Get Over It – the Rage of Bereavement
Goodbye, Dear Friend – Coping with the Death of a Pet
Problems! Problems! Confessions of an Agony Aunt
How to Have a Baby and Stay Sane
Made for Each Other
Distant Sunset
Chelsea Bird

Children's Books

The Huge Bag of Worries
Phantom of Burlap Hall
SpaceBoy at Burlap Hall
Vampire Master
Poltergeist of Burlap Hall
The Human Zoo
Roseanne and the Magic Mirror

Yes!
I can manage
Thank You!

Virginia Ironside

Quercus

First published in Great Britain in 2014 by Quercus Publishing Ltd
This paperback edition published in Great Britainin 2015 by

Quercus Publishing Ltd
Carmelite House
50 Victoria Embankment
London EC4Y 0DZ

An Hachette UK company

A CIP catalogue record for this book is available
from the British Library

PB ISBN 978 1 78206 931 7
EBOOK ISBN 978 1 78429 191 4

10 9 8 7 6 5 4 3 2 1

Typeset by CC Book Production

Printed and bound in Great Britain by Clays Ltd, St Ives plc

For David Collard

JANUARY

January 2

Oh gawd. A whole year flashed by without my writing my diary. I'm clearly a bit of a flibbertigibbet. 'A flighty or whimsical person, usually a young woman,' says Google. So at 66, just about to be 67, that rules *me* out.

But now I'm starting all over again. The new year should begin, of course, with me full of beans, but two grisly things have happened. The first was when I went to the corner shop yesterday to buy some more milk. I always run out of milk on public holidays and, as I hadn't got dressed, I had to hitch my nightie under my coat and race there – as much as anyone over 60 can race – in my slippers. Much to my relief, the road was deserted.

However, as I was hastening back, milk in hand – and I'd also bought half a bottle of Courvoisier on the spur of the moment, remembering I'd used up my last supply in the brandy butter for the Christmas pud – I saw a group of chattering people on the pavement in front of me. Even though it was bitterly cold, it was sunny, and standing on the kerb was a large black guy with no shirt on, cradling a can of Special Brew in one hand and high-fiving a group of lads with the other. All of them were, I guessed, still pissed from the night before. One was dressed as a native dancer, a grass skirt straining under his belly, another wore a huge jester's hat on his head. Sitting on the pavement was a knackered-looking bloke, gloomily sipping at a bottle of lager and dressed as a crocodile. I was about to give them a wide berth when I spotted, coming in the opposite direction, Father Emmanuel, who runs the evangelical church next door. He was heading straight towards me and looked more than usually disapproving.

We met only feet away from the roistering group, and much to my horror Father Emmanuel started pontificating to no one in particular, in a voice clearly Intended to be Heard by the group.

'Drunk! At this hour of God's morning!'

I was just about to utter some non-committal comment and hurry on but was so eager to make a speedy escape, I inadvertently relaxed the clutch on my coat and the hem of my nightie fell to the ground, whereupon I was revealed in all my bed-time glory. There were a few cheers and, I think, a wolf-whistle. Flustered but, I have to say, not entirely unflattered, I tripped and the bottle of brandy slipped from my pocket and shattered on the pavement, filling the air with the reeking smell of alcohol.

As I hobbled past the revellers, the black guy shouted, 'Happy New Year, grandmother!'

I made it back home, sweating with embarrassment.

What would Father Emmanuel think? He'd clearly have me down as a raging alcoholic (not that far from the truth, actually). And as for 'grandmother' – honestly! I spent a small fortune on a facelift a couple of years ago, and look pretty good though I say it myself. To be now addressed by every passing piss-artist as 'grandmother' is a bit much.

I consoled myself with the fact that it would have been worse if I *weren't* a grandmother, but I am – a granny to my adorable Gene who's now all of seven years old.

However, a far more sinister incident was to follow.

Safely indoors, I skimmed the paper: 'New Year Doomsday! Chancellor predicts quadruple dip and worst economic crisis in history. Thousands homeless!' (Yes, I'm afraid I've returned to the *Daily Rant*.) I chatted on the phone with Jack, who rang to wish his old mum a happy New Year while he was out in the park with Gene, trying to fly a kite (rather him than me). I ran my bath and, after checking in the mirror to see that my facelift hadn't suddenly dropped during the night and I'd turned into the heroine in the last chapter of Rider Haggard's novel *She*, I slipped into my bath through the warm bubbles and decided to have a good old luxuriate.

Apart from the minor incidents of that morning, I was thinking I'm pretty lucky. I know my beloved Hughie – one of my best friends – and my beloved Archie have both died, but at least I'm still in fairly good nick. I've had a most fulfilling few years since retiring from teaching art at a girls' school, and I'm still congratulating myself on having prevented the local Council from giving planning permission for a hotel on the tiny strip of green at the top of the road. Gene gets more adorable each year, though how I simply don't know, and he still appears to enjoy coming over to see what he calls his 'old gran' for the odd night. I still seem to be speaking to my ex-husband, David, a fact which appears – considering most of my friends are still at loggerheads with their exes, sometimes 40 years on – to be a total miracle. My great friend Penny, who helped with the hotel protest, lives a stone's throw away; my other great friend, James, Hughie's boyfriend, is a neighbour, and my old school friend Marion and her husband Tim live just down the road. I've got a nice little family of friends around me and I love them all.

As I added more hot water to my bath, I mulled over the list of New Year's Resolutions that I'd made yesterday.

1. Get a new lodger.
Michelle, my old lodger, or rather my old young French lodger, has moved in with Ned, the tree expert who helped us with our campaign to fight the hotel. Everyone thought he was gay to start with but apparently he was only experimenting, and ended up with Michelle – much to the disappointment of James who had rather fallen for him. Oh dear. And much as I like having the place to myself, come night-time I have to say I would prefer to have someone else in the house as well. And I want a man. Don't get me wrong.

I don't want a man *per se* and I'm *certainly* not looking for a partner or a lover. No thanks! I want a man to protect me. And the house.

2. Get fit.

Now I've always been against getting fit. I did have a gym jag, but the place was so smelly! And the music! And the embarrassment of putting on those funny clothes and wobbling around in front of sweating, ebony men – some with bandanas round their heads just to make sure we knew they were 'dudes' who were lifting weights and running on treadmills all day – was too dispiriting and humiliating. 'As we slow down,' Penny once told me, 'we owe it to our bodies to do some work on our muscles and hearts.' She explained there's something that insurance people have identified which means, these days, we all tend to remain fit as fleas till the eleventh hour and then drop dead instantaneously – like falling off a cliff, rather than following a treacherous downwards slope involving the inability to walk, wheelchairs, general gasping, forgetfulness and bonkersness. Sounds a very good idea indeed. So I will start a fitness regime.

3. Do more painting.

A couple of years ago I took up painting again. I did a whole series of pictures of the two trees at the top of the road, trees which had been threatened with being cut down when the idea of the hotel was mooted – and one of which, though I say it myself, I bravely clambered up in order to get publicity for our 'Save the Trees' campaign. Indeed, the pix were so good that my neighbours Brad and Sharmie, the Americans next door, actually bought them for a huge sum of money. Which I still haven't spent.

4. Make a plan.

To be happy, according to a jolly interesting article in the *Daily Rant*, you have to have three goals: one goal that's next week, one goal next year and one goal for the future generally. Now my goal for next week is to start putting my resolutions into action, so I've just got next year's and general future goals to sort out. I have a feeling this proposition was made by someone young, because when you're 66 going on 67 there isn't a hell of a lot of future to look forward to. My long-term plan should be, of course, to move into a more manageable house. Or a flat. Or, heaven forbid, a bungalow. Certainly by the time I've got to the top floor of this place (and I haven't tried for a few months because it's so daunting) I need a slab of Kendal Mint cake to recover.

5. Clear my house out from top to bottom.

I think I made this resolution a couple of years ago but still haven't got round to it. I need to label everything and sort things out and put them in boxes so when the time comes poor old Jack won't be left with the insuperable task of sorting out reams of love-letters and frightful old jerseys, sandwich-makers, broken cat-baskets, moth-eaten cushions and clothes-dryers etc, things I've always thought 'might come in useful one day' but actually have never come in useful ever.

6. Try some new illegal drugs.
It would be a shame not to, wouldn't it, while there's still time? I gather Ecstasy makes one feel incredibly friendly towards everyone, so why not? Just once? I remember taking a few drugs in the Sixties but getting a bit freaked out, after I'd smoked heroin on one occasion, by a dream that I'd covered baby Jack with passionate kisses and woken the next morning (in the dream, this is) to find him covered with the most horrible bruises. Don't think I'll be trying *that* again!

Well, I was just scratching around in my head to think of the next resolution (though surely six resolutions are enough, considering I've stopped smoking, and I'm not going to give up drinking alcohol until I'm 70 and may not even then: I might do the reverse and start boozing like billy-o) when I breathed in, my tummy rose to the surface of the water and I noticed a puzzling sight. One side seemed to be higher than the other.

I checked again and then felt my tummy. Left side, absolutely fine, springy and tummy-like. Right side, however, another story. Swollen and hard. Swooshing away the bubbles, I discovered a lump that was pinkish and had little spots on it. It *really* freaked me out. I've constantly examined my breasts for lumps, but never thought of giving my tummy a going-over as well. I kept pressing and fiddling and wondering how deep it went and wondering if I'd accidentally swallowed a stone or something, which had got trapped . . . was it a very late ectopic pregnancy? The odd thing was that it didn't hurt a bit. But it was terribly sinister.

I lay there with my heart beating and finally got out of the bath, but found that once I stood up the whole room had gone all swimmy. I had to sit down on the edge of the bath because I thought I was going to fall over. I put my head between my knees, I felt so faint with anxiety. What on earth *was* it?

There was only one thing for it. Doctor Google. After giving myself a brief rub-down with my towel, I shrugged on my dressing gown, headed for the computer and got to work.

I must have spent at least an hour hunched in front of the screen. Was it elephantiasis? Could it be a dangerous swelling of the Fallopian tubes? An infected gallstone? Diverticulitis? (Pretty worrying, that, because unless I got it attended to, eventually my bowel might perforate and then it would be curtains.) I went to Google Images and put in 'tummy' – which took me to loads of pictures of grossly fat people who'd had tummy tucks. Far down the pages, there were people with hernias and enlarged prostates. I had pretty much convinced myself I'd got prostate cancer when it dawned on me (spotting all the pictures were of blokes) that prostates weren't things that women had.

I couldn't understand why I couldn't diagnose my problem. I'm of an age, now, when I could quite easily get a job as a doctor. Just give me a white coat and a stethoscope and I'd be able to recognize most ailments. If I haven't had the specific conditions personally, my friends have had them. And as all we do these days is talk about our afflictions and go and visit friends in hospital, we're all pretty expert in the workings of each other's innards, not to mention the symptoms of diabetes, heart attacks, Alzheimer's, macular degeneration, arthritis, detached retinas and polymyalgia, to name just a few. And now I've got the hang of prostates, I think I can count myself fully qualified.

Finally, after scouring medical site after medical site, I came to the unhappy conclusion that it could only be stomach cancer. Which, of course, I'd really known all along.

I was tempted to rush off to the doctor straight away, but it was a public holiday. And because of the way New Year fell this year, today is another. Anyway, I think I'll leave it a few days. I mustn't panic. And who knows, it might just disappear overnight. These things can.

I remember once limping painfully to my doctor with an enormous spot on my left foot which was absolutely agonizing. Every night it suppurated with a discharge so bad that I had to bandage it and change the dressing every night. I could only wear carpet slippers and even they were painful. Eventually it got so horrible to look at, I just swathed it in lint and didn't look any more. When I finally got to see the doctor, some days later, I hobbled in and blurted out the symptoms.

'Let's have a look at it,' he said. So I eased my foot out of the slipper to show him – and blow me if the blasted thing hadn't vanished. It appeared to have healed completely.

'But only a few days ago . . .' I said. 'It was huge . . . it was agony!'

He gave me one of those reassuringly direct smiles you give to mad old ladies who say the CIA are bugging their flats, made a note on his pad (which I suspect read, 'Marie Sharp: Early dementia?') and I crawled away feeling like an absolute idiot.

So I've made a resolution. I'm not going to mention the lump to *anyone* yet, because I might just be worrying unnecessarily and there's no point worrying everyone else if it's nothing. Which I'm sure it is.

I'm *sure* it is.

January 3

Penny came over this morning to have coffee. She's panicking because she suspects her daughter Jill is thinking of divorcing her very nice husband Alan, and they only married last year.

Penny was looking very nice, in a blue cashmere jersey she'd been given for Christmas. (Why is it that everyone else seems to be given presents that delight them, presents they can bear to wear or eat or display, while only ungrateful old me seems to receive presents that hardly leave the wrapping paper before they're bunged straight on the pile for the charity shop or, if they're remotely bearable, into the recycling present drawer?)

'Jill says that, although he's very kind, a good provider and they have great sex, she doesn't love him any more,' she said to me despairingly.

'Love?' I said, incredulous. 'Honestly, to think of how we used to bang on about it! She should be grateful that he's halfway normal!'

'I know,' said Penny, shaking her head. 'And yet I was just like her at her age. Bill was an old sweetie and I fancied him rotten, but I still left him. Can't remember why, now.'

'Just the same with David,' I said, talking of my ex. 'Totally dishy, a soul-mate, funny, generous, faithful. But oh no, I didn't "love" him, so I left him. Sometimes I look back and think I was a bit dotty but then I remember how he used to pick his feet in bed. Not sure how I could stand that, however brilliant he was in every other way.'

David had left about 15 years ago – or rather, I booted him out on account of not 'loving' him – but oddly, after all the understandable bitterness, we've actually become quite close. I think it's because I felt it was such a shame to waste all that friendship and affection we'd invested in each other. And we had a son together, for heaven's sake. Cutting him out of my life seemed ridiculous, like throwing away a perfectly good skirt when just by shortening or lengthening it you could make something eminently wearable for a few more years. Or, as David put it, it's like making stock out of chicken bones rather than throwing away the carcass. Not, of course, that he is remotely like a chicken. Or, indeed, a carcass.

'You've got to get your money's worth out of a relationship!' I said to him jokingly when I'd last seen him. 'I'm determined to squeeze every drop out of you, and I hope you're planning the same with me.'

'Sure thang,' he said in the fake American accent that used to drive me up the wall when we were married. Does it bother me now? Hmm. A little bit. And then there were his frightful right-wing views about the miners' strike. And mustn't forget the fact that he used to come home pissed every Saturday. And the lying. And the broken promises . . . God, when I look back it was pretty frightful. But it's all different when you're not actually living with someone. Not being quite so close means those things don't matter any more. It's Sandra, the younger model he took up with after we divorced, who has to put up with them now, not me. I just have a very nice friendship with him instead.

I often think it's a shame, though, that David didn't end up with someone rather more congenial than Sandra – a girl I have nothing in common with at all. It would be good if he could find someone more on his own wavelength.

Anyway, back to Penny. I told her about Michelle moving out with Ned and explained how I needed a new lodger. Male preferably. 'The reason I want a male lodger is that I'm a bit fed up with women,' I said. 'Having worked all my life in a girls' school, eventually they got on my nerves. Someone told me that when a lot of women spend time together, as they do in convents, they all eventually start to have synchronized periods. So I'd often have to hold my breath in the staff room, just in case any of the lunar hormones, or whatever they were, got to me and I'd start working in some ghastly physical unison with the English teacher, the geography teacher or the biology teacher. Or even, heaven forbid, the daunting headmistress herself.'

'And men are so useful about the house,' gushed Penny. 'They can kill rats, unstick windows, put bulbs into inaccessible sockets and, with their heavy footsteps and booming voices, they can frighten burglars away when they get in.'

'They can also keep burglars away *before* they get in, just by their masculine presence being spotted regularly at the front door,' I added.

'Talking of rats,' said Penny, 'wasn't there some experiment done with the wretched things, to show that if you get a box of male rats and shove a female in, all the males instantly start behaving better, applying deodorant, twirling their whiskers and saying "After you" before entering the sewers? Similarly, take a box of female rats and add a male, and all the females stop gossiping and shopping and instead behave like normal human beings. If a rat can, ever, behave like a normal human being.'

She had a point. I know I'm not a bunch of female rats, but I think the presence of a man improves the behaviour and performance of even a single female (and certainly vice versa). And it would be nice to see if the presence of a chap could force me into getting dressed in the morning, instead of slopping round in an old dressing gown till midday, and maybe even putting on some make-up every morning. Much needed, clearly, after the incident in the street on New Year's Day.

I was absolutely determined to say nothing about the lump on my tummy, and managed to keep my mouth shut until the very moment Penny got up to leave.

'Isn't it your birthday soon?' she asked. 'I must say you're looking very well for someone of 152.'

And suddenly, from somewhere outside myself, I heard a strange sobbing voice. 'Well, actually, I'm not very well,' it said. 'I've got this horrible lump and I'm really frightened and I don't know what to do . . .' and before I knew where I was, Penny was sitting next to me on the sofa and she'd got her arms round me and she was saying, 'Now, what's all this? What lump, where?' and I realized that the disembodied voice had been mine and I'd told her, despite my great resolve to be stoical and keep it to myself.

Honestly, sometimes I feel I'm like a ghastly child who occasionally escapes from the watchful eyes of her strict nanny.

'I didn't mean to tell you,' I wailed. 'I don't know why I did. I'm sorry. I don't want to worry you, and it's so silly. It's on my tummy, I don't even know what it is, but it's probably nothing . . .'

'You must see the doctor,' said Penny, holding my hands in hers. (Pouncer, my cat, was looking up at us warily from his spot on the floor, his whiskers bristling.) 'Of course it's nothing. You probably knocked it, and it's some kind of bruise. And when you're old you get funny lumps in you all the time. We're all like old duvets, you know, bits knotted up, spaces where you can see through to the daylight, it's perfectly normal . . .'

'Oh, God,' I said. 'I think I'd rather have cancer than go around like some ghastly old duvet. What a dreadful idea.'

After making her swear on her mother's grave that she wouldn't tell anyone, not even James, she made me swear on my mother's grave that I would make an appointment to see the doctor tomorrow. Oh gawd, oh gawd, oh gawd.

January 7

The next day, I'd staggered downstairs in my dressing gown, made my usual breakfast of toast and Marmite and a cup of tea, given Pouncer his disgusting food, and begun running my bath. I'd read a bit of the *Rant* – 'Husband butchers wife after wife butchers five kids' – and thought that, as I'd promised, I'd *better* make an appointment with the doctor. I'd finally got through – the surgery seemed to be permanently engaged, no doubt due to everyone trying to wriggle out of ever having to go back to work after the lengthy Christmas break – and was just about to ask for an appointment when I heard a familiar splashing sound and realized the bath had overflowed. Again. This is happening on such a regular basis now, I wonder I don't keep buckets in position in the kitchen. 'I'll ring you back!' I shouted, and raced (quite pleased to find that in an emergency I *can* actually race, old-style) up the stairs to turn off the bath and pull out the plug, then back to the kitchen and up on a chair with a saucepan to put it on top of the cupboard and catch the torrent coming through the crack in the ceiling. Then I raced up again to get a couple of towels from the bathroom, raced down and put them on the floor to soak it all up, and everything was right as rain. Perhaps not the aptest description, considering.

Have decided to buy a little timer – to set whenever I run a bath – so when it pings, I can just nip up and turn the taps off.

When I finally got through to the surgery again, I was told that my usual doctor was away for the next fortnight. So, rather than make an appointment with a complete stranger, I booked in for her first available appointment – I doubt if I'll die in a fortnight – and put down the phone muttering.

How dare these doctors ever go away! I do think they're frightfully inconsiderate. I don't see why they should even have weekends off, and preferably they should stay up all night and every night for emergencies. It may not be physically possible but they should have thought of that before they became doctors. Anyway, I feel better for having made the appointment.

Today I'm invited by Jack and Chrissie, my daughter-in-law, for a special pre-birthday tea. My actual birthday's next week but Gene wouldn't have been able to come if we'd had it on the proper day because he's got a party. (He seems to spend his entire time at parties these days.) I've asked James to come along too. I just hope I don't have to drive all over London in this downpour with the windscreen wipers whining away. It's raining like mad.

Later

I shouldn't have mentioned windscreen wipers. They screeched and smeared and jerked all through our journey and James couldn't stop going on about how ghastly my car is. It's all very well. He inherited masses of money when Hughie died, so he's been able to afford something called a Hybrid. God knows what it is, but I gather it's a car that sings while it dances while it skims along on nothing but air, tells you when you're going to back into something, stops of its own accord when little blonde-haired children run into the road in front of you, and is as environ-bloody-mentally friendly as you can get. The thing is, it's so state-of-the-art that when it goes wrong the garage doesn't know whether to call an electrician, an osteopath, a magician or just give the front bumper a good kick. But the upshot is that it's the coolest thing on the road, with a dashboard covered in dials like a jet aeroplane – and the smuggest car I know.

Mine, on the other hand is absolutely knackered. As James told me again and again, all the way to Brixton.

He'd warmed to his theme when I pulled out my keys to open the passenger door.

'You can't have a car these days that doesn't have central locking, darling!' he said. 'Those went out with the Ark. You'll probably tell me that somewhere you've got an old crank-shaft to start it up with when you break down.'

We got into the car and he fiddled with his seatbelt. As we pulled away, I laughed. 'No, there's no crank-shaft. But at least with this car I know all about it, unlike you, faced with your state-of-the-art engineering. I know about the spark plugs and how to clean them and the fan-belt and . . .'

'What?' said James. 'I can't hear you! That's the other thing – it's so noisy!'

I repeated what I'd said.

'Marie, please! Cars don't have spark plugs or fan-belts these days,' said James. 'Not even this one. Get a new car, please. Not for my sake, but for yours! This is the most frightful old wreck.'

To be honest, I had been thinking of getting a new car for some time. Darling Archie, the love of my life, who died a couple of years ago, had left me some money and so far I hadn't spent any of it. Plus,there was Brad and Sharmie's tree picture money. And as my car was getting increasingly wobbly, it had crossed my mind.

'But my garage man said to me the other day: "They don't make them like this any more"!' I said.

'And you took that as a compliment?' shouted James, sarcastically, over the engine noise, and then he started listing all the things wrong with the car. No power steering. A tape deck instead of a CD player. ('I expect you wind back your broken tapes with old biros, am I right?' He was.) A glove compartment that's lost its flap. A spare tyre (apparently cars these days don't have spare tyres, just some kind of spray gadget that you squirt into the hole and seals it up). Windows that wind up by hand. No air conditioning. Or what James called 'air-con'.

'True, it doesn't have orange indicators that rise and fall

like rabbit's ears at the sides, but it might as well have,' he said. 'Frankly, I'm surprised you don't have running boards and a man with a red flag to walk in front of you as you drive.'

After we'd finally parked outside Jack and Chrissie's house, he examined the car from the outside, peering at it from under his umbrella. 'Tyres nearly bald,' he said. 'Terrible paint-work. Very unsafe colour, black. Rust on the back bumper. I'm amazed it passed its MOT.'

I remembered that the garage man had said something else along with 'They don't make them like that any more!', he'd said, 'But you'll find that out soon enough.' So perhaps James is right.

Seconds after we rang the bell, the door opened. Gene had been waiting for us.

'Happy birthday, Granny!' said Gene. 'We're pretending it's Granny's birthday today,' he explained to James, who came in after me, shaking his umbrella. 'It's not really but we're pretending.'

'Hi, Mum!' said Jack, coming into the hall and kissing me. He resisted kissing James, but enfolded him in a curious mas-culine type of hug. Men are so funny when they say hello these days. When I was young they'd barely shake hands, then they moved on to a kind of friendly knock on the shoulder, then they sometimes performed a curious affectionate boxing match, each punching the other in a mock-fighting way, shouting 'Hey, man . . . good on you! Great to see you!! Cheers, mate, how you doing?' But more recently I've seen straight blokes openly kissing each other on the cheeks and some, horror of horrors, on the mouth. But I suppose Jack can't do that to James because he's actually gay. Golly, it's all so complicated.

'Look, we've made a cake and I did the icing,' said Gene, pulling us into the kitchen. 'Look, Granny, look.' I was dragged over to the table, where Chrissie turned from putting things away to greet me. I thought she was looking very tired – unlike her because she's usually so slathered with beauty products that you can't tell how she's really feeling.

'Not now, Gene, the cake's for later,' said Chrissie. 'Happy birthday!' she added, wiping her hands on a very pretty apron covered with roses.

'Now look at all your presents!' said Gene, pointing to a chair covered with parcels. Then he asked, 'Are you very old?'

'I am rather,' I said, mussing his hair. 'I'll be 67 next week.' He looked at me with a start. 'Well, that *is* old!' he said. 'Are you going to die soon?'

Just before tea, I made the disastrous mistake of mentioning Jack's health. He'd had a slight scare about his appendix just after Christmas – it had started grumbling – and naturally, being his old mum, I'd started to get very worried about it. I know his doctor had advised him to have it taken out. So when I said, 'And when are you having your appendix out?' I wasn't prepared for the prickly response.

'I'm not having it out, Mum,' he said, sharply. 'There's nothing wrong with it. I've been told by a friend of mine, who's a nurse, that it could last all my life. There's no point in having an operation if I don't need it.'

'But what if it suddenly goes wrong when you're on hol-iday? Miles from anywhere?' I asked.

'Look, I'm not having an operation until I really need it,' said Jack firmly. And I remembered how incredibly paranoid he was about being ill. When he was young he'd had to go into hospital overnight for some minor op and a mixture of being left alone and the food had put him off for life, I think.

I felt rather chastened, but relieved when Chrissie, from behind Jack, raised her eyebrows at me and shook her head, meaning she agreed with me.

Once we'd all sat down, the present-opening started. Chrissie, naturally enough, had given me a whole bag of beauty products from the company where she works (another pile of stuff destined for Age Concern as I'm a totally soap-and-water girl myself). I only wished she'd given me a rose-covered apron like the one she was wearing. Jack had got me a huge flat-pack model of the Taj Mahal to cut out and make – I've always been fascinated by paper models – and a real taxidermy duck with a boater on. Now, there's a chap who knows exactly what his old mum wants! I adore this sort of thing!

And then, 'Remember that thing of your dad's,' said Chrissie suddenly – and Jack pulled out another present from behind the chair.

'David?' I said, astonished. 'All his life, he's never remem-bered my birthday, even when we were married! I'm amazed he remembered. How sweet of him!'

I opened it up and found it was a box of the most delicious Turkish Delight.

Not only that but it was the special brand I really love – one that's only available from a Turkish Delight shop down some mysterious side-street in Istanbul. It's Turkish Delight heaven – floors of the stuff, walls of the stuff, Turkish Delight with nuts in it, Turkish Delight with raisins, rose-flavoured Turkish Delight, lemon-flavoured Turkish Delight, Turkish Delight in huge wooden boxes and Turkish Delight in fancy decorated tins.

'How on earth did he get hold of this, I wonder?'

'Oh, some friend of his was going – you know the Widow Bossom woman who lives next door and is always trying to get her claws into him – and when she asked if she could get him anything while she was there, he remembered about the Turkish Delight you liked,' said Jack.

'That was very nice of him,' I said.

Finally, Gene gave me a small packet of Smarties and a home-made card showing a rather serious picture of a tree. 'I wanted to do a tree like you do, Granny,' he said, coming up and showing me. 'Do you like the way I've done the branches growing, like you told me? And there's the shadow of the tree along the ground, like you said. And do you like the Smarties? Can I have some?'

'Not before tea,' said Jack, sternly. During tea Gene was pretty silent as we were in the middle of talking about schools and the problems of finding the right one for the next phase of his life. Then he suddenly interrupted.

'Not now, Gene,' said Jack, 'We're talking!'

'But it's about schools!' said Gene. 'My school wants you to come and talk to us about the war, Granny,' he said. 'Will you come? Were you a Land Girl? Did you drive ambulances? Were you evacuated? Did you know lots of people who died?'

'No, I didn't, darling, because I was born just after the war, so I don't remember anything much about it except for the sirens near my grandmother's house in the country that for quite some time after used to wail twice a day at a certain time. I remember Mummy – that's your great-granny – shuddering with fear.' I felt disappointed that I couldn't come to Gene's school and tell them about doodlebugs and sleeping in Underground stations like those people in Henry Moore sketches.

'It doesn't matter. Just after's okay. My teacher said. You can tell us about . . . um . . . horses and carriages?' he asked, doubtfully. 'Did your dad wear a top hat? Did you have a butler? Did you have a toilet that was a hole in the ground? Did you have to work in a factory making things, with no holidays?'

Chrissie produced a letter and gave it to me. It was from the school. It read,

'Hi Granny, Nan or Granddad!!! We in Year Two are doing a project on the Second World War and we are trying to find out everything about it! We would like to ask you some question's about it. Will you come in and talk to us about what you remember about the War? We will try to make it interesting for you, we will give you coffee and biscuits. Love from . . .' And here Gene had written his name.

'Who wrote this?' I asked.

'The form teacher,' said Chrissie. 'I know, I know. There shouldn't be an apostrophe in "questions".'

'And,' I added indignantly, 'what about that comma between "you" and "we"? Should be a full stop. Well, one thing I can tell them about the old days is that at school we were at least taught how to punctuate properly.'

'You can tell Mum used to be a teacher, can't you?' said Jack, grinning at James. 'By the way, Gene, have you done your homework?'

'Uurrr,' said Gene moodily, mooching off into the other room.

When it was time to go – me feeling very happy and yet sad to leave them, of course – Gene brought his teddy out onto the step to say goodbye. It was the old one that I'd had when I was young and had passed on to Jack who'd passed it on to Gene, and I could see my little darling making the battered creature wave his stuffed paw as we drove into the darkness. Little had I imagined, when I was Gene's age and hugging my teddy to me, that I'd be seeing it in the arms of my grandson, waving to me.

The rain, thank God, had stopped, leaving the roads glistening with silver wetness.

'Now let's get down to your real birthday,' said James.

'Marion and Tim are giving me supper,' I said. 'As you know. The usual. Hope you'll be there.'

'I'll take you out for dinner some time soon so we can have something delicious to make up for Marion's cooking,' said James. 'But first you've got to tell me what you want as a present.'

We spent the next ten minutes wrestling over what I want.

So tricky. When you're 12, there's no end to what you want for your birthday. When you're 67, there is no beginning to what you want – because you want nothing. He and I were both in agonies trying to think of something I might like.

Eventually I said, 'Look, this is mad. I'm in agonies, you're in agonies. I really don't want anything, I'm so sorry.'

'I can't give you *nothing*!' said James indignantly. Not sure why he can't give me nothing, but still.

'Look, you're taking me out to dinner, and that in itself is a lovely birthday present. And if you like you can get me some flowers. I love flowers,' I added. 'But not orange ones.'

He seemed relieved. 'Very nice of David to get you the Turkish Delight,' he added. 'Wonder if Sandra knows?'

David insists on calling Sandra his 'squeeze'. She's miles younger than him, nearly half his age, and although she's quite nice, she's a bit of an airhead. Originally they had horses in common, because David's always been keen on racing, but neither of them seem that interested now. And I've noticed she's always going off on holiday on her own. I imagine they have a brilliant sex life – at least I can't think of anything else that would keep them together – and though David's vastly improved since the old days and has at least cut down on the drinking which makes a lot of difference. I can't imagine why she wants to stay with him. He's virtually retired and has always been adamant he doesn't want more children, so she's just hanging about, going to the gym, having beauty treatments and doing nothing much else as far as I can see.

'Very nice of the Widow Bossom, rather,' I said. 'She's the one who's bought it. I bet there's some ulterior motive.'

'Trying to ingratiate herself with the ex-wife?' suggested James.

'Something like that. David would never do anything along those lines off his own bat. Anyway, good luck to her. To be honest, the Widow Bossom would be a lot better than Sandra – at least she's a jolly sort and more his age.'

'So what's the plan for the coming year?' asked James as we trundled along. 'Apart, of course, from getting a new car. Would you like me to research what's available for you? I'm quite good at that sort of thing.'

At this I perked up considerably. 'What about a Mini?' I said. 'I like them. I used to have one in the old days.'

'They're not like the old ones,' he said. 'I'll do some research.'

'My plans are just to keep on trucking,' I said, thinking suddenly of the lump on my tummy and wondering how long I'd got to truck (though I've never seen the verb used this way). Funnily enough, I could actually feel it, Being A Lump, under my seatbelt. I wondered briefly whether to tell James about it or not, and then decided against it. I must try to keep as quiet about it as possible. 'And you?'

After Hughie died, James has tried his hand at all sorts of things – he's only in his fifties – and a couple of years ago he decided, much to my fury, to be what he calls 'an artist'. His first project was to do an installation of yours truly, a huge and frightful affair constructed of barbed wire, old plastic bags, a walking frame and plastic Coke bottles. It was only a couple of months ago that, after the judicious placing of it in the most exposed part of the garden and gently loosening the wires every so often, the thing conveniently collapsed and I was obliged to chuck it in the bin – much to my regret (as I told James) and much to my delight (as I told everyone else).

I must say, I find his artistic ambitions infuriating. It's because, as someone who's spent her entire life learning how to draw and paint, then teaching people how to draw and paint (and I'm talking here of trees, faces, hands, bodies, landscapes, still lifes – or is it still lives? – you name it); and also as someone who really can draw, though I say it myself, like an angel, it's pretty irritating to hear a chap who hardly knows which end of a pencil to use calling himself an 'artist'. It implies a measure of accomplishment that James simply does not possess.

I have even heard him – across the table from me at a dinner party, when someone's asked him what he does – replying, 'I'm an artist!' I mean! Surely it's only *other people* who can declare that you're an artist? Calling yourself an artist is rather like describing yourself as incredibly attractive, creative and clever.

Anyway, I didn't let on. And yes, he said, he was going to devote this coming year to making more art. He'd got some ideas about lines, spaces and colour, he said, and he thought he could make them 'relevant'. I felt like saying, 'What is any visual art but lines, spaces, colour and some kind of relevance?' but bit my tongue and we talked about cars the rest of the way home.

'See you on your real birthday, darling,' he said as he got out. 'Lots of love, my angel.'

Then I thought, as usual, what a creep I'd been with my thoughts about him being an artist. Why shouldn't he call himself an artist if that's what makes him happy, for God's sake? I went back home feeling loathsome and wretched but, after a large glass of red wine, cheered up.

January 15

My birthday! And I'm 67! Golly, it sounds a lot older than 66, I must say. I got lots of cards, including one from Penny which said 'Holy Shite! You're 67!' with a woman screaming on the front. Penny had written in '67' in felt-tip pen over the '40', because presumably you can't custom-make cards for every age. I also got a lovely one from Brad and Sharmie, with 'We'll miss you lots!' written inside it. (They're moving to India, where Brad has a new job.) James had sent me one which had on the front 'The older you get, the better you get' and inside 'Unless you're a banana.'

James rang the bell just before I was going to have my bath – it gets later and later these days, not just because of laziness but because I'm so reluctant to confront the ghastly lump – and came in with a large bottle of champagne.

'I didn't bring it this evening,' he said, 'in case everyone else drank it. Once Penny gets her hands on it . . . well, you know . . . I've got another for tonight. This is just for you to drink all by yourself in the lonely watches of the night as you contemplate life at this great age. Though they do say, of course, that drinking alone is one of the sure signs of being an alcoholic.'

'Drinking alone is the *only* time to drink, my darling,' I said. 'The sprightliness of other people's conversation usually gets one by in a crowd, but on one's own, one needs a pick-me-up.' I felt very touched. He stared at the array of cards on the mantelpiece. 'You have so many friends,' he said. 'How do you do it?'

'You've got just the same number of friends,' I said reassuringly. 'But I've picked mine as the types who send birthday cards.'

The lump seemed slightly bigger today, and I'm anxious about what the doctor will say.

Later

Just back from Marion's. She'd said, 'You do want me just to ask the usual suspects, don't you – Penny and James and us?' and I'd replied, 'Absolutely!' I said it rather loudly because she's such a generous person that she's always asking waifs and strays and if you don't watch out, you turn up and discover she's so busy feeding the huddled masses that you might as well not be there at all.

Anyway, this time, it was indeed 'just us' and she'd made an enormous lentil stew, which was absolutely par for the course. Marion's cooking seems to have stopped in the poverty-stricken student days of the Sixties and she is a complete stranger even to mozzarella. I'd be amazed if she's ever heard of garlic or an avocado pear. She's a stranger to fennel or chicory as well. The lentils had been boiled in water flavoured with a chicken cube, to which had been added many tins of tomatoes and some curious tinned mushrooms. As an accompaniment she'd laid out slices of ham from a packet, several tomatoes cut in halves and a salad of a floppy lettuce with dressing on the side, served in a bowl that looked like a lettuce leaf itself – surely a relic from the Fifties – which meant that you had to add the dressing on your plate and it never quite covered the leaves. The dressing itself was that stuff created, oddly, by Paul Newman, the actor. I would have been very surprised to find Nigel Slater cast as Butch Cassidy in a Hollywood movie, but there we are. There was a large sliced loaf on the table, some 'spreadable' stuff that pretended to be butter but was actually a ghastly yellow substance made, probably, from whale blubber, and no salt and pepper to be seen.

Tim, her extremely kind but stodgy husband, tucked in, declaring the whole thing delicious. 'I don't know how my wife does it!' he said. 'She has a real knack for cooking!'

Marion smiled. 'I don't believe in recipe books!' she said, smugly. 'I just throw in any old thing and pray, but it always seems to come out right!'

Penny and I – who both pore over fashionable cookbooks, marinating, weighing, tasting and seasoning all the way through – exchanged looks and it was difficult not to laugh, particularly after Penny'd given me a posh new cookbook for my birthday earlier in the day – but after a few glugs of James' champagne, it didn't really seem to matter any more and even I was persuaded to have a second helping of the cheerful slops that were doled onto our plates.

We chatted of this and that. Marion asked how I'll cope

when Brad and Sharmie leave, and I said I was dreading it. Then she told me she'd heard the house had been sold to a woman called Melanie Fitch-Hughes – whereupon Tim said, 'Not Roger's wife?' and Marion said, 'Ex-wife by the sound of it,' and he said well, if it *was* ex-wife then lucky old Roger because she was a nightmare, and Marion said she was sure it wasn't her, and James said there couldn't possibly be two people called Melanie Fitch-Hughes.

Then Marion got onto Syria. Oh dear. If there's one thing I can't stand, it's people banging on about the dreadful state of the world when there's absolutely nothing at all one can do about it. After she'd gone into a long spiel about how the government was repressing the rebels and how children were dying of chemical weapons and their eyes were falling out into their mothers' laps, and how families were starving in camps, I held up my hand.

'Look, Marion,' I said. 'I love you, and I know Syria's ghastly, but could we possibly keep off the subject on my birthday? I'm trying to have a happy day.'

Tim butted in, rather crossly, I thought.

'But we *should* talk about Syria,' he said. 'We can't just put our heads in the sand. This is real life, Marie, birthday or no birthday.'

Then I was struck by a brilliant riposte. 'Tim,' I said, seriously. 'I think about Syria and the starving refugees all day and all night. I can't sleep for worrying about them. I send money to them and there isn't a moment when I don't offer up thanks that I live in a civilized country, with no war and no guns and no insurgents. But perhaps just for an hour or so, on my birthday, we could have a small moment when I'm not dogged with guilt and misery and compassion? Just a moment?'

Sensing things were getting tricky, James wisely clapped his hands and said: 'I second that! Now for the presents!' And he produced an envelope. I thought it was going to be just a card since he'd already loaded me with champagne, but inside there was a piece of paper which read, 'I promise to introduce the bearer to the pleasures of Facebook any time she wants.' Hmm. Not really sure I want to be on Facebook but everyone assures me that once I get going I'll never be off it, so perhaps it's worth a try.

And then Marion produced her birthday present.

It's always difficult opening a present from Marion. I love her to pieces but she never gets presents right. A couple of years ago she gave me a card telling me that she'd donated a goat on my behalf to Africa which drove me wild with rage, though I never let on, and I suspected this was going to be another howler.

Well, although this wasn't in the goat class it was pretty near. It was a yellow and orange scarf. With fringes at either end. I had never seen anything quite so hideous in my life and I knew that the moment I put it on, my skin would turn a green colour and people would start asking me if I was all right.

But there was nothing for it. Not so much as a split second of horror crossed my face. I radiated delight.

'I love it!' I cried, winding it round my neck. 'Marion, it's brilliant! Thank you *so* much!'

Marion looked incredibly pleased. 'You're so difficult to buy presents for,' she said. 'I'm so glad you like it. I can tell you really do, too ... I know you sometimes pretend ... but I thought it was such a cheerful colour!'

'How right you are!' I said. 'I'll wear it all the time! You are a total angel!' I got up and kissed her.

And felt like Judas.

Later still

Hours have passed in contemplating the scarf. And as I looked back on my performance of delight tonight, I wondered if I wasn't a psychopath. I can be so charming and manipulative sometimes. Then I thought that maybe I was being hard on myself. There was a bit of me that was acting, but the pretence was inspired by a real feeling of warmth to Marion who'd tried so hard to get it right. My acting was prompted by a strong desire not to hurt her and to make her feel okay about the present. So it was an act of kindness to her. At the same time, a bit of me thought: First, has that poor darling ever seen me wear the colour orange? No. (Marion wears orange, true, but not me.) Second: Has she ever seen me wearing a scarf? Again, no.

There are two reasons why not. One is that I always think, on an older woman, they look as if they're hiding a wrinkly neck. And since, after the facelift, I don't have a wrinkly neck, wearing a scarf is pointless. I want to advertise my youthful neck, not hide a wrinkly one.

The other reason is that I have a huge bust, like a shelf. So if I wear a scarf and let it hang down, the result is that, rather than looking like the svelte yet curvy person I really am, I could be mistaken for a gigantic refrigerator. In this case, an orange refrigerator.

It's as if someone were to give me a pair of trousers. I am adamant about not wearing trousers. I think that, as they get older everyone looks increasingly sexless – men and women. Women's voices deepen while men's rise. We start growing faint moustaches and sprouting the odd single hair that sticks out of our chins. Men's beards get mangier as they age. And that's why wild horses won't get me into trousers. I look too much like a bloke in them.

Anyway, I was about to put the scarf into the present drawer, which is where I put little knick-knacks that I think I'd like to give to friends, and occasionally presents I'm given that can be recycled, but then I realized it was one of those presents I couldn't give to anyone because it was so hideous.

So it was bunged in the cupboard under the bathroom sink where I keep all my stuff for Age Concern. Honestly, despite what I say about thinking it sweet of Marion to buy me a present at all, I have to say that when a present is so completely badly judged it's more like an insult. It shows that the giver knows you so little, and has examined you so cursorily, that they don't really know you at all.

I am a horrible, ungrateful, vile person and I don't deserve presents at all. OR NICE FRIENDS.

January 16

Wrote Marion an email and found I'd written 'Thank you for the scummy supper' when I'd meant to write 'Thank you for the scrummy supper.' Oh God.

January 21

Went to see the doc. It was an oddly sunny, freezing day. Even though I was on time, billions of people seemed to have appointments before me, including one woman with a little girl who had a small graze on her knee. To my amazement, after they'd been called into the consulting room and stayed there for what felt like an hour, they emerged, the little girl now with a plaster on her knee.

'I've been so worried,' said the woman to Edna, the receptionist. 'She's never fallen before. I didn't know what to do. The doctor was wonderful!'

After she'd left, Edna looked around the waiting room in general and raised her eyebrows to no one in particular. 'Comes in with her child over a graze! Wouldn't believe it, would you? Some mothers!'

'When I was a boy, me knees was bleedin' all the time,' offered an old gentleman with a hacking cough, sitting on the other side of the room, 'We never 'ad plasters then! Broke both me legs *and* 'ad concussion but we just carried on, didn't we, in them days? Never 'ad no plaster casts or 'ospitals then, my mum just made a splint out of a couple of old broomsticks, bound 'em up with pipe lagging, and next day I was off doin' me paper rounds at four in the morning as if nuffin' 'ad 'appened.'

'They 'ave it too easy, they don't know how lucky they are,' said another old woman, an outsize, spittle-drenched creature with a bandaged arm. 'We just got on wiv it, didn't we? I 'ad ten bruvvers and sisters, all of them carried off with the Spanish flu, just me left, 'ad to look after both me parents, they 'ad TB, *and* I was only eight.'

For a moment I thought how incredibly stupid and wet I was wasting the doctor's time with a trivial lump on my tummy. I should probably just have ignored it or chopped it out with a vegetable knife while biting on a whisky-soaked gag, then dished it up for supper with a bit of parsley, and just carried on. But I was there now and eventually I was called.

Like all doctors these days, mine didn't even acknowledge me as I entered the room, so engrossed was she in the computer screen where, hopefully, she had assembled all my notes. Of course she might have been just sending off amusing pictures to her friends on Facebook, of elephants dancing with owls on their heads, but I gave her the benefit of the doubt.

'Yes?' she said, finally looking up. She's a nice enough old bird, but a bit too reluctant to give me the drugs I'd like. And a bit too alert to such trivial things as high blood pressure, diabetes and cholesterol – but today, apparently, all was well. At least, so far.

I explained my anxieties and she asked to take a look. After unpeeling about a million jerseys, vests, slips and tights, we arrived, like a pair of archaeologists, at the suspect site and there was the lump. Smaller than it had been this morning, of course, because it knew it was coming to the doctor and had decided to downsize itself in order to humiliate me.

'Hmm,' she said, poking and prodding at it. She got me up on a table so she could feel it properly, pressing down with both her palms and getting out a tape measure. She looked puzzled.

I suppose I was secretly hoping that, when she saw the evidence, she'd give a light laugh and say, 'Ho ho! Looks nasty, doesn't it, but actually it's extremely common! It's just a mild eczema-like allergy. Use this cream and it'll be gone in a week!' Or, even better, 'Well, to be honest, it's perfectly normal. In fact I'd be worried if you *didn't* have a lump like that! It usually arrives when you're 50, but in your case, because you're so fit and well, it's come to you rather late. *Lumpus Agealis*, it's called, and if at your age you don't have at least a couple we have to perform an operation to insert them.'

But no. She said nothing. She frowned. She said, 'Hmm,' several times. Finally she said, 'I've never seen anything like this before. You haven't been to the Far East recently, have you, or any exotic location?'

'No further east than Shepherd's Bush,' I said. 'Though no doubt there are some weird diseases around there since the mosque was built. Not,' I added quickly, bearing in mind that she might well be a Muslim herself, 'that I'm being racist. It's just that with a big influx of people from other lands it's inevitable there'll be a big influx of new germs as well.' I imagined the germs lining up at immigration, all wearing tiny hijabs and all bearing false germ passports.

She looked a bit sour.

'And you haven't bumped into anything on that area recently, have you? Fallen down?'

'No more than usual,' I said, lightly.

She looked even more sour. 'I'll take a swab from the rash on the surface,' she said. 'But that might just have arisen because of pressure on your clothes. As for the swelling, I'm sending you for a scan and then on the basis of the results we can see what the next step should be.'

She got out all her kit, scraped away at one of the spots, and put the result into a bottle. 'You can get dressed now,' she said, as she walked back to her seat in front of the computer.

'Everything else all right at home?' she asked. Since 'home' consists only of Pouncer and me, I wasn't sure quite what kind of upsets might qualify, except perhaps a feline uprising against the 'tender salmon pieces in jelly and creamy gravy' that I've been putting before my cat recently. Still, it was kind of her to ask. Then she said, 'Hmm. I see your cholesterol levels were slightly raised last time. I think we'd better do another blood test to make sure they're not rising any more.'

By the time I left the doctor, clutching various pieces of paper, I felt I'd been given a thorough going-over. It was difficult to feel reassured, of course, because I hadn't had an instant diagnosis, but at the same time I felt a sort of load off my mind because now, at least, I didn't have to worry about it too much myself. It was all in the hands of the experts. I hoped they were experts, anyway.

January 22

Got an email this morning from David. No surprise there, but he's coming up to London because he's got to put Sandra on a plane to Goa. As I don't live too far from the airport, he hoped he could take me out for lunch before he drives back to Somerset.

Most odd. What does Sandra do on these solo holidays? And can David really enjoy being left on his own? I wonder if the Widow Bossom is thinking along the same lines as me.

January 24

I'd just got out of the bath this morning – and morning's not the best time for me, never having been a leaper out of bed and yeller of 'Hello, you beautiful day! How lucky I am to be alive!' – and when I saw the lump again, I felt increasingly worried. Every time I look at it or feel it, my heart starts thumping and I get incredibly anxious and frightened. I can't think why, really, because I'm not afraid of dying – and anyway, surely most people in the old days died long before they were my age? Three score years and ten – wasn't that what the Bible said? – and since that's 70, I'd only be three years short. I've done most of the things I want to do in my life. And though I'd love to see Gene grow up, and it would be an awful wrench to leave Jack and Chrissie, we've got to part one day – and besides, it would be good for them not to have a burdensome old mother around. But as I was drying myself, I felt tears of self-pity rolling down my face. And when the phone rang, I assumed it would be Penny – she often rings about this time – so I was rather devastated that, having rushed, rather damply, to pick it up, I heard Marion's voice on the line.

'What's the matter?' she said as she heard my choking 'Hello'.

At the sound of her sympathetic voice, I couldn't pretend any longer and I sobbed and sobbed.

She sounded terribly worried, as well she might.

'It's nothing,' I kept saying. 'Don't worry. It's so silly.'

'But what is it?' she said.

'It's just that I've got this lump,' I said. 'I'm sure it's nothing.'

'Lump?' she said. 'Why didn't you tell me?'

I get jolly irritated if people ask, 'Why didn't you tell me?' when I'm in the middle of telling them.

'I *am* telling you,' I said, through my tears. 'I've got this lump and I've been to the doctor and she's sending me for a scan.'

'Well, you don't have to snap my head off,' said Marion, clearly rather hurt. 'I was only being sympathetic. And anyway, what do you mean, "lump"? What kind of lump?'

'It's weird. It's kind of a lump on my tummy, like a ping-pong ball,' I added. 'And . . . and . . . and it's got these kind of spots on the top . . .' And I burst into tears again.

There was another silence at the end of the phone. Then I heard a sniffing sound.

'Oh, I do hope you haven't got . . . I mean I hope it's not . . .'

'Hope it's not what?' I said, astonished that she should be jumping the gun quite so quickly.

'Well, you know, I know I shouldn't say . . . but you must have thought . . .'

'Thought what?' I said, becoming increasingly irritated.

'That it might be . . .'

'What?' I snapped, irritably. *I* was the one who should be weeping, not her.

'You know, I shouldn't say it, but the Big C!' she blurted out. 'Oh, I can't stand it, all my friends seem to be getting ill or dying, but I couldn't bear it if you . . .' And she started crying again.

I have to say I was completely flabbergasted by her reaction. I felt utterly confused. First I'd blurted it all out to her when I hadn't meant to and now, when she should be comforting me, I found myself expected to comfort her. I felt a bit tetchy.

'Who's talking of dying!' I said. 'And what's all this talk about the Big C? Who is this character? Are you talking about cancer? If so, say the word. Don't disguise it and make it sound like the Jolly Green Giant. God, I'd never have told you if I thought you'd start reacting like this. This is so unlike you, Marion. I was hoping for some sympathy not a load of self-pity!'

'I'm sorry,' she said. 'But you don't understand . . . I couldn't bear it if . . .'

By this time I was so confused and angry, I'm ashamed to say I slammed the phone down and burst into tears again myself. Honestly, you tell someone and expect them to say,

'Oh, poor you, but don't worry, it's going the rounds. I've got a friend whose whole body was a huge lump covered with suppurating spots and it turned out she just had a virus and after two days it went. Everyone's got it at the moment,' and all you get is lots of moaning and idiotic talk about the Big C. Thanks a lot!

The phone rang again and I imagined it must be Marion, but I was too upset to answer.

Oh dear, oh dear. Must try not to think of it. But oddly, Marion's reaction upsets me far more than worries about Big – or little – Cs. Let alone As or Bs.

Later

Sat down to get my act together and send out a round robin email to all my friends asking if they know of anyone who wants a room in Shepherd's Bush. I felt I couldn't actually put 'man' in the message in case I was had up for racial prejudice or whatever it is. I tried putting 'man preferred' and then 'both sexes welcome, but it would be nice to have a man for a change'. But it either looked sexist or it looked as if I were gagging for a bloke. Which I'm not. Or rather, I am, but not in the way it might be interpreted.

I'd barely pressed the 'send' button when a reply came flying through.

I'm desperate for a room! My friend Marion forwarded me your email. I've been recently evicted from my flat (entirely unjustified, I might add) and I'm currently sleeping on friends' floors. I'm a very respectable piano teacher, I am creative and sensitive to other people's needs. I'm 55 and suffer from arthritis (who doesn't?) so am hoping it isn't too far up the stairs, and I can cook a mean Spanish omelette!

Let me know when I can come round and have a look.

Love and Peace and God Bless, Bronwen

PS I would be happy to install a stair-lift at my own expense.

She sent me a link to her Facebook page, which was just full of petitions against GM crops, more petitions to allow the NHS to use complementary medicine, lots of 'Support the Palestinians' campaigns and a long rant about subsidizing arts centres. None of it stuff that I completely disagreed with (except the complementary medicine one) but nothing I felt very strongly about, to be honest. I'm such a political lightweight, I'm ashamed of myself. I meet someone who argues against GM crops on a Wednesday and I'll support them up the hilt; then on Thursday I meet someone else who says GM crops are the answer to world famine and I'm voting for them. I never feel I can get the full picture. Anyway, there was, suspiciously, no photograph of the potential lodger. She appeared to be represented by a tulip. And I realized that the last thing I wanted was an arthritic old piano teacher who looked like a tulip lumbering upstairs and stinking the house out with her Spanish omelettes. I was also wary of that phrase about her eviction – 'completely unjustified'. Hmm. I'd like to hear the landlord's side of the story first.

I wondered what other people would make of me if I were

to ask for a room. 'Retired 67-year-old art teacher, amusing, quiet, recently involved in a campaign to save trees on the local common, has adorable old cat called Pouncer (!) . . .' I think I'd be pressing the 'delete' button pretty swiftly.

I'm afraid I wrote back saying that there were 102 stairs up to her floor and – being a sensitive artist myself, like her – I had a particular prejudice against the visual aspect of stairlifts in my home. Also, I needed complete silence. And anyway, the room was already taken. I bet the friends who are putting her up will gnash their teeth when they hear I've turned her down.

How the room could have been taken in the few seconds between my sending out the email and her replying, I have no idea. But that was up to her to work out. It was, as people so unkindly say these days, *not my problem*.

January 26

Got rather a tear-stained letter from Marion, apologizing. But not quite apologizing enough. There was still a hint of 'poor me' about it. Will reply, but will let her stew for a few days. I know it's mean, but I still feel terribly hurt by her reaction.

January 29

Another reply to my round robin from a bloke called Graham. Now, I like the sound of him. He says he's 35, just separated, looking for a flat to live in and needs 'a perch from which to search'. He works as a lawyer – so that means he's bright – and from his email he sounds amusing, too. Also pretty desperate. He added, 'I'm quiet, reliable and always pay my bills. (I prefer bankers' orders.) I've read the works of Shakespeare, I'll water plants when you're away or feed cats/ walk dogs. I'm always pleasant to visiting workmen. I don't have a car or a bicycle and never want anyone to stay over for the night (at least for the foreseeable future)! I eat out most of the time, but am very good at fixing things. If there is anything more you are looking for in a lodger, please just let me know and I'll add it to the list.'

He's working in Paris at the moment but will be over briefly this week so I've asked him to drop by then. Can't wait to see what he's like. At least there's one thing I know. Even if he looks like Quasimodo and makes Spanish omelettes for breakfast, lunch and tea, he's certainly an utter charmer. On paper, anyway.

Later

Having had another near-miss with the bath, I was delighted to find, popping through the letterbox, my timer. No more leaks for me!

January 30

This morning the bell rang and there stood Marion on the doorstep, holding a big bunch of supermarket roses and looking very tear-stained and sorry for herself. To be honest,

I still felt extremely angry and didn't feel like talking to her at all. I felt she'd hijacked my lump and was going round telling people she felt miserable because 'my friend has a lump and I don't know if it's cancer or not' – and everyone would be very sympathetic towards her, leaving me, the one with the lump, completely isolated and uncomforted. But she's an old friend, she did look particularly contrite and I'd decided to make up soon anyway. So I had to let her in and listen to her apologies.

'I'm so sorry,' she said, as she sat down and sipped the coffee I'd made for her. 'I shouldn't have reacted like that. But my mother died of cancer at this time of year, and I suppose I've been thinking about it. And only the evening of your birthday I heard that Jill's husband has got some kind of skin cancer – and you know how it is – and when you said you had a lump it was the last straw. I'm so sorry, I'm a terrible friend. You must think I'm awful, only thinking about myself. Oh God, oh God. You're never going to speak to me again, and I can't blame you.'

And she burst into tears again.

Well, of course, at this outburst I couldn't help forgiving her on the spot. I started to laugh, sat down and put my arms round her.

'Don't be silly,' I said. 'I think I might have over-reacted because I was so worried myself. God, you do seem to be surrounded by the Angel of Death, poor you.'

'That's how it's going to be from now on, isn't it?' she said, dabbing her eyes. 'We'll only meet friends at funerals!'

'And if you have your way with Mister Big C, you won't even

be meeting me for long either!' I said, jokingly. 'Look, you're just feeling low. No one's going to die round here, I promise. Besides, if I'm going to die it's going to be at a time of my own choosing – so sucks to the Grim Reaper. As for the funerals, we'd better make sure they're the very best, smartest, and jolliest funerals anyone's ever had in their lives.'

She smiled wanly.

'The thing is,' she said, 'I'm so frightened of death. I always have been. It absolutely terrifies me. I don't know what I'd do if I died.'

I was tempted to point out that if she died she wouldn't have to do anything at all, but I didn't because it would have been too mean. And I thought: isn't it odd that some people are so terrified of death?

I'm a bit apprehensive, I must say, but not terrified. I think it's the idea of chemotherapy that scares me more than anything. Dying – well, we've all got to go one day, haven't we? And personally, since I can feel the leaves falling off my particular tree, I can already see that it's not such an awful thought after all. When one's young of course, the idea of dying fills one with terror. But I think the peculiar thing about most people's attitude to death is that, the older they get, the less scared of it they become. They see it's part of a natural progression.

Of course, in one way, it's very touching that Marion's so upset. It shows how much she loves me. But in another, it's tremendously irritating. Because when you have a huge, unexplained lump, you want lots of love and kindness not weeping and wailing.

It's one of those maddening things about your nearest and dearest. I remember one art school friend suddenly abusing me with a torrent of horrible accusations. Naturally, I felt like never speaking to her again, but most of my friends said I should take it as a compliment, as she'd only been able to say those things because we were so close. Hmm. I find it pretty hard to accept that kind of reasoning.

FEBRUARY

February 3

It is one of the dankest, most miserable, lowering days I've seen in ages. So dark that even when I woke at 8.30 am (late for me) I still thought it was the middle of the night, I drew the curtains and then tried to draw the curtains. (Well, I know what I mean!) Anyway, I looked out and it was as if the End of the World were Nigh. Pouncer was just a dark blob on a grey lawn, looking like an inkblot in a Rorschach test. Everything seemed to be drawn in pencil and ink, in a kind of grey chiaroscuro (as we painters call it). There was a watery glimmer of light behind one of the less grey clouds, hinting at a sun feebly trying to poke its way through, like the light from one of those torches I keep for emergencies whose batteries are on their last legs. And generally there was a feeling of menace and gloom in the air. I saw the inkblot suddenly scamper inside, heard the rattle of the cat-flap and the first great drop of rain landed splat on the window in front of me, followed by a horde of others, like giant tears of rage shed by some vengeful god in the sky.

Later

Graham, the potential lodger, is coming over tomorrow. I did a quick check of the room to make sure it wasn't too grotty and all the light bulbs worked and the sheets were clean and aired and so on. Looking under the bed, I found an old pack of tampons left by Michelle.

February 4

Well! Can't believe my luck! The fabulous Graham came round! Admittedly he was an hour late but kept sending apologetic texts. I could see him through my nervous spyhole when I peeped through the front door and instantly liked what I saw. He was one of those people who beams even before you've opened the door, and the moment he stepped in I knew he was Mr Right as far as being a lodger went. Frankly, had I been 20 years younger or he 20 years older, he would have been a potential Mr Right in every way, but having pretty much given up looking for Mr Rights he was the next best thing. I'd already had experience of a younger Mr Right in the shape of the horrible Louis a couple of years ago, and I've had a Mr Right my own age who, natch, being a bloke, went and died on me, men always dying sooner than women. And as I don't want to be with anyone who I'm going to have to look after to the end of his days, and nor do

I want to be someone who's always chasing after younger blokes and making an elderly fool of herself, the most I can ask for is a lot of good male friends of every age – which is, actually, what I've got.

Graham was about Jack's age – perhaps a bit younger – and wearing the most gorgeous Paul Smith suit, revealed when he removed his snazzy fitted overcoat. Admittedly he's a lawyer, but he's an extremely cool lawyer and not at all fusty like my own solicitor, Mr Rankle. The moment he stepped through the door he spotted one of my pictures and stopped in his tracks.

'I like that!' he said. 'Beautifully drawn . . . who did it, might I ask?'

Well I was already completely bowled over, covered in a layer of charm dust.

'Oh, just a little thing I . . .'

'You?' he said. 'Gosh, I wish I could paint like you!'

And so we continued for about an hour. He sat down and told me his life story. It appears he was with his wife until recently. They'd been together for seven years and after a while it emerged – as it so often does – that he was actually extremely unhappy underneath all the cheeriness. His wife had chucked him out after he'd confessed to having a one-night stand when he'd been drunk, something he bitterly regretted, and she'd told him she never wanted to see him again so here he was, trying to 'find himself'.

'Not,' he added sadly, 'that I'd know what to do once I found myself.'

He was trying to get back with his wife but for the last few weeks she'd refused to answer letters and barely spoken to him on the phone.

Oh dear. It all reminded me of the last days of my marriage to David. I remembered that however much he tried to get us to talk or consult a therapist, I totally refused. The problem was that we'd never really talked properly – both of us probably too frightened to risk a major row – so everything built and built until I finally exploded. And then it was too late.

I took Graham up to see the room – kicking my bedroom door shut on the way up – and he didn't seem to notice anything except how delightful the house was. He adored the room and he couldn't think of anything that would suit him better. Frankly, I was weak at the knees from the moment I saw him at the door. It was a mixture, I'd say, of thinking 'What a cracker!' and 'He's so like my son!' and having those feminine and maternal feelings all rolled into one was rather confusing but at the same time delightful.

The slight problem is that he doesn't want to move in until April but he said he liked the room so much he'd be happy to pay February and March's rent just to secure it, which is fine by me. So against all my principles, because I usually always want a few days' waiting period on either side, I just said yes. He promised to pay in advance, and was peeling out a month's rent from a wad of notes before I even had to ask.

On his way out, he met James, who'd popped over. When the door closed, James clapped his hands and gave a little squeal.

'Well, I hope you've snapped him up at once!' he said. 'He's an absolute dish! I'm in love! Honestly, if I could get a lodger like that I'd move to a bigger house specially.'

February 8

Having rung Gene's school last week to say I'd be very happy to go over and talk about the war or, rather, the aftermath of the war as far as I remember it – being only 18 months old at the time, and with a memory that had barely got off the ground – I got a letter from them confirming they want me to go over next month. 'If you can bring any photographs or artyfacts or perhaps some of your old toys we are certain this gesture would be much appresiated.'

Of course my hair practically fell out when I saw the spelling, but I accepted and set about collecting some interesting, ahem, artefacts.

February 11

I still haven't got a letter about the scan. One bit of me says that I should let sleeping dogs lie: if they're not worried enough to contact me, then there's nothing to worry about and obviously everyone thinks I'm making a big fuss about nothing and the doctors know best. The other bit, however, says that doctors do *not* know best, they are just as hopeless in their way as the teachers at Gene's school, and that I don't want to be one of those statistics I read about in the *Daily Rant*. 'Retired art teacher visited ten doctors in ten months. Six told her to go away, and four offered her paracetamol. Now the 67-year-old professional has been told that, with cancer raging through her body, she only has five minutes to live!'

'Why don't you ring up?' said Penny. 'You know what they say: "The squeaky wheel gets the most oil."'

'Shall I ring up and squeak, then?' I said.

'Yes,' she said. 'Start squeaking right now.'

February 14

Marion, in another effort at peace-making, had suggested we make marmalade together, so she came over this morning laden with oranges and jars. (We'd agreed that the shop-bought varieties always contain too much sugar.) She clearly thinks I should be seeing an acupuncturist rather than a doctor. Or a herbalist. Or sticking coffee enemas up myself. Or going to sleep on a crystal pillow. Actually, I've seen enough acupuncturists in my time. I still remember the one I went to see in Oxford Street a couple of years ago who, although enthusiastic, was utterly hopeless and didn't even know North from South, let alone, I imagine, where anyone's chakras were – if, indeed, a chakra even exists, chakras sounding rather like those odd dry kosher biscuits they sell in special sections of supermarkets. So I have no intention of going down the alternative therapy route.

We had a pleasant enough afternoon chopping and boiling and straining and dropping bits of marmalade onto saucers and sterilizing the bottles and writing the labels – I like doing them in proper italic hand-writing – and eventually we had 30 jars all lined up. What a chore! And what fun!

Amazingly, in the post this morning there was an anony-mous Valentine's card. Quite baffling. As far as I could see the postmark was Somerset. And the only person I can think of who lives there is David. It couldn't be him of course. Oh – I wonder if Gene sent it to him to send to me so it had a mys-terious postmark? I bet that's the answer. How sweet!

February 15

Tried the marmalade this morning. It tasted absolutely perfect. Just like marmalade. Shop-bought marmalade.

I rang Marion. She agreed. 'Perhaps we put in too much sugar,' she said. 'Next time we'll try with less.'

But frankly I think I'll stick to Waitrose marmalade in future. My fingers are aching with chopping.

Everyone bangs on about how brilliant home-made stuff is, but on the whole I'd rather buy my clothes, furniture, curtains, alcohol, butter and milk etc from shops than make them myself at home.

February 18

Rang up to ask when the scan would be and the hospital said they'd never received anything about a scan and perhaps I should get back to my doctor. God, I could shoot her! I sup-pose I must be quite anxious about the lump because I do feel tremendously angry when so-called professionals simply fail to do even the simplest part of their job properly. Got the doctor to fax me a copy of a new letter – not a word of apology – and then faxed it myself to the hospital. The nurse there said dismally, 'Oh well, now you've joined the queue', which enraged me even more because if the letter had gone off at the proper time in the first place I'd be halfway up the queue, making long noses at the people who'd just joined and crowing, 'I was here first!'

Must say it's difficult keeping this lumpy thing secret. Particularly after Marion's reaction. The thing is I don't want everyone throwing their hands in the air and screaming or rushing round and telling me to rest or recounting dire stories about people who had cancer which raced through their bodies and they were dead in a week. I do so long to tell Jack – and perhaps I should because he's the one who'd be most affected after all. But at the same time I feel I can't worry him. He's got enough on his plate.

February 19

'Could ketchup cure cancer?' This is the latest headline from the *Daily*. I read the article closely and it turns out that ketchup may or may not cure cancer and research continues.

February 21

Brilliant day. Outside it's like Switzerland, or how I imagine Switzerland. (I've never been able to understand how people prefer to whizz down a mountain on two thin planks of wood instead of doing it far more safely in a car down a proper tarmac-ed road.) But anyway, it was one of those extraordinarily bright February days, gleaming with frost, with the buildings and trees looking chiselled out of the clear air, all braced and refreshed, as if they'd just had a cold shower.

Next door I can hear the sound of banging and yelling from Brad and Sharmie, who are packing up to go to India. Outside their house each evening sits a pile of rubbish left out for the binmen, but each morning it has disappeared – presumably because passing desperados have decided an old rack for storing CDs is just what they want, or a clothes-horse or a mattress or a frayed carpet or an old mixing machine with a note saying 'Yes, it works! Please take!' attached.

I spent most of the morning looking at old photograph albums of me when I was small, trying to remember what life was like just after the war, so I had something to show the pupils when I went to Gene's school. I found one of me with a hoop. (Does anyone have hoops these days, and bowl them down the street? I think not.) And there was a sweet picture of me in a toy pedal-car, a real old-fashioned model. There was my mother, in a ludicrous hat and long pencil skirt standing beside me holding, I was certain, a ration book. I even started painting a huge chart of all the things I remembered, making illustrations of the New Look, bomb-sites, old confectionery like Fry's Five Boys – all the things that no one can remember any more.

What else can I tell them? That ordinary people like us

didn't have a telly or computers or mobile phones or washing machines or refrigerators, and there weren't any motorways or antibiotics and you could park your car where you liked, and if you saw a woman with a burka on in the street it was hot news. That's about all. Though actually, when I write it down it seems rather a lot.

Later

James has done his back in, and asked if I'd get some shopping for him. Before I went out I looked at the *Daily Rant* and saw that it featured one of those wonderful psychological tests. This one was called 'Are you a psychopath?' They always have tests like these – 'Are you a good mother?' 'Are you a great lover?' Always fun to do, because invariably you come out top of the league and it makes your day. It was simply a matter of answering yes or no to eight questions. And as I'm always worrying about whether deep down I'm a psychopath, this was the test for me.

I sat down on the sofa, Pouncer came and curled up on my lap, I got out the old pen and started.

1. Are you charming and, on occasion, manipulative?

Yes. Well, I certainly can be if I want to. And, though I wouldn't describe it as manipulative, I have been known to get my own way now and again. Look how brilliantly I'd persuaded James that the best place for the ghastly installation he did of me was in a part of the garden that nobody apart from my unfortunate neighbours could see. And charming? I can be quite charming when I want to be. Surely it's a morally defensible situation? I want to spread sweetness and light and avoid confrontation.

2. Have you ever committed a crime and tried to cover it up?

Yes. If I'm honest. Last year I stole Brad and Sharmie's wind-chimes and I didn't own up when they accused the mosque next door. I suppose 'stole' isn't quite the right word because I didn't want them for myself, oh no. I gather that when Americans want to torture prisoners in Iraq they play them non-stop heavy metal music. Well, the sound of those wind-chimes was, to me, as intolerable as the sound of Motorface or AB/CD or whatever they're called. When I heard them I felt like a captive inside a jar with a wasp. So naturally I nipped over the wall, brought them back and chucked them in the bin. Result, complete peace and quiet. And a permanent sense of guilt.

3. Have you ever been accused of being cold-hearted?

Yes. My friend Penny down the road was horrified I wasn't more upset than I was when Hughie died. But the thing was, since I'd known he was going to die for months, when it happened it didn't come as a shock. So although it's true I've been accused of being cold-hearted, I don't think I really am. Still, I'm determined to answer the questions accurately – and accused, yes, I have been.

4. Do you get upset when you feel people around you are behaving badly?

Yes. Indeed I do! Having, a couple of years ago, actually shinned up a tree to protect it from being chopped down by developers, I'm proud to say that when I see a high horse, I scramble on it and start galloping.

5. Did you have a close family who expressed their affection openly?

No. Close, yes, but no one ever said 'I love you' like Gene does now, all the time, to his parents. And they to him. Even hugs were thin on the ground. But wasn't everyone's family like that in the old days?

6. Have you ever shoplifted?

Yes. I did once steal an olive from a supermarket. Felt dreadful about it for weeks.

7. Do you believe you have special abilities?

Yes. After what I've written about my ability to draw, I'd be lying if I said I didn't think I had certain abilities. Still, just because I think I can draw like an angel doesn't mean I don't have moments when my self-confidence is at an all-time low and I think I'm the scum of the earth and wonder, quite frankly, why I have any friends. But I do have this one ability. Draughtsmanship. It'll have to be a yes to this one, too.

8. Did you ever torture animals when you were young?

No. No, no, no! Honestly, that's a psychopath question if ever there was one.

And yet, working out how I scored, I was horrified to discover this!

Whoa, steady on there! Although you're not a fully-blown psycho-path, you're heading in that direction, so watch out! Chances are that most other people don't even realize just how sick you are. This is deeply concerning, but there is a faint chance that with therapy and medication you could be a productive member of society.

By the time I got to James with his newspaper, milk and eggs and bacon, I was feeling pretty low. I should never have done that test. I should never even have started getting the *Daily Rant* again. It always scares the daylights out of me.

As I stomped up the stairs to his flat, I kept wondering if he knew 'how sick I was'? Was I such a cunning psychopath I kept my deadly personality hidden from even my closest friends? Not, I reflected glumly, that I could have any close friends, because psychopaths don't have close friends.

'Welcome!' cried James at the top of the stairs after he'd opened the door. 'You're an angel!' he added as he took the shopping. 'I thought I'd have to starve.'

'I'm not an angel,' I said, sorrowfully as I followed him into the sitting room. 'Apparently I'm a psychopath.'

James stopped on the landing. 'Did I hear you right?' he said. 'You're a psychopath? You can't be, darling! I've just done one of those tests myself in the *Daily Rant* and . . . oho,' he added, shaking his head. 'You failed to look at the answers before you started, didn't you? Didn't you know that all psychopaths look at the answers first? That's why, with their low cunning, they're always able to be one ahead of the psychologists examining them. I, having been sensible – and perhaps psychopathic – enough to check first, came out as a warm and sensitive soul. No, look, darling, look at me.' He held my shoulders and turned my head so I was staring into his eyes.

'You are not a psychopath. You could not possibly be a psycho-path. You're the most lovely granny, friend, retired teacher, spreader of sweetness and light, moral, gorgeous and sensitive person on the planet. Good heavens, if I were straight I'd ask you to marry me! And you know something? Psychopaths just aren't my type.'

'Are you sure?' I said.

'Of course I'm sure, you big bundle of darlingness,' he said.

I've been treasuring that phrase for the last couple of hours.

MARCH

March 1

Worry worry worry.

How long do I have to wait now for the scan date to come up? After all, the documents already seem to have got lost once, so how can I be sure they won't lose them again? Or, if they find them, give me the wrong result and tell me I've got emphysema or something?

I can hardly bear having a bath these days because there is the lump always grinning up at me, saying, 'Hi! I'm here to scare the living daylights out of you! I might be benign or I might be cancerous! And you don't know. I know, but you don't know. Tee hee hee!!'

To make matters worse, a couple of the other little spots or blisters have burst and now it looks as if they're turning into some kind of sore. The lump underneath still appears to be huge and hard – I say huge, it's probably about the size of a small orange now. Tumours are always described as being the size of an orange, or a melon. But you never describe an orange or a melon as being the size of a tumour. Odd.

Anyway, this morning, I'd just got out of my bath and was drying myself when I heard the most frightful racket outside. Was someone having a fight at ten in the morning? It seemed unlikely. Tucking my towel round me so it didn't fall off (they always make it look so easy in films, but I've never got the knack), I slunk up to the window at the front and peered out. There, outside the door of the house opposite – a council house, which has been unoccupied ever since George, the old black guy, died, years ago now – was a woman. She looked as if she'd slept in her clothes. Slept in her clothes for years, actually. Her hair was greasy and knotted, when she turned I could see she had very few teeth, and she generally looked poverty-stricken and, it has to be said, rather frightening. She reminded me of one of those witches in the kind of books that used to stop me getting to sleep when I was Gene's age. Anyway, there she was, cursing and shouting, trying to get a key in the lock. I imagined she was either drunk or high on drugs. Or, more likely, both. Anyway, wrapped round her wrist was a chain, and at the end of this chain was a very large, mangy Alsatian who was barking his head off. Every so often she swore at the dog and kicked it, pulling on the chain so its throat was caught and it started choking.

Oh, I do hate these sights. I get all panicky and miserable. Oddly, it wasn't the woman I felt sorry for, though no doubt she'd had her fair share of misery, poor soul. It was the dog.

I hated seeing it being ill-treated. Eventually the woman got inside the house, slammed the door and I could hear them inside, banging about, barking, screaming and generally causing havoc.

I'm not very sentimental about animals, really. When one of my cats has died, I've been curiously unmoved. Oh, God, maybe I really am a psychopath. But if I see an animal being ill-treated I can't bear it. The idea of being a pet and being left alone for too long, or hit, or starved . . . it's one of the reasons I can never go to Morocco again, because of all those wretched donkeys being beaten. Actually, there are very few countries I *can* go to because of this problem. Greece is full of starving kittens, the US is teeming with de-clawed cats which aren't allowed into the garden, France is chock-a-block with chained-up barking dogs . . . And China! Well, don't get me started! They eat dogs there and everyone has a bird in a cage. When I went on a package holiday to China our guides suggested we go to a tiger zoo and feed the big cats live rats. It's not just abroad, either. If I go into a fish restaurant I'm nearly always stuck sitting at a table next to some tank full of lobsters with their claws bound up, and I have to leave.

Actually, I'm so sensitive about all this, if I go to a restaurant and see a plant that hasn't been watered, I'll pop up to it on the sly and tip water from my glass into the earth – yes, even if it's expensive fizzy bottled water. I have even been known to water plastic plants by mistake.

So I felt very nervous about this dog. I hope it either goes away or shuts up. Otherwise, knowing me, I'll have to Do

Something About It, and I don't fancy Doing Something About either of that pair, the owner or the wretched dog.

Later

It's 11pm. I heard more kerfuffle from outside and when I looked out of the window I saw the ghastly woman opposite staggering out of the house and getting into a waiting car. A car that made mine look like a brand-new Rolls Royce. No dog. From the terrible barks and yelps it's clear the poor thing has been left inside the house. And it's starting to go mad.

Thank God my bedroom is at the back of the house. I can't imagine sleeping with that racket going on. As it is, I'll have to use earplugs.

Later

Having searched high and low for earplugs, I can't find any so will have to resort to Gene's Play-Doh.

March 9

David came up for lunch. To my amazement Gene arrived with him. Apparently David had dropped Sandra off at the airport at the crack of dawn, popped in to see Jack and Gene this morning, and then, because Gene insisted, brought him along to see me for lunch. David had actually brought me a bunch of flowers, which surprised me because he's not a flower-bringing sort of person. And he seemed tremendously relaxed and perky, which was even odder. For the last few years he's always seemed rather downtrodden. Over coffee, while Gene was watching old Popeye cartoons in the other room, I discovered what had happened.

It seems Sandra met someone when she was on holiday in Goa last autumn and he's dying to marry her and also dying to have children, and it's really Sandra's last chance.

'Oh David!' I said. 'I'm so sorry! You must be feeling terrible!'

'Well, I'm rather surprised to find that I'm not,' he said, sheepishly. 'It was all wonderful to start with, as you can imagine and I was really chuffed to have this much younger beautiful girl in love with me, but recently, although I'm terribly fond of her, I've discovered we haven't got a lot in common. The truth is, she never reads books. And although I'd be more than happy for her to stay, I'm aware she's desperate for kids. It's always been preying on my mind and I feel guilty, and to be honest now she's found someone I'm really happy for her. Isn't it odd? Though I bet I'll feel very lonely down in the country all by myself after a while.'

'Oh don't be silly, David,' I said. 'You won't be alone for a moment. She'll go out of the back door and someone will step in the front. I bet there are regiments of widows down there just waiting to snap you up. I bet the Widow Bossom is waiting to pounce, I just know it. After all, you're good-looking, you're funny, you're kind . . . you're Mr Eligible.'

After that there was an uncomfortable silence and I wondered if I'd gone too far. I hope he didn't think that *I* was interested. Because the last thing I'd want to do is get together with David again.

David gave me a funny look and then said, 'Well, that's very kind of you Marie. Particularly after our break-up.'

'Oh, come on David. That was then,' I said. 'I don't think you liked me very much either, now I look back on it. Anyway, you haven't answered my question. Has the Widow made her move yet?'

'Edwina's been very kind to me, I must say,' said David. 'She's always popping in and doing things when Sandra's away. But really, I don't think she's at all predatory.'

'Edwina is it now?' I said. 'Not predatory? Honestly, men. They think they're good at hunting but they never have a clue when they're being hunted themselves. Watch out for Edwina, I'd say. Though, to be honest, you could do worse. Glam old widow. I like her anyway. You should encourage her. But you mustn't make any hasty decisions. You're not to jump into anything until the lady in question has been thoroughly vetted by your old ex-wife.'

Pouncer then padded into the room and jumped on David's lap as if David had never left home.

'Pounce! Me old mate!' said David, stroking him delightedly. 'Haven't seen you for a while! Glad you remember me!'

Gene, bored with telly, sauntered in.

'I've never seen you both at the same time, Granny and Granddad!' he said, climbing up onto a chair and swinging his legs as he picked at some grapes.

'That's true,' I said, feeling rather awkward. 'But your granddad and I do see each other sometimes for lunch and things, even though we're divorced.'

I wanted to ram home the idea that even if parents separate they can still remain friends. You never know.

'Why did you get divorced?' asked Gene. And David and I stared embarrassedly at each other.

'Was it because we didn't agree on so many things? Like the miners' strike?' I asked David. I felt a bit silly.

'I thought it was because you suddenly decided you couldn't stand the sight of me,' said David. 'One day, Gene,' he said, 'your granny just announced she never wanted to see me again.'

'Well, there was the drink,' I said, rather miffed. 'And that night he never came home. And your granddad wasn't exactly generous – I don't think you ever took me out to dinner after we'd been married!' I added, turning to David, suddenly remembering. 'And you always forgot my birthday and our anniversary!'

'Well he's brought you some flowers today,' said Gene, looking rather puzzled. 'And didn't he give you some Turkish Delight?'

'I think that was more the Widow Bossom than Granddad,' I said, jokily, glancing at David who looked rather sheepish. 'But thank you very much for them. They were absolutely yummy!'

'Anyway, you're good friends now,' persisted Gene.

'Yes, we're good friends now,' I said and David heartily agreed. 'But that's quite different.'

'You've got to be more than good friends to be married,' I added.

Gene looked baffled, pushed away the grapes and went off to play with the terrible plastic Superheroes I'd bought for him six months ago. David told me he wasn't sure if he *had* been right about the miners' strike and I said for God's sake what did it matter now. And unfortunately we couldn't quite get over our embarrassment and grumpiness before they had to leave to get Gene home for supper.

March 10

Mother's Day. As usual, a late-night text from Jack saying 'Hi Mum! Hope you had a good day!'

March 12

Today was weirdly spring-like. It smelt like spring and I only had to look out of the window and see the blue sky to feel cheered up. Of course, go out in it and it's a different matter. Bloody freezing. Bit of a downer. Like meeting some lovely new man and then he suddenly says he's married. Or turns out to be a psychopath.

The dog's stopped barking, thank goodness, so maybe the woman came back last night or has taken it away.

Brad and Sharmie have asked me over to drinks next week to say goodbye. Gosh, I'll miss them – and Alice, their little girl. I wish they weren't going. I hate getting new neighbours because you have to start from scratch. And every time my neighbours go I always think they couldn't be as nice as the neighbours I've got at the moment – and yet, oddly, they always are, if not nicer.

But I don't like what I've heard so far of this Melanie creature. Will try to find out more from B and S when I see them.

Later

I got so anxious waiting for an appointment for my scan that I rang up again to find out what's going on. Turns out they'd sent me a letter for an appointment a week ago and I hadn't got it. But apparently I can't make a date for the scan without the reference on the actual letter so I've still got to wait for it. And they can't give me the reference because of the Data Protection Act. I kept saying 'But I'm me! This is me! Marie Sharp! I am she! I can give you my date of birth, my national insurance number and my postcode!' but they refused to believe me or, rather, chose not to. So I'll have to wait for the letter to arrive. Barmy. Well, at least I'm in the system now. I keep telling myself that if my doctor had thought it was anything serious she would have got all the machinery cracking right away, so obviously there's nothing to worry about, but oddly that argument doesn't seem to convince me. Recently I've been trying not to think about it. But it keeps popping up. And anyway, everywhere I look there seems to be mention of cancer. Especially, of course, in the *Daily Rant*.

March 15

Went to a jolly party of old art college friends and drank too much. The plan was to lie in today but I was woken early this morning to hear, even from my bedroom at the back, the tragic barking of the dog in the house opposite. I know a lot of people can put this sound to the back of their minds with a muttering of 'Bloody dogs!' but unfortunately I can't. I imagine it, locked up in a room, knee deep in its own piss and poo, hungry, frightened, lonely . . . in an agony of mental and physical distress.

Wonder if I should ring up the RSPCA?

Oddly enough, I'd be happier if I knew it were dead – it's just this non-stop suffering (or what I imagine is suffering) that's so hard to bear.

Stared at my lump again in the bath. Now it seems to be getting bigger and bigger. Eventually I can imagine that I will consist only of lump, a huge rolling thing that finds it hard to get out of the door, and the rest of my body will be stuck on the side like some unnecessary appendage. Having nothing better to do, I wondered if this anxiety about the dog wasn't a displacement anxiety for the lump. Perhaps I'm in even more of a panic than I think, but I'm transferring the anxiety to worrying about the dog. The problem with this kind of thinking is that, even if it's true, it doesn't really help.

Later
Much cheered when I opened my post and found the letter for the scan appointment. Rang up triumphantly and made

my appointment. Thank God. Soon I'll know exactly what it is.

Or, of course, not.

March 18

Spent the morning buying plants. It was pouring with rain at the garden centre, so no one was there, and I was able to browse happily by myself. Bought masses of foxgloves, tobacco plants and delphinium seedlings and then, since the sun came out this afternoon, spent a happy hour or so bunging them into the damp earth. Pouncer sat on the wall above me, occasionally looking extremely irritated that there was another being hanging about his territory.

Later

It was so sad saying goodbye to Brad and Sharmie this evening. They're off in a couple of days – to India where Brad has got his next posting as some kind of planning advisor in Allahabad.

Just stepping into their house was like walking into a ghost town. There were packing boxes everywhere, no pictures on the walls – just the dirty outlines of where they'd been – and in the kitchen, only a few cooking essentials and piles of black binbags full of rubbish. There was an eerie light because they'd taken all the shades off the lamps, and we sat on the few chairs remaining in the sitting room while Brad cracked open a bottle of champagne. We drank it out of transparent plastic cups.

They'd sweetly invited James and Penny too, but Penny couldn't come because she'd been asked to the theatre in Greenwich where her god-daughter was appearing in a non-speaking part as a maid. (She'd had to set off practically this morning to be there on time.) James could, though, and jumped up the moment I arrived – just as Sharmie entered the room with some delicious nibbles. 'Here we are,' she said. 'Alice!' she shouted. 'Come and say goodbye to Auntie Marie!'

This was a title I'd reluctantly acquired – reluctantly because I don't like to be called something I'm not, being such a psychopath (or is an obsession with literalness an autistic trait? Must find out). If I'm an aunt, fine, call me Auntie, but if I'm a neighbour, let's just stick to Marie. Or maybe it's something to do with being English.

Alice came into the room shyly holding a card. I opened it and she'd stuck a photograph of herself on the front and inside she'd written 'LOVE YOU!!!! Alice (your friend)'.

That's more like it, I thought.

Brad poured us all more champers and raised his. 'Here's to us!' he said. 'And may we never lose touch! Oh, it breaks our hearts to leave you, Marie,' he added. 'We had a great time in London, and that's all down to you (Isn't it, honey?) You made us feel – what? "Part of the community". (Didn't she though, honey?)'

'And we're taking all your pictures with us,' said Sharmie, jangling her bracelets as she reached for another smoked salmon nibble. 'And we do *not* want to say goodbye, Marie, we want you to come over to India to visit us.'

'And paint the trees over there,' added Brad. 'What do you say to that? Our "tree painter in residence"! Then we can have a memory of every place we stay round the world. Don't they have special trees out there? What are they called? Banban or something?'

'Banyan,' I said. 'I'd love to do a banyan . . . but you think it over when you're there. I bet you'll be far too busy to have a guest.' Though secretly I felt rather excited – I've never been to India. 'Maybe James could come, too . . .' I said, nervously. 'Then I wouldn't be round your skirts all the time.'

'Don't look at me,' said Brad. 'I'm not wearing skirts yet.'

'You will in India,' said Sharmie. 'You'll be forced to wear a dhoti.'

'No, that's one of those nappy things that Gandhi wore. They don't wear those these days. Dhotis are *so* 1940s,' I said. Oddly, no one laughed and I was left with that funny feeling of a joke hanging in the air like an unfinished sneeze. Americans are so nice but they have no sense of humour at all. 'But I'll miss you so much. We mustn't lose touch.'

Secretly, I fear that's exactly what will happen. Americans are notoriously charming and when you meet them you feel you've made friends for life. Then they pop back to the US or wherever they're going and you never hear from them again. I still feel a bit hurt about Martha, Louis' godmother, who I met in the States. Louis was a younger man I had an unfortunate crush on. He was utterly charming and kept implying that if only he were older or I were younger, how different things would be, but it turned out he said the same charming things to every woman he met. Anyway, I remember Martha announcing me as her 'new best friend', and did I ever see her again after that moment? Not a squeak, even though I emailed her.

'So who's the new neighbour?' asked James. 'She'd better be up to Marie's standards. This girl's very exacting, you know.'

'Hmm,' said Sharmie. 'I hope you'll like Melanie.' I noticed she tried to catch Brad's eye, but he turned away.

'She's quite a piece of work,' he said.

My heart sank. I know that expression. I'd been hoping they'd have a nicer slant than Marion and Tim on my new neighbour. It seemed that was not to be.

'Piece of work!' I squawked, panicking. 'What does that mean? In my book no one wants to be called a "piece of work"!'

'She certainly knows what she wants,' said Sharmie, clearly trying to be tactful. 'Very feisty.'

'Oh dear, not "feisty"!' I said. I'd once looked up the word on Google and found its origin lay in a word for something called 'fart dogs', irritable creatures that 18th-century *grande dames* held on their laps and which they could blame for all the dreadful odours that emanated from beneath their skirts. So whenever we call a woman 'feisty', instead of it being a compliment, it actually means a ghastly yapping smelly old bat.

'She made an offer on the house,' continued Sharmie, 'and just as we were exchanging she suddenly dropped her price. Nothing we could do. Tickets all booked. Job starting. We had to give in.'

Alice interrupted to insist I admire her new pink skirt. It

was covered with hearts embroidered in sparkles. 'Very nice,' I said. 'Lovely. You look gorgeous.' And she did.

'I think she's got plans for an extension at the back,' said Sharmie.

'Doubt if she'll get planning permission,' said Bill.

'Don't say any more,' pleaded James, who'd seen my stricken face. 'Marie will commit suicide and then we won't be able to come to India to see you.'

'I don't think you'll like her plans for the garden,' said Brad. 'She wants to gravel it all over and have pots.'

'Do you like my necklace?' asked Alice, one little hand on my arm and the other reaching to show me a sparkling heart on a chain.

'Oh, it's so pretty!' I said, smiling at her, and then turning to the others in horror. '*Gravel?*'

'And didn't she say she wanted to put in a hot tub at the end?' said Sharmie.

'Oh, well, as long as she doesn't put up wind-chi . . .' I bit my tongue and coughed. 'Water features,' I said, hastily. 'I hate the sound of running water.' I blushed to my roots remembering the wind-chime incident. (After I'd stolen them, it turned out they'd been a present from Alice's granny . . . oh, the shameful tale.) But a hot tub! I did hope Melanie wasn't going to have naked orgies every night and cram her hot tub with middle-aged men with hairy paunches and women with sagging boobs, who'd shriek into the early hours. What with the dog one side and the hot tub squeals the other, I wouldn't be able to get a decent night's sleep ever again.

So now I've got barking dogs, gravel, hot tubs, extensions and a feisty neighbour to worry about.

Puts the lump into perspective, though.

Today is the day the *Rant* Weekend Magazine comes – called, in an effort to be trendy, *Vibe* – and before I read it I always give it a shake to get rid of the advertisements they sneak in. They fall to the floor like lice. This time there was only one flyer, asking for contributions to the Macmillan cancer support charity. Sometimes I think the *Rant* knows I'm worried about cancer and fills its pages with cancer stories and supplements about the subject just to terrify me. For some reason the word 'Macmillan' had been set in a childish font, which made it look like an advertisement for Play-Doh. Odd, isn't it, the assumption that when you get ill you want to be treated like a child? It's bad enough *being* ill without hospitals wanting to put you in wards decorated in 'cheery colours', the walls covered in yellow smiling suns, with happy music playing and staff all addressing you by your Christian name without so much as a by-your-leave. I'd prefer to be left in a eerily lit room, a large profile of the Grim Reaper on the wall and the slogan 'In the Midst of Life we Are in Death' stencilled round the border. The way I see it, however ghastly you felt, you'd think 'Well, I don't feel as ghastly as *that!*' And perk up no end.

Actually, now I come to think of it, when I had a major op a while ago, I was for some reason bunged into a Catholic hospital – and there, hanging on the wall to greet me every morning, was a crucifix. With blood pouring from his hands and feet, the dying Christ certainly didn't make me feel much better.

Later

Penny rang to say that, after hiking all the way to Greenwich to watch her god-daughter appear for only a couple of seconds as a non-speaking maid, it turned out her seat was in the one part of the theatre where she couldn't see the stage. So she had to pretend she had. 'Which of course I could have done sitting at home,' said Penny, rather sourly. I told her about the prospect of the feisty woman next door who had plans for extensions and the garden.

'Which reminds me,' said Penny. 'We must have a meeting of the Residents' Association. First, to keep the whole thing alive in case it needs to spring into action at any time. Second, to keep an eye on people's neighbours when they want to build large and hideous extensions.'

'Good point,' I said, and spent the afternoon trying to work out how to do a group email.

Ate a whole packet of pork scratchings. Felt very sick.

March 19

Can't believe it. I was just beavering away this morning, sorting out my clothes in my bedroom, when I heard the all-too-familiar drip-drip-drip of my bath emptying itself onto the kitchen floor. Rushing down, I went into my flood defence procedures and afterwards scratched my head, trying to understand how, with a timer, this could possibly have happened. I worked out that I'd heard the timer, rushed down and turned it off but had failed, like a complete nincompoop, to turn off the bath itself. I sometimes wonder whether I shouldn't simply section myself.

Spent the whole evening polishing old brass pennies that I'm planning to give to everyone in Gene's class at school. I'd hoarded quite a few before the currency changed in the Seventies and it was nice to see they'd finally come in useful. Golly they do look *huge* now I look at them. And so heavy! Heaven knows how we managed to lug them round with us. We might as well have been carrying gravestones.

March 20

'Ketchup sales rocket! "We can't meet demand," say supermarkets' (*Daily Rant*)

Checked in my cupboard to see if I had any ketchup and when I discovered I did, toasted a piece of bread and slathered it on. You never know.

March 21

James came over this afternoon to install Facebook for me. I still can't see the point of it, but he swears it'll be terribly useful. 'You could organize the residents' meetings on it,' he said. 'And let everyone know about local affairs.'

I said I somehow didn't think Sheila the Dealer, our local

drug-dealer (and a key committee member of the Residents' Association) would be on Facebook, but James said no, loads of drug deals were done on Facebook and drug-dealers were now on eBay and how out of touch could I get, and I said I thought he was talking out of his hat and surely drug-dealers hung about on street corners and didn't want to do anything that might leave an electronic trail, and he said I was living in the past and no one knew what a street corner was any more . . .

Anyway, the upshot was that he came over, eager to get his hands on my computer, and I felt terrified.

'I'm not sure I want to do this,' I said, when he arrived. 'What if it turns out I have no friends?'

James scoffed. 'You'll have plenty of friends. Remember all those birthday cards.' And then, as he came into the light, I noticed that his chin wasn't as smooth as it had been the last time I'd seen him, a few days before.

'What's that?' I said, pointing to strange greyish spikes on his upper lip.

He blushed. 'I'm growing a beard, darling,' he said. 'But first I'm trying out fashionable stubble.'

To be honest it looked as if his chin was some forgotten piece of old bread that you'd found at the back of the bin, growing bits of grey mould on it. I mean, dark fashionable stubble is one thing, though I always imagine kissing it must be like kissing burnt toast. And if it got to be more than kissing, surely it would feel as if your body was being sand-papered all over? Doesn't bear thinking about. But I didn't say anything.

'You don't like it?' he said.

'I didn't say I didn't like it,' I said.

'But I know what it means when you don't say anything,' he said. 'Your silence speaks volumes.'

As I made him a cup of coffee I changed the subject back to Facebook. 'Friends. Hmm. Those cards were from people who send birthday cards. No one I know does Facebook.'

'They will,' said James. 'It's such fun. You can post all kinds of things – bits of films, random thoughts, photographs . . . you could photograph all your pictures and have a virtual gallery!'

We went upstairs to my computer and James fiddled about and asked me what I wanted my password to be. Oh God, I hate all these passwords! Well, I thought *Michelangelo* might be good, but he said no, because there weren't any numbers in it. I decided against suggesting *1shavethatbeard2shavethatbeard3shavethatbeard* because I thought he might be cross, so I said what about *Georgethe3rd* but he said no, because it meant something and it has to be gobbledygook. So finally we agreed on *b9Pl5901Vxj*, which of course is incredibly secret but unfortunately so secret that I'm sure I'll forget it, particularly as he said the one thing I mustn't do is write it down where a burglar might see it.

'But surely a burglar wouldn't want to hack into my Facebook page!' I said.

'You never know. He might take it over and pretend he was you and then say he was ill and ask for donations from all your many friends,' said James darkly. 'Or he might post pornographic images of little boys being . . .'

'No, no no!' I said, putting my hands over my ears. I'm very feeble about people describing horrible things to me. I can cope apparently okay, but then in the middle of the night some bony finger comes out of the woodwork and says 'Wake up! Wake up! Can you imagine what it must be like for those little boys ... or caged birds ... or tortured prisoners or barking dogs ...' And then I'm awake for hours trying to purge the horrible images from my mind.

It was pretty difficult understanding Facebook, anyway, because James insisted on sitting in my computer chair, and I was squinting at the screen from a chair at the side and seeing everything from an angle was particularly tricky. I couldn't see what keys he was pressing on the keyboard so new boxes and menus would spring up here and there and I'd have no idea how he'd got there. I pretended to understand everything James said but, although I can just about log in – he forced me to do it about ten times – I've no idea what to do once I've done so.

'Post something like "Hi guys! I've got myself onto Facebook at last! I'm 67, live in London, retired art teacher with one gorgeous grandson Gene, a lovely son Jack and daughter-in-law Chrissie ... "'

'Hang on!' I said. 'I'd never say "Hi guys!" And Jack would never forgive me if I wrote about him. I can't think of anything to say ... it's difficult speaking to nothingness, anyway, because I haven't got any friends yet.'

'You'll get the hang of it,' said James, though I thought he sounded a bit more dubious than he had before. He said he'd go home and suggest himself as a friend and that I must accept him as a friend so he can be the first, and before I know where I am I will be making friends with hundreds of people and I will have an entirely new virtual social life.

'I don't think I want an entirely new virtual social life,' I said. 'But thank you very much, anyway.'

'You'll love it once you get the hang of it,' said James, knowingly, as he left. He stood on the doorstep smiling at me. 'We'll have to tear you away in a couple of months! You know sometimes I think I know you better than you know yourself, darling!'

I bridled. *'No one knows me better than I know myself,'* I said, extremely crossly, feeling, I'm afraid, a surge of rage. It was the sort of thing a nanny says when you're tiny.

James laughed. 'I knew you'd say that!' he replied, smugly.

'And I,' I shot back, in a pitiful riposte, 'knew you'd say that, too!'

So childish! Luckily our spat was interrupted by the really appalling sound of barking and, looking across the road, I saw that the Grisly Woman was hauling the dog out of the front door of the house opposite, kicking it and struggling. She was on a mobile phone and looked as if she'd slept rough the night before. Her hair was matted and, even though it was a particularly chilly day she had raw, red, bare legs and was wearing flip-flops (never a good look in March). Part of me was delighted she was taking the dog away and part of me was terrified she was only taking it away to enter it into some ghastly dogfight. I told James.

'Rubbish!' he said. 'She's taking it for a lovely walk in the park and then home to sit in front of her crackling fire after a delicious bowl of dog biscuits. Why do you always look on the dark side, Marie?'

'Because I'm usually right,' I said, ruefully. But after warmly kissing him goodbye – ouch ouch ouch! – I gave him a big hug and went back inside.

One thing I *won't* be doing today is logging onto Facebook. I've already forgotten the password.

March 22

Put my alarm on for really early because today was the day I was talking to Gene's class about life in the old days. Haven't got up at such a time since I was teaching at school myself. You get into bad habits, being retired. Pouncer wasn't even in from his nightly escapades – he seems to stay out all night – so I left him his food, checked I'd got my notes and my bag full of artefacts and pennies, locked up and set off for the bus. To my horror, I could still hear the poor dog opposite barking away, and then starting to whine pitifully. The Grisly Woman must have returned after the dogfight and was leaving him to starve till the next one. I can't let this go on.

It's odd to think that I used to brave the rush hour every day when I was working. Now I wonder how on earth I did it. All those people, squashed up against each other, staring at their iPods – or is it iPads? I never know the difference – or listening to music through their headphones. Suddenly I remembered how smelly we all used to be in the old days. You'd get on a bus or go down to the Underground and it would reek of old sweat and unwashed hair and chip fat. Now, everyone reeks of scent and aftershave. I have to say that, though I regret the passing of a lot about the old days, the pong isn't one of them. Did we ever clean our clothes? I remember washing my hair only once a fortnight. And we didn't have baths more than once a week, when we were only allowed to run the water until it was six inches deep. I made a mental note to tell the children. Children are all very keen on smells and find them hilarious.

The school was miles south of the river, a sprawling Victorian building set at the top of a steep road lined with plane trees. I found a wrought-iron gate and tottered, gasping, up a disabled walkway beside a wretched-looking children's garden where seeds had clearly been planted – you could tell by the little seed packets threaded through with sticks – though whether they'd ever come up or not was another matter. There was no bell on the wall, so I pushed open a great door to find no one there at all. Finally, after wandering down several corridors, I came across an office where a dismal typist was hammering away at a computer keyboard, and announced myself.

The dismal typist told me to wait, so I found a chair and sat there, beside a wastepaper bin in the shape of a huge plastic frog, under lists of school trips and kids' paintings pinned on a noticeboard. All around was the pervasive smell of school – poster paints, pencil sharpenings, a slight whiff of floor polish and steamed fish. On the wall was a notice:

OUR SIX GOLDEN RULES.

At this school we promise to

1. Be kind to other people.
2. No hitting.
3. Offer help to everyone.
4. Never talk to strangers.
5. If you are worried about anything, tell a teacher.
6. Stay safe.

Oh, the grammar! I tried not to think about it, and dwelt on the message instead. It's odd, this modern preoccupation with 'staying safe'. It wasn't a phrase we used in the old days. As for strangers, I remember that, every day we walked home from school, we had to brave the ghastly old flasher who stood on the corner as we passed, keeping his dirty brown overcoat wide open to reveal a mangy, beige-coloured penis, sagging sadly from the flies of his stained grey trousers. 'Put it away!' we used to shout. 'Tiny!' And he'd go on grinning mindlessly. If that happened now, everyone would have a nervous breakdown. However, I thought as I sat in that dingy office, perhaps this was one memory I *wouldn't* be sharing with Year Two.

'Mrs Sharp?' A tall and gorgeous black girl, her hair swept up in a complicated cornucopia of knots and swirls, suddenly appeared in front of me holding a clipboard. She looked more like an escapee from the *X Factor* than a teacher. 'I'm Miss Grendel, Year Two's form teacher. Will you come this way?'

'Well, this is certainly a change from when I was an infant,' I said, as she led me down several concrete passages until we reached an airy forecourt, off which I could see several class-rooms. 'All the teachers then were dreadful old hags.'

Miss G smiled. 'No doubt I look like a dreadful old hag in the eyes of my class,' she said.

'Surely not!' I said. 'You look utterly gorgeous!' Then I felt silly. I did hope she didn't think I was chatting her up. Age gives you a kind of prerogative to say nice and flattering things to young people, but I suddenly thought what I'd said was rather creepy. I suppose I was nervous. I was surprised to find how anxious I felt at the idea of addressing Gene's class, despite having been a teacher for so long myself. I really didn't want to let him down in front of his friends.

'Have you got any objects to show the children?' she said, as we went in.

'Yes,' I said, producing my large chart. 'And I thought that I'd give them each an old-fashioned penny at the end because I kept a lot of them when we changed to decimal currency.'

'That's a nice thought,' she said. Then she added, 'But we don't encourage children to take presents from strangers, so perhaps it might be best if you give them to me and I'll dis-tribute them at the end of the day.'

Stranger? I thought. But I'm Gene's granny!

None of the children showed the remotest interest in my arrival as they were all pinching and pulling each other. There were about 30 of them, all around six or seven years old, sit-ting cross-legged on the floor. Miss Grendel clapped her hands and they gawped up at me. I searched the sea of children for Gene and there he was – most odd to see him in his uniform, staring out at me. I could hardly recognize him in his white shirt, green blazer and grey trousers. Naturally enough he hadn't rushed up and kissed me but he seemed too shy even to catch my eye. Then, I realized to my embarrassment, that it wasn't actually Gene at all. It was a little boy who looked exactly like him. Indeed all the boys looked exactly the same in their uniforms.

I cast around again for Gene and then I saw him watching me, and he waved his hand very low down so he couldn't be seen. Out of politeness I played it very cool, too, only giving him a perfunctory nod. But I found I was starting to sweat. I had to make it good – for Gene's sake.

I pinned the chart to the wall and began by telling them that, when I was small, they still used to do twice-daily tests of the air-raid sirens – explaining what they were – and then described a little of what it had been like during my childhood. No television, computers, mobile phones. No central heating. No frozen food. No fish fingers. No McDonald's. Indeed, no burgers at all, and no pasta, except in special restaurants. No fridges, just iceboxes. No fruit except apples, oranges and pears. Only a tiny bit of butter, meat and eggs each week because they were rationed by the government. The same with sweets – only a few each week, and the shop put a stamp in our ration books.

An incredulous murmuring came from the class.

I told them that in the old days everyone was much thinner

than they are now and that we walked everywhere because there were hardly any cars.

I did also mention the smell, which made them all laugh. And how the streets were full of dog poo. And that in the towns in the winter we had big fogs, when you couldn't even see your hand in front of your face. And when we walked in the country there were loads of birds and butterflies and insects and wild flowers.

And though I say it myself, it was a roaring success.

But when it came to questions, I realized how little they could even comprehend life in what to me is only a recent past.

'How did you wipe your bottom if you didn't have toilet paper?' asked one.

'We had toilet paper, but it wasn't soft like it is today. It was cold and hard, like greaseproof paper,' I said. But then I realised they probably had never heard of greaseproof paper. 'Like tracing paper.' But no one had heard of that, either. 'Like shiny wrapping paper,' I said, eventually. 'It was a bit cold and scratchy,' I added.

'Did you have a horse and carriage?' asked another.

'No,' I said, 'but when my granny was young, she had one . . .'

'Were you evacuated?' For some reason – they've probably done a project on it – they were obsessed with the life of evacuees.

'No, that only happened in the war.'

'Did you ever meet Mary Seacole?' asked one little Asian girl.

'No, she died before I was born. A long time before I was born,' I answered.

Curious. I think it's only adults who have any sense of the past. Not much point in teaching history to little people Gene's age, really. It's difficult enough for them to cope with yesterday, today and tomorrow without understanding years into the past as well.

'Did you ever meet Hitler?' asked a boy sitting next to Gene. But a very fat girl on his other side said, 'Of course she didn't meet Hitler, silly. He'd committed suicide in his bunker before she was born.' Which was rather odd considering she can't have been older than seven. Obviously going to be a genius.

I'd brought with me an old, rather bald, stuffed toy badger I used to have when I was small – which all the little girls thought was 'sweet'. And I showed them a couple of old exercise books I'd kept, filled with my neat pencilled handwriting, with which they were very impressed.

Then I produced the pennies, and they went down a storm. I loved doling them into their small, grubby hands – and I was sorry when Miss Grendel told them they all had to hand them in and she'd give them out again at the end of the day. (No doubt after she'd checked each one to make sure it was 'safe'.)

When it was all over I gave a discreet wave to Gene, who grinned at me and made a thumbs-up sign, which was extremely gratifying. Then, as it was break-time, I was invited for a coffee in the staff room, a curiously smoke-free zone compared to the old days when I'd been a teacher. And what amazed me was that, on our way there, Miss Grendel herself said that she'd learned a lot from my talk. 'I didn't realize about the smells and the dog poo,' she said. 'That must have been very unhealthy!'

I was completely ignored by her colleagues until I revealed I'd been an art teacher all my life. Then they all started moaning on at me about how things had changed for the worse, and teaching wasn't like in my day, when it had been easy. Not wanting to be impolite, I didn't disagree, but clearly they had a rose-coloured view of what things were like in the past. I've been twice threatened by pupils with knives – and once a parent actually got his hands round my throat before he was pulled away by the geography teacher, who happened to come by in the nick of time.

'Did you say you taught art?' said Miss Grendel. 'Are you qualified?'

'Of course I'm qualified,' I said. 'Got my Child Protection Checks. I've spent my whole life teaching!'

'Do you miss it?'

'Sometimes. Why?'

Miss Grendel said, 'Wait there . . .' and, rather mysteriously, slipped out of the door and down the corridor.

'I think she's just gone to ask the Head something,' explained one of the other teachers. I thought it was all very odd. I wondered if I'd transgressed some ghastly new school rule, like not talking about dog poo to six-year-olds in case they were traumatized for life, and I'd be clapped in irons, vilified for the rest of my life and never allowed to be alone with children again. I'd be put on some kind of register or have to wear a thing on my leg and observe curfews. I'd only be able to see Gene with a responsible adult in attendance on neutral ground. Or perhaps they'd discovered that the pennies weren't 'safe' after all.

However, Miss G returned with the head teacher – or what I would have called 'headmistress' – another bizarrely young-looking creature with spiky purple hair. And eventually I discovered that Year One's art teacher has some kind of post-viral syndrome and can't work at full steam. How would I feel about helping her on a regular basis?

The job would be unpaid, said the Head, the children would be much younger than I'd been used to – and luckily the year below Gene – but, she said, it would be wonderful if I could do the job.

Normally I never make a decision without waiting 24 hours, but this time I had no doubt in my mind whatsoever. 'I'd love to!' I said, immensely pleased and flattered. 'It's just what I need at the moment!' It would take my mind off the lump and it would get me back feeling useful again. 'When can I start?'

She said they'd got someone covering the next month, but after that things were looking pretty desperate. Could I start in May?

I've been away from teaching for too long. It would be good to get back. And I do love those little people!

March 23

I told Penny all about it this evening, over a glass of white wine. (She'd come over with some weird new ready meal from Waitrose which, to be honest, wasn't very nice, but at least we didn't have to cook it ourselves.) And she was very envious.

'You're very lucky,' she said. 'One of the things about being retired is that you don't feel useful, or that you matter to anyone.'

'Well, you do if you've got grandchildren,' I said and then bit my tongue because I realised Penny didn't have any. It's very difficult, when you've got grandchildren, not to bang on about what a joy they are and then, as you watch the other person's face get stonier and stonier, realize that not only do they not have grandchildren but perhaps they don't even have any children. 'But of course Gene's going to be grown-up soon and won't want to come and see his old granny and then I'll be up a gum tree. Sometimes I feel that, now Archie's dead and Louis hasn't been seen for dust, I haven't got any close relationships with anyone at all – except you and James of course. And maybe Marion. My only new relationship,' I said sourly, 'is with a lump.'

'And that's nothing new,' said Penny, with surprising acerbity. 'Much the same as a husband.'

'Do you know,' I said, 'when I look back on being married to David, I'm not sure that having a lump isn't, to be frank, slightly better.'

'How is David these days?' asked Penny, helping herself to another glass of wine.

'Well, Sandra's left him and now he's all ready to be snapped up by someone else,' I said. 'The widow next door has already got her eyes on him. What about you, Penny? I think you'd make David a very nice wife. Maybe we should get you together?'

'Hmm,' said Penny, looking rather sly and twinkly. 'Who knows? I'd love to see him again, anyway.'

Later

Was just thinking about Penny and David and remembering Penny's husband, Bill. He was a different matter, a drunken bore who was congenitally unfaithful, and she was well rid of him. But David . . . he'd never been horrible. We still liked each other. I just think we'd married too young and when we got to a certain age we both thought that it was our last chance to have a new life. So I'd ended up on my own – which actually was rather interesting and exciting, even if it was on occasion lonely – and he'd ended up, poor sap, with Sandra. Who now was leaving him in the lurch. I must see he's fixed up with someone nice. Nothing I like better than playing marriage-broker.

March 24

Forgot to put the clocks forward so was an hour late for lunch with Penny – or would have been if she hadn't rung me. Can't think how I'd been so stupid. I'd even written myself a little Post-it note and stuck it on the mirror last night to remind me, but it had dropped off.

APRIL

April 3

An email told me that I might have missed lots of 'activity' on Facebook, so I gingerly logged in. (Having forgotten my password, I had to reset it and plumped for one of a long line of European kings – work that out, snooping burglars!) And arriving at my page, I discovered I had four requests to become 'friends'. One was James. One was Penny. One was Marion and one was some mysterious Singhalese man called Wu who I'd never heard of. He didn't have a picture of himself, just a photograph of a brass bell. I 'confirmed' them all. What the hell.

Next, I thought I'd take a peek around other people's pages. But oh, the misery of looking at them! Golly, what rubbish they post! Marion had several holiday snaps, mainly of meaningless mountains, and an incredibly dreary picture of a snowflake with the words 'Amazing what nature can do!' written under it. She also had an image of a rainbow under which she'd written, simply, 'Wow!' Several of her other friends had clicked 'Like' underneath.

Even Penny let me down, with a photograph of a statue with a pigeon on its head, underneath which someone had written 'hahaha'. There was a cartoon reproduced from the *New Yorker* of a cat on a desert island. Couldn't make head nor tail of it. And a video of a penguin being tickled and making an odd noise, which she commented was 'hilarious'.

Later she'd written, 'Happiness is something that sometimes comes through a door you didn't know you left open.'

I scratched my head. Then I checked her name. Yes, it was Penny. My Penny. Amusing, witty, sympathetic. And there she was writing incredibly soppy things about happiness. Last month she'd posted the Serenity Prayer. Crikey!

Glad to see, however, that she had 'shared' the Facebook Valentines that her daughter and husband had sent each other. Presumably, then, they're not getting divorced.

April 4

It seems most of the committee can make the residents' meeting, which is going to be here, next month. Will have to think of things to talk about – though Sheila the Dealer can usually be relied on to regale us with accounts of her sister's many operations and Marion can bore for Britain about the filthy state of the streets and the fact that she's found used needles in her garden. Drug users seem always to select Marion's garden as the one in which to dispose of their paraphernalia. I've never found a used needle in mine. It's not fair.

April 5

Met Marion at the National Gallery. Very tactfully, I dragged her scarf out of the charity cupboard and, gritting my teeth, draped it round my neck. She'd said she wanted to see an exhibition of Goya drawings, which interested me, but it soon emerged that the whole outing was really an excuse for her to sit me down over coffee and offer me advice on how to cure the 'cancer' she'd decided I'd got, by any method possible except for ones proven by drug trials, doctors and science, all things of which she is deeply suspicious. Rather than have an operation to cut a tumour out, she prefers coffee enemas. Rather than admittedly clumsy but often effective chemotherapy, she prefers sticking tincture of wheatgrass up your nose, and lying slathered with damp sage leaves for hours on end.

'Look, I don't even know if it's cancer, yet,' I said. 'It's probably nothing.'

'This friend of mine, she was told she was going to die in two weeks, but she got this book, I'll get the title if you like, and she followed the instructions to the letter and she's been alive now for two years! Every day she gets up at 4am and meditates for an hour, then she has a coffee enema, then she liquidizes 17 different fruits and drinks them all in a special order, then she meditates again – this time visualizing the cancer as a block of ice, which melts as she radiates these golden vibes over it. She's cut all her nails because they store all the toxins, and turned all her furniture in her house round so she's sleeping to face west . . .'

'Marion!' I said sharply. 'I am not going to get up at 4am, meditate, bung coffee up my bottom or anything. I would rather die,' I said firmly. 'Do stop it. Anyway, ten to one, the lump will turn out to be benign.'

Whatever that means. When people say they have a lump that is 'benign', it means it's simply nothing at all, that it's not malign. But I always consider the word 'benign' to mean that it's actually doing good. I'd love it if this lump were to turn out a happy, friendly, jolly lump that had arrived at just the right time to protect me from my enemies. A benign lump that made me tea in the morning and said of course I was right when everyone else said I was wrong, and who sang me to sleep and produced extra tenners when I was short.

Marion looked very disappointed when I refused to listen to any more mad remedies, commenting, as a final barb, that I wasn't looking at all well (would anyone, wearing an orange scarf, except for some proud Namibian tribeswoman?) and I changed the subject to when the next residents' meeting should be held.

April 8

'Water to be rationed by next year! "One shower per week if lucky!" predicts Minister' (*Daily Rant*)

April 9

I didn't tell anyone I was having a scan today. I couldn't bear the idea of Marion insisting that she came along and either taking over the whole thing, as if I were a child or worrying herself sick and shaking and holding my hand. And no doubt trying to persuade me not to have the scan at all, since, she would assure me, it was full of evil rays that far from detecting anything would actually *give* me cancer. I didn't even want Penny there chattering on about nothing 'to take my mind off it all'. James would have been okay, but somehow it was something I wanted to do all by myself. No fuss, that's me.

I'd parked with difficulty in the exorbitantly expensive hospital car park – it was in Fulham – a vast area with practically no spaces at all. Being an old parking hand, I spotted a man cautiously wheeling an Asian lady swathed not only in a burka but also in bandages, down an endless aisle of cars, and noticed he had car keys dangling in his hand so I followed him, very slowly. I'd been right. He opened his car, and I waited for him to lift in the patient, then fold up the wheelchair and stash it in the boot – quite a process – before he got into the driving seat and switched on the engine. (I could tell that when the rear brake-lights came on.) But what is it that drivers do between turning the key and actually pulling out? Quite honestly, this one had enough time to dial a phone-in radio show and give his detailed thoughts on MPs' expenses before he decided, at last, to reverse out.

I finally managed to park and, pulling my coat around me

because it was a bitterly cold day – bleak and wretched, just right for a scan – I plunged into the hospital, past scores of sickly smokers puffing away outside the entrance, some even attached to drips, others in their pyjamas and nightdresses, shivering with cold.

Hospitals are like foreign countries, and there were signs for all kinds of departments I'd never heard of: Ancillary X-rays (GSA), Orthopaedic Gynaecology (P2), Paediatric Genesis (xii). Eventually I showed my letter to a bored woman at the desk who was glued to her screen (no doubt 'liking' a picture of a crocodile wearing an apron on Facebook). And she, naturally enough, told me I was in the wrong building. She gave me a baffling map that was the sort of thing that Jack would construct for Gene's friends on a birthday treasure hunt. 'You are here,' she said, jabbing a fat finger in the middle. So I set off.

By the time I arrived at the Scanning Centre, I was ten minutes late and frantic. It was no bad thing because at least I'd forgotten all about the lump in my panic. But of course I was made to wait another hour until I was seen. I noticed, on top of a cupboard, a sinister box on which was printed 'Cervical Spectroscope with Locking Nut'. Yikes.

Finally a nurse showed me into a cubicle and – after I'd taken off all my clothes, stashed my watch, my ring and my specs into a locker, and put on a gown – she sat me down to grill me.

'Do you have any metal fillings?' she asked. 'Any pacemakers? Pins in your legs or anywhere in your body?' She had to ask this because, apparently, the scanner is hugely magnetic and if you have anything inside you that's metal, it either drags it out of your body, through your flesh, or sticks you to the roof of the machine, leaving you there until the thing's turned off. Once, a patient suffering agonizing stomach troubles had an MRI scan to find out what was wrong, and practically died of pain when it transpired that a very sharp scalpel had been left inside her during her last operation. You can imagine what happened. Or so goes the urban myth.

'Any tattoos?'

Tattoos? Apparently there is metal in some of the tattoo ink. Not much fun when the carefully etched tiger on your chest starts slowly to pounce, pulling all your flesh skywards.

'Nothing at all. The only bit of metal in me is a will of iron,' I said.

'A will of iron?' she asked, looking up briefly, puzzled.

'Don't worry. Only a joke. You've probably heard it before,' I said, though clearly she hadn't.

Next she said, 'Now, I have to ask you this. Is there any reason to think you might be pregnant?'

Feeling immensely flattered that anyone could possibly imagine I was pregnant at my great age and congratulating myself yet again on the result of the facelift I had a couple of years ago – which still doesn't seem to have collapsed – I jokingly replied, 'No, of course not! Unlikely anyway, because I'm 103.'

Far from laughing lightly, she really did start at this revelation. 'You're not!' she said, staring into my face. 'Not really?'

'No, not really,' I said, suddenly flattened again. 'Come on, let's get this over with.'

Taking me into another room, she hoisted me onto a bed, positioned just outside an enormous white metal tube. She placed various lumps of plastic around me and told me that the whole thing would take 20 minutes. 'You must stay still,' she intoned. 'If you move a fraction of a millimetre, the scan won't work. So even if you have an itch, don't move. And I suggest that, since many people find this rather claustrophobic, you close your eyes.'

She gave me a flex with a soft plastic bulb attached – which I was to press if I couldn't stand it – warned me that the whole procedure was incredibly noisy, and left to switch the contraption on.

I had decided, long before submitting to this torture, that I would keep sane by counting the number of seconds in 20 minutes. It would keep my mind occupied and stop me freaking out, thinking, 'How long have I been in here? Hours or days? What if there's a fire in the hospital and everyone's evacuated and they forget about me? What if my particular nurse has a heart attack and dies and no one finds her body till the following morning, when they'd discover me scanned to a crisp inside the machine, all my fillings embedded in the lid.'

And was it noisy! (Imagine operating a power drill in the middle of Oxford Street without protective earphones.) But after a while I started to get into it. I discovered that there was something utterly blissful about lying there, the centre of attention, with nothing, absolutely nothing, to do. I felt like a much-loved sleeping baby being stared at by its adoring relations.

In fact, when it was all over and I was hauled out, I said, 'God, I could have stayed in there all day!' and at that point the nurse looked even more astonished than she had when I'd said I was 103.

'No one's ever said that before in all my ten years here!' she said. 'They usually come out absolutely gibbering!'

The results will be 'posted to my doctor', she said. So I suppose it will be next year before I get any news.

April 10

Ate an entire Family Pack of Maltesers. Felt very sick.

April 11

Had a really scary thing happen to me today. I went to the newsagent to get some more milk, but when I looked for my purse I couldn't find it. I told him I'd go back and get it but when I got back home, there was no sign of it. I was almost certain that I'd had it last night, and even this morning, but couldn't for the life of me imagine where I'd put it. All my credit cards were inside so being without it would have been the end of the world.

Then I thought maybe I'd got it in my hand when I went to the newsagent and put it on the counter, and then looked in my bag for it – a kind of batty move. So I went back. Nothing.

I returned home again and scoured the house, even looking in rooms that I haven't been into since last week. And looking in weird places like the lavatory. And pockets of clothes I hadn't worn since last year. But nothing. I started to imagine that someone must have nicked it from my purse between here and the newsagent and I realized that I'd have to ring up the bank pretty soon and cancel all my credit cards. Otherwise at this very moment people would start ordering flat screen televisions and exotic handbags on my account. Then I thought, 'Maybe it's in the car!' It might have fallen out onto the floor. So I went out and had a look – but nothing.

Back I came to the house and again looked in every room, under every chair and bed and cushion, even in the garden, mad as it was. I was just about to ring my bank to cancel the cards – I was holding the receiver and looking for the number in my address book – when I suddenly thought, 'Why don't I pray to St Anthony, the patron saint of lost things?'

So even though I have no religious faith at all, I bowed my head and sent up a fervent prayer to Old Tony. I sat down for about a minute to give him a chance to find it and then, giving up, turned to the telephone again. But as the number was ringing I was hit by a sudden thought. Perhaps it was in the pocket of my dressing gown?

I went upstairs, put my hand in the pocket, and blow me, there it was! What it was doing in there I have no idea. Why would I put my purse in my dressing gown pocket? Honestly, the power of that monk.

Still, oddly, even though I'd found my purse, the panic

chemicals that had gone whizzing round my body remained with me until about teatime.

April 13

What a brilliant day – or so it seemed to me – though actually it was no more brilliant than yesterday. I couldn't understand why I was so happy, but I felt all spring-like and energized and for some reason all the aches and pains I usually have in my body had simply vanished. I actually *ran up the stairs* for the first time in weeks. In the garden the first daffodils were out and when I leaned down to smell them I was exhilarated. Even Pouncer, not known for his leaping abilities, was jumping about on the lawn like a spring lamb, trying to catch a baby frog no doubt.

And, thank God, no noise from the dog. Actually, haven't heard it for a while now and hoping, rather selfishly, that it's either been taken away or died. Either way, I wouldn't have to hear it suffering any more.

April 14

I was just sorting out my freezer when the bell rang. Sorting out the freezer is rather like Christmas for me. I discover things I simply can't remember ever buying – and they're usually, by now, whitened with freezer burn around the edges. There was a packet of chicken livers (*maybe*; they might just as well have been a collection of benign and cancerous lumps placed there by some strange surgeon who was passing and saw the door open). Also a French loaf that was brittle with age – at least I think it was a French loaf, it might have been a thin leg of lamb – plus a pack of extremely old what-looked-like-stewing-steak. Then there was a rigid green cardigan I'd stuffed in months ago, to try and cure it of moths. Forgetting this, I'd later spent hours ringing up theatres, cinemas, restaurants and friends to ask if I'd left it on their premises – little knowing that, like a woolly mammoth lodged in the permafrost, it was here all the time, buried in the ice.

What else? Some iced lollies I'd made for Gene, about six packets of frozen peas and a plastic box of something brownish-grey with a label on it which started 'Delicious ...' and was then smudged beyond recognition, so I'll never know what it was. No good serving it up as a pudding and finding that actually it was guacamole or aloo gobi. There was one sad chicken leg – can't imagine what I was going to do with that but I kept it anyway, for stock in the future – and, triumph of triumphs, a ring that my lovely Archie gave me years and years ago. It wasn't anything like the valuable one he'd given me, which I'd sold to help pay for the facelift, but a cheapie from the early days. It must have fallen off when I was stuffing the cardie in the freezer drawer.

Anyway, as I say, I was just wiping the drawers out, and about to put everything back in some kind of order and make a list of what was where, when the bell went.

Cursing, and wiping my frozen hands on my apron, I opened the door to find an alarming creature on my doorstep, dressed in flowing green and gold, with wild curly red hair bursting from beneath an elaborate flower-laden straw hat, covered with rings and emanating a powerful smell of patchouli oil. She – I imagined it was either a 'she', or a very elaborate transvestite – wore bright red lipstick, was clasping her hands in front of her in a pleading gesture and had on her feet an enormous pair of blue Crocs. For one moment I thought the Romanian gangs that the *Daily Rant* insists are waiting to pounce on vulnerable middle-class women had well and truly arrived, and that this supplicating figure was just stage one in a dastardly scheme to appropriate my house. But this person didn't look too dastardly. She was bursting with smiles and, the moment she saw me, reached out both hands, took mine in hers and pulled me forwards to embrace me, kissing me warmly on both cheeks.

'Surprise!' she said. 'I've been told all about you! Straight away I knew we'd be friends! And now I've seen you it's true! Oooh, your hands are cold!' she said suddenly, pulling hers away and making a face.

'Sorry, I was just cleaning out the free . . .'

'I need to ask you a teeny favour,' she said, 'before you ask me in.'

My mind was whirring, riffling through the files, trying to imagine who the hell she was. Her voice was low and intimate and at the same time powerful, like one of those old actresses who, despite having drunk gin and tonics all their lives and smoked like chimneys, still have whispers that carry to the gallery.

Then suddenly the penny dropped. It must be the new neighbour!

'Oh, you're Melanie from next door!' I stammered.

'Indeed I am!' purred Melanie. 'We have so much in common! You're David Sharp's ex, aren't you! Oh, I remember David. We had a little fling a long time ago. Before he was married,' she added hastily, giving a naughty smile and then covering her mouth coquettishly. 'Terrible in bed, wasn't he? Now, my removal van's waiting at the end of the road – he's a darling and so cheap – but we can't park the van because your little old car is in front. If you moved it, there'd be just enough room.'

'Of course!' I said, going back into the house to get my keys. But how on earth did she know it was my car? And what was all that about David? I'd always enjoyed sex with him. Very much, actually, as far as I could remember. However, I resolved to keep an open mind. And in order to shift the power balance further in my favour I graciously asked if she'd like to come to supper tonight. (She could always have that weird brown thing called 'Delicious . . .'.)

'My dear, you're an angel!' she said. 'There is nothing I'd like more. I shall be exhausted! I'll pop over at 8.30 just after I've done my meditation. And you won't mind if we park some of my pots in your front garden just temporarily, will you? No, I know you won't. Word of your great kindness has spread far and wide. I've just got so much *stuff. Stuff*. Isn't it dreadful! It's the curse of our age group.'

Pots in my garden? I was certain my hackles were rising,

but unfortunately I have no idea what or, indeed, where, my hackles might be. We could sort it all out later.

Will she make a new wife for David? I think not!

Later

Melanie arrived half an hour late, a brilliant, jangling, gasping burst of smells, bells and scarves. She carried a nearly dead spider plant in a pink and white striped pot. The earth was as dry and brown as something out of my freezer.

'I brought this for you, darling,' she said, handing it to me. (Then she deposited an overflowing straw bag by the door and unfurled a lacy shawl from her shoulders, hurling it onto the stairs before she came into the sitting room. Rather unnervingly, she didn't remove her hat.) 'I found it behind the kitchen door and I thought, 'if there's one person who can bring this back to life, it's the lovely Marie. I hear you have a wonderful way with plants.'

I thought back to the time, a few years ago, when I'd ordered vast quantities of flowering plants from a garden centre and only one had come up, but if she'd heard I had green fingers, so be it. 'And I've brought you this as well,' she added, producing from her bag an already-opened bottle of white wine which had about a third left. 'I've been drinking it all day to get through and I thought it was a shame to waste the last bit. No . . . you have it all. I've had enough.' Melanie had already followed me into the kitchen. I poured the remains into a glass and took a great gulp while she deposited another glittering golden stole over a chair and then somehow managed to open the garden door at the back, allowing a huge draught to blow in. I couldn't work out how on earth she knew where the key was. Even though it was pitch black, she started to poke around, jumping up to see over the wall into her own garden.

'I've got such plans for this place, Marie,' she yelled through the open door. 'I'm going to gravel over the lawn, and make a maze of box hedges at the bottom, and then put the hot tub at the end, and a great mirror so we can all see ourselves – you must come over when it's summer, we'll have such fun, you and I – and I'm getting a sprung dance floor laid in the kitchen, and I've got this marvellous old jukebox . . .'

'But how can you have a maze when it's only a small garden?' I shouted, turning the potatoes on.

'Oh, anything's possible,' said Melanie, airily, as she came back in. 'You just have to ask your angels.' She shrugged off a scarlet scarf and draped it over one of the kitchen chairs. 'I'm like a child, you know, Marie,' she added. 'I have these child-like qualities and I bring out the child in everyone I meet!'

'I see,' I said coldly, thinking privately that it would be a long time before she brought out the child in *me*.

I opened a new bottle of wine, to which she gladly helped herself. And discovering, after a slightly precarious tasting moment, that the "Delicious" was a bit of old kedgeree I'd made a couple of years ago, I perked it up with some cream and lemon and it wasn't bad. Over coffee in the sitting room, Mel, as she insisted I call her ('Mar and Mel, we'll be like Starsky and Hutch or Laurel and Hardy') flung off her shoes and swung her feet onto the sofa. I heard about her three failed marriages, her daughter in rehab, her disastrous pottery venture in the South of France, and the time she was asked to give evidence at a Parliamentary Committee on homeopathy. She'd also lived in Nigeria, escaped prison when she was with a heroin dealer in Paraguay and done a course in reflexology. There was nothing she hadn't done, no one, it seemed, she hadn't slept with – she'd had one lover for every year of her life, 60 in all – and no experience she hadn't had. I felt like an unadventurous and spinsterish old pudding. She also told me about her two children – the rehab one lives in the US and the other in Delhi. Can't blame them, frankly. I imagine the moment they turned 16, they booked tickets for countries as far away from their mother as possible.

She has three grandchildren who naturally have no idea who she is, since she can barely afford to visit them and they hardly ever come here. But she announced she hadn't given up on men: 'You never know, do you? There's life in the old girl yet! The pilot light hasn't completely gone out, if you know what I mean!'

At this point I informed her that any idea of sexual relationships with men was completely out of the question as far as I was concerned and she raised her eyebrows till they disappeared under her hat.

'Never say never, darling,' she said. 'You might get lucky any time. Fate is a wonderful thing. You and I still scrub up pretty well, and wouldn't look too bad on a dark night with the moon behind us, as my grandmother used to say. We've just got to look stylish enough. You know what the saintly

Mandela said, a natty dresser if ever there was one: "Appearance constitutes reality." What say you and I go out on the pull one night?'

Finally, 'Enough about me,' she said, bestowing a charming smile on me as I opened another bottle of wine. 'You must tell me all about *you*. I hear you're a brilliant artist. Now, for a start, how are we going to cheer up this dreary street? I was thinking of starting a Residents' Association once I get settled, but then I heard that there is one already, but it must be pretty dozy, to be honest, because it hasn't done anything for the . . .'

'I am the chair of the Residents' Association,' I said, acidly. Melanie was momentarily nonplussed. But she recovered quickly, waving a hand covered with rings. 'Well, that's marvellous! We can do great things! We'll transform the street! Parties! Hanging baskets! And we must do something about the appalling parking situation! Is there a date for the next meeting? I want to be on the committee!'

When she finally got up to go at midnight I was exhausted. Then, while she kept me chatting in the cold outside my front door, to my immense fury, James passed by on his way back from dinner somewhere. He hung over the gate and naturally he had to be introduced and Melanie turned to me and said, 'You've kept him hidden from me! You have such a dishy neighbour, you lucky girl. And he's got a beard! I love beards, they're so, so sexy!' She reached out her hand to stroke James' stubble, giving a kitten-like growl as she did so.

'Sadly, I'm gay,' said James, half-flattered and half-embarrassed. She opened the gate and pulled him onto the front path, putting her arm through his. 'We'll soon see about that, darling,' she said. 'But I promise not to try without your permission. Otherwise I might be said to be "inappropriate". Dreadful word that, isn't it? Inappropriate. I love being inappropriate, don't you, Mar? Now I must be off. We've had the most wonderful evening, Mar and I. I have talked most selfishly about myself the whole time, but I'm so happy to be here and have Mar as a neighbour – and you as, I hope, a new dear friend when we get to know each other better.' She made a 'mewing' face at James and finally, making her way past all the pots she'd dumped in my front garden, wound her way to her house and shut the door.

'What an absolutely lovely person!' said James, through his beard, his eyes glittering delightedly. 'So warm! And she obviously adores you! Aren't we lucky to have her here! You must be thrilled! Better than boring old Brad and Sharmie, nice as they were!'

'Hmm,' I said.

'She must have been very pretty when she was young,' he added as he left.

When I came back into the house I found Melanie (I refuse to call her 'Mel') had left a silvery scarf on my landing, and the whole place reeked of her patchouli oil. She was like a cat, I decided, marking out her territory. Pouncer was probably having a fit. Indeed, he was sitting on the middle of the carpet looking distinctly cross. His fur was all smoothed back, and he looked as if he'd been hiding somewhere while she'd been round. Now he ventured up on the sofa where she'd been reclining, giving disapproving sniffs from time to time. I'd have to watch out for her, I thought. 'Mar!' 'Dear friend!' 'Must do something about the street!' What a nerve!

As for her being pretty when she was young, I know quite a few people who everyone thinks must have been pretty when they were young but when you look back on the old photographs they often looked like the back of a bus. I bet she was one of those.

April 21

'Ketchup cancer cure claims "rubbish", say experts' (*Daily Rant*)

April 22

Maddeningly, at midday, when Graham moved in, who should be in her front garden fiddling about but Melanie herself? She draped herself over the wall, gawping as he and another young man unloaded boxes from the back of a large car they'd double-parked outside.

'And who are you?' she asked, from under her hat.

'I'm just moving in to Marie Sharp's house as her lodger,' replied Graham, nodding to me.

'Oh, *are* you?' said Melanie, giving me a horribly sly look. 'Giving up men, eh? That's what she was saying last night, and now look who she's got moving in. He's just gorgeous,' she added, to me. 'Very fit. You like them young, don't you!

Only teasing!' she added, seeing Graham's laughing grimace as he staggered in with yet another box of books.

'Do forgive her,' I whispered to him in the hall. 'She's only just moved in. She's an absolute nightmare!'

But Graham for some reason simply grinned. 'Oh she's a game old girl!' he said. 'Doesn't mean any harm. Must be lovely to have her as a neighbour. So warm.'

I bridled. Presumably these men only say that Melanie is warm compared to icy old me. Or was I just getting paranoid? Quite possibly. Or could it be that she is literally warm? There she was on a freezing April day, standing outside with only a dressing gown on as far as I could see, happily gossiping away, while I was inside the house covered with vast jerseys, my teeth chattering.

Anyway, Melanie refused to leave them alone as they humped box after box into the house.

'You don't do it by halves, Mar, do you!' she purred. 'I think you two gorgeous hunks need a drink after all that work.' And she slipped inside her house, arriving back with two beers, which she handed to them. They downed them gratefully. I was left feeling ungrateful, and mean.

'Can I offer you a cup of tea?' I said nervously when they came into the house. And bless them, even if it was just to humour me, they both said that was what they *really* wanted.

'Mar!' yelled Melanie, from the front. 'Mar!'

'What?' I asked tetchily, as I peered round the door.

'Forgot to ask . . . do you think I could borrow your hunks to move a bit of furniture around here? I've got a large wardrobe that needs lifting upstairs and an old oak chest that doesn't look right on the top floor . . .'

'Melanie!' I said reprovingly. 'Give them a break! *You* ask them if you're so keen.'

'What are they called?' asked Melanie.

'Graham and William,' I replied.

'Gray and Bill! Gray and Bill!' she shouted through my door. 'Will you come and help a damsel in distress!'

'By the way, when are you going to move your pots?' I asked.

'Oh, very soon,' she said casually. 'But I think they look lovely in your garden. Makes the house look really chic. Still, don't worry about them. What I want to know is: what's that dreadful barking? Does it come from across the road? That house with the alley down the side? It sounds as if a dog is being murdered on an hourly basis.'

I'm afraid to say that the dog *hasn't* gone away. I've been kept awake for the last two nights, first by its barking and then by just thinking about its horrible situation. 'Oh, it's ghastly, isn't it?' I said, relieved that at last we could share a mutual outrage.

'Well, personally, if it goes on like this I'm tempted to get some poison, inject it into a steak and chuck it over the garden wall,' she said. 'It makes such a racket! Particularly when I'm trying to meditate!'

'I was thinking more of rescuing it,' I said nervously. 'But I don't know where I'd keep it.'

'I'll keep it,' said Melanie. 'For five minutes. Then I'll take it to the local vet and get it put out of its misery. But seriously – do you mean what you say about rescuing it? I'm game, darling. Tonight?'

'No, no, not tonight,' I said, hastily. 'I've got people coming round, I'm busy . . . let's talk soon if it doesn't stop.'

April 23

Today is St George's Day, which the English have never worked out how to mark.

The *Daily Rant* celebrated in its own way with the headline 'Britain will be "Little Romania"! Ruthless gangs invading!'

Underneath was a photograph of a group of unspeakably unsavoury characters, some with knives in their clenched teeth, boarding a boat and bearing a banner on which was written, 'Brian! We coming!'

Think they meant 'Britain'.

MAY

May 6

First day teaching at the school. They wanted me a week into term so they could get themselves sorted out first. I was nervous, naturally, but rolled up with a whole kit of art-work suggestions: autumn leaves, stencils, potatoes for potato-printing, newspapers and magazines to cut up and make collages from. Angela, the recovering art teacher looks like someone whose plug has been pulled, rather as I used to feel when I had a particularly stupendous hangover. This morning she did hardly anything except introduce me in a soft and piping voice and then slump at her desk.

There were 25 children in the class, all about five years old, and a very noisy bunch they were. Luckily I don't have much problem in keeping control. It was a help, too, that they were dead keen, but I realized after quarter of an hour that I'd completely misjudged their capabilities. I'm used to teaching much older children. When I looked at the class, they all seemed to be glued together with leaves and bits of coloured paper, doing potato prints on their hands and cheeks and getting into a frightful muddle. I resolved to do one project per lesson in future, though this first time it was interesting to see who had some kind of interest and talent and who were just the muck-abouters.

There was Ollie, a ginger-haired monster who was trying to glue his fingers to the desk to see what would happen, and Ahtel, a thin, morose Indian boy who, you could see already, was destined to an excellent future in accounting or computers. He stuck leaves in rigid patterns on his bit of paper and joined them all together with lines. But Barbie was a little girl who seemed to have real talent. For a start, she cut her paper into a circle to make it a different shape from the others', and produced a tremendous collage of prints, leaves and faces from magazines, encircled at the end with a border of red and yellow glitter.

There was only one child I worried about. This was Zac, a very thin, white-faced boy who reminded me of Oliver Twist. He stuck one leaf onto the corner of his piece of paper and simply refused to do anything else. No matter how I encouraged him to put a bit of colour in and add some glitter, he just put his hands by his side and said nothing. He seemed completely out of sync with the rest of the class. Indeed, his behaviour was so peculiar that I asked about him in the staff room during break.

'Oh, Zac,' said Miss Grendel, Gene's teacher. 'He's so sad. He used to be fine but then his parents broke up and he just hasn't got over it, poor boy. Nothing seems to help. He's really devastated by his father leaving.'

'Doesn't he see his dad?' I asked.

'No, Zac refuses to see him. He's extremely unhappy and angry. And the mother doesn't help, to be honest.'

My heart did rather bleed for the little chap, and I resolved to keep a special eye on him. A lonely adult is sad enough, but a lonely child is so pitiful because they don't have any of the strategies or resources we adults have to get help, or cheer themselves up. They don't even have access to drink and drugs, poor mites.

When I got back, I couldn't resist taking a quick peek at Graham's room, as he wasn't yet back from work. Exceptionally tidy, full of files, his computer all set up on the desk, shirts folded neatly and the bed beautifully made. Just my kind of guy. Wish Jack were like that.

Later

When I heard Graham coming in, I popped out just to check that everything had been okay the night before.

'Everything here is perfect!' he said. 'The only problem is that there seems to be a dog barking. Do you know anything about it? It doesn't sound very happy.'

'It's a nightmare,' I said. 'But let's hope it stops soon. Otherwise, I can guarantee I'll be on the case.'

May 8

The most ghastly thing happened this morning. I was lying in bed, listening to the dog and wondering how I could stop myself getting obsessed by it when, breaking into the barking, there came the most stupendous crash. I sat bolt upright in bed, and immediately various car alarms started going off and I could hear the murmur of voices outside.

Pulling on my dressing gown, I rushed down to the street, to find everyone out in hushed groups, gawping. As I stared, there was the 'nee-naw' of a police car, which swerved to a halt. It turned out that a stolen car – driven, everyone imagined, by druggies – had raced down the street, ricocheted off the cars on each side of the road and ended up smashed into a car parked outside the house on the corner. The one with the dog. And it was making the most fearful racket as a result, poor thing. The occupants had apparently leapt out of the car and fled.

'Golly, who's the owner of that?' I asked, pointing across the road to the pile of tangled metal on the corner.

'Don't know,' said a man standing next to me. 'But it's not just that one. It's this one, too.'

He pointed, very worryingly, to my own car.

'Was it bumped into?' I asked nervously. It looked perfectly okay from where I was standing. 'Did it get a scratch?'

'If you look on the other side, you'll see it's a total write-off.'

Despite being in my dressing gown, I walked around to have a look. And was horrified to find the whole left side of my car completely buckled, the wheel askew, the entire thing looking totally done in.

Alerted by the noise, Melanie had by now come stumbling into the street in her dressing gown, a whooshing Indian affair of orange and yellow silk, her head done up in a towelling turban.

'My God, oh my God!' she said with a little scream. 'And that's *your* car!' she said, pointing. 'What are you going to do? Would you like to borrow mine? Please do. You'll have to get a new car . . . but do borrow mine . . .'

Feeling a wave of affection for the old nightmare, I said it was very kind of her. After giving some details to the police and on their advice taking everything I wanted from my car before they called a tow-truck, I went back into the house feeling very shaky. What if I'd been sitting in the car? What if I'd been sitting in it with Gene? But that's a pretty silly question, I told myself. I *wasn't* in it and nor was Gene. I rang James. Thank God he's always there to rely on.

'Well, don't be too disappointed, darling,' he said. 'You were thinking of getting another and you wouldn't have got anything for that old heap. Now we can go looking seriously for a new one.'

I spent part of the evening sifting through the rubbish I'd removed from my old car. An empty bottle of anti-freeze. Some twisted jump-leads. A rope. Four maps falling to pieces, one dating back to the last century (1998, that is). Some funny bits of see-through paper you're meant to stick on your headlights when you go abroad. A dried-up plastic bottle of windscreen wash. A First Aid book. A spare petrol can. A rape alarm. I was about to throw it out, then thought: you never know, it might come in useful one day.

Later

The dog appears to be able to bark every 30 seconds, come what may. How it does this, I really don't know. I don't think it ever gets any sleep. I'm starting to read words into its barks now. I can almost hear it shouting, 'Help me! I'm so lonely and cold and hungry! Please, for God's sake, help me!'

May 9

Got a letter today – at last – from the hospital. They want me to go and see a specialist next month. God, finally, I might get this sorted out. And the fact it's next month means they can't be too worried. The lump really has been preying on my mind – even though in reality it's been preying on my stomach. It's just *there* in a very worrying way. I keep panicking that it's starting to show through my clothes and people will start asking me if I'm pregnant. But actually, on second thoughts, no one but a myopic MRI nurse would do that.

I was so pleased about getting the appointment that I couldn't help telling James about the lump. He was round to look at possible new cars on my computer and was horrified that I hadn't told him before.

'But Marie, we're old friends,' he said, obviously mortally offended that he hadn't been the first to know. I do wish that when I told people they didn't always think of the news in terms of *them* rather than me. Sometimes I wish I hadn't told anyone. Other times I wish I'd put an ad in the paper so that everyone knew at the same time. Or perhaps Facebook would be a better means of communicating such news. Not sure you're allowed to post stuff about lumps on Facebook, actually. People would be hard-pressed to 'like' a picture of a cancerous (or not) lump, though I'm sure there'd be a few mindless 'friends' who would. I've never seen anything on the blasted website that wasn't full of jollity, smiley faces and the word 'Like!' 'Like!' 'Like!' everywhere. I wish you could click on something that said, 'Hmm. Not sure about this.'

'I'm sorry,' I said, not sorry at all. (Not only do I have a lump but I have to apologize for not telling people about it. Bats.) 'I didn't want to worry you.'

'But friends are for sharing worries,' he said. 'And you know I'd want to be first to know – particularly after Hughie . . .'

'Well it was because of Hughie I *didn't* want to tell you,' I said. (Honestly, now I was having to justify myself on top of everything else.) 'Anyway, James,' I added curtly, 'it's bad enough having this thing without being nagged by my friends for not telling them. We all deal with this kind of news in different ways.'

'But who does know?' he persisted.

'Marion, Penny – no one else. I haven't told Jack,' I said.

'You mean you've told Marion and Penny *before me*?' said James, looking up from the computer at me, apparently quite angrily.

'I wish I'd never told you now!' I said, tears coming to my eyes. 'I've got a lump! I'm worried! Stop shoehorning yourself into some hierarchy with our other friends. They're women, for God's sake. They're different. You're the first *man* friend I've told. And the first person I've told about my next appointment. Okay?'

That seemed to calm him down and he laughed when I told him about the MRI scan.

'Well, good luck with the doc,' he said. 'And from now on, I want to be told every single detail, okay? Spare me nothing, nothing at all.'

I gave him a big hug, even though when our cheeks met I was scared of getting my face sandpapered off. Though actually now his beard is getting a little more silky. Rather like one of those pupa-skins that you find on hedgerows in the country, which a revolting insect has just crawled out of and left behind. The problem with beards is that all the people with them look exactly the same – usually like a doctor who's been struck off for unspeakable behaviour or a clergyman who's eloped with the church warden's husband. James is actually an extremely good-looking man, and now he's got a beard his features are hidden. You can't see his gorgeous mouth or his white teeth, just a mound of old undergrowth in which, I'm afraid to say, the odd crumb occasionally rests.

Talking of teeth, I'm getting very worried about mine. Smiling at myself in the mirror – as one does – I noticed my teeth were remarkably yellow. I've got one crown in front, which has remained gleaming white while all the others are like old gravestones. Have made an appointment with the dentist to have them whitened. No point in having a lift, after all, if every time you open your mouth, your face suddenly looks like the entrance to Hades. Of course this vanity is all occasioned by the presence of dishy Graham who, though he's far too young for me, I don't want to frighten on the stairs. Sometimes, as I'm pottering down to the kitchen in my towel, he'll call out something flattering like 'You're looking very glamorous today, Marie!'

This morning he popped down to borrow some Sellotape and stood chatting at the door for hours. I didn't ask anything about his wife, though I'm dying to find out how it's going.

But back to James. Apart from his beard, there is his wretched Art. He's got completely carried away this time and is into taking photos on his camera, blowing them up, painting them over with washes of colours and then sticking on things like pix of the entrance to Auschwitz and skulls and enlarged images of the atom bomb. He gives the results titles like *Want*, *Lack*, *Need*, *Desperation*, *Yearning*, *Calling* and *Silence*. One particularly bleak example features ropes of metal chains called *Nobody Came*.

'I'm thinking of having an exhibition,' he'd said, before he left. 'What do you say to a joint one, you and me together? Very different kinds of art, of course, ancient and modern, but perhaps the contrast would highlight our strengths?'

Ancient and modern! I tried hard to say nothing but it must have shown on my face.

'Oh, I didn't mean that, Marie. Sorry! Oh dear, silly old me. No, not ancient. I meant, um, traditional.'

'I honestly haven't got any work to show,' I said, trying to keep the ice from my voice. 'I sold the last lot of trees to Brad and Sharmie and now I'm so busy with the school . . .'

Narrow escape there. Ancient and modern, my foot!

Later

James made me feel so guilty about checking Facebook – or rather not checking – that somehow I managed to summon the energy and found David had asked to be my friend! Oddly excited by this though, for God's sake, if David isn't already my friend I don't know who is. Still, it meant I could go on his page and snoop around, and thankfully it was more interesting than most. He'd put on some brilliant YouTube clips, and a very handsome pic of himself.

Even later

Forgot to say that James was most sympathetic about the car, which is being collected tomorrow. He looked around it thoroughly and said there was no way it could be repaired because the front wheel-shaft had obviously cracked, or something. He's done loads of research and come up with this idea that what I need is a Fiat 500. Have to say it looked utterly charming when he showed it to me online. Oddly enough, I had a Fiat 500 when Jack was small and I remember driving down to Cornwall in it and breaking down three times on the way. It was just like a bubble car, with only room for a baby seat in the back, but I loved it. Perhaps I shall be returning to my roots!

May 13

'Ketchup claims "unproven" – Mayonnaise Makers' Association' (*Daily Rant*)

May 19

I'm so worried about the lump. I mean, is it really worth buying another car? Should I just take taxis or buses from now on, considering there might not be a lot of time left? I did feel strong enough to visit a Fiat showroom in town this morning. I needed to feel strong because I'm always baffled by car salesmen who assume that I'm the sort of person who watches *Top Gear* and knows about back axles and gears and torque, when in fact I know nothing.

The showroom was mostly glass, like an enormous fish tank. Gleaming Fiats in various shapes and sizes, with wonderful shining paintwork in reds and blacks and creams, were displayed in the windows and, as I went in, the doors opened magically by themselves. (I'm of a generation that can still be impressed by this. There was a time when my school friends and I all used to queue up at of the Science Museum in South Kensington to have a go at walking confidently through the magic automatic door in the basement. Recently, I was delighted to find that it's still there, staunchly opening and shutting a million times a year – although Gene wasn't impressed.)

I finally attracted the attention of a mini-skirted girl who took down hundreds of details from me before leaving me perched on a designer stool in the middle of the showroom. After ten minutes, I was starting to feel like an exhibit myself (admittedly a second-hand one) when a man came up and asked for my details all over again.

'I just want a normal no-frills Fiat 500,' I said. 'Something as simple as possible that'll get me from A to B.'

'You *think* you want a simple Fiat 500,' said the salesman, 'but what I think you *actually* want is the "twin-turbo" model.' His name was Mike Lomax and he was a spotty youth with, horror of horrors, a white plastic belt holding up his trousers. 'You live in London and the twin-turbo means you only have to pay half the congestion charge. It also has a lower tax-rate, on account of it being more green. And on top of everything, it has an air-filtering system powered by an ecologically friendly fuel-to-oil ratio.' Or something. It would also, he added, 'hold its price'.

As I'm planning never to have another car again in the whole of my life – I'm very much hoping this one will 'see me out', as the expression goes – I couldn't care less if it holds its price or not. But somehow, before I knew where I was, I found myself at the wheel of this twin-turbo affair, zooming round the centre of London and feeling like a professional rally-driver.

It was undeniable. I did rather *enjoy* feeling like a professional rally-driver.

As we turned into Wigmore Street, a well-dressed young woman stepped into the road, ignoring the traffic as she fiddled with her 'smart' phone. 'Watch out!' said Mike Lomax nervously, making me brake and stall.

'Oh dear, am I not driving this very well?' I said, nervously.

I noticed he made no reply, as I crunched the car back into gear. His silence spoke volumes.

'With the sun-roof, tinted windows and self-heating seats, this would only set you back £22,000,' he said later, recovering his composure and running a hand over the dashboard as if the car were a prize race-horse.

'I don't want a sun-roof!' I said. 'I hate the sun on the top of my head. Nor do I need self-heating seats. No tinted windows either. At my age I need all the light I can get.'

Mike Lomax looked rather disappointed. I'd discovered, during our roaring escapade round the West End, that in real life he was an actor and had played Widow Twanky in Bournemouth last Christmas. I couldn't help wondering whether he wasn't actually playing the part of a car salesman at this very moment, and if I'd asked him, could have transformed himself into Hamlet at the click of my fingers.

'Fair enough,' he said. 'But remember that the turbo-hybrid has the double-accelerator fuel expander.' Or something. 'With the extra mph you will be able to increase the GBH to 100 miles per hour.' Or something. Then he showed me a different model, with non-reflective glass, automatic gears and special tyres that were smaller than usual. 'This doesn't have a spare tyre,' he said. 'But an aerosol is provided to seal the inner tube in an emergency.'

'Does the twin-turbo have a spare tyre?' I asked. I always feel safer with a spare tyre.

'No, it doesn't. Very few cars do these days,' he added, looking at me as if he were a modern hotelier and I'd asked for a stone hot-water bottle in my bed.

I explained that I didn't want an aerosol spray. I wanted a simple old spare tyre. Nor did I want non-reflective glass. I just wanted a very simple car that would get me from A to B . . . but now it was he who couldn't understand what I was talking about.

Finally, clearly in despair, and not knowing the meaning of the phrase 'getting from A to B', he said that I could design a car for myself, online. I said that I didn't want to design a car for myself online. Did I look, I asked him, trying to get through to his inner humanity, like someone who could design her own car online?

No, I wanted to buy a very simple car that would get me from A to B. I didn't know what a twin-turbo was, or a hybrid, and didn't care about the air-filtering system. Could I just please have a simple . . . He stared at me, baffled. Then, thinking mistakenly that it was the price that was the problem, he dropped it by £500. And, feeling rather depressed, I came home.

£21,500 seemed a hell of a lot for a car, much as I had enjoyed the powerful feeling the old twin-turbo had given me. So I went online and found another dealer in some god-awful suburb miles from anywhere. Anyway I thought I might track down a second-hand twin-turbo there.

'Why do you want a twin-turbo?' asked the suspicious voice

at the other end of the phone when I rang, after having made myself a strengthening lunch of scrambled eggs on toast. It was a woman who'd announced herself as Kim. 'If you don't mind my asking?'

'I'm told,' I said desperately, a sob starting to enter my voice, 'That it's a half-hybrid, that you don't have to pay the congestion charge, that the tax is halved . . .'

'Could you tell me, do you often drive into central London?' asked Kim.

'Hardly ever!' I said. 'But . . .'

'So you don't want a twin-turbo,' said Kim. 'No, I'm guessing from what you tell me, that what you really want is a little run-around car. A car that gets you from A to B.'

'Yes, YES!' I said, incredulous that I had found someone who understood my language. 'But I'm not sure now, having driven a twin-turbo – it made me feel like a rally-driver.'

'But if you don't mind my asking, *are* you a rally-driver?' asked Kim.

'No, I'm not, I'm a retired art teacher . . .'

'. . . who wants a run-around car that gets you from A to B,' insisted Kim. 'I've got just the thing for you, love. It's a Fiat Pop. I've got one, and my two daughters have got one each and we all swear by them. Nip down and we'll go for a spin.'

I decided to borrow Melanie's car and look in as soon as possible.

May 24

Met David in John Lewis today. It was a muggy grey day and Oxford Street was like an undredged river, with muddy-looking crowds moving sullenly along the clogged pavements. The reason he wanted to make the store our rendezvous was because he was looking for a lawnmower, and it seemed sensible to meet there rather than have him hike out to Shepherd's Bush. Anyway, I couldn't bear the thought of Melanie popping out of her house and winking at him over the wall and reminding him they'd spent the night together. As for the night before, he'd spent it with Jack and Chrissie and reported that they were very well.

We queued dismally at the counter in a café which seemed to be stocked solely with carrot and pasta salad, lentils, chickpeas and broccoli, smoked mackerel, something unspeakable called a 'tuna bake' and various quiches. The soup was 'butternut squash', a vegetable I've always avoided in supermarkets so successfully that I wouldn't know one if I saw it. Marion would have revelled in the fare.

'Did Jack say anything to you about his appendix?' I asked, as we sat down at a table and, after we'd wiped the remains of the last customers' lunch onto the floor with our napkins, unloaded our own from our trays. Stumped, I'd opted for a plain yoghurt, an apple, and a piece of walnut cake.

'I did ask him, but he's adamant about not having an operation,' said David. 'I think he's stupid and I told him so. It's dangerous having a grumbling appendix and it's hardly a major op.'

I wasn't reassured because David's father – my ex-father-in-law – had been a doctor and so he knows quite a bit about medical matters.

We chatted on about our mutual friends and suddenly I couldn't resist mentioning my new neighbour.

'She's ghastly,' I said, as I opened what I thought was going to be my plain yoghurt. To my dismay it turned out to be pinkish and, looking on the label, I saw that it contained 'cranberries, vanilla and rhubarb'. (Why can't they just leave things alone?) 'She said she'd slept with you!'

David stared at me, dumbfounded. 'Melanie? Melanie?' he said. 'I simply can't remember . . . what does she look like?'

I told him of her flowing robes, her scarves, her necklaces, her smell of patchouli . . . and finally something seemed to dawn.

'I think I do have a dim memory,' he said. 'It was a party. We were both dreadfully drunk and she forced me back to her place. I didn't even fancy her. It was a disastrous night. I'm surprised she hasn't drawn a veil over it.'

'I know. She's got enough of them, for God's sake.'

David laughed. 'One of these women who seem to have a psychic flex they plug into you to drain you of all your energy,' he said.

I asked him why he'd come up to London to look at lawn-mowers when he could easily find one online, but he explained that he wasn't an online person. 'I've never got the hang of it and I never will,' he said. 'I like looking at the machines themselves, anyway. I like to feel them in my hands.' Understandable really, considering he'd spent his life in engineering. A very good man to have around if your motorbike broke down, David. Unfortunately there were very few broken-down motorbikes around during our marriage, or it might have been a different story.

'But if you're not an online person how are you going to meet new potential wives? Or girlfriends?' I asked. 'That's the only way you can meet new people these days, apparently. If you don't watch out, the Widow Bossom will just wade in without any opposition.'

David looked a bit guilty. 'Let's draw another veil over the Widow Bossom,' he said. 'Let's just say you were right when you said she was predatory. The trouble is, I really like her, but I just don't fancy her.'

'Aha!' I said, victoriously. 'You see, I'm vindicated! I really can read people's minds!'

David laughed.

'Now what about Penny?' I asked. 'She's single now. You always liked her.'

'Hmm, I haven't seen her for ages,' he said. 'Well, it's a thought. Perhaps you can arrange something. I'd like to see her anyway.'

'I'll do that,' I said. We were then talking of this and that, and lending the salt to the next-door table and going up to get more napkins and finally some coffee, topping up the cups with those tiny little pots of milk that contain about a drop each, when I suddenly had an urge to tell him about my lump. It's so strange. We've been divorced all these years and yet in some ways he's still one of the closest friends I've got.

So when he said to me, 'And how've you been keeping? Tip-top as usual?' I found myself pausing. I was about to speak but, just as I was going to open my mouth, my throat constricted and I felt my eyes fill with tears.

'What?' he asked, looking anxious.

'I shouldn't really tell you,' I said in a rush, and paused.

'What shouldn't you tell me?' he asked, looked even more alarmed.

'Oh, it's so silly. I don't know why I'm saying it. But I've got this weird lump on my tummy and no one seems to know what it is.'

Before I knew where I was, I was crying – yes, in the middle of the John Lewis café, so embarrassing – and David was reaching out for me with one hand and scrabbling in his pocket for a hankie with the other. Finding nothing, he picked up a crumpled paper napkin covered with quiche crumbs and offered it to me.

'Marie,' he said. 'You should have told me earlier!' (Yes, even he fell into the old trap.) 'Have you seen the doctor? What did he say?'

'I'm going to see a specialist next month – everything takes so long these days.'

'Look, come down to Somerset! There's a brilliant man I know there – old friend of the family – a retired oncologist. I'm always helping him with his vintage cars, so he won't mind doing me a favour, and he can tell you everything you need to know about lumps without making you feel patronized or scared. How long has this been going on?'

'Since the beginning of the year,' I said, managing to stop the tears for a minute, but still gasping in that funny way you do when you've been crying deeply, as if you've been rescued from drowning.

'But you've told people, haven't you? I hope you've got a lot of support.'

'Well, yes and no,' I said. 'Everyone seems so angry. They all say I'm not taking care of myself properly or that I should see some crystal therapist or they get cross I haven't told them before . . .'

'. . . when all you want is a good cry and some good advice,' said David. I must say I'd forgotten how sympathetic he can be when he pulls the stops out. 'I expect they're all frightened and don't know what to do. That's usually why people are angry. Doesn't stop them being shits though. What does Jack say?'

'I haven't told him,' I said. 'And please don't say anything. I really don't want to worry him. I mean, what's the point if it's nothing? They've got enough on their plate anyway. But I feel better now I've told you,' I said, gratefully. 'You've been sweet.'

I blew my nose rather damply and realized everyone was looking at us. They must have thought we were some sad old couple and David had just told me he'd been having an affair and wanted a divorce or something. I got the mirror out of my handbag and started some facial repairs. The only problem was that the tears kept rolling down my cheeks, getting in the way.

'I'm so glad you told me!' said David. 'I can't bear to think of you worrying about this by yourself. You don't know how much I worry about you, sometimes, on your own. I know we had our bad times, but we had our good times too, didn't we?'

He put the spoon into my pink yoghurt – after I'd seen the colour I'd pushed it away uneaten – and put it towards my mouth. 'Eat up,' he said. 'It'll make you feel better.'

I couldn't help smiling. It was so odd being treated like a child. Even though the yoghurt was cranberry, rhubarb and vanilla, I managed to choke it down.

'Good girl,' said David, smiling, 'Now another one. Watch the aeroplane!' I couldn't help laughing.

'You are an angel,' I said, as I swallowed the second mouthful. 'No, no more, thanks so much. Actually, I wish I *had* told you before. I'd forgotten what a good man you are in a crisis.'

'That's me,' said David ruefully. 'Crap at all other times, but great in a crisis.'

'No, don't be silly,' I said, and I had a memory of what it had been like when we'd been in love and had thought that just sitting in each other's company made us the luckiest people ever. For a moment our eyes met and I suddenly knew he was thinking the same. Then it all faded away.

'Now, shall I contact my doctor friend?' asked David.

'I think I should wait to see my man first,' I said. 'It's in a couple of weeks so I may be clearer then about what's wrong.'

'Well, all I can say is I hope he's got a VTMK.'

'What's a VTMK?' I asked.

'A Voice to Melt Knickers,' he replied. 'Bedside manner stuff. I always remember Dad telling me all these phrases – NFN – Normal for Norfolk . . . oh, it was hilarious. "Pumpkin positive" – that was when he shone a torch in the patient's mouth and the eyes lit up – signifying no brains. Then there was Dagenham, which meant three stops beyond Barking . . .'

By now I was giggling so much that the other customers were looking at me again. 'You do make me laugh!' I said to David and, reaching for his hand, kissed the top of it affectionately.

He looked at me, right in the eyes. And I could feel all the affection zooming in from his eyes into my heart. I felt a real connection. I squeezed his hand and he squeezed mine back. And I suddenly fully realized how lucky I was to have David as a friend and how sensible I – and he, actually – had been, despite everything, to keep our friendship alive all these years.

Then he said, 'Well I've got to catch my train. I'll ring you every week from now on to see how you're getting on. And if you're worried, Marie, any time of the day or night, just give me a ring – and I mean that – and if you want I'll come up like a shot. And if you want me to come up and take you to the hospital or come with you to any appointments, I'll be there. Don't forget now. Promise?'

'Promise,' I said.

Tonight I know I'm going to sleep better than I have for ages. Everything seems clear and calm, just like the weather after a storm. Every so often, about once every four months, I'll get a blissful feeling of peace, knowing that everything's okay. I feel I'm living in the present, the house appears to be on my side, the air caresses me and I enjoy everything in what I imagine is a Buddhist way. Even emptying the washing-up machine feels fulfilling and meaningful. Rising from my chair seems to me pregnant with purpose and when I sit down, the cushions plump themselves up to welcome me. I know all this sounds potty, but it happens so rarely it's worth recording when it does.

JUNE

June 3

When push came to shove, inevitably there was a problem with Melanie's car. I wasn't insured to drive it. She said it would be fine, but I was far too nervous to do anything illegal. God knows, I might have an accident. Then I'd have to spend the rest of my life under a bridge, in a cardboard box with Pouncer, having been forced to sell my house to pay for some hapless wounded bystander, who would have been forced to spend the remainder of *his* wretched life in an iron lung. I did try to get it insured but in the end it would have cost £30 – and for that I could have got a taxi to the showroom and back. So I did.

From the taxi-driver's rear-view mirror hung a little veined leaf with a Buddha imprinted inside it, and during our conversation he told me that Buddhism could be explained simply. 'With a butter-knife you can spread the butter on the bread. But with the same knife you can also kill someone. That is Buddhism.'

I couldn't imagine killing anyone with a butter-knife. The last time I used one, it was a small blunt object with a rounded end, the sort you could give a baby as a plaything in its cot, but I thanked him for his homely wisdom and, at the end of my journey, added a tip to the fare, simply for being Buddhist, whatever he did with his butter-knife.

This car showroom, in Hounslow, was a much more homely affair than the London one, tucked away in a leafy side street. The moment I stepped over the threshold, a well-preserved woman with blonde hair and a tight black dress came up to me.

'You're Marie!' she said. 'I knew it was you! Now sit down, have some coffee, love.'

We had a nice chat. She didn't baffle me, like Mike Lomax had, with talk of the car's engine capacity or its diesel particulate filter or its torque at 106lb on 1900 rpm. She just said, 'You'll love this car, Marie, it's just you to a T.' There was something reassuring about the way everything here was reduced to letters of the alphabet, A B and T. 'Now let's go for our drive.'

She led me out to the forecourt and there, parked as if it was waiting for me, was a little blue Fiat 500. It immediately reminded me of the car I used to have and, though it was a different shape, a whole host of memories came flooding back. David had first kissed me in that car. I'd taken my first cat, poor old Bob, on his final visit to the vet in that car. I'd driven that car when I'd bought my first dress from Biba and I remembered being so thrilled by it that I'd tried to put it on at the traffic lights.

'Hop in, love,' said Kim. 'Isn't it a darling?'

It *was* lovely. It turns out to be what is known as 'intelligently designed'. In other words, it is *on your side*. It's got a proper spare tyre, hidden away, and air-conditioning, which I've never had before. Ten seconds after you've started driving, it locks all the doors for you *by itself* so no one can reach in and nick your handbag. It switches its passenger airbag off if you have a baby in the front, and when you get out, the lights stay on for a while to let you get to your front door and then slowly dim. I'd forgotten what a real pal a nice car could be.

As we cruised about the streets I had the feeling that this car was actually mine.

'You drive beautifully,' said Kim. 'Not like some of our clients, I must say. Sometimes I can't wait to get back to the office. I think this car was designed for you, Marie.'

'Kim, you're too kind!' I said. I was conscious of using her first name as much as possible, as she'd been so very keen to use mine.

I came to a decision the moment we'd parked back on the forecourt – a process made extremely easy by the fact that there's a button you can push to make the steering lighter so it's easier to get into a tight spot.

'I'll have it, Kim,' I said. 'I love it.'

'I knew you would,' she said. 'This car – it's got a certain X quality.'

And I wrote out a deposit right away. The whole thing is less than half the price of the other one, too. Apparently

I can pick it up next week, when all the paperwork's been done.

Feel rather excited!

June 7

'Whose human rights? Serial killer freed by European Court to kill again!' (*Daily Rant*)

June 9

Jack rang to ask if I could have Gene for a day at the start of next month's school holidays. Slightly embarrassed, he explained that Chrissie was forcing him to have a second opinion about the appendix and as the appointment is on his looking-after-Gene-day, he wondered if I was free.

June 10

Have to admit that Graham is such a charmer, I try to get up a bit earlier than usual these days, so that if I meet him on the stairs I have, at least, got my make-up on, even if I'm not yet fully dressed. He's no older than Jack, so there's no question of my being after him, but I'm one of those girls who do perk up a bit when there's a man around. My mother was like that. I remember in her final days she'd be lying on the sitting room sofa groaning in agony and refusing all offers of help, tears of self-pity pouring down her cheeks, but when a courier popped round with some flowers and helped me in with the vast box, she somehow managed to sit bolt upright, flash him a charming smile, and twinkle her eyes with all the pleasure of one who has, at last, met Mr Right.

'You are *too, too* kind,' she'd say, tilting her head in a flirtatious way and stretching to put a hand on his arm as he approached. 'And how marvellous and clever of you to find me here – so few people can discover the address – and you've brought these wonderful flowers! You are quite amazing! Isn't he quite a marvel, Marie?' she'd add turning to me. 'And tell me, how do you do it?'

The courier had barely pranced out of the room, marinated in flattery, than my mother would slump back on the sofa, weeping and groaning.

Funny how you turn into your mother as you get older, come to think of it. Though actually I'm now quite a lot older than my mother was when she died so I'm entering uncharted territory. Looked into the mirror the other day and saw my old mum staring out at me. Gave me a nasty shock, I must say.

Anyway, following in my mother's footsteps, I sent my dressing gown to the cleaners the other day, so now there is not a single toothpaste stain on it. I've scrubbed some grease marks off my slippers and now put on the full slap almost the moment I wake up – partly so as not to give poor Graham a terrible fright on the stairs before he goes to work and partly because the old male hormones clattering around the house have this effect on me. Put a bounce in the step.

June 13

Dentist agrees with me that my teeth are not quite as white as they should be, so he's made me a special mouth-guard with some peculiar stuff to squirt into it and he says that if I wear this all night for three weeks, my teeth will soon be back to their sparkling best and neighbours will have to shield their eyes as I flash them dazzling smiles in the street.

June 16

Went down to the car showroom again today to collect the car and drove it home very nervously. It kept cutting out at the lights, which worried me to start with but then I remembered Kim had said it was meant to do that. 'When it's on eco-drive, it automatically cuts out when you're in a traffic jam or at the lights, saving you pounds in petrol. If you put your foot on the clutch it'll start again. Try it. And if you want to drive it the old way, just press the button and it goes back into the normal mode.'

Is there nothing that this wonderful car doesn't do? Talk about benign. Now there's a word you really can apply to the Fiat 500. It's got a little hook for you to hang the petrol cap on when you're filling up, and a little strap to pull the boot lid down so your fingers don't get filthy on the paintwork when you yank it down.

I parked it, clicked the key to lock it, checked it . . . walked a few yards, clicked again to open it – it seemed actually to be winking at me, like my mother in the presence of an attractive man – and locked it again. When I got in, I gazed at it out of the window, to see what it looked like from above. Just as adorable.

Later

I've bunged all the rubbish that I need into the new car. (Jump-leads? You never know.) And popped the rape-alarm in the glove compartment. It might be useful in a road-rage incident.

Penny dropped by to have a look so I gave her a demonstration drive. And we'd just got back to my house when there was the sound of jangling bracelets and Melanie swooped out through her gate.

'Mar, it's divine!' she said clapping her hands. 'I'm so jealous! I've been staring at it all afternoon . . . aren't you over the moon? And who's this? Is this another fascinating resident?'

Penny put out her hand and introduced herself.

'No relation of Bill Martin?' said Melanie, cocking her head. 'J Walter Thompson? 1967?'

'My ex-husband,' said Penny.

'Oh, you lucky girl! I remember him well. Only went out with him once, but always used to fancy him rotten!' said Melanie. (How is it that she seems to know everyone's ex-husband?) 'Now, you're on the residents' committee, aren't you? Well I'm aching to become involved . . . why don't you both come and have a drink?'

Of course I was longing to see the inside of her house and so in we trooped.

It's not even half-finished, but she's managed to make it look like the inside of an Indian bazaar, with Eastern hangings looping from the ceiling, a smell of joss-sticks, huge cushions round the room . . . all very Seventies. In a clip-frame on the wall was a copy of the *Desiderata*. Starting with 'Go placidly amid the noise and haste . . .' and ending with '. . . Be cheerful. Strive to be happy', this is the text that everyone thinks was discovered in some church in Baltimore in the 16th century but in fact was written in the 1920s. Load of codswallop if you ask me. The *Desiderata* is always featured in houses owned by people who couldn't be less peaceful. What with Marion's house down the road, which is like a rock-pool from the Sixties, and Melanie's, a rock pool from the Seventies, we could charge people entry to come and have a goggle at period pieces.

We were chatting away, when I suddenly heard a familiar sound outside. Barking. The dog again.

'Oh, yes,' said Melanie, noticing me pricking up my ears. 'Hope we don't have to put up with it for too long.'

'What dog?' said Penny – and we explained. Then Melanie suddenly jumped up.

'Let's go see what's going on right now!' she said.

Penny, being a dog person, was game. So, after persuading Melanie to take off her bangles – a dead give-away on a covert operation – we stole across the road and, waiting outside the house, listened. It was a golden afternoon and mothers were hurrying past to collect their children from school.

I bravely tiptoed up to the front door and peeped through

the letter-box. 'It doesn't seem to be in the house,' I said. 'I think it's in the garden.'

We walked around to the side of the house down the little alley. Though the wall was extremely high, Melanie, who was the tallest of us three, could catch a glimpse if she jumped.

'It's chained up,' she whispered. 'It's horrible. I'll nip over to my house and get a chair, so we can all have a look.'

My heart was pounding. I remembered all too clearly the day I'd stolen the chimes from Brad and Sharmie's garden when the chair had broken as I clambered over, so 'Make it a sturdy one!' I whispered.

Once we'd got ourselves organized we took turns to look over the wall. The garden was a wasteland, full of old rubbish, cans, a broken bicycle, a smashed television, and plastic dustbins. Weeds were crowding through the cracked paving, and big bushes of elderflower were starting to reclaim the land. And there, chained up, pitifully thin and looking pretty crazed, was this tragic Alsatian. In the shadows, it was just a brown shape, but you could see an empty bowl for water and the outline of a kennel, so presumably it didn't have to sleep in the open. When it noticed me peering over the wall it went berserk, straining at its chain, mad with rage or, perhaps, desperate for company.

At the sound of a car drawing up outside, I scrambled off the chair and hurried back onto the road, all gasping and dishevelled.

Out of the car stepped the nightmarish woman, who said goodbye to the driver with 'And you can fuck off, too!' and then slammed the door. As she was fumbling with her front door key I decided to be brave. I broke away, while the others were tumbling into Melanie's house with the chair. 'Excuse me!' I said attempting to sound confident. Unfortunately my voice had turned rather mouse-like and croaky.

'What?' she said. She appeared to have very few teeth.

'We were wondering, er, whether your dog is all right,' I said, nervously. 'We were worried whether he might not be, er, ill. He seems to be barking more than usual.'

She glared at me. 'It's none of your fucking business!' she yelled. 'My dog's fine. Don't you interfere in fings you got no business interfering in!' Then she opened her front door, stepped inside and slammed it in my face. The dog's barking increased for about 20 minutes and then there was silence.

June 17

Can't sleep for thinking of the dog, still barking even though it's 3am. Decided to look at a few Facebook pages to take my mind off things.

Melanie had put up a picture of herself in her new house with the caption: 'Home at last!' Penny had posted a picture of someone apparently holding up the Leaning Tower of Pisa with one finger (did that myself with Jack on a trip to Italy when he was small) and Marion had written, 'Do try Gingon Veta herbs. They are marvellous for bringing down cholesterol.' James' page showed weekly photographs of himself with his beard, getting longer and longer, interspersed with quite a few of his abstract pictures.

Still unable to sleep, I went upstairs and looked through an old bookcase until I found a PG Wodehouse I hadn't read for years. Made myself some Horlicks, got into bed and turned on the electric blanket. (It's a comfort even in the middle of June.) Started reading all about Blandings Castle and Lord Emsworth and was soon transported into a safe and cosy world.

Later
Woke at 6.30 with the Wodehouse over my face and the lights blazing.

June 19

Latest on Penny's Facebook page: 'If you're having a bad day, remember, there are people out there who have their exes' names tattooed on themselves.'

Jesus Christ.

June 20

This morning got gum-shields for the tooth whitener from the dentist. Dog continues to bark. Lump appears to be growing again. Worried sick. Can't wait for the hospital appointment.

No paper delivered yet so was forced to read yesterday's rather more thoroughly than I had the day before.

'My J-sized breasts suffocated my ex-love during sex!'

The worst thing about newspaper obituaries these days is that you don't just see ancient Spitfire pilots have died, people you'd never heard of. Oh no. They're stuffed with people who I still think of as hip young groovers. Just today Alvin Lee from Ten Years After went to the great gig in the sky. There was a picture of him with long, black (presumably dyed) hair, a haggard face like an old leather handbag, studs in his belt and the tightest jeans you've ever seen, still rocking on his last tour, a couple of months ago. I muttered to myself that he'd probably died so young because of his sex, drugs and rock'n'roll lifestyle – but blow me, it turned out the man was 70! Hardly in the class of Jim Morrison, Jimi Hendrix or Janis Joplin.

Later
This afternoon, and about time too, I rang the RSPCA to tell them about the dog. Apparently the area manager was out, but the nice woman at the end of the line assured me he'd ring me back as soon as he came in. Feel much better.

Rather nervous about putting in the plastic gum thingies tonight and hope they won't hurt. But will I be able to sleep with a mouth full of plastic? Might take a Valium just in case.

June 21

Felt extremely dopey in the morning as a result of the Valium, and groped my way to the bathroom. Bumped into Graham as he was coming downstairs and said good morning to him.

'Are you okay?' he asked, rather worried.

As I was reassuring him, I realized my mouth was feeling rather bulky. I hadn't taken the gum thingies out. Oh gawd! Not only had I flashed him a huge plastic smile but I was talking as if I were quite half-witted. 'Gooth Morthig! Yeth I'm fithe!'

Unable to face yanking them out in front of him, I covered my face with my hands as I tried to articulate, 'Haff a thice jay!' and hurried into the bathroom.

June 22

At last! The hospital appointment is tomorrow. Hooray!

June 23

Got to the hospital and as usual needed a native guide to lead me to the right place. But eventually I found the correct department and waited, in a low-ceilinged, brightly lit, windowless corridor for what seemed a couple of weeks. Finally a nurse called out my name and told me to follow the blue line. This was painted on the floor, punctuated occasionally by a sinister black footprint. So anxious was I about my appointment that I found myself giggling slightly hysterically as it reminded me of the Yellow Brick Road. I wondered if the doctor at the end might not be some shrivelled-up old con-artist like the Wizard of Oz. When the line ran out, I found myself in another waiting room and this time, in only a matter of hours, I was called to a cubicle and introduced myself to a Mr Melchett.

Well, all I can say is, I was jolly glad old Melanie wasn't with me. She would have had Mister M for breakfast. His tall slim back was turned as I entered the room, but when he moved back to greet me I felt like one of those girls in a hospital drama, eyes bulging out of my head at the sight of him. I mean, dishy or what! The best thing about him, apart of course from his firm mouth, noble nose and pointed cheekbones – well not very pointed, but certainly accentuated – were his incredible twinkling blue eyes. He must have been about Jack's age.

'Jack Sharp?' he said, as I sat down.

'No, Marie,' I replied, rather discomfited. I mean, a doctor who can't tell what sex you are doesn't inspire much confidence, however dishy he is.

'I mean Jack – he's your son, isn't he?'

'Yes?' I said, now wondering if this man didn't have psychic powers and was going in a minute to tell me that my mother was standing beside him and did I remember the broken cup in the cupboard above the cooker.

'I'm Ben, Ben Melchett – do you remember? I used to come round?'

I was dumbfounded. Of course I remembered Ben. 'Brainy Ben' we called him, on account of his academic prowess. He had been a great pal of Jack's at school and I remember how, once, he'd left a great lump of dope in the back of the car and I'd had to give it to Jack with a big ticking off about how I didn't want to throw it away because I knew it cost money, but in future I'd prefer it if he could ask his friends to keep their dope to themselves. Ben, Jack and I had had a lot of laughs when I'd driven them back from school, and Ben was always a delightful guest when he came for a sleepover.

'I don't believe it!' I said. 'But you're so big now! And so glam! Jack will be amazed!'

'Glam! That's the nicest thing anyone's said to me in weeks,' he said. 'I usually get insults from my patients. How's Jack these days?'

'Oh, he's fine, doing really well – married with one little boy. Only problem is he's got a grumbling appendix and refuses to have the operation. He's phobic about hospitals.'

'Don't blame him!' said Ben. 'I wouldn't let any member of my family go near one if I could help it. Oops, perhaps I shouldn't have said that. And David? His dad? I always enjoyed seeing him.'

'I'm afraid we broke up,' I said. 'Just didn't work out. But I still see him. Oh, I'm trying to find a nice partner for him. You don't know any charming single women in their fifties or sixties, do you?'

'Can't say I do,' said Ben. 'Not really my age group. But I'll keep my eyes peeled. Now, let's have a look at your notes.'

He pulled over a pile of papers on his desk.

'Oh God,' he said. 'Hope I'm not having a 404 moment.'

'What's a 404 moment?' I asked.

'Error message 404 page not found?' he said. 'Computer stuff . . . . Oh no, here they are.'

He stared at the notes, and then looked at his computer and inserted a disc.

'Would you mind not watching DVDs while you have desperately ill patients in your consulting rooms?' I said. I found myself making all these jokes just to cover up my nervousness, I suppose. I had an awful feeling that I actually had one of those Smiley Faces you get in texts instead of a real one.

'MRI,' he said. 'Stands, as you know, for Major Revealing Inspection. A dark look into the depths of the human body. Or, in your case,' he added reassuringly, 'not so dark. Can't see anything there. Have you had an ultrasound? If not, I think we'd better book you in for one of those. Now let's have a look at the old object itself.'

'What other acronyms do you use?' I asked, before he politely left the room, leaving me to undress in private. 'I mean, I know NFN – Normal for Norfolk – but I've never heard the MRI one before – or the Error 404. I love the different language you doctors use.'

He gave a dazzling smile.

'I'll tell you some more when I get back, so long as you don't sue me,' he said.

As he went out of the room, a nurse came in with a towel, to protect my modesty. I suppose someone had to be there, in case I claimed Ben assaulted me or something. Quite mad. I undressed in front of so many strange men in the Sixties, I couldn't care less any more. And I'm sure Ben had often seen me in my dressing gown if not worse when he came to stay with Jack. Besides, at least I knew this bloke's name – which is more, I seem to remember, than I did with several of the chaps I'd slept with in the past.

Anyway, once my towel was strategically placed and I was lying down, in he came again.

'Nothing like a quick smoke,' he joked.

He started pressing and kneading. 'A GOK, don't you think?' he said to the nurse.

'What's a GOK?'

'God Only Knows,' he answered. 'I wonder if, as well as the ultrasound, we hadn't better have a hope and scope as well. It could just be a harmless lump, but we'd better take a biopsy to be on the safe side. And if you could ask Marie for some shits and spits,' he added to the nurse, 'that would be good. How about that for doctor-speak?' he said. 'If you can understand that, I'll let you join my team.'

We went through the routine of him going out and me pulling on my tights and him coming in again, and I sat down again in front of him.

'I don't think there's anything to worry about at the moment, Marie,' he said. 'But I'll see you again in a month and we can have another chat. There could be something nasty in the woodshed. But there again, it could be something benign. Still let's be on the safe side, get those tests done and see what the results are.'

'Before I go,' I said. 'There's a phrase that's keeping me off your team. What's a "hope and scope"?'

'Hope and scope's a laparoscopy,' he said. 'We just hope it won't be a peek and shriek, of course, but I'm pretty sure it won't be. Shits and spits . . . stool and sputum samples. Love to Jack. And really good to see you again, Mrs S.'

I came home feeling a lot better. The hope and scope's next month, as is the ultrasound, so perhaps after all that I'll be given the all-clear. DO hope so. Can't tell Jack I saw Ben, as I haven't told him and Chrissie about the lump yet – and at this rate I'm not going to. No point in worrying them if it's nothing.

Later

Residents' Association meeting next week. Penny came over for supper and we discussed the agenda and whether to have Melanie on the committee or not. Penny had brought the curious remains of half of a pudding she'd made with pears, crushed up amaretto biscuits, cream and pomegranate seeds. Not entirely successful, we both agreed, as we picked the pomegranate seeds from our teeth.

We decided that the topics at the meeting should include: the drug-dealing in the alley opposite, which backs on to Barking Dog Garden; parking (because there are thousands of disabled stickers on the cars in our street – and we have never, except once, seen anyone remotely disabled hobbling or wheeling down it – we're certain there's forgery afoot); violence to the trees, since the Council, no doubt in a money-saving measure, have lopped them so that they look like those withered remains in a Great War landscape painted by Paul Nash. And finally, the provision of litter-bins at the end of the street.

Then we came to the tricky subject of Melanie and the committee.

'She seems very enthusiastic,' said Penny, doubtfully.

'I think she'd be ghastly, but I can't quite see how we can leave her out,' I said. 'Every man who meets her loves her. And James would be bound to tell her we'd had a meeting. Perhaps we could ask her to attend this one not as a committee member but as a visitor – for the moment. And see if anyone proposes her for the committee.'

'Bet Tim proposes her as a member,' said Penny, gloomily. No question, Tim, Marion's husband, is a sucker for women and would probably throw his weight behind Lucretia Borgia if she applied.

'Bet James seconds her,' I replied, moodily.

'She's started to call me "Pen",' said Penny, crossly. 'And when you were out the other day she came over to my house, forced her way in and demanded to borrow my mixer. I haven't seen it for days now. I posted her rather a stiff note on my way round.'

'She wants me to call her "Mel" but I've resisted so far.'

'Perhaps we could call her "Melon",' suggested Penny.

'She calls me "Mar" and James is "Jimbo", believe it or not,' I said. 'I even spotted him on her doorstep last night, looking very shame-faced. Turns out she'd asked him to supper.'

'Well, she won't get very far with *him*,' said Penny. 'Any news of the dog, by the way? It was barking its head off as I came here.'

'It never gets a walk or anything,' I said. 'It's too cruel. I've rung the RSPCA and they promised to ring back but they haven't.'

'I don't think it's exactly illegal,' said Penny. 'I imagine it's not being starved and it's got shelter. But it's certainly incredibly cruel.'

June 27

'"Milk more dangerous than smoking," claims Nobel Prize-winner!' (*Daily Rant*)

June 28

We had the residents' meeting here. I got out a couple of bottles of wine, and I'd asked Marion to bring some snacks. She and Tim were first – Tim bearing a dozen packets of Walker's salt 'n' vinegar crisps. (I'd been hoping for a posher variety.)

Sheila the Dealer came next, fag in mouth. Every Residents' Association should have its own drug-dealer – scary and repulsive with unwashed hair and a smell about her of old cooking fat – just to scare their enemies, so she's our secret weapon in wars that require upfront confrontation. James came next – well, I think it was James, but it could have been anyone behind that beard, which I told him rather sharply – but he was bearing a bunch of lilies, which was sweet of him. Father Emmanuel from the local evangelical church, the Holy Rock Mission, came as well. Though far too religious for my liking and always swearing everyone will go to hell – I sometimes hear him preaching damnation when I'm sitting in my garden of a summer afternoon, trying to relax – it's good to have him on the committee because he's from the West Indies and we like a spot of cultural diversity round here. And he usually goes along with most of our plans. He leads his flock of huge Caribbean families by the nose, and I think that it's only when he's at a residents' meeting that he's outnumbered.

No Brad and Sharmie, of course. I really miss the old neighbours. They were lovely when they were here. And Brad was a particularly authoritative presence, being trained in law and having one of those loud American voices that can be heard across the Atlantic. (I've had one email from them, with promises of invitations to India to follow, but so far nothing. Ah well.)

Finally, late as ever, and bearing a sheaf of papers under one arm and an enormous carrier bag containing Penny's food mixer under the other, came Melanie. She unpeeled a few layers and sat down. Sometimes she reminds me of that children's game, Pass the Parcel. I imagine that, if she were unwrapped all the way down, you'd eventually get to a tiny little Melanie in the middle, someone you could hold on the palm of your hand. Or perhaps there'd actually be nothing there at all.

Sheila the Dealer started telling us about her son's operation – no doubt for shotgun wounds – and Marion chimed in with news of her daughter's latest pregnancy. Even Penny, I'm afraid to say, suddenly joined in with stories of her sister's bad back. Eventually I banged the table and called 'Order! Order!'

in the most humorous impression of a parliamentary Speaker I could manage. Thank *God* I'm chairman.

Well, we got through most of the items on the agenda. I promised I'd write to the Council about parking badges and litter bins and Marion said she'd follow up the druggies in the alley by writing to the police and the Council, and Father Emmanuel declared that they'd all go straight to hell. And we were just about to wind up when Melanie, who'd been remarkably silent, pushed in.

'I'd love to propose myself for the committee!' she said. 'I'm so keen on the community, and I feel so much could be done to improve this area. I'm full of good ideas. Street parties, Neighbourhood Watch, music festivals in the street, humps in the road to slow traffic and cause less noise and fewer accidents . . . and I love you all, Mar and Pen and Jimbo and Father Em and Marion and Sheel and the gorgeous Timmy – what a thrill to meet you,' she added, throwing him a dazzling smile. 'It feels like *family* here! I feel I've come home!'

'I'll propose you!' said James, enthusiastically. It sounded enthusiastic. I couldn't really see behind his beard.

'And I'll second you!' said Tim, slapping the table with his hand several times.

'And I will third you!' said Father Emmanuel, surprisingly. Bet no one's dared called him Father Em before. Perhaps he likes it. Well, at least she didn't call him Daddio.

There was a palpable silence from Penny, Marion, Sheila the Dealer and myself.

'Well, I think that's passed, then?' I said. And then, feeling

I'd sounded a bit sour, I added, cheerily, 'Welcome to our world, Melanie!'

Afterwards, when they'd all gone, Penny, who'd stayed behind, sighed. 'She's even ghastlier than I remember from last time,' she said. 'Timmy! Jimbo! She's captivated Father Emmanuel, a man trained to put all thoughts of sex behind him as the Devil's work. And she doesn't even bother to bring my food processor back to my house! No, she leaves it here, expecting me to lug it all the way up the road. Grr!'

'I'll give you a lift,' I said. Any excuse to drive the lovely Fiat 500. Outside it was so dark at first that I couldn't find it – but then I remembered my special key and, feeling like a character in a fairy-tale with a magic token in her hand, I pressed and, lo and behold, my little car gave a reassuring wink from the end of the street. I just love it!

I'd been given a new satnav free with the car, and I'd rather dangerously left it out the last time I'd driven. So after stuffing it into the glove compartment, we set off down the road – and just a couple of minutes of being sheltered in the car's kindly and friendly interior made me feel a lot better. Arriving home, I even sat there for a while with the engine turned off before I went in, and listened to the end of a very interesting discussion on climate change, featuring an excellent man who said that it was something to embrace not to fear.

And so to bed.

June 29

No word from the RSPCA even though I rang a second time. I opened the door this morning to get the milk and was horrified to notice that the dog's barking has turned into a terrible kind of yowling. He does sound as if he's in agony. Will definitely do something about it when I've got a minute. Not sure what, but will do something, that's for certain.

JULY

July 2

Opened an email this morning from Penny. It was headed 'Emergency!!!' Imagining the food processor had been broken by the ghastly Melanie or her bath had overflowed, I opened it up to read:

> GoodMorning!
> I really hope you get this fast. My family and I made an unan-
> nounced trip to (Philippines) for a program. The program was
> successful, but our journey has turned sour. everything was going
> fine until last night when we were mugged in an alley by a gang
> of thugs on our way back from shopping. All our money, phones
> and credit cards was stolen away including some valuable items, It
> was a terrible experience but the good thing is that they didn't hurt
> anyone or made away with our passports. I've report the incident to
> the local authorities and cancelled all our cards.
>
> I'm really having some difficulties clearing our hotel bills. We're

financially strapped due to the unexpected robbery attack. I'll be indeed grateful if I can get a loan of £1,750 from you. This will enable me sort our hotel bills. but anything you can spare pending when we get things straightened out will be appreciated and I promise to refund it back as soon as we arrive home safely. Let me know what you can do so I can tell you how to get the money to me.

Thanks. Penny

As I'd only seen her last night, I thought all this highly unlikely. Also I doubt if she'd ever refer to a holiday as a 'program'. Or to herself as 'financially strapped'. Or talk about 'refunding back' anything. So I rang her up and she wasn't in the Philippines at all. Her email has been hacked.

'Oh God!' she moaned. 'First Melanie on the committee and now this!'

Still, at least the scammers know how to spell 'appreciated'.

July 3

Spent the evening watching a programme about a horse whisperer on telly. Rather cosy in my dressing gown, curled up with a special supper that I like but no one else does – strips of raw fillet steak, shredded pear, an egg yolk and sesame oil. It's a Korean concoction called Yuk Hoe and I have never met anyone else who will give it the time of day. I wonder if we all have some special secret food vice that we don't tell other people about? I don't mean buckets of Ben and Jerry's ice cream – too obvious – no, I mean weird little comforting food combinations that are just special to us.

Anyway, this programme. It was all about some guy called Chuck who'd been brought up as a child lasso artist on a remote ranch in the States. He and his brother were experts but were beaten by their father within an inch of their lives. After a priest had noticed Chuck's little seven-year-old back was covered with weals and welts, the child was finally rescued and sent to live with a kindly family, who also had a ranch. There he discovered he had Strange Talents with horses and, now he was adult, went round the entire country sorting out equine problems. Show him a horse who wouldn't go near anyone without kicking and biting him and Chuck would quietly mosey into the paddock, mutter a few words in horse language and – presto! – before you knew where you were, he'd be riding the beast, getting it to do tricks, walking backwards, sideways, and leaving it as a horse full of peace, calm and serenity.

Wondered if I could somehow get to look into the Alsatian's eyes and fill him with peace and love.

After these kinds of programmes I always wonder – as must everyone else in the world, now I come to think of it – whether I have such Strange Talents myself. Spotting Pouncer sitting on the floor, I fixed him with what I hoped was a calm and reassuring gaze and tried to penetrate his catty mind, sending out waves of love and peace.

Needless to say, he gave me a withering look, put back his ears and immediately walked away. In a couple of minutes I heard the decisive click of the cat-flap.

What I'd like would be to possess an animal that was a person whisperer. Then, if you were in a terrible state about having a lump which no one seemed to be bothering about enough, or worrying whether it was time to stop getting your hair coloured or seething with rage about the latest Melanie incident, you would be instantly transformed, after they'd suddenly uttered some gnomic soothing phrase in perfect English, into a pool of bliss.

July 8

So far things are going really well at the school. I'm getting to know the class and Barbie, who increasingly reminds me of little Alice, Brad and Sharmie's daughter, even brought me a picture she'd made at home. I announced that if anyone else wanted to bring in things they'd made themselves we'd put them on show. Then they could all decide which three were the best, I'd have the casting vote, and I'd give the winner a prize of a set of felt-tipped pens. Everyone extremely excited.

Thought this was reasonable enough but when I ventured into the staff room I got a lot of disapproving looks. Apparently Angela had just been conscious enough to hear my plans and had reported me to the headmistress – sorry, Head – who later summoned me to her office.

'We don't give prizes here,' she said. 'We don't like to think in terms of which pupil is "best". I'm afraid your ideas went out with the Ark. I have to say your art classes are a great success and we're very grateful for your contribution to our school. But in future, if you have any plans like this, would you please check with me to ascertain what our policy is?'

Dumbfounded, I asked if I was able even to judge one picture better than the other.

'No. I suggest you ask the children to bring things in that they've made at home, but then you consider the individual merits of each. We don't like to judge here. After all, what is "best" in art is only a matter of opinion.'

Here she gave what I read as a patronizing snigger.

A matter of opinion! I wondered what Michelangelo or Leonardo would have said if someone had admitted that their *David* or *Mona* was great but 'only in their opinion'! I choked back my fury and returned to the class. What a total idiot that woman was, I thought. I was actually wondering if I could bear to continue teaching at the school. That's the trouble with me. I don't have the ability to understand someone else's point of view, accept it for what it is, and then proceed as if nothing has happened. My fury was compounded when it became clear the whole class was terribly disappointed when I told them the competition was a nonstarter. Still I managed to get over it and by the end of the session we'd produced some very nice designs using only food glued onto card – lentils, sugar, rice, pasta shells, bay leaves and so on – and some of them had started on sections of a large piece that I'd planned, whereby each of them was given a piece of paper and had to design or paint something about the school. Could be a portrait of the Head (I'm learning!), how they feel when they're in the playground, pictures of school lunches . . . Then the idea is that I'll mount them all on a huge bit of hardboard and we can display it in the school corridor, rather like a patchwork quilt. Surely no one can object to that?

The only one in the class who was reluctant to participate was sad little Zac. He just downed tools. In the end I said he needn't take part in the project, but couldn't he please do *something,* so he began a picture of his house. Checking on him throughout the lesson, I found he'd started off with a happy family. Daddy was working on a computer, Mummy was indoors washing up and the child – there was only one – was playing on the lawn. But as the minutes went by, Zac seemed to get angrier and angrier. Suddenly he got out some red paint and sloshed great streaks across the picture.

'Now everyone's in bed and there's a fire and everyone's dead,' he said, sounding more enthusiastic than I'd ever heard him before.

'Oh, that's a pity,' I said, feebly. 'Can't they be rescued?'

'Daddy's gone away,' he said. 'He's here . . .' and he pointed to the edge of his desk, 'but everyone else is dead. And now,' he said, dipping his brush in the black paint, 'it's night-time.' Before I knew it, the whole picture had become as black as a wall in the Rothko Chapel in Houston, Texas. (Brilliant place, incidentally.)

I have to say, I was rather alarmed. It did cross my mind that the little chap was seriously disturbed. Was this how homicidal maniacs were formed? Dad leaves home and the children left behind become so angry they eliminate entire families?

At the end of the day I asked if I could have another word with the Head.

'I'm so sorry to bother you,' I said, poking my head around the door. 'But I do have a concern that I'd like to . . .'

Perhaps thinking she'd been rather harsh on me earlier that morning, she welcomed me in. Poor woman. She looked incredibly harassed and I wondered if this 'no prize' nonsense was really her idea or whether it was a rule laid down by the governors. I explained about the large collage of images of the school and she was suddenly all over me. And then I mentioned Zac.

She put her head in her hands. 'Oh, God,' she said. 'It's tragic, isn't it? We're thinking of having him statemented as a special-needs child. But the truth is, before this family trouble, he was a lovely little boy. His father just left and hasn't been in communication at all with him. Zac used to be happy, he'd play, he had lots of friends. But now no one can get through to him. I've had the mother in and we've talked to her, but frankly she's so angry that it's very difficult. The father seems to have no interest in getting in touch with Zac, and the mother refuses to speak to the father. Why can't parents behave like adults once in a while? Why do they always think about themselves?'

'I wonder,' I said. 'Do you think I might have a word with her? I could show her his picture. And I'm much older than her. I might not seem such a threat. You know – play the harmless old lady card?'

The Head smiled at this. 'I don't think anyone sees you as a harmless old lady, Marie,' she said, with something like awe in her voice. I was surprised to sense it, that awe. I get moments, now I'm older, of being aware that sometimes I'm seen not as a shy retiring worm – which is what I've always felt I am deep down – but rather, a tough old boot. Indeed, sometimes a terrifying tough old boot.

I didn't disabuse her and point out that I was actually a shy retiring worm disguised as a terrifying tough old boot, but I didn't think there was a hope in hell of her going along with my idea. No doubt there was some dreadful rule about parents and teachers consorting. But oddly, after she'd hummed and hawed, I saw in her eyes a ray of hope – though it didn't last for long.

'As I said, Zac used to be a lovely, friendly little boy,' she said. 'I've begged his mother to take him to see a therapist but she refuses. She's only been in to discuss him once and that ended in a screaming match. Frankly I don't look forward to a repeat performance – but you never know. Even though I can't see it will have any effect, I think we owe it to Zac to give it a try. I'd have to be in on the meeting of course, but if you think it might help . . . I doubt, to be honest, if she'll come. But I'll send her a note saying you're disturbed and would welcome a talk.'

'Don't say I'm disturbed,' I said. 'It's her son who's disturbed.'

The Head smiled again. 'We're all disturbed really, aren't we? When you get down to it?'

And then I revised my view of her. Funny how quickly one can revise one's views once someone is on your side.

Suddenly from being a raving idiot, full of spoon-fed ideas about equality and untenable views on art, she'd turned into someone compassionate, rational and efficient. And with a sense of humour.

Later
Checked Facebook and found Marion had posted a picture of a rainstorm and underneath the words: 'Life isn't about waiting for the storm to pass, it's about learning to dance in the rain.'

Load of bollocks.

July 9

Dog still barking its head off. I will have to do something about it soon. I sometimes wish it would just die, to stop it worrying me so much, but I know that's very selfish of me. I feel so sorry for it, all alone, straining away at the leash, with hardly anything to eat. What's the point of having a dog if you don't look after it or love it or take it for walks? I've often thought I'd like a dog, but I'd always feel guilty if I went out, leaving it staring at me with its wet nose and big doggy eyes, wondering if I was ever going to come back. Anyway, there's Pouncer to consider. No word from the wretched RSPCA. Will ring them again. I'm sure it's against the law to keep a dog in those conditions.

Have asked Graham to supper tonight. After all, he lives in the house and, although we have cheerful chats as we pass each other on the stairs, it seems only friendly to meet up now and again and have a gossip. He arrived at 8.30, straight from the office, very apologetic about being late and bearing a bottle of wine.

I'd cooked a chicken because I thought it was the thing he might miss, not being at home – odd how you can never get roast chicken when you go to a restaurant – with delicious bread sauce and bacon and tiny sausages, and after we were stuffed to the gills with deliciousness, I made him some coffee and he suddenly started talking about himself. He'd hardly opened his mouth when the bell rang. It was, naturally enough, Melanie from next door.

'I just wanted to say I've got this great idea for the street,' she said, walking straight into the hall. 'I say, that smells good! Have you got guests?' She peered down the corridor to see if she could make out who I'd got for dinner.

'Yes I have, Melanie,' I said very firmly. 'Can we talk another time?'

I somehow managed to get her out of the house and hoped Graham wouldn't have changed his mind about baring his soul.

'Melanie!' I said, as I sat down. 'I simply refuse to call her Mel. Have you met people like that before? They're such snoops and leeches ... basically warm-hearted,' I added, in case Graham thought I was too unpleasant, 'but talk about hard work.'

'She practically ate us for breakfast when we went over to move those bits of furniture. If she'd had her way, we'd have both moved in with her,' he said, grinning. 'I know what you mean.'

Anyway. The saga of Graham. It turned out that he'd been happily married for ages and then one night he'd gone abroad on a trip, got drunk, and slept with someone else's PA. Waking up full of guilt, he immediately confessed all to his wife on his return and, rather than be understanding, she blew a fuse and chucked him out the house.

'It wasn't even as if I fancied this girl,' he said. 'And I've never done it before and would never do it again in a million years! It was just because I was pissed! I went up to my hotel room and then there was a tapping on the door and there was this woman in a dressing gown with nothing on underneath, and she flung herself at me, and what was I to do? I mean it was only polite. I didn't even fancy her! I didn't even enjoy it!' he protested. 'I mean why would I want to leave a woman like this?' And he pulled out a photograph from his wallet of an extremely glamorous-looking blonde, with a very white face and scarlet lipstick. Very modern.

'Have you thought of marriage counselling?' I said. 'Would your wife agree?'

'I think she might in a few months, but at the moment she's still furious,' he said, giving the photograph a lingering stare before he put it back in his wallet. 'And what's worse – oh, never mind . . .'

My heart went out to the poor chap. I remember my own parents going through a bad patch and the absolute misery they felt when there was talk of them breaking up. Luckily, though, they stuck together – divorce was practically unheard of when I was young – and in the end they seemed pretty fond of one another. Sometimes I think marriage is like the Grand National. If you can get over Beecher's Brook and Lovers' Leap, or whatever the jumps are called, then you're in for the long stretch to the finish. But so many people fall at the first hurdle.

July 10

'Home Counties gran chokes to death on ketchup' (*Daily Rant*)

July 11

Have been feeling a bit wan recently so went to the chemist to ask if they had any pills to stop me feeling so tired. The woman there assured me that I lacked Vitamin D, which is something you manufacture when there's lots of sunshine around. As there's been no sunshine for weeks – it's been one of those summers that never comes – I thought she might have a point.

'If you need sunshine to make Vitamin D, how do women in burkas cope?' I asked, for a moment forgetting that, although she doesn't wear a burka, she's Muslim.

'They don't,' she said. 'They get very tired and depressed. They are very stupid.'

Fearing a minefield, I nodded sympathetically and took the pills home.

The problem with pills these days is that they're so incredibly difficult to get out of the wretched wrapper. In the old days you used to get pills in bottles. They rattled. Now you get silent blister-packs and you need thumbs of steel simply to release one from its plastic prison. Sometimes, you've even pierced the metal foil on the back, but they still won't budge. You have to push and shove to persuade them to pop out and then, of course, when you succeed, they leap across the bathroom, into the basin and down the plug hole.

After about quarter of an hour, I managed to get most of them out and put them in a box, and I threw the packaging away. Then, thinking there didn't seem to be many pills in the box, I hauled the metallic strips back out of the bin and blow me if there weren't five more hiding in there like cornered rabbits.

Have planned to take Gene to the zoo tomorrow. I find zoos pretty grim places but hope he'll enjoy it. What grannies do for love! It's costing me an arm and a leg, but still.

Watched a very old DVD that came free with a newspaper years ago and I'd never got round to viewing. Halfway through, I realized I'd watched it before and it was rubbish. Can't remember the title.

July 12

The collage is turning out extremely well and we'll definitely have it finished by the end of term. Even Zac finally has contributed something – a dark picture of a child sitting in a deserted classroom, looking out of the window at other children playing. Oh dear.

July 14

Couldn't find the car in the street yesterday, so wandered up and down until I saw the reassuring wink of its little lights. I felt it was smiling at me. A surge of affection came over me. Golly I *must* be a psychopath if I'm having an emotional relationship with an inanimate object. Like those American farmers in the remote Midwest who get married to their tractors.

Anyway, I was just about to drive off to collect Gene for our zoo trip and sleepover when who should I spot leaving Melanie's house next door but James, looking very furtive?

'Computer meltdown,' he explained apologetically, leaning through my window. 'Urgent early morning call-out.'

'What was the problem?' I asked, tartly.

'Hadn't plugged it in!' he said. 'Mad old Mel!' he added, affectionately. 'Car looks great!'

Don't like the way things are shaping up at all.

Later

When I got to Jack and Chrissie's they were looking rather strained, I thought. I wondered if they'd just had a row about the appendix appointment. Poor old them. I can just imagine it – Jack full of fear about an operation and Chrissie full of fear that he could die if he didn't have his appendix out. Each accusing the other of being selfish.

So I scooped Gene up as quickly as possible.

'I love your car!' he said, as he got in. 'It's the nicest car I know.'

He settled in on the special safety cushion in the front.

'You soon won't be needing that, will you?' I said.

'S'pose not,' he said, gloomily. He seemed a little down. Then, after we'd driven a little way, he said, 'Mum wants Dad to have this operation. And Dad doesn't want to. Do you know anything about pendickses, Granny?'

'It's "appendix",' I said, automatically. 'To "append" is to add – it's an addition.'

Then I thought I was being ridiculously pedantic. 'Not that it matters, darling,' I said. I felt we hadn't got off to a good start.

'You mean like an app?' said Gene. 'But not,' he added, puzzled, 'like an apple. Anyway, Mum – I mean Granny – they're very interesting. I'll do a drawing of one when we get to your house. You don't need it, you know. God just put it in by mistake.'

Wasn't sure if I should start a discussion about whether God had anything to do with it, then felt it best to let sleeping gods lie.

It wasn't the best day to go to the zoo, I have to say. Summer had arrived in a one-day burst, it was boiling hot and everyone was clearly feeling frazzled. Also, whenever I approach the place, I feel a shudder of misery go down my spine. It's all those cries and the roaring and trumpeting that give me the willies. While Gene was very excited, all I could hear were the sounds of imprisoned animals screaming for help. We bravely pushed through the crowds – extremely fat people pushing enormous buggies in which were lolling podgy babies far too young to know what a zoo was.

We saw some rather mangy gazelles and a couple of giraffes, and were just staring at a gorilla who (or should it be which?) was drearily pushing a rubber tyre to and fro, when Gene became quiet. I thought the aquarium would cheer him up, but he pressed his nose glumly to the glass and said, 'These fish are very big for such a small space, aren't they, Granny?'

My thoughts exactly. But I said something trivial like, 'Oh well, they probably don't know any different.'

Later we passed a pair of zebras and a llama and then, round a corner – past a signpost covered in grotesque cartoons of grinning tigers with thumbs up and crocodiles winking, all very Facebook – we walked over a bridge and from the top of it we could see a real tiger. At least it had a bit of green space and a pond, but it was just walking up and down, up and down, pressing itself to the glass boundary of its enclosure. It looked desperately anxious and stressed, but I tried to put a bright spin on it all.

'Much better than when I was young,' I said encouragingly. 'They were in tiny cages then.'

But Gene by now had grown silent. 'It's not very kind, is it?' he said. 'I'm sure they'd be happier in the wild. I don't really like seeing them like this.'

Half of me felt delighted that, though he was so young, he had such exemplary compassion for the animals and half of me was jumping up and down thinking, 'For God's sake, I spend a fortune on giving you a treat and you just regard it all as some kind of torture!' Revealing neither of these emotions, I took the third, coward's route.

'Well,' I said, 'London Zoo does do very good work with endangered species. Lots of these animals are only alive because of zoos. And they do breed some to put back in the wild, you know.' I drivelled on about the usual ecological rubbish, and felt a mixture of dismay and relief to find that Gene, poor love, seemed to take it on board and cheered up. Which was the idea, of course.

The rest of the day was taken up by me trying to paint a bright picture of all that we were seeing, and attempting to repress my feeling that we had just paid an arm and a leg to go round a hideously brutal prison camp. I was jolly relieved when we got back, after an extremely expensive and very inadequate tuna sandwich.

Later, Gene had a bath, and then we watched some Tom and Jerry cartoons before he went to bed.

'I love coming here, Granny,' he said, when I tucked him up.

'And I love you coming here,' I said. But oh dear. Soon he'll be too big to take to the zoo, I can already imagine it. He'll be on his mobile all day, doing his hair with gel, embarrassed to have me in the bathroom with him – all silent and moody – and he won't have any time for his old grandma. Oh well. Best make the most of this short time I'll have with him. He'll start looking back on it all when he's much older – perhaps when he has children of his own – and remembering, I hope, that days with Granny were pretty good fun. I think of my old grandmother nearly every day – making cakes with her, going on special picnics to the park, playing snakes and ladders with penny bets on who'd win. We'd go round to the shop and get sweets (she managed to wheedle some out of the shopkeeper even though we were on rations) and she'd painstakingly read me children's comics from cover to cover, even though she must have found them incredibly boring.

While we were at the zoo, someone in my street had been cutting the grass and it threw up that lovely sweet smell. For a moment I was transported back to the times when I used to help my grandfather mow the lawn – I'd go ahead and pick up stones to stop them getting in the way of the mower's blades – and my eyes filled with nostalgic tears. What's so weird about these memories is that I don't recall feeling anything particular while I was helping my grandfather. It's the memory that brings out the poignancy, not the actual event at the time.

After I'd taken Gene back home today, I stayed for supper with Jack and Chrissie. And when Gene had gone to bed we talked about Sandra, David's girlfriend.

'Poor old Dad,' said Jack. 'He seemed quite cut up about it, didn't he Chrissie, when he was round here?'

I'd obviously been given a slightly different spin.

'I thought he was nearly crying,' said Chrissie. 'There were definitely tears in his eyes. I think he suddenly felt past it. Perhaps it was the fact that she was so desperate for children – and he really feels too old to be a good father – that upset him, because they were very fond of each other, despite the age difference.'

'Yes, she's found some glam beach boy, I gather, and is going to live in a hut on a Goan beach. Can't imagine it'll last very long. But it's sad about Dad. I said he should go for it and have kids with her, but he said it wouldn't be fair on them, and he'd be the oldest father in the playground and so on. But he was always a great dad.'

'If she does come back, it'll be too late,' said Chrissie. 'He'll have found someone else.'

'Well, apparently the Widow Bossom is off the scene,' I said. 'He doesn't fancy her. It's a shame, because I liked her – she was a good sort – so I've told him he's not to get involved with anyone else until I've had a good old vet. I was wondering – what do you think about Penny?'

Jack made a face. He's never seen the point of Penny, but Chrissie thought it was a good idea.

Jack's appendix wasn't mentioned and I thought it wisest not to bring up my lump.

July 15

The great school collage is going fine. We've started to lay all the pictures out on the floor and arrange them, and I'm surprised how visually aware these little people are.

'Don't put all the dark pictures in the corner!' said Annie, a little blonde girl. 'Mix them up with the light ones!'

'No!' said Ned, whose parents are designers. 'If we get all

the dark ones in one corner we can put the light ones on the other corner and it will look like a big pattern with shapes instead of lots of dots!'

Later

Marion, Tim and I went out to see the old French film *Breathless*, starring Jean-Paul Belmondo, which Marion's been dying to catch for ages. As we came out of the cinema, we both agreed it was odd that he'd seemed so extraordinarily attractive when we were young and now appeared to be a dull poseur with over-blubbery lips. Of course Marion didn't put it like that – she was a lot more charitable – but we agreed that he didn't make us flutter in the way he'd done in the past.

Afterwards I managed to guide Marion and Tim to a place in Notting Hill that serves halfway decent food compared to the 'cheap and cheerful' Italian dump they prefer. Cheap it may be, and the proprietor always puts his ghastly dried-up old pasta in front of you with a huge smile and loads of talk about 'bellissima' while pinching together his thumb and forefinger, but it doesn't alter the fact that the food is muck. I suspect he reheats his pasta dishes in a microwave, which means (and trust me, I know) that it comes out tough and rubbery and all glued together. And his lasagne is like eating mince separated by sheets of cardboard.

Unfortunately I discovered too late that this whole evening was merely a pretext to grill me on the subject of my lump. Marion wanted to know exactly what the doctor had said, and she urged me to 'fight' it.

'I have no intention of "fighting" it,' I said, over a delicious veal escalope. (Marion had been very disapproving: 'Have you seen how they raise the poor calves? It's so cruel!') 'Not my style,' I continued. I'm more likely to befriend it. And it might be benign for all I know. Not be a lump, just a pocket of air on its way to my lungs. But the doctor did make a diagnosis, actually. He said it might be a GOK.'

'What on earth is a GOK?' asked Marion, worriedly, putting down her knife and fork.

'What do you think?' I asked.

'Gerontological Organ Keratosis?' suggested Marion.

'Glandular Ovoid Kinesis?' offered Tim, as he tucked into his prawns with garlic.

'God Only Knows!' I said. 'By the way, the specialist turned out to be a friend of Jack's, believe it or not! I used to take them about in the back of the car when they were small. Really weird finding he'd suddenly turned into such a distinguished figure. He's a fund of medical jargon, too. And extremely dishy – which makes having a lump almost worthwhile.'

I felt a bit bad about saying that because Tim, for all he's a sweetie, is definitely not in the dishy category. He has, as they say, 'let himself go' and, at the point where his waistband started, I noticed his shirt had parted, revealing a tiny triangle of white tummy covered with hairs.

'I don't think that's funny,' said Marion, stiffly, helping herself to a large glass of house red. 'Are you sure he was a proper consultant? He sounds far too young.'

'Well, Jack's 40!' I said. 'That used to be ancient when we were 20.'

'I don't think you're taking this seriously enough,' said Marion.

If only, I thought to myself, she knew how seriously I took it. The nights I lie awake worrying and the days I spend trying to cover up my worries. I just want to distract myself from the wretched thing until I know exactly what it is.

'You don't take enough exercise,' said Tim ponderously. 'Exercise, that's what you need. Gets the blood going.'

'How much exercise do *you* take, Tim?' I asked, astonished, considering the size of his tum.

'I walk everywhere,' he said. 'No bus, no tube. I've never used my pensioner's Freedom Pass in my life. I know London like the back of my hand.'

('And all the pie shops en route, by the look of you,' I thought unkindly.)

'And I do Pilates,' said Marion. 'You should try it.'

So many people bang on about Pilates and nag me to try it that I've got a terrible teenage-like aversion to it. The more people tell me, the more adamant I become that I won't go near a Pilates class.

'And you eat too much salt,' said Marion, wrestling the salt-shaker from me as I sprinkled it over some delicious cour-gettes in batter. 'I don't think you eat properly. What have you had today, for instance?'

'Two oatcakes and some coffee for breakfast – okay?' I said defensively. 'Then for lunch, tomatoes with garlic and herbs on toast,' I added. 'Some mango bits from the supermarket, some orange juice.' Luckily it was a day on which I'd eaten very healthily. (Oh – and a Crunchie bar . . .)

'Beans, lentils, brown rice – that's what you should be eating,' said Marion, who is no stranger to The Pulse. 'And you never walk, you're always driving.'

'Well, my car is so lovely!' I said, coming to the defence of my adorable little Fiat.

They both looked very disapproving. They clearly thought that the lump was entirely my own fault and that if I lived their kind of lifestyle – not a word that ever ventures into my vocabulary – I wouldn't ever be ill, let alone have a mysterious GOK.

Eventually I managed to change the subject to David and Penny, which got them going. Neither of them thought she'd be at all suitable, but Marion had some terrible old schoolfriend she said would be perfect. Golly, there are so many single women of our age around – men having a nasty habit of dying first – I'm surprised David isn't already besieged.

July 21

I was trying to get into the drawer where I keep all my presents but it was so packed with stuff that I couldn't open it. I had to find the breadknife and slowly ease it in, to flatten everything, before I could slide the drawer out. It is with such trivial tasks that my day – and my life, come to think of it – is filled. Sorting through, I decided to shift half the things into the pile for Age Concern, including Marion's scarf. Dropped them off in Notting Hill Gate this afternoon. (Surely no chance of Marion ever going up there and seeing it?)

July 22

As I was leaving for school today, Melanie popped out of her house. 'The dog!' she cried. 'I can't bear it! What are we going to do about it?'

'Let's talk about it this evening,' I said. 'Must rush now, though.'

'Okay. I'll chuck it something over for now. Till tonight.'

As it's nearly the end of term, the great collage has finally been put up in the school corridor and I must say it looks fantastic. I've made a frame for it out of drawing pins and rulers – I bought 100 cheap at Ikea – and now it's like some kind of Grayson Perry tapestry. The Head is thrilled and wants to get it laminated so they can keep it for posterity, which is very pleasing. 'Pleasing.' One of those strange words like amiable, congenial, convivial. Doesn't really mean anything.

Later

Incredibly relieved to hear the dog was quiet. So when I went over to Melanie's for a drink, I said, rather admiringly, 'What have you done? Drugged him?'

'No. I chucked over a box of chocolates actually. I thought I'd give him a treat. I can't eat chocolate, so I hope he's having a good time!'

I reached over and clutched her arm. 'Chocolate? But didn't you know that chocolate is poisonous for dogs?' I said. God, that woman.

'Is it?' she said. 'I thought it would be nice for him.'

'No, it could kill him. Oh Christ, we've got to get him to the vet! Straight away!'

'Are you sure?'

'Of course I'm sure!'

Melanie said she couldn't help because she was going to a meditation class and she'd already missed the last two. It seemed to me a poor piece of logic because surely, if you've missed two, you can miss three? But still. All very typical.

I rang Penny and James and they said they'd be over right away – James with a ladder, though how on earth we'll be able to get the poor dog up a ladder I have no idea. Though there's a small gate in the garden wall, it's always locked. Anyway, we all piled over, but when James got up to the top of the ladder and peered over, he wasn't very hopeful about the situation..

'How is he?' called Penny.

'He looks fine,' said James. 'But I can't see how we're going to get him over the wall. The only thing would be to wait until he gets very ill then bung him in a sack and haul him up in a basket. But by that time he'd be nearly dead and besides, who's got a sack strong enough or a basket big enough to put an Alsatian in?'

I suggested we break down the gate but James, although he rattled it and said it wasn't very secure, was reluctant actually to put his shoulder to it and break in.

'It's against the law,' he said. 'I don't want to be had up for breaking and entering.'

'What about waiting till it gets dark?'

'That won't be for a while,' said Penny. 'The dog could be dead by then.' We were already attracting strange looks from mysterious bearded men, and even the burka-clad women's eyes were bulging through their slits as they passed us.

'If only we knew a locksmith who could pick the lock on the gate, that wouldn't be so bad,' said James. 'It's only a simple Yale.'

Then Penny thought of Sheila the Dealer. 'Surely she must know someone who picks locks,' she said.

'But we can't ring her and say, "Surely you know someone who picks locks?"' I said.

'Just ask her round and get her advice,' said Penny. 'She was concerned about the dog at the last meeting, remember?'

So within a few minutes Sheila the Dealer arrived, fag in hand and carpet slippers on feet. The smell of chip fat had been replaced by a smell of paraffin. Great improvement.

'So 'oo giv 'im the choclit?' she asked us, accusingly. 'Everyone 'oo knows anyfink abart dogs knows they can't eat fuckin' choclit. My son 'ad a dog and 'e ate a Christmas decoration – all choclit – and 'e was dead in an hour.'

We immediately protested that we were innocent and were delighted to inform her that Melanie was the culprit.

'Fucking idiot! Ought to be poisoned 'erself if you arse me,' said Sheila the D.

Eventually she stopped chatting and assessed the situation.

'Well obvious, innit?' she said, looking at James. 'You got to get froo that door.'

'But how?' said James, despairingly.

'You got a big plastic bottle, love?' she said to me. 'You bring it 'ere wiv a pair of scissors and I'll get froo that door. It's only a Yale, innit?'

I rushed over the road to my house and was going to pour a brand-new bottle of fizzy water down the sink but my Scottish ancestry kicked in and instead I poured it carefully into a jug. Back at the door Sheila got to work. She cut off the top and the bottom, as well as a long strip down the side and, throwing those away, was left with a wide, curved sheet of plastic. Carefully, she inserted the edge between the door and the frame and pushed it round, jiggling the door as she did so. Soon we heard the latch slide back, and – *voilà!* – the door was open and the dog was leaping on us all, barking and whimpering. If I had been a dog whisperer I know he would have been saying, 'My saviours! Free at last!'

'Now, you ain't seen me, rart? I 'ad nothing to do wiv this, innit?' said Sheila, the excellent woman. 'You let me know 'ow you get on. That poor dog! Good luck! And good luck to you, too, me old chummy!' she added, giving the hysterical dog a rub on his head. And then Sheila the D went shuffling off down the road like any other innocent old woman – back to her drug den, I presume, to do some more bagging up.

While Penny and James struggled to keep the dog under control, I rang round vets on my mobile and found one in Chelsea who would take an emergency appointment. After only about ten minutes the poor animal was starting to flag, presumably with the creeping effects of the chocolate. But that helped us because it was quite easy to get him into James' car. (James did insist on a blanket, though, because he didn't want Chummy to be sick all over his hybrid interior.)

We had a precarious drive, Penny in the front, me in the back with the dog, James at the wheel, saying he hoped the dog wouldn't suddenly go mad and start biting everyone. Finally we got him to the vet – the only one I could find open late was near Sloane Square, and of course incredibly expensive – so Penny and I lugged poor old Chummy (the name seemed to have stuck) out of the back of the car and managed to half-drag him into the waiting room while James parked nearby.

'What are we going to do with him after the vet?' asked Penny.

'God knows,' said James, gloomily. 'Perhaps, with any luck, he'll die first.'

'James!' said Penny. But I think we all knew what he meant.

After subjecting Chummy to the briefest of examinations, the vet, an energetic young man in a white coat, naturally started giving us a good ticking off.

'How could you let a dog get into such a condition!' he said. 'I'll be surprised if he lasts the night. He's half starved, dehydrated, he's full of ticks, his mouth's in a frightful condition, half his teeth are rotten! I've a good mind to put him down, poor old chap!' he said, stroking him, affectionately. The Alsatian looked up at him pitifully and his mangy old tail started wagging. 'And now you say some idiot gave him a box of chocolates! You can see he's already got the beginnings of Theobromine poisoning. He'll have to go on a drip but I doubt he'll make it. I'm half inclined to report you to the police. Who actually owns this dog? Whoever it is isn't fit to own animals!'

I don't think he believed us when we explained the situation but at least he calmed down.

'It won't be cheap,' he said, glowering. 'But I'll do my best.'

We all crawled out feeling small and cowed.

'Honestly, I feel like a criminal now,' said James on the way back in the car – its interior still smelling horribly of sick dog – 'when rightly we should all be feeling like heroes.'

'Well, maybe he won't pull through,' I said, hopefully. Penny said nothing but we clearly were all pondering if it wouldn't have been better to leave the dog where it was to its own wretched fate.

'I wonder how much it will cost,' said Penny, articulating again what we were all thinking but too embarrassed to say.

'Can't be more than £500, surely!' said James. 'That's about £170 each.'

I asked everyone back for a drink. Because we were all feeling so shaky and low, we cracked open a bottle of Prosecco and after a couple of glasses each we were starting to feel more heroic. I said I'd keep the dog until we'd found a home for him – if he lives, that is – because Penny was going away and James lives in a flat. But we agreed that I couldn't keep him for ever.

'And then it's Battersea Dogs' Home for Chummy,' said James. If he survives. Which, fingers crossed he . . . er . . . will? Won't?

July 23

'More deaths from dog attacks than cars, cancer and heart attacks put together!' (*Daily Rant*)

According to the vet, Chummy should be kept in for another couple of days or so, to sort out the matted lumps in his fur and see that he's fit enough to come home, but on the whole things seem to be looking up for the animal. I must say it's a huge relief not to hear him barking all day. The road seems like an oasis of calm now.

July 26

'Mad Alsatian mauls toddler, 3' (*Daily Rant*)

James collected Chummy from the vet in his glam hybrid car. He was reluctant but no taxi-driver would have taken him. Apparently he (Chummy that is) started whimpering as soon as he arrived in our street but when he realized James wasn't taking him back to his ghastly old house he perked up. Poor old chap. He's still pretty sickly but he's been given a real wash and brush up by the vet, not a tick in sight. His nails have been trimmed, his poor old teeth cleaned and pulled (the very bad ones) and, although he's tragically thin, he'll feed up in no time. The vet says he's basically a nice animal who's been ill-treated, but unless you raise your hand (when he obviously thinks he's going to be hit) he is peaceful and friendly. He pottered around checking everything out, and is quite house-trained, though he finds it hard to go into my huge garden for long periods. You have to stand by the door making comforting noises all the time because he's obviously frightened he's going to be abandoned there.

'What are we going to say if the ghastly woman comes knocking at my door?' I said nervously to James.

'Don't worry,' said James, 'Mel says she saw a policeman banging on her door this morning, and she was last seen being hustled down the road towards the police station. So hopefully she won't be around for a while.'

Chummy didn't even seem to mind Pouncer so he's obviously been used to cats at some point in his life. Can't say the same for Pouncer, who went into full-blown Mrs Rochester mode, screaming, spitting and arching his back like a Hallowe'en cat. Since this very unpleasant stand-off, Pouncer has been slinking around with his tummy close to the ground and his ears back, occasionally glaring at me with such a look of resentment and betrayal that I can hardly look him in the eye.

Later

Golly, I'm never going to have a dog permanently! Chummy is round me all the time, following me about when I'm up and, when I'm sitting down, putting his great slobbering head on my lap. It's awful. I really don't like dogs, though I can't help but feel a great sympathy with Chummy. Still, sympathy or not, I don't really *get* him. Luckily, Graham is very good with him, and pats him and calls him 'old man' and has even offered to take him for walks when he gets back from work, which is pretty decent of him. The last thing I want to do is to go out for a walk round here, roaming parks that are swarming with gangsters and drug-dealers.

Just had a brilliant idea. Archie's daughter and son-in-law! I wonder if Sylvie and Harry would like Chummy? They live in the country and I know Hardy, Archie's old dog, has just died. Bet they'd love another one. Or, failing that, what about David?

AUGUST

August 1

This morning, I was just in the middle of doing my exercises, which involve lying on my back stretching a long blue strip of what looks like an enormous rubber band around my knees, when there was a knock on the bedroom door and it was Graham, asking if he could borrow some of my milk.

Felt a total chump lying there like a maniac.

August 2

Thought I'd clear out all the junk email on my computer. And couldn't resist having a peek to see what it was. It all appeared to be emails from people promising to make my penis longer. 'Make her scream when she sees your dick!' said one. Another, oddly, asked me, 'How do you feel about enriching yourself by means of war? It's the very time to realize this. As soon as the military attack Syria, oil prices will rise as well as MON-

ARCHY RESOURCES (MO_NK) share price!!! Go make cash and buy MO_NK shares!!!'

Later

I was just popping out to buy some dog food for Chummy when who should I see coming down the road towards me but Melanie! For some reason, I simply couldn't face her. I didn't want to have to stand there with her moaning about how guilty she felt about throwing chocolates over to the dog and as I was just passing my lovely Fiat, parked by the kerb, I gave a friendly wave to the old monster, hopped into the car, revved up and drove off. I was waiting at the lights, wondering how long I had to drive around before Melanie got into her house – a minute or so – when I noticed a string hanging out of the glove compartment. I turned into the Uxbridge Road, trying to open the flap – but failing in that, tugged at the string. To my horror, the air was filled with an ear-shattering shriek. The whole road turned to look at me, because clearly the racket could be heard outside.

To start with, I thought that maybe the car had caught fire and the alarm had gone off, until I remembered it didn't have an alarm. Then I realized what I'd done. I'd pulled the string of the rape alarm, which I'd stuffed inside the glove compartment. I couldn't stop in the main road because everyone would stare at me, so I turned off into what would have been a peaceful side-street had I not been there. Feeling dreadfully guilty, I opened the car door, flung the shrieking rape alarm into the gutter and shot off as fast as I could, hoping that no one had noticed me.

Came home and let myself in. Could still hear the rape alarm from several streets away, although the battery appeared to be running down. I felt awful, imagining the people who lived in that street and had now had their day ruined. Perhaps some of them were asleep after gruelling night shifts, or in bed recovering from operations, or worrying about dying loved ones, or dying themselves. And perhaps there were babies woken up from afternoon sleeps, their poor mothers staggering around looking for milk bottles, the dads grumbling and an argument brewing.

Still, I got over it eventually.

August 3

'Orphan sex slaves on offer in high street!' (*Daily Rant*)

August 5

Keep feeling awful about leaving Chummy when I go out. Every time I shut the door he sets up such a wretched howling that I want to turn back and simultaneously shoot him and hold him in my arms, breathing sweet nothings into his pointed furry ears. God knows how Melanie can stand the noise but she's been surprisingly understanding so far. I should think so too – considering, for all her whinges, she never did a thing to help us rescue him.

Even though school has broken up, they're continuing weekly holiday art classes for those whose parents are working. There's also chess and sport, and gym and break-dancing, and the atmosphere is much more fun and relaxed. The only problem with all this is that there's less time to do any of my own work. But I must say it's all tremendously jolly.

Today, when the class was over and Zac was still sitting there – everyone else having gone off to have their packed lunches in the playground, as the canteen was closed for the hols – I pulled up a school chair next to him, feeling rather silly because the chair was about half normal-size and my knees were up to my chin.

'Why doesn't he go out and play with the other children?' I said, pointing to the child in his picture and coming over all therapeutic.

Zac turned his pale face to me and stared at me with watery blue eyes. He didn't look as if he'd washed his hair for a while or even combed it, and his clothes were crumpled as if he'd slept in them.

'He doesn't want to. He's sad,' he said. Not being a therapist, I didn't really know how to move the conversation along, though I felt I had grazed an emotional seam.

'What would make him happy?' I asked, gently.

Zac was silent.

'Would seeing his mummy or daddy make him happy?' I asked, feeling like a terrible psychic bull lumbering into this little boy's china shop.

Zac stared at me again, gave a bleak smile and turned away.

'His daddy doesn't love him,' he said suddenly. 'And the little boy doesn't love his daddy.'

Poor Zac. I wished I could do something more for him. I wished I'd been trained as a genius therapist so that I could guide his feelings somewhere but I couldn't. Despite dire warnings from the school about not getting too close to the children, I instinctively put my arm round his cold, bony little shoulders and hugged him.

There was absolutely no response from him at all. I released my grip.

'I hate coming to school,' he said suddenly.

'I know you do,' I said, after a pause. 'I used to hate going to school. But it won't go on for ever. And this isn't really school, is it? It's holiday school,' I added, pitifully trying to put a happy gloss on the fact that his mother was working her socks off during the day.

'I don't mind art,' he added. I wasn't sure if he was just being polite. I assumed that he meant it and put my hand over his on the desk. I was struck by how big and wrinkly my fingers looked compared to his slim and delicate little ones.

'Thank you,' I said. 'Well,' I added, hesitantly, 'I very much enjoy seeing *you* every week.'

I felt utterly hopeless. All I'd done was to go crashing into his emotional interior with no idea of how he worked and now I was leaving him high and dry. And the worst thing was, what I'd said wasn't even true. I *didn't* enjoy seeing him every week. He was like wretched Chummy had been – every bark had tapped into some uncomfortable bit of me that simply felt guilty and frustrated that I couldn't do anything to help.

Zac looked up at the clock. 'I'd better eat my lunch,' he said, with no particular enthusiasm, hoiking from his backpack a lunchbox covered with pictures of Shrek. (One of the more loathsome cartoon creations.) 'But I'm not hungry.'

I nodded and paused before speaking.

'Some time soon, I'm hoping to have a chat with your mum, so tell her I'm looking forward to seeing her,' I said. I hadn't thought this out but, as I said it, I realized it was a good tactic. The woman hadn't even agreed and there was the risk that, if she knew I'd told Zac I was going to see her, she might become even more furious. But perhaps, I thought, that fury would propel her in to school, if nothing else.

'Are you going to talk about me?' he said, and for a moment his eyes met mine, flickering with interest.

'Yes,' I said. I had the strong instinct that few people in the past had ever been honest with him. 'I am.'

But he'd slumped again into a kind of affectless stare.

'It won't make any difference,' he said.

'No harm in trying, is there?' I said. 'I think you're sad because your dad's gone away. For the moment,' I added – and as I said it, I realized I might be letting too much hope steal in. But all the same, I was determined that he should at least take on board the possibility of a meeting with his father.

Zac turned his head and stared at the wall. I got up, ruffled his hair, and said I'd see him next time. And as I got to the door Zac spoke. 'I don't want to see my dad,' he said. 'He's not my dad any more. I hate him. He promised and promised he wouldn't go away again and he broke his promise.'

As I walked down the corridor my heart was breaking. But

I was glad I'd had that conversation. It gave me something to fight for. And having spoken to Zac, I felt there was hope somewhere. He had opened up to me a little bit. I could see the crack in the door, even though it was on a heavy chain. Maybe it would never open again but I had spotted a glimmer of light, even if I hadn't got very far at all.

August 13

Just had lovely card from Gene. He's gone to a summer camp in the Lake District *on his own* and is having a 'brilliant time!!!!!' Apparently they spend all their time singing camp songs and whittling sticks. Whittling sticks! For some reason I feel incredibly proud of him, being able to whittle a stick.

Later

Came back from school to find that Chummy had not only chewed through my copy of the *Rant*, which I'd been looking forward to reading over a cup of tea, but also appears to have eaten Gene's card. God, no wonder that woman kept him howling in the garden all day! But I realized that it's no good – I can't have him prowling round the house. He's too big and slobbery and every time he wags his tail he breaks something. Pouncer is absolutely miserable, poor chap, and just sulks around the edges of the walls or hides under the sofa, scared out of his poor little feline mind. The only place he's really happy is my bedroom because I won't let Chummy in there, so Pouncer sticks around on my bed. I've even had to put a cat-tray in there – which is, of course, totally disgusting. I hear him in the middle of the night sometimes, scratching away, throwing those tiny bits of grey rubble all over my carpet, but it's a small price to pay.

Not sure how long he'll want to stay at home, actually.

Later

Rang Sylvie and Harry to see if they'd like Chummy. They're used to dogs, so it wouldn't be difficult for them to incorporate another one into their life, I'm sure. But they were away, so then rang David who said he'd be delighted to look after Chummy – temporarily, at least – until we can find someone else to have him. He's coming up to London in ten days on some business errand, so he'll pick him up on the way back. Only a few more days till Chummy goes, then. I'll be glad to see the back of him.

August 17

Got back from my weekly trip to Waitrose not only to find a letter from the hospital giving me the date next week for an ultrasound scan – relief! – but also to get a call from my cousin Bella who lives in Suffolk. She rang to say she'd found my old doll's house in her attic – she'd inherited it when I'd grown out of it – as well as a shoebox full of furniture and little people.

'Is there a bendy man in it?' I asked, trying not to sound too excited. He'd been the 'father' of the house, with brown wool bound round his tiny wiry limbs. Brown, of course, because he was a man and in those days men never wore anything but brown. 'And a dressing table, with a tiny round bit of glass stuck on?'

'Yes, it's all there,' she said. 'Next time you come to stay we'll play with it together!' she added, jokingly.

I was thrilled. But whatever she'd said, one of the major problems about being an adult is that you *can't* play with things. I suppose you could, self-consciously, in an earnest therapy group. But every time your teddy hit another person's stuffed rabbit, a ponderous counsellor would be on hand to tell you that it signified the rage you felt for your father. Thanks!

A lot of my granny friends clearly don't go in for playing. Marion, for instance, loves her grandchildren but, beyond a bit of colouring or making biscuits together, she can't join in the fun. She's quite prepared to go to the park and feed the ducks, or read endless books to them. She'll help them collect dried leaves and stick them into a chart and buy them toys galore. But she won't actually *play* with them.

I remember, when Gene was small, pretending the sofa was a boat, and the cushions we'd thrown on the floor were fish. We used a string bag to catch them with and every so often he'd dive onto the carpet to kill a shark, which I would then 'cook'. (This always involved a stirring motion over a pretend pot.) After putting it in the 'oven' – under the footstool in front of the fire – we'd take it out and eat it. Unless, of course, the shark escaped from the 'oven', as it so often did, and we had to start all over again.

Once, we built an entire city out of cardboard boxes on the lawn. There was a prison (his) and an art gallery (mine) and a hospital and a post office, and luckily I took a photograph before a huge monster (Gene) came down from the sky and destroyed it all by jumping up and down on it until it was flattened.

When Jack was tiny, we used to play dinosaurs in the bath, into which I'd poured gallons of bubble stuff. I'd make my hands into a couple of these creatures – my little, ring and index fingers and thumbs as legs and my middle fingers as their waving heads. This pair would walk along the edge of the bath making rude remarks, occasionally pushing each other into the water and constantly demanding hats and coats from Jack, who'd obligingly cover them in bubbles. Jack talked to them as if they were real, in a completely different voice from the one he used to me.

I think that, until they're about six, children do regard their grandparents not as adults like their mums and dads, but as huge playmates. Gene was always saying things like, 'You be the bad bear, Granny, and I'll be the good bear.' Or 'Watch out, Granny! He's coming to eat you up! I'll save you!'

But I'm afraid those days are over now. (I borrowed that phrase from an elderly friend of Penny, who says she uses it whenever she's asked to something she doesn't want to go to. Rather a chilling remark really, and sad, but incredibly useful. I think a lot of 'those days are over now' for me too.)

August 18

Went to the hospital to have the fabled scan. I lay in a darkened room until a woman finally came in and introduced herself as my radiologist. She rubbed some gel on the lump and passed a kind of plastic wand over it, all the time staring at the screen.

'Any monsters in there?' I asked, genially (but inside, of course, frantic with worry that there *were* monsters in there).

'It has rather an unusual structure,' she said, frowning at the screen. 'But I don't think you have anything to worry about. You've had an MRI scan, haven't you?'

'Yes.'

'And you're having a laparoscopy?'

'Yup. A peek and shriek,' I said, so nervous I could hardly stop the jokes coming.

'*You've* been to see Mr Melchett,' she said, turning to me and smiling. 'He's dreadful, isn't he? He shouldn't talk like that to the patients.'

'To make things even odder, he was a friend of my son Jack, and I used to pick him up from school occasionally and bring him home for tea. Rather strange to find he now has the power of life and death over me,' I said.

There was a long silence and she seemed absorbed in staring at a screen while she rolled the scanner over my tummy. The gel was cold.

'I know – you're not looking at my tummy at all,' I said.

'You're catching up on the latest episode from your boxed set of *Breaking Bad*.'

Finally she turned and gave a wry smile. She put her instruments away and handed me a tissue to wipe the gel off my tummy.

'Thank you so much!' I said as I climbed down from the table. 'What a relief. But back to the lump – nothing creepy?'

'Not that I can see. But you'll have to talk to Mr Melchett about the results. I'm not really meant to tell patients what I see. But when patients are really worried, like you, I sometimes break the rules.'

'How did you know I was worried?' I said.

She paused. 'Happy face,' she said with a sudden look of kindly sympathy. 'Jokes. Always a sign.'

August 20

I didn't sleep well. Was it because of what the radiologist had said? No matter how reassuring she'd tried to be, the phrase 'unusual structure' kept playing over and over in my mind. Did she mean some weird cancer or something like a building by Zaha Hadid? I know she said she can't see anything wrong but I have a feeling that, although I'm not aware of being very worried, I am deep down. It would be odd if I weren't. I'm just so exhausted these days. I start to worry about whether it's the cancer – if, indeed, it is cancer – that's making me knackered or, more likely, the anxiety about the cancer. I keep waking up in the middle of the night, aching all over and with what feels like an incipient migraine.

August 21

This afternoon I took Gene to see a matinee performance of *The Mousetrap* as his birthday present. It's been running, incredibly, for over 60 years – in fact for so long that I realized my own grandmother had taken me to see it when I was about Gene's age. Indeed the audience was jam-packed with grannies bringing their grandchildren as a holiday treat.

I found it a bit tedious because I knew all along whodunnit the second time round – and it was very old fashioned and slow – but Gene was captivated. He loved booking the drink at the bar for the interval, browsing through the programme, getting the opera glasses out of the little gadget in front of the seats. He'd finished the tube of Pringles we'd bought before the curtain went up (something we'd never had in my day and very noisy) and as the lights went down and the sinister music started, he reached out and squeezed my hand. In the interval, after our drink, he queued for ice-creams by himself – proudly handing me mine and showing me where to find the little plastic spoon which was, mysteriously, hidden in the lid under a piece of cardboard.

A huge success and we came back on the Underground saying, 'I loved the bit when . . .' and 'I thought it was the old woman at first, didn't you, Granny?' It was so peculiar to think that, all those years ago, my grandmother and I probably had exactly the same conversation. Only of course in those days we'd have come back in a cab.

August 22

This morning I did what I'd promised myself I'd never do – I locked Chummy out in the garden. I really didn't know how he'd behave with children, and I couldn't risk Gene getting bitten. Gene was rather distressed to see Chummy barking away and trying to get in but I was adamant. He'd be let back in the minute I took Gene home.

Everyone I know says I'm completely stupid about dogs, but whenever I'm in the park with Gene and he goes up to one to pat it, I pull him back with the words 'Never touch strange dogs!' – much to the fury of the dog owners, who always insist their dogs are 'lovely with children'. They get quite angry, as if I've insulted them personally. And of course their dogs may be fine with children, but they can also inflict horrible damage if they're in a bad mood, and I don't think stroking strange dogs is worth the risk. After all, all the dangerous pets I read about in the *Rant* who have chewed the faces off golden-haired toddlers have always been described by their owners as 'great big softies who wouldn't hurt a fly'. So Chummy was put in the garden for Gene's visit, howling and barking just as badly as he ever did across the road – but because he's nearer, and I know him better now, it's worse.

This morning we decided – or rather I decided – to make butter. I had a vague memory of being young and my grandmother putting some milk into a jar, screwing the lid on and leaving me to shake it for hours like Mick Jagger working his maracas, until finally a tiny pat of butter appeared. I doubted the dreadful super-skimmed stuff that seems to be the only milk you can get these days would have enough cream in it to make enough for a goblin's breakfast toast, so I'd bought some cream from the local supermarket and Gene got shaking.

He'd been going for about half an hour, and I'd helped with the odd burst till my wrists hurt, but nothing seemed to be happening. Finally I put the liquid into the whizzer, but again it remained the same old white slop. Gene was, at this point, getting bored and was on the kitchen floor practising some of the moves he'd learned at break-dance class the week before. I felt frustrated. What on earth was I doing, getting my grandson to make butter when all he was interested in was break-dancing? I might as well have suggested making a pen-wiper. I smiled to myself as I remembered the pen-wiper I'd made for my own mother at school, a square piece of felt hemmed with blanket-stitch around the sides. Crikey. Gene probably wouldn't even know what a blanket was, let alone a pen-wiper.

As I was mulling this over and Gene was trying unsuccessfully to do a back flip, I noticed that on the cream carton there were some tiny letters printed before the word 'cream'. The word 'Double' was written big, as was 'Cream' but between them lay the ominous phrase 'alternative to'. 'Double alternative to Cream'. No wonder it wouldn't make butter. It probably wasn't even made of milk. Most likely it consisted of an amalgam of trans-fats, whale oil, products of nuts from several countries and whitewash.

'It's not real cream!' I cried to Gene, who appeared totally uninterested in the whole proceedings. 'We must go out and get some!'

We returned with the proper cream and, plastering a fresh and enthusiastic smile on my face, I said, 'Now! At last! We can finally get cracking! Butter, here we come!'

Gene, clearly by now bored stiff with shaking, made a desultory attempt before saying, 'This doesn't work either, Granny. Can I go on the computer?'

'Come on, we can't give up now, not after all this effort,' I said, gamely. 'Never say die!' Curious how great is the sense of failure when something doesn't work out with a grandchild. I went on shaking and then we put on some music so that Gene could shake and break-dance at the same time. What seemed liked hours went by, but I suppose it was just minutes, and still the consistency of the cream remained resolutely the same.

'I'm bored with making butter,' said Gene. So as it was a glowing summer day we went to the park, and I had kittens while he climbed up huge bits of scaffolding in the adventure playground and shouted, 'Look at me, Granny!' from some pinnacle above while I did nothing but imagine what would happen if he fell and – if the worst happened – What Would I Tell Jack and Chrissie or Would I Kill Myself First, but nothing happened, thank goodness. (Just read this back. Kill Myself First? i.e. Kill Myself and Then Tell Jack and Chrissie? I'm going bonkers.) We fed the pigeons, and several clustered on our hands as we held out the seeds, a very unpleasant scaly feeling. Then we came back home. And still the butter preyed on my mind.

'No, I don't want to go on,' said Gene, when I suggested it. 'It's not going to work.'

'Let's watch it on YouTube!' I suggested, finally. 'There must be films of people making butter on the computer! Maybe we're doing something wrong!'

The word 'computer' seemed to gee him up, so we scrambled upstairs and, after watching several videos of butter being made effortlessly using exactly the same method as we'd been using, I let Gene play a couple of games before insisting we made one last effort.

'Do we have to?' he said, yawning. 'It's so booooring.'

'Just five minutes,' I said. 'If it doesn't work after five minutes, we'll stop.'

Five minutes later, with both our wrists collapsing, I said, 'Okay. Okay. I give in. A mystery.' I put the jar down despondently.

Gene looked at me. I could see a look of sympathy crossing his face. He felt torn. He was bored – and yet saw I felt glum and didn't want to let the side down.

Suddenly, his face burst into a cheeky grin. 'Come on, Granny!' he said, using just the same kind of voice that I'd used earlier. 'Come on! Never say die! Butter, here we come!' He picked up the jar and gave it a last shake. And after about ten seconds a thumping sound came from inside the jar. Gene stopped shaking and looked inside, astonished.

'BUTTER!' he shouted. 'GRANNY! GRANNY! BUTTER! IT'S BUTTER! WE'VE DONE IT!'

I know it sounds ridiculous but I felt like crying with joy. We'd spent so long trying, and I'd gone through so many emotions, that succeeding in making butter was, to me, like winning in the Olympics. We both marvelled at the pale golden lump of lardy butter that we'd created. I found a piece of muslin in an old baking drawer, squeezed the liquid out of the lump and we put it in the fridge. Every so often, Gene opened the door to look at it and gloat.

We examined the whey and I said I might make scones out of it. (Fat chance but you never know.) And from then on, the rest of the day went with a swing. It was punctuated every half hour or so by Gene saying to me smugly, 'I made it, didn't I, Granny? You were going to give up, but I said "Never say die"!'

'You did indeed!' I said, smiling to myself.

We took the butter back to Jack and Chrissie's and we'd barely got through the front door before Gene produced the butter with a flourish. 'Look Mum, look what I made!' he said. 'I made butter!'

We all ate it on small pieces of toast and declared it the best butter we'd ever eaten. And I drove home feeling vindicated, relaxed and totally fulfilled, quite looking forward to Chummy's slobbering company. Even the fact that I won't see the family for a while, because they're going to Spain for the last week of the holidays, couldn't put a blight on my pleasure.

Later

Worried the rest of the street might be driven mad by Chummy's barking when I'm out at school, but no word so far. And at least he doesn't do it at night now.

August 25

Rang Penny to suggest that she 'pops over' tomorrow afternoon as David says he'll be dropping by to take Chummy back to the country. (He's been staying in Jack and Chrissie's house while they're in Spain.) Suddenly got rather cold feet about this idea of setting him up with Penny as not certain, actually, that Penny and David *would* be the ideal pair. Also not sure, but this is mean, whether I really *want* them to be the ideal pair. It's quite fun having David around as a stray man looking in now and again, and do I really want to engineer some big romance between two of my best friends? If it came off, I'd lose both of them – which would be no fun at all.

August 26

Have to say David was looking particularly debonair. Most of my friends' husbands have completely gone to pieces as they age – they've let themselves go – but David, perhaps because he's always riding and digging and ploughing and strimming or whatever people do in the country, always looks fit and trim. He walked in bringing a breezy freshness with him and holding, very sweetly, a big bunch of flowers. A proper bunch, too – not one of those skimpy multi-coloured affairs, full of orange daisies, that you can pick up in supermarkets.

After he'd given Chummy a good going-over, and told him, 'You're coming back with me, old boy! Yes! Aren't you a lucky chap?' he looked approvingly at the pile of stuff I'd put aside for him to take – his lead, dog bed, chews and various treats and toys that Penny and I had bought him over the past few days.

Then, 'But how's the old lump?' he said, finally. We were sitting in the garden, looking out over the lawn, and I'd made him a cup of *real* coffee, which was rather nice of me as normally I just give people instant. 'Any news? I've been worrying about you.'

'I had this ultrasound the other day,' I said. 'And though the woman said she was sure it was nothing, she added that it had an "unusual structure" so I can't help worrying. I don't want to have something inside me that's got an "unusual structure"!'

'Understandable,' said David. 'How big is it now? I can't see it from here . . . so it's obviously not gigantic.'

'Have a look if you like,' I said, standing up, half-pulling up my top – and then hesitating. I mean, David's seen me undressed so many times it was hardly a come-on, but then I thought maybe he'd feel a bit funny, since we're divorced. But David, with his GP dad background, didn't turn a hair.

'Come on, let Dr Sharp make a full examination,' said David, leaning forward.

I tugged down my skirt and the top of my pants and he put out his hand, resting it on the skin on my right hand side. He leaned forward and felt around professionally. 'I see exactly what you mean,' he said. 'Yes, not normal, is it?' Then he smiled, and gave it a little affectionate pat . . . 'Ah, happy days!' he said, with a twinkle, before withdrawing his hand. And as he said it, I felt the most embarrassing spark of desire shooting up inside me. It came from absolutely nowhere and I only hoped it hadn't showed. I briskly pulled down my top and gave a light, rather croaking laugh.

At that moment the bell rang, I answered it – and it was Penny 'popping in'.

'Well, this is a lovely surprise!' said David rising, smiling, from his seat and offering it to Penny.

'Oh, don't worry about me,' said Penny, rather dismissively. 'I can sit on the grass!'

'No, come on, I'll find another chair,' said David. 'Let me . . .'

'No, I'm fine,' said Penny, rather ungraciously I thought, as she made herself at home in a patch of sun. 'Stop fussing!'

'So what have you been up to since I last saw you?' asked David.

'Oh, we don't have to go through the chit-chat, do we?' said Penny, looking up and grinning. 'Fuck off to small talk, I say.'

After a bit more of this, I suddenly remembered. Penny was absolutely hopeless at flirting. Like a schoolboy in the playground who clicks a rubber band at the legs of the girls he fancies, Penny always delivers this rather mannish banter, designed to completely put off any man worth his salt.

Finally, she told a rather bullish story about what she'd said to the man who'd pinched her parking space, ending up with the alluring words 'So I said, "You don't mess with me, arsehole!"' and to be honest my heart rather bled for her. She never spoke like this normally. I suppose she was just panic-stricken. Well, that's the kindest thing I can think of.

After she left, David got up, raising his eyebrows slightly.

'What was all that about?' he asked. 'Did I do something wrong?'

'No,' I said shaking my head ruefully. 'I think she was just petrified. Most odd. She's not normally like that at all.'

'Poor old thing,' said David, kindly. 'Well, keep me posted, my old darling,' he added. 'And I'll be ringing you. Keep your pecker up, won't you?' And he enveloped me in a huge bear-hug which again had rather an odd effect on me. He kept me close to him a little longer than usual. 'Mmm . . . takes me back!' he said, giving me a peck on the cheek. 'Lots of love, darling. Bye! And,' he added, 'keep on the case! I'm relying on you to find the next Mrs Sharp! Are you sure Melanie's a no-no? Come on, Chummy old boy,' he added as he clipped a lead on the old dog. And he made for the front door.

But just as he grabbed the handle, there was furious knocking and ringing of the bell, and a great yelling going on. Pushing past David, I opened the door, only to find, right there on my doorstep, the frightful old hag from across the road. She looked even madder than usual, and gave off the most stomach-churning pong of cheap wine and cigarettes. She stood there, heaving and shuddering with venom, her eyes glittering.

'You stole my dog!' she said, shaking a nicotine-stained finger at me – something you don't often see these days. 'I'm gonna sue you! 'Ow dare you! There 'e is! Tyson!' she added, spotting Chummy in the corridor. 'Come on, Tyson, you're comin' wiv me!'

At that moment, Chummy, recognizing his previous owner, gave a fearsome growl. As she approached he began to whimper – but at the last minute, before she could get hold of his neck, he suddenly sprang up at her and bit her hand. She screamed and tried to beat him off, and it was all David and I could do to stop him biting her again.

'He's not Tyson, he's Chummy,' said David in a low, even voice. 'And,' he went on, his tone becoming very menacing, 'if you don't leave this minute, I'll set my dog on you right now!'

Taking one look at Chummy, the woman backed away, down the path shouting, 'Fuck you! Fuck you!' As she tried to wrap her bleeding hand in an old tissue she'd found at the bottom of her bag, she continued screaming abuse at the three of us while we loaded Chummy into David's estate car. Locking the dog into the boot, he put a protective arm round me as he watched her go down the street.

'You'll be okay now, won't you?' he said, anxiously. 'Promise you'll ring me if she comes back. I'd better get Chummy off now before he destroys the inside of the car.'

But just as he'd got into the car and driven off, I saw the mad woman running back up the road towards me. She was about to march up my garden path, her bleeding hand wrapped up in the fold of her filthy tracksuit top, screaming and swearing, when Melanie opened her front door.

'Not one step more!' she said, fiddling with her mobile

phone. 'I'm ringing the police this very minute and we're going to tell them what you did to that poor dog! And if I ever see you here again, I'm going to put a spell on you! I'm a fully qualified witch, and if you don't go away and never come back, you and all your mates will die within a week!'

The word 'police' didn't seem to frighten the mad woman a bit, but at the mention of the word 'spell' – coming from a person who, covered in scarves and necklaces and bangles and wearing a turban, seemed almost as crazy as herself – she looked distinctly frightened.

'You don't put no spells on me!' she said. 'Sod off!' But she backed away down the street, mumbling, and I found myself turning to Melanie with admiring amazement.

'Thank you! And thank God you were there!' I said. 'I was really frightened. Where did you get the idea of a spell?'

'You've been amazing, Mar. I wasn't going to let her terrify you. You've done wonders with that dog. Now come in and have a cup of strengthening coffee and I'll throw in a dash of brandy. You must be in shock.'

And to my surprise I found myself tottering into Melanie's house and being pretty grateful for a stiff coffee, if there is such a thing. Even the sight of Pouncer curled up on her sofa – so that's where he went when he got fed up with Chummy! – didn't faze me.

So I now find myself back at home slightly pissed. Have to say that old Melanie's certainly turned up trumps. But I double-locked the front door in case the mad woman returned with a band of brothers.

Later

For some reason, David's phrase – 'Are you sure Melanie's a no-no?' – kept repeating itself in my mind. Of course she's a no-no! The idea of David getting together with Melanie would be a total nightmare. And actually, if truth be told, I was incredibly relieved that the encounter with Penny hadn't gone too smoothly either.

I couldn't be feeling jealous, could I? Surely not!

Even later

Penny rang me this evening, sounding very apologetic.

'I can't think what got into me, Marie!' she said. 'As soon as I'd left I felt so stupid! For some reason I just felt so frightened in front of you both, knowing I'd been set up, and these horrible remarks kept coming out of my mouth like toads! Sometimes I think I must have Tourette's! David must think I'm quite awful! I didn't even accept his offer of a chair. Honestly, I think perhaps I've just forgotten how to behave with men any more. Did he say anything?'

'You were a bit, er, forceful,' I said. 'But don't worry. It was obvious you were nervous. No, he said it was lovely to see you again,' I added, thinking a small lie wouldn't harm anyone and could only make things better.

'Marie, I hope you don't mind my saying this,' said Penny, rather nervously, 'but have *you* thought of getting back together with him? To me, he did seem inordinately fond of you, you know. I'm sure he's still got feelings for you.'

'Me?' I said. 'You must be joking. God, if ever there were

a case of "those days are over now" this is that case. Not in a million years.'

'Well, think about it,' said Penny. 'Just a thought.'

Later

Email from David to say Chummy appears to have settled in absolutely fine, and he can't wait to take him for a walk tomorrow. Ended up 'Take care, lots of love, David x'. After what Penny had said I stared at it rather long and hard. 'Take care' – that was nice. 'Lots of love' – well everyone says that. But the 'x' at the end. That was a bit extra-affectionate, wasn't it? I mean, on top of everything else?

Oh, stop it, Marie. He's your ex-husband, for heaven's sake. Hopeless when it comes to relationships. Well, he used to be anyway.

August 27

Oh dear. Missing Chummy already. I know he was irritating, but he was a curious kind of company, and it was comforting hearing him, in the mornings, scratching at my bedroom door to try to come and say hello. Or whatever dogs say in the mornings.

Took my mind off things by spending the morning in Penny's garden, trying to help her with some weeding. It was a glorious, still day, and a whole host of green parakeets, the plague of West London, was squawking away in the bushes. Apparently they arrived here when they were used in a pirate movie made in some London studio.

As she stuffed weeds into a plastic sack, Penny told me that Melanie has suggested calling another residents' meeting.

'She didn't say anything to me about that yesterday!' I said. 'She probably knew what my reaction would be. Anyway, we've only just had one! We usually try only to have one a year – if that – except in emergencies! We can't have one every couple of months!'

'That's what she's suggesting,' said Penny. 'She says we could transform the road into something special if we all put our shoulders to the wheel.'

'The street's quite nice enough as it is, isn't it?' I said. 'I don't want it to change, anyway.'

'Nor me,' said Penny.

August 28

Felt so much better after a day spent gardening with Penny that I decided I should take some more aerobic exercise. I would walk up and down the stairs of my house every morning to get the old heart rate going. Started this morning and met Graham on my third trip up. I was in my dressing gown, puffing and wheezing away.

'You okay?' he asked. 'Can I fetch anything for you?'

'No,' I gasped. 'I'm just trying to get in some aerobic training. Take no notice.'

He looked rather alarmed and continued down the stairs and out to work. What a chump I am. I must wait till he's left before I do any of these things. Too humiliating to be caught exercising or walking up and down stairs by a fit young lodger.

It reminded me of the time Gene had asked me, 'Do you go upstairs slowly because you *like* it, Granny?'

August 29

'An apple a day can kill you, claims think tank' (*Daily Rant*)

James dropped by to pick me up on our way to an exhibition of Whistler paintings at the Tate. I'm resigned to his beard now. It's a shame. He's such a good-looking guy – well he was, before he let this ghastly foliage grow over his features. Wondered what I could say to make him shave it off. I remember an old boyfriend of mine wearing a little rabbit's foot on a piece of cotton round his neck and I tried everything to get him to take it off, it looked so weird. Finally I said it made him look like a rent boy. He never wore it again.

I remembered, too, how I'd got Jack to cut his long hair when he was a teenager. I'd begged him to get a haircut but he'd refused to listen to me. Then, one day I hit on a plan.

'Darling,' I said, as he mooched into the sitting room with his hands in his pockets, his laces undone and his hair straggling round his neck. 'Do you know, I'm coming round to your look. I especially like the hair. I'm starting to get the point of it. It looks really nice.'

That afternoon he came back with an army cut.

Unfortunately, James and I go round exhibitions at completely different rates. He looks for about three minutes at every picture while I race round until I find one that's really special and then I can look at it for hours. But it usually works out about the same in the end. Have to say, going to exhibitions does rather give me the willies these days. Talk about the halt and the lame. Everyone seems to be on crutches or wheelchairs, or else being escorted round by their carers. Is it really only old people who are interested in art these days? Or is it just that all the young people are at work? I had the weird feeling at one point that I was actually inside that picture of the Resurrection by Stanley Spencer where everyone is crawling out of their graves.

The air resounded with the sound of muffled recordings about each picture that the oldies were squinting at while listening on their earpieces. Funny, because the people using these are exactly the sort of people who give disapproving looks to kids on trains when they have rap music leaking out of their headphones.

'Did Penny tell you that Melanie's proposing another meeting?' said James later, over a delicious lunch in Borough Market. 'She's not so bad, you know. She's got some good ideas for the street.'

'You seem to be living in her pocket,' I said rather sourly. 'She winds men round her little finger.'

'She's a harmless old thing,' said James. He probably says the same about me to Melanie.

'So what's her latest wheeze for the street?' I asked.

'I think she's got some kind of colour scheme she'd like to implement,' said James.

'Oh really?' I said tartly as I rolled up a piece of Peking duck in a pancake, having slathered it in hoisin sauce. 'Well, we'll see how far she gets.'

'You've forgotten the spring onions,' said James as I was about to bite into it.

August 30

When I got back from the school this evening, I found a note from Melanie. She appears to be taking part in a 'fun run' for Cancer Relief. And, naturally, wants me to sponsor her. On the note she'd written, 'I'm doing this for you! James says you'll need all the support you can get, Mar! Here's wishing you all the luck in the world! We'll beat the Big C together! I'm praying for you! Mel x.'

I was so angry I stamped my foot. 'Bloody James!' I said out loud and then I thought I sounded a bit too much like Penny with David.

I rang him at once.

'What on earth do you mean confiding all my problems to Melanie?' I said. 'It's outrageous!'

'I only said you had a lump,' he said. 'She's jumped to conclusions! I'm so sorry!'

'No wonder I don't confide in people!' I said. 'She says she's doing this fun run for Cancer Relief all because of me,' I added. 'I wish you'd keep your mouth shut. I'm never going to tell you anything ever again!' And I cut him off.

Suddenly rather missed old Chummy. He would have been

there to nuzzle up to me and console me. And now there wasn't even Pouncer who, ever since the arrival of Chummy, hasn't spent as much time at home as usual. I hope Melanie isn't seducing him.

SEPTEMBER

September 4

Back at school, the very first day of term and the Head asked me into her office. She looked fraught and drained, like a portrait by John Bratby.

'Bad news,' she said. 'I've heard from Zac's mother. She says she's dealing with the situation perfectly well at home and would appreciate it if the teachers at the school would – where's her letter,' she scrabbled around on her desk and then picked up a piece of paper, 'would "give Zac the space and normality he needs after his father left home rather than upset him by discussing with him his problems in school".'

'Oh dear,' I said. 'Perhaps I shouldn't have mentioned anything. I'm sorry.'

'How could you not say something?' said the Head. 'It's difficult when you're faced with a sad child like Zac. But I'm afraid in future the subject of his father is definitely off limits.'

'What do I do if he mentions him?' I asked.

'Change the subject or ask him to discuss it with his mother,' said the Head.

'The coward's route,' I said.

'The coward's route,' replied the Head, with a sympathetic smile. 'But who knows, she may be right.'

September 6

The next residents' meeting was planned for today. Everyone came round including Marion and Tim – he bearing a clipboard, a large briefcase in which were several different coloured folders and a laptop, which he opened on the table. Ever since he retired he's been trying to convince people that he's still 'working' in some kind of way and he imagines, I think, that if he goes around carrying the accoutrements of his old job, he'll still be seen as a professional.

Father Emmanuel commented that people were throwing rubbish into the front garden of his church. Sheila the Dealer said if there were no litter-bins it was small wonder people used his garden as an ashtray. James said the drug-dealing had decreased, and Sheila the D looked quizzical at this. Then Melanie asked if she could say a few words.

'I think we need to establish more of a sense of community round here. It's very ... very ... urban,' she said, adjusting one of her scarves. 'I want to turn Sheldon Road into a village, a place where we can all feel safe. After all, we are a village, aren't we? Just looking round this table, I feel I'm part of a community, a family ...'

There was a stony silence from the 'family'.

'I propose that we make a start by asking people if they'd all consider painting their front doors the same colour. That would unite the street. We'd be one. One street, one town, one country, one nation, one world.'

There was another silence as we all tried to absorb this.

Then, 'It'd be like a fuckin' school uniform,' said Sheila the Dealer, stubbing out her fag in the ashtray I'd provided. 'Most of the 'arses in this street are owned by the fuckin' Council, anyway.'

'Exactly!' said Melanie, and here she scrabbled in a file and produced three letters. 'But I've considered that. The Council *and* the various housing associations who own some of the houses in this street are on-side. I've talked to them all. And if we agree to carry out the work for free, they'll provide the paint. At least for the houses they own. So what do you say? They've given us a colour-chart to look at.'

Marion looked rather earnest. 'What colour were you thinking of?' she said. 'I don't think we'd like anything too sombre – black for instance!'

'No!' said Melanie. 'But not anything too garish, either.'

'Something dignified. Stylish. Peaceful.'

'What about a very good grey?' said James, dragging one of the colour-charts towards him.

'Grey?' said Sheila the Dealer. 'Bloody hell!'

'Magnolia, I was thinking,' said Marion. 'That's a lovely kind of greyish, whitish, pinkish colour, and yet slightly beige.'

'You're not talking about any colour at all!' I found myself snapping. 'It's all "ish". All those colours are so tentative and bland. Like Pepsi instead of Coke.'

'Oh do shut up, Mar!' said Melanie, suddenly turning on me. 'You're so pessimistic! Just because you teach art doesn't mean you know anything about doors. I'm trying to do something new here, and there you are looking on the negative side.'

I was so taken aback I could hardly speak. Not only did I feel furious about being ticked off in my own home, but I felt hurt because she'd never have said that to me if we'd just been on our own. Even David had never told me to shut up, and I could see that everyone was very embarrassed.

Only Tim, who naturally hadn't noticed a thing, looked up from the colour-chart. 'Look, there's this new colour on the other side,' he said. 'It's a kind of mixture of grey and beige and they call it "greige". What about that?'

James looked round the table optimistically. 'I like that idea!' he said. I could see that everyone was trying to show enthusiasm because they didn't want to be snapped at by Melanie.

Father Emmanuel raised a solemn hand. And Tim nodded vigorously.

'Hold on,' I said, getting my confidence back. 'I'm not so sure. I like to be an individual. I like the colour of my door – it's a very dark blackish grey and it has a particular sheen on it. I don't want this street to look like a middle-class ghetto. Because it isn't.'

Penny stared down at the table and so did Marion. Wretched women. Too cowardly to stand up for themselves.

'How about we leaflet all the residents and see what they say?' said Melanie. 'I think greige is a great idea. I've got an old pal who'd do the work for half-price. And I think doing this would add substantially to the values of our properties, which is something to consider. Let's agree to leaflet the residents at least. There can't be any objection to that.'

It was true. It was hard to find an objection, so we were forced to agree. But after the meeting, surprisingly, Sheila the Dealer stayed back.

'Fuckin' Nazi!' she said. 'I'm not going to paint my door any colour that Melon woman wants! Wha'ever the residents say. Fuck 'em! And fuck 'er an' all! An Englishman's front door is his castle! Innit?'

I'm sorry to say that I'm tempted to agree. I can see that to have all the doors in the street painted, say, alternately electric blue and red and black, might look rather smart. But clearly that's not the colourway Melanie has in mind.

September 7

'My family,' Gene once declared, as we were in the middle of a game of goodies and baddies, involving dreadful plastic figures from his repulsive Planet Protectors game, 'is Mummy and Daddy and the cats.' Then he paused. 'What's *your* family, Granny?'

I moved a figure called Ice who repeatedly boomed from his tiny plastic body 'I am Ice! Protector of the Arctic!' 'Well,' I said, taking care not to show the hurt I felt about not being included in his list, I think *my* family is *your* family. *You're* part of my family.'

Gene looked unconvinced.

'No,' he said, decisively. '*Your* family is Michelle [who was my lodger at the time] and Pouncer and,' he thought for a while, 'your *house*.'

Oddly, while I'm not certain about the first two, the last is true. My house, in which I've lived for nearly 40 years, is rather like my family, hung as it is with pictures my friends and I have painted from way back, and endless bits of brown furniture from my grandparents, brass heads brought by my mother from India, not to mention samplers stitched by me, chairs caned by me, and cupboards stained by me ... It's a heritage, in the middle of which I live, like a great Sharp spider. Indeed the other day, when I told Jack I was going to have a huge clear-out (I really must do it – I've been talking about it for long enough), so he wouldn't be too confused about everything when I die, he just said, 'Oh don't worry, Mum, we won't be taking any of it. We'll just turn it into a museum and have a man on the door to sell tickets.'

It does need a clear-out, though, and I've been meaning to do it for yonks. So I've decided I'll start next week. Don't think I can do it by myself, though. Wonder if Penny would help? Or Marion? Just the presence of another person will make the whole task easier. I remember, ages ago, getting an interior designer friend to cast his eye over my house and give me a bit of advice about what to do, and he only had to come into the sitting room, look round disapprovingly and say, 'Mmm', through pursed lips for me to know at once what should go. All the hideous things suddenly leapt out at me, like objects in a 3-D picture. The old spider plants, the clip-frames, the ragged throw on the sofa . . . which should anyway be moved to the window.

Penny's coming in a couple of days, but she's going away after that, so I'll have to ask Marion. I'm not sure how helpful she'll be at de-cluttering, considering her own house is one vast compost heap which, as far as I can see, goes back to the 1960s. I wouldn't be surprised, digging deep into her clutter, if you found an ancient dried-up hippie snapping his fingers and saying, 'Man, man', in a spaced-out way to no one in particular.

When I rang Marion to book her in, I was answered by her machine. 'Hello! This is the Evans family. Please leave your short message after the tone giving the date and time of your call.'

There's something about the word 'family' in Marion's answering machine message that always makes me feel suddenly extraordinarily lonely. I imagine them, dozens of Evanses all crowded round the telephone as she records her message, arms round each other in a group hug, lit by a friendly roaring fire to one side, united in love and kinship. And it makes me feel very excluded and uptight, all on my own.

I'm tempted to record *my* message as 'Hello! This is Marie Sharp, single and free as a bird and loving it. So *ner* to all you families out there. Sorry I'm not in but as you've discovered I'm *out*, having a great time painting the town red because I'm single! Yahoo!'

Reminds me of those single women who say, 'We're not at home, but we'll get back to you as soon as possible', under the tragic illusion that a burglar, on ringing the number – do they ever do this anyway? – would be put off by the word 'we'. 'Oy, mate,' he'd say, gruffly, to his fellow burglar. 'Turns out there's two of 'em in that perishin' gaff. Better lay off.'

Golly, must stop ranting on. They're only phone messages, for God's sake. Get a life, Marie!

Later

Facebook again. Marion has written, under a picture of a child holding a daisy, 'Seek the wisdom of ages but look at the world through the eyes of a child.'

Bloody hell.

September 9

Letter arrived today from the hospital booking me in for the peek and shriek. Or is it peep and weep? God, will this never end?

I was stopped on my way to school by Melanie, but I'm afraid I was so pissed off with her for telling me to shut up at the residents' meeting that I cut her dead. First the fun run – I pointedly hadn't sponsored her – and then that outburst. It wasn't good enough.

David rang and said Chummy was in his element in the country and I needn't worry about him at all. Didn't like to say I was rather missing him (Chummy, that is.) I asked if he could hang on to him for a while because I'd just got hold of Mrs Evans, Sylvie and Harry's housekeeper, who tells me they're away on some huge African trip, and won't be back for a couple of months. But when I mentioned another dog, she sounded extremely pleased.

'Oh, they're missing Hardy,' she said. 'I like the idea of another one. I'm sure they will, too.'

September 10

Penny came over to help me on the first day of my huge clear-out. I suppose it's the lump that's got me going on all this sorting. *Tempus fugit* and all that. Given me a sense of mortality. Or something. We both put our aprons on, and our rubber gloves, and got going. We began with the kitchen cabinets, stuffed to the gills with herbs and spices and jams, plus quite a few jars of that marmalade Marion and I made earlier in the year.

Everything shop-bought was past its sell-by date. But luckily, we agreed on the ridiculousness of these things. "Smell-by dates" is what I go by,' said Penny, 'but some of them are terribly stale. And are you ever really going to use a tin of Fray Bentos Steak and Kidney Pie? It must be as old as the Ark.'

We weeded out the ones I didn't want, washed the jars of the ones I did, and bunged them back into the newly cleaned-out shelves.

When we got to the dozens of plastic containers I'd carefully hoarded from Indian take-aways over the years, she didn't say,

'Ugh'. She just asked, rather kindly, 'When did you last use any of these?' So out they all went. Upstairs in the spare room she simply said, 'How old is that blind?', pointing to a stained, ramshackle affair hanging lopsided in the window. Or 'Do you really need *two* spare keyboards?', as she rummaged through my computer drawer.

But doing all this sorting and tidying has been bliss. And what makes it even better is the row of plastic binbags in the hall, all waiting for me to take them to Age Concern. In fact there's nothing for Marion to help me with but the bathroom and bedroom. And I've got a list of things to do on my own: get all my pictures put into acid-free mounts; label each one on the back; organize my drawers of unsorted photographs; sort through a desk full of meaningless memorabilia; re-arrange my bookshelves so that the books are lined in serried ranks rather than piled one on top of the other all over the place; get the curtains cleaned . . .

Over a large glass of white wine at the end of the day, Penny confessed she was rather scared of death. 'I sometimes think about it and then I don't know what to think about it so I don't think about it,' she said, sweetly. Then she asked if I'd made my will.

'Of course,' I said. 'And done my power of attorney.'

'Hope you've given it to someone young,' she said. 'Wouldn't it be awful if you gave your power of attorney to someone who got Alzheimer's before you and they gave all your money to a mad cult?'

September 11

Marion arrived half an hour late but, very sensibly, with a roll of black binbags. She was wearing even older clothes than usual and her hair had been tied up on top of her head and covered with a knotted scarf. She looked like a charlady straight out of the Thirties – and, naturally, she wasn't nearly as ruthless as Penny. Anything I said I didn't want, she stuffed into a black plastic binbag, saying, 'Are you certain you don't want this? I'm sure I can find a home for it.' I wouldn't let her take my collection of old toothbrushes home, though. Some things *have* to go in the bin. And she was dead keen on chucking out an unpleasant-looking small purple plastic figure that we found behind a curtain. As she picked it up, it spoke to her. 'I am Kat! I protect the Rainforest!' it said, many, many times. I recognized it as one of Gene's Planet Protectors figures that we'd searched for for ages.

'Are you sure about this?' she asked, staring at it.

The only embarrassing moment was when we went through my scarf drawer. I was about to dump them all into the Age Concern bag, saying, 'I don't know why I've kept these, because as you know I never ever wear scarves, but all these idiots keep giving them to me as presents', when I suddenly remembered her Christmas present.

'Yours isn't here because I left it at Jack and Chrissie's when I was last over,' I explained. Hope she believed me. But have an awful feeling she didn't. Do hope she never goes up to the Notting Hill Gate Age Concern. I should have burned it rather than risk her ever seeing it for sale in a shop window. What a wally I am.

September 12

Today I received this extraordinary email out of the blue with 'Attn: Beneficiary' in the subject line.

It read:

Payment notification of your funds.

I am Mr. Paul Jones, the secretary to Dr. Lamido Sanusi; the executive governor of the central bank of Nigeria (C.B.N), the central bank of Nigeria is the parent bank of all commercial banks here in Nigeria. I was instructed to initiate contact with you by my boss the executive governor of the central bank of Nigeria (C.B.N) on an urgent issue, kindly note that your funds were re-called and re-deposited into the 'federal suspense account' of the cbn last week, because you did not forward your claim as the right beneficiary.

My boss the executive governor of the central bank of Nigeria (C.B.N), was visited in his office by three gentlemen today, really these men were unexpected by him because their visit was impromptu. He had to ask them why they came to see him in person and they said that they came to collect the inheritance/ contract funds bill sum of us$20 million which rightfully belongs to you as shown in your file with us, on your behalf and by your authorization. Note that they actually tendered some vital documents which proved that you actually sent them for the

collection of these funds. Below is list of the documents which they
tendered to this bank today . . .

I skipped the rest. I can't imagine that anyone would actually fall for this kind of scam. It's obviously a con – I mean obviously, isn't it? What I don't get about these people is why they always announce the fact that they're Nigerians. I'm not saying that all Nigerians are con-artists but 90 per cent of the con-emails I get purport to be from Nigerians. Someone should tell them they'd be a lot more convincing if they said they were Austrian or Australian. Or from the Outer Hebrides. Even Kenya or the Cameroons would make a change. I'm sure we'd all be much happier to give them the time of day if they'd only change their country of origin.

September 13

'5000 villages to disappear in global warming floods' (*Daily Rant*)

Today I had the laparoscopy. I'm starting to become too familiar with that hospital. I've now got such a confident look on my face when I arrive that new patients ask me for directions.

Not much to report because they bunged a little thingy in the back of my hand – some kind of needle – and said I'd soon be asleep. The next thing I knew I was asking them when they were going to start and they said they'd not only started but it was all over and I could go home as soon as I'd had a cup of tea.

Came home feeling absolutely terrified about what they might discover. Have to go again tomorrow. Oh dear oh dear.

September 14

Appointment with Brainy Ben. (But oh GOD, I wish all this would be over.) He flashed me a gorgeous smile when I came in, and said, 'Ah, you've had your peek, I see. And I'm glad to tell you there hasn't been any shrieking, so let me put your mind at rest.'

The moment he said this, I felt as if a huge weight had been lifted off my shoulders. Tears started coming into my eyes. I even laughed with relief. And it wasn't a 'happy face' kind of laughing, it was real. But I'm afraid my euphoria didn't last long. He still couldn't pin down what exactly was wrong.

'I can't say categorically it isn't cancer, but I certainly can't say categorically that it is,' he said. 'Whatever it is, it seems to be dormant, not active – so you needn't worry about anything just now – but there's something slightly odd about it. It's definitely not normal.'

I asked him what could be done and he said, 'Well, usually, we indulge in a bit of shot gunning – that's ordering a vast array of medical tests in the hope that we come up with something – but what I'd like to do at the moment is to discuss this with Dominic Sheridan – he's our top oncology man, but he's away at the moment – and then see you again in a month. Obviously be in touch if anything changes, but otherwise, you needn't worry. I think the worst that could happen is that we'll have to operate – but because of the size of the thing, and because it's quite near some vital organs, it's not something I want to do unless it's growing. And obviously there's no point in giving you chemotherapy if it's not cancer. I'm so sorry, Mrs S, I know this isn't satisfactory, but I'm sure you'd prefer I was honest with you.'

Not sure I was very keen that he'd be honest with me, actually. I'm at home now and acutely aware of this sinister growth. I keep pressing it and wishing it would go away.

I wouldn't mind if he'd said it was cancer and I'd got three days to live. (I mean, it would be sad, but at least I've got the house sorted and I've lived a jolly long time and when you get to a certain age, death doesn't hold so many fears.) Or if he'd said it wasn't cancer and I could have gone out dancing into the sunlight. That sort of honesty doesn't worry me at all. But being honest about not having a clue what's going on – that's a bit *too* honest.

Should I live 'each day as it comes' and try 'living in the moment'? That's what people who are about to die always say they do (though actually I've always suspected they just say it to make themselves feel special so all we people who aren't dying feel dreadfully trivial and envious). Or should I just mooch along as I always have? I don't feel I'm about to die. But at the same time I don't feel as if I'm *not* going to die. Quite honestly, I just feel as if I'm going mad.

Later

David rang. He's been keeping his promise and ringing every

week, and I've now got to the point where I really depend on his calls to keep my sanity.

'Dr Sharp here,' he said, as he always does. 'Just checking up on the patient.' After I'd told him the latest, there was a pause the other end of the line.

'I do worry about you, Marie,' he said, quite softly. 'I don't want anything to happen to you. I had a dream about you last night, and it made me realize how – even in spite of everything we've been through – there's still a lot we can't erase, isn't there?'

I slightly wondered what the dream was, but didn't like to ask. 'There is,' I said, carefully. 'Lots. Sometimes I think what we had was more special than we realized at the time.'

'*Si jeunesse savait, si viellesse pouvait*,' he said. 'If only old people were able, if only young people knew.'

'I don't think I'm that old yet,' I said, smiling. 'I feel it's a time when I'm starting to know and understand more and yet I'm still young enough to be able to act on that knowledge. Not for long, though,' I added, wryly.

There was another pause. A significant pause. And when I say 'significant', I don't know exactly what it signified.

'Good,' said David. 'I feel exactly the same way.'

I wasn't quite sure what we'd agreed on, but there was no doubt some weird kind of subconscious step seemed to have been taken between us – although of course it couldn't have been subconscious because it was conscious. A mystery.

He said he was coming up to London and maybe we could have lunch next week as well. He seems to be constantly on my doorstep. Very nice, but very odd. Oh dear. Perhaps I should be a bit more cool and not so available. Wouldn't like him to think I was a Widow Bossom.

September 16

When I told James about the email I'd had from the Nigerian and said how stupid it was of Nigerians not to say they were from another country, he told me that they stick to calling themselves Nigerians because they want to weed out the sceptics. Even if the scammers *aren't* Nigerians! How sinister!

September 17

Most extraordinary thing happened today!

I'd left school after my class and was waiting for Jack to ring me with a telephone number, but I didn't want to get in the car and drive back because I wouldn't be able to take the call. So I popped into the local caff where I could get a signal before I set off. Plus I had an absolute longing for a Danish pastry. (Not something I often desire. For a brief and crazy moment I wondered if I might be secretly pregnant and Having a Craving, but immediately pushed that from my mind.) Anyway, I went into the one opposite the school – one of those groovy caffs with leather sofas – and found myself in a parental hell crammed with prams, mums, au pairs and lone dads, everyone texting and gossiping, with the odd loner staring glumly into a laptop. Amazingly, I found a sofa to myself and was just winching myself down into it when a woman came up to me.

'Do you mind if I join you?' she asked, pointing to the empty place beside me, the only one in the room. In one hand she held a brownie on a plate and in the other a cappuccino. 'I'm just waiting to pick up my son from school.'

'Not at all,' I said. The joint was so crowded I was surprised people weren't asking to sit on each other's knees.

She was in her late thirties, and extremely pretty. She had short blonde hair and her face was extravagantly made up – white skin, scarlet lipstick. She reminded me of someone but I couldn't put my finger on whom. But her eyes looked sad and I could see the strain behind the make-up.

As she was about to sit down, her hand must have trembled because the cup slipped on its saucer and her coffee slopped all over the floor. The other customers shifted their chairs imperceptibly. I grabbed as many napkins as I could from the neighbouring tables and began mopping.

The blonde, however, was doing nothing. She just stared, like a rabbit caught in the headlights, her eyes brimming with tears.

'Oh fuck fuck *fuck*!' she was muttering.

'Don't worry!' I said, looking up from a pile of soggy brown napkins. 'It's not too bad. It doesn't matter!' Everyone had turned to look.

Eventually my guest sat down, pushing the brownie away from her, looking as if she might cry. She fumbled in her bag for a handkerchief, and after I'd given all the wet tissues to a waitress who'd hurried up to see if she could help, she looked up.

'I'm so sorry!' she said, sniffing. 'Everything's going wrong. Sometimes I just don't know how I can cope.'

'Tell me about it!' I thought I'd said it in a casually friendly American way. '*Tell* me about it!!' That sort of way. Not a 'Why don't you calm down and tell me about it, my dear?' way – which is how she took it. 'My life's a mess,' she said. 'Do you really want to know?'

'Of course,' I said, putting my hand out to touch her arm. 'You do seem so sad! Tell me, what's the matter?'

There was a pause while she closed her handbag and gave a little shake of her head. 'My husband's left home and I'm trying to cope with one very unhappy child. My son's so angry, he won't even see his dad. I just don't know what to do for the best! Everyone gives me different advice!'

I said nothing. I didn't need to be Mystic Meg to realize who she was talking about. It was Zac. Poor sad little Zac. My Zac. Her Zac.

'It's all his father's fault,' she said. 'He's been having this affair with another woman, and Zac refuses to see him. But after trying a couple of times, my ex has just given up and refuses even to attempt to see his son. The problem was, his work kept him away and that week he'd given his solemn prom to Zac that he wouldn't go away, and then I chucked him out and Zac thinks it was all his father's fault. Which of course it was. And the school keeps trying to get me in to talk. I suppose it's because he's so sad. And he *looks* so sad, too. He refuses to have a bath or even comb his hair, I don't know what to do.

'I thought everything had settled down at school, but now there's some dreadful old art teacher who's become "disturbed" about him, and wants to have a chat, but what she thinks she can do I don't know. Probably wants to send him to a psychiatrist and put him on pills. To be honest I'm in such a muddle. Part of me thinks I should insist Zac sees his father and part of me thinks that it would be best if he never saw him again.'

My mind reeled at all this. I mean, what are the odds of bumping into this woman? Is there some vast cosmological coincidence engine that sometimes kicks into life and plays around with us mere humans like so many puppets on strings? But I was brought back to earth when she asked, 'Do you have children?' She looked up slightly and suddenly I didn't see a woman, I saw an unhappy child.

'I do,' I said. 'And I think I do know how you feel, my dear.' I don't know where the 'my dear' came from, but it seemed the only way to address her. I reached over and took her hand and her eyes filled with tears. 'And I also know how that dreadful old art teacher feels, I'm afraid. She doesn't want to put him on pills. That's the last thing she wants to do. Oh, I wish there were something I could do to help you and make everything all right. I know how very painful it is, splitting up.'

'You know this teacher even told Zac that she was going to see me! And talk about him! You can imagine what effect that's had on him. He can't sleep, he keeps begging me that he doesn't have to see his father, does he, and apparently she's implied he might come back! And this woman isn't even a teacher, she's just some busybody who thinks that sticking leaves onto bits of paper is somehow creative! These teachers, they know absolutely nothing at all about what's going on at home.'

'I'm very sorry,' I said, feeling absolutely rotten. 'But I'm sure they're only trying to help.'

She sighed. 'I suppose so, but they've got a funny way of doing it. I'm sorry to burden you with this. You've just got a sympathetic face.'

I looked at my watch. Ten minutes to go before the bell went. I took my courage in both hands.

'I'm afraid you don't know who I am,' I said, deciding that total honesty was now the only option. 'I hate to tell you but I'm that dreadful art teacher you're talking about. My name's Marie Sharp. I'm awfully sorry.'

Zac's mother looked at me with horror. She started to say something but then changed her mind. 'But you seem very nice!' she said eventually, with a puzzled look.

'I *am* very nice!' I said laughing. 'But I'm also terribly stupid, now I look back on what I've said to Zac. I just wish there were something I could do to help, but if you think that you've got everything under control, obviously I'm very sorry to have barged in and upset things. You're quite right. I had no idea what upset I was causing and I'm very *very* sorry. I have behaved completely . . .' and I hesitated before using the over-used word, but there didn't seem to be another one around at the time, 'inappropriately.'

She shifted in her seat rather awkwardly. Then she looked me in the eye. For a moment I thought she was about to be angry and then her expression changed to one of despair.

'No, it's me who should be sorry,' she said. 'I had no idea! I didn't mean you were dreadful! Zac enjoys the art classes! It's just . . . well, I'm sure you can understand . . .'

'We all know Zac is unhappy,' I said. 'He says he hates his father, but I suspect he doesn't mean it at all. Have you thought of asking the school if they could contact the father? That would take all the emotion out of it – the emotion between you two, that is. Would that help?'

'He couldn't give a shit,' she said.

'Let me have a go,' I said. 'Look, though I'm only a part-time voluntary helper at this school, I was a proper teacher for 30 years and have a lot of experience. I've charmed a lot of angry parents in their time – not all, but lots. Do let me write to Zac's father or talk to him. I mean, he's not the only father to have left home. Sometimes fathers are so upset they can't think straight either. Most children are upset, but after a while something can usually be worked out.'

She looked at me. My delicious Danish was only a quarter eaten. Her brownie was untouched. She checked her watch and gave a little gasp.

'Oh God, I'm late,' she said, getting up. 'Let me think about it.' She gathered up her bags. 'I know you're only trying to help, and I'm sorry I exploded. Honestly, I don't think anything will make any difference, but thank you.'

Then she got up to make her way to the door.

'Look, take my phone number if you want to chat,' I said, scrabbling in my bag for a piece of paper. At that moment Jack decided to ring. I ignored the phone and thrust my details into her hand. As she left, I sighed. So much for my brilliant intervention. Diplomat Sharp – ho ho bloody ho. I just seem to have made things worse all round. I stared at my Danish pastry and pushed it to one side. Time to go. I paid, and headed for home. Oh God, what a horrible muddle. What with this and the lump, I felt extremely depressed. I thought a bath might be a treat, but I only cried in the bath.

September 23

Off to school today. On my way out Melanie looked over the wall and I gave her a frosty smile.

'What have I done?' she asked, rather helplessly.

'I don't like being told to shut up,' I said, icily. 'I don't like it at any time and particularly not in front of my committee.'

Melanie looked astonished. 'I can't believe . . . Talk about over-sensitive! Well, pardon me for living and all that, but really, if you can't take an old friend being honest with you . . .'

'You're not an old friend,' I said, coldly. 'You're a new neighbour. And as I say, I don't like it.'

Melanie shook her head in exasperation, and then turned and went inside her house, banging the door.

I felt quite shaky, and immediately thought, 'Perhaps I *am* over-sensitive. Perhaps I should just have yelled back at her at the time.' The problem is, I'm not made like that. I just don't do shouting. I do silence and sulking and plotting and scheming. It's not as if one way is better than the other. It's just different. Though of course, secretly I admire shouters because they always seem to be able to have rows and get over them in a few minutes while with me they fester for weeks, sometimes for years.

No doubt we'll get over it in time. If nothing else she won't be telling me to shut up again in a hurry.

At school, Zac was looking particularly glum, poor soul. The awful thing is, although my heart bleeds for the poor chap, it has to be said that he isn't the most prepossessing of little boys. His pallid face and lack of energy all conspire to drive his classmates away at precisely the moment when, I suspect, he needs every bit of friendship he can get. I keep thinking of his mother and our meeting and hoping she'll give me a ring – though I don't hold out much hope.

Got back to find an answering machine message from Penny. I know this makes me a dinosaur, but I still love my landline. Conversations on a landline still sound more important and significant than ones on a mobile. Particularly if the call is to another landline. Because then I know the other person is at home and possibly sitting down and concentrating, whereas with a mobile they could be walking across busy roads, or buying bread at the same time as they're talking to me.

But back to Penny's message. 'Just wondered – for Marion's birthday – can you think of an extra man I could ask? I'd ask David, but I can't face it after my weird performance the other day. Or shall I just leave it?' So I rang her and said what about Graham, my lodger, as he's feeling pretty low these days? It's only the usual suspects – Marion, Tim, and James. Can't think why Graham would want to spend an evening in the company of five ancient old grey-heads (well, not in my case because I keep my hair dark brown, come what may, by means of various potions) but will ask.

Anyway at least I'll know everyone.

Spent the evening watching a documentary on Jimi Hendrix. Really odd, because it was all filmed in the Sixties, the time of my youth. I'd even been to the Isle of Wight Festival where he'd played, and kept looking in vain for myself among the crowd of flower-waving hippies and pot-smoking beardies. Not that I ever was, I hasten to add, a pot-smoking beardie.

Just before I went to bed I checked into Facebook. Marion had posted a photograph of some ancient megaliths she'd discovered in a field somewhere and underneath she'd written, 'If only these old stones could speak . . .'

Somehow, I doubt they'd have anything of great interest to say, except perhaps 'Hot, isn't it?' Or 'Chilly for the time of year.'

September 24

Just reading John Ruskin's *The Elements of Drawing*. I've always thought of him as this bony old bore who married some young girl who was later spirited away by Millais. A tedious obsessive who liked nothing more than to go round Venice logging every building, every stone and every fern. But how wrong I was! He's totally riveting and explains why trees grow the way they do, and that they shoot out of the earth to get as much sun as possible, their branches reaching out, their leaves flat against the sky – to suck in as much energy as they can – in the same way that roots spread underground to suck up as many nutrients as possible. As a result of reading him, I wondered if trees turned upside down (branches in earth, roots above ground) would be the same as they are the right way up, and I think they would, pretty much. Leaves apart, of course.

In my time I've been a mad-keen tree painter but I've been aware, a lot of the time, that I've only *copied* trees. Ruskin explains that you have to understand how they grow and get life in order to draw them with real understanding and I can't wait to have a go.

Later
When I mentioned Marion's dinner to Graham, he said he'd be delighted to come. He must be desperate. From the number of large flat boxes I find in the rubbish, I suspect he lives on take-away pizzas and would be glad of a good meal now and again.

Even later
Thought I'd just listen to the radio while preparing myself for bed when the announcer said, 'The time is half past eleven. After the news we will be broadcasting the first in our ten-part series of short plays on child sexual abuse.'

Jesus! Turned that off pretty quick, I can tell you.

September 25

Wondered what I should give Marion for her birthday. Thank God her ghastly scarf's already gone to the charity shop so there's no chance of my accidentally giving it back to her (which is the sort of thing I used to do until I started making lists of the things in my present drawer). Finally hit on the excellent idea of doing a little watercolour of the outside of her house, particularly as it's got a very nice lime tree in the front garden. All I had to do was discover when Marion and Tim would be out, and nip down to take a photograph and make a few pencil sketches. So I rang her to make discreet enquiries – and luckily she said they were off to Peter Jones, so I was able to get cracking right away.

OCTOBER

October 5

Penny went to huge trouble with her dinner. I don't mean it was all knives and forks and separate glasses for the various wines, but she's got the cosiest of houses and she always makes an effort, with real napkins instead of the dismal bits of kitchen roll I usually hand out to my guests – and very good lighting so that, although we all may be 103, we don't actually look it.

'Thank God you haven't brought flowers!' said Penny as she greeted me at the door and I thrust a bottle of Prosecco into her hand. 'Such a bore! Just when you want to welcome people, you have to cut off the stems and bash them and then find a vase . . .'

The doorbell rang behind me and in came Graham straight from work – bearing a large bunch of roses.

'Flowers! How lovely!' cried Penny seamlessly. 'Aren't these beautiful! Nothing I like better! Look everyone!' she added, as she took them into the sitting room, waving them about enthusiastically. She pulled it off so well I almost believed she'd had a sudden change of heart.

Everyone was there already and I was, as always, very touched when James actually rose to his feet to kiss me, even though he knows me so well he doesn't have to be polite. I do think that everyone ought to leap to their feet when anyone comes into the room. I once met an old Etonian with these impeccable manners and I said how nice it was that he got up when anyone came into the room, even other men. And he said, 'And I always get up for children, too. Children most of all. It makes them feel acknowledged and respected.' And from then on, I decided that, however wobbly my knees are and however low the seat in which I'm stuck, I would always get up whenever *anyone* entered the room. I can only say the decision has gone down a storm.

Supper was absolutely delicious bouillabaisse and bread which had been warmed up (golly, what a difference it makes!). After, it was birthday-cake time and we all sang and then Marion opened her presents. A scarf from Penny, a book (a baffling bit of 'new writing' by some Irish woman who'd won all the prizes) from James, nothing from Graham – who said, 'Oh, nobody told me!' and everyone said it didn't matter at all – and from me, the watercolour of their house that I'd been secretly painting all week. I'd managed to get it very nicely framed at a cheap Indian shop round the corner and, though I say it myself, it wasn't at all bad.

Marion was clearly touched. She got up, and kissed me.

Then she said, in a low voice that only I could hear, 'Well one thing's certain – *this* isn't going to go to a charity shop!'

Thank God no one else heard it – but I did. I was absolutely knocked for six. I found myself blushing and blushing and I just couldn't think of anything to say. Obviously she'd seen the scarf and must have realized I'd just given it away . . . oh God!

Came home, went to bed but couldn't sleep. So I've had to get up and write my diary. I am a loathsome, critical, smug human being. I have not one hint of generosity or kindness in me. I am ungrateful through and through, cut me where you will, like Brighton Rock. I may have a sweet outside, but inside I'm just a pit of rotting, writhing worms. Psychopaths are saintly compared to me. I would like to die. I would like to die right now. I want to die immediately, preferably of a slow and lingering death, if the forms of extinction are compatible.

Forgot to say, as I left, I remembered to take with me a catalogue that Penny had promised to lend me of a Goya exhibition she'd been to on a weekend to Spain. 'Don't worry, we're not having an affair!' I called to everyone as I clutched on to Graham while we went down Penny's front steps.

And Graham added – very gallantly I thought – with a big wink, 'Yet!' Very chivalrous and charming. But he wouldn't even have made a joke like that, had he known the person hanging onto his arm was a piece of sick-smelling slime in human form.

October 8

Slowly emerging from the cloud of shame that has enveloped me for the last couple of days. Keep wondering if I should email Marion to explain it, or just say nothing. Penny thinks I should let sleeping dogs lie.

'Who knows, she might just have been referring to all that clearing out you've been doing recently – nothing to do with the scarf,' she said. 'And anyway, she hasn't said anything to me. Are you sure she said it at all? Or perhaps she said, "I'll certainly put this in pride of place!" and your guilty conscience just misheard it? Whatever, emailing her to apologize would only make things worse, particularly if she still doesn't know you gave the scarf away. But next time you give something to a charity shop,' she added, 'do get a train north and dump it in Newcastle. Not in Notting Hill Gate where you can be certain she'd see it. You know Marion and charity shops!'

David, who's recently been ringing almost daily to see how I am, was much more sympathetic.

'Well of course you gave it to a charity shop!' he said, loyally. 'She's known you for longer than me and she's female and even I know – and I'm a man – that no one can buy you anything to wear.'

'Particularly not orange!' I said.

'Particularly not orange. Anyway, think of it like this. At least you didn't just throw it away. At least you didn't try to palm it off on someone else. And at least you didn't sell it on eBay. Think of what she'd have felt if she discovered you were flogging it! No, it didn't suit you, you didn't want to hurt her feelings by saying she had the worst taste in the world so you gave it to charity for nothing, hoping that your unwanted gift might bring joy and warmth to someone less fortunate than yourself.'

'Well, put like that . . .' I said, starting to feel less like a worm.

Oh dear oh dear. I do just love hearing David's voice. Just the sound of it makes me feel more secure and at home.

Later
Think I've got a cold coming on. Or perhaps the start of the long and lingering illness I've brought on as a punishment on myself.

October 9

Gene rang me after school today to tell me he'd been voted as his Class Representative.

'It means I can go to conveniences, Granny,' he said. Then I heard a muffled correction in the background and the sound of Jack talking. 'I mean conferences. My class tell me what they want me to say and I go and say it at big meetings we have so we can say how the school is run.'

'Clever you, darling,' I said. 'And what do you have in mind?'

'We want to be let to wear our own clothes on Fridays,' he said. 'And we want to be let to bring our own snacks in to eat at breaks.'

'Allowed,' I corrected. 'Allowed to bring your own clothes.' Then, 'Oh, that's nice,' I said, not quite knowing what to say next.

'But we can't bring scones, not even in our lunchboxes. Miss Grendel has a phobia about scones.'

'A phobia about scones?' I said.

'Yes. We're let – allowed – to bring them if it's by accident, but we're not let to bring them in if it's on purpose,' he said.

'What happens if she sees a scone?' I asked, amazed.

'She dies,' said Gene seriously. And as I laughed, he said, 'No, Granny, I mean it, it's serious. She dies if she even *sees* a scone.'

October 11

Popped round to return Penny's catalogue this morning, and when I rang the bell the door was opened by a complete stranger with a lot of dark growth on his chin and wearing a pair of torn old trousers. He appeared to be holding a poker.

I started back but he gave a broad grin and said, 'I was the last person you were expecting, wasn't I?' and drew me to him, kissing me on both cheeks. Not wanting to be rude, I reciprocated and, as I stuffed the catalogue into his hand, I stammered, 'Could you give this to Penny? Good to see you!' and practically fell back down the steps. At the corner of the street I frantically rang Penny on her mobile.

'There's a strange man in your house!' I said. 'Are you all right?'

'What do you mean a strange man?' she said. 'I'm in Wait-rose. Call the police!'

'But I can't!' I said. 'He kissed me on both cheeks!'

'But Marie, it's a ploy! It's what burglars do when they're interrupted! He's a con-artist! Call the police! Are you sure it was my house?'

'Of course! I'm not mad! He was brandishing a poker!'

'Well, I'm coming back right away,' she said. 'Wait there. Keep an eye on things. I'll be back in ten minutes. We'll go in together.'

I stood on the street corner, trying not to look like an old drug-dealer, keeping a nervous eye on the house. After what seemed like several hours, Penny's car came rolling round the corner and she parked.

'Come on,' she said. 'Let's see what's going on.'

'I've dialled 999 but I won't press the green button till I actually know he's a burglar,' she said.

'Good idea,' I said.

Penny had wrapped a Waitrose cucumber in a plastic bag so it looked like a cosh, and I'd dug around in the boot of the car and found a long yellow plastic thing that contained the emergency triangle you put on the road if you break down in France, but despite being armed with these, I felt terri-fied as we walked up her steps. My heart was beating like a drum from a military parade. Penny put her key in the door. She went in first and I followed. She looked into the sitting room. Nothing. Then we got to the kitchen and there was the intruder, kneeling on the floor with his back to us.

As Penny approached, a floorboard creaked. I let out a yelp and was about to lunge at him with my European danger triangle when the terrifying figure suddenly reared up. 'Alan, darling,' said Penny. 'How lovely to see you! But what are you doing here? You remember Marie, don't you? My son-in-law, Alan. You met him at the wedding. She thought you were a burglar, Alan,' she added.

I was so overcome with a mixture of fear and relief that I had to sit down. Turned out he'd popped in to try and fix her sink because she'd mentioned it the day before to her daughter. His mobile had run out of battery so he'd just walked in using the family key.

'You all right, Marie?' he said to me, worriedly, as I sat there, looking drained and faint. 'I thought you seemed a bit surprised! I'm so sorry! Now, now, deep breaths.'

Deep breaths. Imagine all those poor Pompeians in their togas, stricken with panic as the volcanic ash rained down on them. No one would have thought of saying to them, 'Deep breaths.' Has breathing deep breaths ever calmed anyone down? If anything it just revs up the old heart, incensed that anyone could offer such a ridiculously simple remedy for such a major nervous catastrophe.

It's like the Indian man in the newspaper shop. I went to get a copy of the *Daily Rant*, which hadn't been delivered yesterday – they sent me the *Guardian* instead, much good it did me – and he said I looked pale.

'I think I've got a cold coming on,' I said.

He leaned over his high, no-reaching-over-to-put-your-hand-in-the-till counter and beckoned as if he was imparting a great secret to me.

'I have a special remedy for colds,' he said, looking around the shop nervously as if frightened anyone could hear. 'It is old Indian remedy handed down for generations, from father to son. My grandfather to my father. My father to me. And now me to my son. And it always works.'

'Oh yes?' I said.

'You must take it three times a day without fail,' he murmured conspiratorially. 'For a week. This is only way you can kill colds.'

'Tell me!' I said. I was waiting for him to prescribe ground-up heels of cockroaches, a fresh wing of grasshopper, a ray of moonshine and a dash of dew from the first morning glory to open its petals to the sun, stirred together with a cinnamon stick that had been dipped in goat's blood the night before.

He leaned forward and whispered in my ear.

'Honey and lemon!' he said. 'That is the secret! You take a spoonful of honey and the juice of half a lemon and you mix them together in hot water, and there you are! Take it every day for a week and you are cured! Guaranteed!'

October 12

Had a call from Zac's mother! I must say I had never thought she'd ring. She sounded very nervous and awkward, and spoke quietly as if she lived in a small flat and didn't want Zac to hear.

'I've been thinking,' she said. 'You're right. Zac is so unhappy. Can you see if you can get his dad to come and see him? Or take him out? Or something? I know Zac's going to refuse to go, but I'm sure we could sort that out if Graham – that's his dad – would only ring and make a plan.'

'Graham?' I said in a strangled voice, coming out in goosebumps.

'Yes, I'll give you his address – he's staying with this woman, probably the one he's having an affair with . . .'

And then she gave me my own address! Which, like an idiot, I made a point of writing down, even double-checking the postcode!

'I'll see what I can do,' I said, covering up my tumultuous feelings with a friendly calm. 'We'll be in touch. Let me have a go. And in the meantime, *don't worry!*'

When I put down the phone I was shaking. It seemed too much of a coincidence to be true. But Zac's dad was my Graham – a Graham who'd never admitted even to having a child! What on earth was going on?

I was tempted to beard him straight away. Why had he never mentioned Zac?

Don't worry, I'd said! But I'm worrying myself sick! I've got no idea what to do. I can hardly face Graham on the stairs now. I'll need to have a think for at least a week or so, while I work out my tactics. Crikey! What have I got myself into?

October 13

Lying in bed this morning and trying to make out, through a crack in the curtains, whether today was going to be grey and muggy or bright and muggy, I came to a decision. And that decision was to do nothing. I used to think that doing nothing was the coward's way, something passive, but the older I get the more I realize that doing nothing can actually be a very positive thing. In my experience, if you deliberately place something on a high shelf in the back of your mind and simply wait for the right moment to take it down – or more likely, for it to fall off – the right moment will come along of its own accord. So for the next couple of weeks I shall just see how I can worm this new information into my brief chats with Graham.

My decision was helped by glancing at the horoscope page in today's *Daily Rant* (headline: 'Today's teenagers can't spell their own names!'). 'Trust your judgment and bide your time,' it read. 'Mercury in Scorpio will lead you to the right decision this month. Trust to the planets.' And so, though normally I wouldn't trust any prediction – let alone one rustled up by a planet – I thought that since the star of Sharp was obviously in line with Mercury in Scorpio, I'd be well advised to stick to my decision.

October 15

Got a letter from the hospital saying I had to come in for a 'procedure'. It seems they inject something into the lump and then photograph or scan it to see if they can identify what it is. I have to go in overnight. This is a huge bore, but still, at least I've got into the hospital system and they appear to be taking it seriously.

This cold has developed into an absolute stinker. And the worst thing is, colds aren't like they used to be. In the past they'd clear up in two or three days, but now they can go on for weeks or – even more sinister – go away and then return with a bang two days later, and two days after that, like some terrible operatic diva appearing for encore after encore. The only benefit is that at least it takes my mind off the lump. I actually had to cancel going in to school this week because I was feeling so rough. I wish there were someone else to do it. The ringing up, that is. However ill you are, when you say you're too ill to come in, it always sounds as if you're lying. I always imagine they're thinking, 'Well, you don't *sound* ill!' or 'If you're well enough to make the call, surely you're well enough to come in?' Even worse is when they say things like, 'Oh don't worry, that's fine! Just rest and get better soon! And if you're not better next week, that's fine too. The important thing is to get better!' when you really wanted them to say, 'God, how frightful, how will we possibly cope? Hope you can come in next week, or the whole world will collapse without your essential presence.'

Later

Having gone straight back to bed after breakfast, I woke up and opened my eyes and breathed and checked for headache, cough and aching nose – and found to my dismay that all symptoms were still present. No change at all since this morning. In a vain attempt at positive thinking, I checked for a single milligram of energy that might have sprung up, like a snowdrop, to give me a smidgeon of hope. Nothing. I feel as if some dark psychic power has dragged a huge lawn-roller over my soul and then got a giant to jump on it in hobnailed boots. Not a scintilla of life.

Pulling myself out of bed, I staggered to the mirror to see if any single sign of recovery could be observed in my face but the creature that stared back at me – though stare is rather too active a verb for the kind of half-hearted goggle that was reflected in the glass – had greyish-white skin, lips the colour of ash and eyes like those of a dead fish. There was not a glint to be seen in them, the give-away sign, as cookery writers are so eager to tell us, of a fish that is definitely off.

And none of my friends are any help. Penny rang this morning and I only had to croak, 'Hello' for her to say, 'Oh dear. I can hear you're no better. No change then.'

I feel so ill, actually, I think I'm going to die. I checked Google for symptoms of ME and once I'd decided I had that, I then changed my mind and thought no, it was far more likely to be linked with the lump on my stomach. It's leeching out its poison and soon I will just be one huge lump of sweating, pulsating horridness. Oh God, when I'd said I deserved to die of a slow lingering disease after being caught out by Marion, I didn't really mean it!

Now I have developed a sharp pain behind my ears. Clearly a brain tumour.

October 17

Still feel lousy. Honestly! It never used to be like this. When I was ill in the old days, I was put into my parents' bed and given a jigsaw puzzle to do on a large tray. Occasionally my mother or father would come up to read to me, after placing a mug of warm milk and a peeled and cut-up apple on a saucer by my bed. My temperature was taken by a doctor, who would look at his pocket-watch as he felt my pulse and prescribe something called Veganin. Every couple of hours someone would whisk my hot water bottle away and top it up with hotter water. Someone else would come in with a clean nightie. My hair would be brushed by unseen hands and if I was lucky my face would be sponged down before lunch was served to me – chicken soup, a yoghurt with sugar, and a jelly.

As I slowly got better, my father would bring some paper cut-out book he'd bought at a craft shop and we'd make a model fairground full of seals and clowns – with me having to keep my knees very still in case the pieces slid into one corner – or we'd play card games like Beggar-my–Neighbour or Halma.

Now it's all changed. All I do is drag myself from room to room feeling as if I'm in prison, stare at the ceiling wondering what will happen when the world runs out of water or if there's a terrorist plot that makes the Internet crash and everything grind to a halt. I tried to change the sheets, which are all dank and sweaty, but had to give up halfway through, gasping.

Marion rang and asked if she could get me anything. 'Listen to your body!' she said, but even though my ears are on stalks, as it were, I don't hear it speaking to me. Or if it is speaking, it's in such a low and morbid whisper that I can't hear it. The dreadful thing about being ill on your own is that you have to be nurse, doctor and patient all at the same time. I often find myself one minute groaning and crying out, 'Oh God, I don't want to live!' and starting to cry and then countering it with a sensible, 'Come on Marie! You've had a cold before, and you're not going to die! Now get up and have a bath and put on a clean nightie and brush your hair and you'll feel heaps better in no time!'

Later

Jack rang to see how I was and I heard myself saying, 'Fine! Just a little cold! Nothing to worry about! Feeling a bit low, but it'll go! How are *you*?' We are so desperate not to be a burden on our children. However, I did have to say I was not feeling quite up to having Gene over this Saturday, which disappointed me terribly. Then David rang. Thank God for David. I'm afraid that now, so long after this cold came on, I was feeling so sorry for myself that I heard my voice breaking when I heard him say hello.

'Oh poor old pudding!' said David, using, to my surprise, an old expression of endearment I hadn't heard since we were first married. I could hear Chummy barking in the background and I felt a pang. 'Now don't worry. This is going the rounds. Everyone's got it down here. Let's do a checklist. Headache, dry mouth, aching back and dizzy spells?'

'Yes,' I said, surprised that he seemed to know so much about it.

'Going on for days and days and you think you'll never get better and get struck down with dreadful depression?'

'That's me.'

'And a strange sharp pain behind both your ears, plus feeling sick in the evenings?'

'How do you know?'

'Because everyone's got it. I told you. Don't worry. I suspect that tomorrow it will have disappeared. It just flies in, causes havoc like some ghastly hurricane, and flies out. Bet you a fiver it's gone tomorrow!'

October 18

He was right. This morning I leapt out of bed feeling right as rain. Well, not leapt, because I never leap, but I felt remarkably better. Thank God!

Honestly, whoever gets their hands on David in the end will be a very lucky woman. Though I'm starting to hope that no woman does. I like things just as they are.

October 19

'When exactly will you die? Do you dare to take our lifestyle quiz?' (*Daily Rant*)

October 23

Off to the hospital today for my 'procedure' and feeling dread-fully anxious. Marion has very sweetly said she'll drive me, which makes me feel all the worse about the scarf, but as Penny says, let sleeping dogs lie.

Nipped out for a pint of milk – but just before I managed to get back inside, Melanie, swathed in shawls and exotic dressing gowns, popped her head out of her front door, and said, 'Mar! How wonderful! And a very good morning to you! Now, when are you going to paint your door greige? I've got all the housing associations on board, I'm getting mine done tomorrow and Penny promises she'll do hers. But we need you to join in!'

I haven't communicated much with Melanie since the 'shut up' incident, so thought I ought to mollify her. Even I, the Greatest Sulker on Earth, can't keep up feuds forever.

'I – um,' I said, 'I'm not sure I really like the colour. I've got to think a bit more about it,' I said, apologetically. 'Also, to be honest, money's a bit tight at the moment, and I'm not sure if I can afford it. I'm sure I'll get round to it at some point, but it's not a very good moment,' I added, deciding to play the sympathy card, 'because I'm just going into hospital.'

'Oh no, is it . . . is it . . . ?' said Melanie holding up her hands in horror.

'No, they still don't know what it is. They're going to do another test but I have to stay in overnight and I can't really think about doors.'

'Oh really? Overnight? And when will you be out?' asked Melanie, rather too interestedly, I thought.

'Some time tomorrow afternoon, they say,' I said. 'But now, if you'll excuse me . . .'

Later

Left strict instructions for Graham on the feeding of Pouncer, and various rules about security so that burglars will imagine I'm at home tonight. I added that he was welcome to make himself at home downstairs while I was away that night. ('*Mea casa est sua casa,*' I said, only realizing later I'd muddled up not only language but gender.) I know I should tackle him about Zac, but quite honestly I feel I've got so much on my plate at the moment I can't face it. I'll do it soon.

Marion very kindly arrived in the car to take me to the hospital and I stumbled as I got into the front seat.

'Old age!' I said. 'Inability to get in and out of cars gracefully. First sign.'

'Now, have you tried Pilates?' said Marion. 'I know I've said it before, but I swear by it.' She was so busy easing her way out of the parking space and into the road she didn't notice the look of menace and fury that had come over me. 'It was devized by a prisoner of war who had to invent a way of exercising in his tiny cell space so he did these series of movements around a metal bed . . . it stretches your *inner* muscles, you see . . .'

'Watch out!' I cried as she narrowly missed Pouncer, darting across the road to Melanie's house, and I seized the opportunity to change the subject. 'I had Melanie banging on about painting my door greige this morning. Honestly! It's the last colour I want my door. All front doors should be dark grey or black, a nice dignified colour. Not greige.' And then I remembered that Marion and Tim's door was a light aubergine. I hoped for another cat but sadly none appeared.

'You are an angel to drive me,' I added. And I meant it.

I'm just typing this in hospital on my laptop, but they're going to perform the 'procedure' in half an hour so I probably won't write any more till I get home. Gosh, I do hate going away, even if it's only for a night. I always imagine that without me there to care for it, my house will turn into one of those fashionable urban wastelands that young people love photographing, with broken windows and willow-herb growing out of the roof and buddleia springing from the walls. Possibly an old leaflet, advertising a long-gone circus, pressed against the brickwork by the wind.

Even later
Had a very sweet email from Penny wishing me 'loads of luck' with the procedure. She ended the email with the words 'Lots of love, dead Marie, and take care of yourself!'

I think she meant 'dear'.

October 24

I can hardly speak or write for fury! While I was away yesterday, Melanie had the fucking cheek – and I don't often use that word because I never think it sounds nice for an older person to swear, but I'll stick with it – *fucking* cheek and nerve to paint my front door greige!!! Not only that but she obviously sees it as some kind of favour, a little 'present' to cheer me up when I got out of hospital!

As Marion drew up outside my house, she said, 'Oh, I thought you said you hadn't succumbed to greige, Marie! Surely your door wasn't that colour this morning, was it?'

'I haven't succumbed!' I raged. 'Someone did it behind my back! And I bet I know who!'

I was so upset that Marion was thinking of taking me back to hospital. Talk about deep breaths. My eyes were bulging, my heart was pounding and, had Melanie appeared at that moment, I would have happily killed her.

What was worse, she'd obviously got some painter to come *into* my house because the inside edges of the door were all done, which they couldn't have been if it had just been done from the outside.

On the table was a note from Melanie. 'Hope you like the new look!' it read. 'I thought it would cheer you up! Hope you don't mind but Graham let the painter in to do the bits inside, but I was there all the time so don't worry about security. And no worries about payment – it's on me! My little treat! Everyone agrees it looks gorgeous! Looks like a brand-new house! Hope everything went well at the hospital . . . masses of love, Mel. x'

I now think I know what it feels like to be assaulted – well a little bit how it must feel, anyway. It was as if I'd been burgled, diminished, erased, violated and generally painted out.

'I'm not going to let it be like that for one minute longer!' I said to Marion after I'd read the note. 'I'm going to paint right over it!'

'But you've just had a general anaesthetic!' she protested.

'I don't care!' I headed to the cupboard where I keep old paint and found a battered pot of black gloss. I yanked a brush out of the cupboard and put on an apron. 'First of all, this is going on and then I'm going to tell Melanie she's got to get the whole thing stripped back to the wood and redone professionally. How *dare* she!' I prised open the lid with a screwdriver and then used it to bash down the leathery skin of black that had formed over the remains of the old paint.

Marion faffed around, saying she was sure it was all a mistake and Melanie must have thought I'd wanted it done, and not to be too hasty, and actually, Marie, it didn't look too bad, you might get used to it, but I wasn't having any of it. Eventually she went away, protesting that it was far too dark, anyway – which was true – but somehow I managed it by putting the light on in the hall and jumping out onto the front path now and again to keep the security light on the alert. It didn't take long to finish the job and, though it was dreadfully streaky, at least the worst of the greige was covered.

I was still in a towering rage when Graham came back from work.

'How could you have let that ghastly woman do this to my front door!' I yelled. 'You had no right to let anyone into the house, let alone that frazzled old hippy and her ghastly painters!'

'But she said you wanted it!' stammered Graham, looking genuinely shocked as I ranted on. He stood in the hall like a statue. 'She said you'd had a little falling-out and she wanted to make up and you couldn't afford to do it yourself so she did it as a present. She said you'd like it!'

'Like it? How could I like it? It's horrible! You've deceived me.' And it was at that moment I thought I should have everything out with him.

'I need to speak to you!' I said, sharply, and I led him into the kitchen and poured him out a large glass of red wine. To start with, he refused it, still looking shocked and confused, but, 'You're going to need it!' I said firmly. 'Sit down!'

Then I unfolded the entire saga of meeting his wife, and her telling me all about Zac and, as a result, exactly what I thought of him.

'And why have you never even mentioned him?' I said. 'He's desperately unhappy, longing to see his dad, and you're too involved in your own misery and hurt to even consider his feelings. Quite honestly, now I've heard the full story, I'm starting to think I wish I'd never let you into the house!'

Graham didn't say anything. He started, 'But I . . . you don't understand . . . no idea you'd met my wife . . . I never thought . . .'

'No, you never thought!' I said. 'That's the trouble with you. You never think. Abandon your little boy, paint my door behind my back – you just don't think, do you?'

Graham rose to his feet, downed the wine in one gulp and said, 'I think I'd better go.' Then he left the kitchen, slamming the door behind him.

In a few moments I heard him upstairs in his room, then clumping down the stairs, opening the front door and closing it behind him. The gate clicked and he was gone. And I was left, feeling absolutely terrible.

Penny was out and not answering her mobile, so in desperation and floods of tears, I rang David. 'Oh, I've behaved so badly!' I said. 'I'd just got out of hospital, and the wretched Melanie had painted my door because she thought it was a kindness – did she get that wrong! – and then I told Graham about his son and I was horrible and I never listened to any kind of explanation and I didn't mean it and . . . oh, I wish I were dead!'

Calmly David took me through it all, item by item, reassuring me that I wasn't a monster. 'She should never have painted your door and you were quite right to repaint it,' he said. 'As for Graham, it might not have been the best way to tell him – but at least now you have, perhaps you can encourage him to see the little boy. He's probably gone to stay with a friend. I doubt he'll be back tonight, but in the morning everything will be better and you can have a proper conversation. You've just got out of hospital and a general anaesthetic makes you feel terribly vulnerable, and also there's the worry

in the back of your mind about what this lump might be . . .'
Here I just collapsed completely and sobbed my heart out.
'Marie? Pudding? . . . I wish I were there, darling, so I could
give you a big hug. Go on, cry, it's okay.'

'You won't tell me to take big breaths, will you?' I asked,
gasping through my tears. 'Because they never work.'

'No, I wouldn't dream of it,' he said, laughing. 'I suggest you
have a large glass of wine and take a big pill and go straight
to bed. Right now.'

'But it's only six o'clock!' I said.

'Just go to bed. You'll sleep like a log and tomorrow everything
will look better. I promise. I was right about the cold, wasn't I?
I'll be right about this. And I'll ring you first thing.'

Oh dear, I do feel so VERY fond of David. Too fond, actually.
Feel very muddled indeed.

October 25

Well, of course David *was* right. I woke this morning feeling
miles better. I realized that actually it was a very good thing
I'd painted the door yesterday, however bonkers I was feeling,
because at least I'd got my territory back. And I rang a builder
friend who said he'd pop over at the weekend to do it properly.
I really can't ask Melanie to pay for stripping it back etc, much
as I'd like to. I know she's a manipulative old creep but I do
think her motive was kind and there's a bit of me that thinks
that I'm too old to be falling out with neighbours. So I wrote
her a little note and popped it through the door.

'Dearest Melanie,' it said. 'It was lovely of you, but at the moment I'm really unable to cope with change of any kind, so I hope you'll understand I've repainted my door as it always was. I know you'll understand. Masses of love and thank you so much for such a sweet thought. Marie x.' Of course I didn't mean the 'est' in 'dearest', 'sweet thought' or 'know you'll understand' (which actually I was certain she wouldn't). Nor the 'masses of love' or the 'x' but the diplomat in me realized that it didn't matter whether I meant it or not. She'd got her way, but I'd now got mine and we were back to square one. I must try to put it behind me. I KNOW it's better to love your neighbours and, although she's a complete NIGHTMARE, she's not a really horrible nightmare. She's quite a kindly old nightmare.

Graham was a different kettle of fish. I found a long email waiting for me.

'Dear Marie, I am very sorry about the door. I genuinely believed I was helping to give you a nice surprise and if I'd known you didn't want your door colour changed I wouldn't have dreamed of letting Melanie's builder in. Please accept my apologies. I am sorry not to have told you about Zac. I really didn't think you would be interested to hear about it, and it is also such a painful subject I cannot think about him even now. I respect and understand your no longer wanting me as a lodger any more so I will collect my things later, if I may, and also leave a month's rent in advance. Thank you for being so very kind to me and letting me stay in your lovely house, and I am sorry to have turned out to be such a lousy lodger. Graham.'

I rang him at once. His phone was on voicemail.

'What's all this about you leaving?' I said. 'You can't go! I need you here to frighten the burglars away! And I've loved every minute of having you, so no more talk about moving out, please. I'm very sorry I exploded but I was completely thrown by the door, and I'd just had a general anaesthetic and I should never have burst out about your little boy. Let's have supper soon. What about tomorrow or the next day? And we can start again.'

Finally, I feel in charge again. And funnily enough, I'm breathing deep breaths whether I want to or not. And at least the whole palaver has meant that my mind had been taken off the hospital procedure. No doubt Ben will explain to me what the results are.

October 26

Graham has returned. When I heard him coming in the door, I ran downstairs and actually gave him a big hug. Luckily, he smiled. 'The door looks great!' he said. 'Much better! And thanks for your message. I really appreciate it, Marie.'

Tomorrow he's off to Dubai on work for a couple of weeks but we're going to have supper the minute he gets back.

In the meantime, Melanie has said absolutely nothing about the door, which is, in the circs, the best thing. I'm actually amazed at her tact. She just said when I saw her in the street, lugging back huge bottles of water, 'How did the test go, Marie? I was so worried about you!' And I said that it went fine and I'd have the results in a couple of weeks.

November

November 1

Was sitting at my computer this morning when the phone rang and one of those familiar Indian voices came on the line, amid a lot of bleeps, bells, jabbering and time-lag – the unmistakable sounds of the call centre.

'Yes?' I said tetchily.

'Are you Miss Marie Sharp?' she said. 'Have I got the right telephone number?'

'Yes,' I said, warily.

'I am calling from Total World, ma'am, your international internet provider,' she said. 'I am ringing you because we have an error message coming up on our screens with every email you are sending out, and we would like to rectify this problem before you lose all your entire data.'

I gibbered a bit, and said I'd never heard of Total World and how did I know they were genuine, but then she said they could verify that they were authentic because they had my 'csl' code.

I had no idea what a 'csl' code was (the lower case was, apparently, essential) but she assured me that the fact that they had the 'csl' code, my name and phone number should be enough to satisfy me that they were genuine. I blustered and blustered and eventually she put me through to her manager.

The comforting sounds of Vivaldi's *Four Seasons* came wafting through the phone and then another Indian person came on the line. He was called Sonny. This made him all the more authentic. I once spent a morning chattering to an Indian rep from Dell called Elvis.

Sonny sounded in a rush. He told me that he could see the error messages on his screen coming up all the time and it was only a matter of seconds before my entire computer crashed. I suggested I ring him back but he said that would be very difficult. Possible, but difficult, because he was so busy putting this error right in other people's computers around the world. Then he asked me to press a few buttons to reach my 'csl' code.

'You can't be serious, Sonny!' I said. 'I wouldn't dream of it! I mean, I've been told from the year dot that I must never divulge this sort of information. In fact, it's so secret I sometimes forget it myself. I mean, I bet you tell your mum never to go into her computer and give out her codes on the phone to complete strangers, don't you? Or,' I added, considering he was probably younger than Jack, 'your old granny?'

Sonny chuckled in a friendly way. 'I am very glad you are so security-minded, ma'am!' he said. 'I tell my mum this all the time! But I am not asking you to tell me your PIN number, I am just wanting you to confirm your "csl" code. If you are consenting, I will read out the number I have first, and hopefully they will tally. This is the reason we have your name and your telephone number, ma'am, because we are your internet international providers and we are here to rectify all problems . . .'

So, chuckling back, I followed the instructions he gave me and – sure enough – there on the screen was my 'csl' code. He then read me out a string of figures and numbers in upper and lower case and, blow me, they matched what was on the screen exactly.

'You see we have your details correctly,' he said. 'So now I must ask you to follow a few directions.'

God knows what divine intervention struck me at the time but I suddenly said, 'Look, I'm so sorry, I know I'm mad, and clearly you're genuine, but I just want to ring up a friend and check, because I want to be doubly sure you're who . . .'

'Of course, ma'am, I quite understand but you must be very quick, only two minutes . . .'

I dragged out my mobile to ring James, first hoping to God I'd got it topped up and second hoping to God he'd be in. He was. I explained the situation.

'For God's sake, Marie, hang up on them!' he shrieked. 'You haven't done anything, have you? They'll be draining every penny out of your bank account if you don't watch out! Just slam the phone down on them! I can't believe . . .'

I slammed the phone down and started taking – yes, I really did – deep breaths. But I'm still shaking.

Later

Still feel utterly wobbly and sick. The thing was that Sonny sounded so nice! The way he'd giggled and talked about his mother . . . ugh!

November 4

Gene's coming over today. I've lined up a whole raft of things to do, starting with some scientific experiments. On the internet I've found how, by adding bicarbonate of soda to vinegar, you can make carbon dioxide and then, if you waft the stuff over lighted candles, they go out immediately. (It's difficult to explain this – all you are doing is 'pouring' out an invisible gas, not anything you can see – but it looks like magic on YouTube.) Then we're going to try to make a vortex with two plastic bottles and some water. I've spent quite a while trying these out to make certain they work because, after the near-disastrous butter incident, I want to be sure there is no possibility that they'll be disappointing.

I'm also hoping Gene will help me sweep up the leaves to make a bonfire. So odd how a grandson can jump up and down with excitement at the idea of collecting fallen leaves because it makes him feel like a man, while the man he will grow into just skulks in the corner with his newspaper in the autumn, muttering about fallen leaves making natural compost and how one shouldn't touch them.

Later

Jack brought Gene over and I felt bad not telling him about the lump. But my thinking is that one of the worst things a mother can do is cause worry and anxiety to her children. And as I'll probably be causing a lot of worry in the future, I feel I ought to cause as little as possible while I'm still able.

I airily asked about Jack's appendix problem, and he assured me confidently that he'd been to a doctor who'd told him categorically that the chances of it flaring up again were absolutely nil, and that there was no point in worrying at all. I'm not so sure, though.

Just before he left, as Jack was wiping some coffee he'd spilled on the work surface and said, 'You really ought to give this wood a good clean and varnish, Mum. It's pretty yukky!'

I groaned. I've been meaning to do something about it for ages. Jack shifted the microwave and peered underneath. 'There's a dead fly here, too,' he said. 'And it's all scraped away . . .'

Gene immediately rushed up to stare at the dead fly.

'Pooey pooey pongy pongy!' he said, holding his nose. 'It's yuk!'

'Shall we clean it and varnish it and make it nice?' I asked Gene. 'That'd be fun, wouldn't it?'

We went out to the shop and bought varnish and brushes, and Gene and I got going on moving all the stuff off the worktops and rubbing and scrubbing until the wood was gleaming. Then, after leaving it to dry for a little while, we got cracking on the varnish. Halfway through, in his enthusiasm, Gene flicked his brush and a great splodge of varnish landed on the floor. He looked mortified and went very quiet.

'I'm very sorry, Granny,' he said in a small voice. He looked as if were about to cry. 'I didn't mean it. It was an *accident*.'

'Of course it was,' I said, briskly. 'Never mind. Can't be helped. It's only water-based – I'll just wipe it up. Just try to be a bit more careful. You've done marvellously so far!' I added.

As I mopped up the splash, Gene continued painting happily. 'Why are you never cross, Granny?' he asked.

'I don't know. I just never feel like being cross with you!' I said. 'You never make me cross!'

We finished it off, gave it another coat and, once it had dried and we'd moved everything back on, it did look magnificent. As we were having tea, Gene said, 'I like your house, Granny. And,' he added, rather surprisingly, 'I like your toilet.'

'Why?' I asked.

'Because it's got a handle. We've got a thing you press in the wall and sometimes I can't do it.'

'I can't do it either,' I said, casting my mind back to only last week in a restaurant when I had to stand with my feet apart and lean with all my weight on a little button in the wall, using both thumbs to get even a dribble of water out of the cistern. The new flushing buttons are meant for men with muscular thumbs. Pinball champions, perhaps. Men who can pop pills from blister packs.

In the evening we watched a French animated film entitled *A Town Called Panic*, which featured little plastic toys – a tiny cowboy in a checked yellow shirt, a brown horse and a Red Indian in a headdress, still stuck to their little plastic bases. Not having had a television at home until I was about 14, I never experienced the pleasure of cuddling up with a parent to watch cartoons and laugh together. Lovely feeling.

Then he went to bed.

November 5

Woke this morning with my heart pounding. I'd dreamed the cowboy had become life-size and greeted me as I left my house on my way to Penny's. He offered to exchange a piece of music he was holding for my 'lovely coat'. I laughingly brushed him away, but then he pursued me down the street, wobbling on his plastic base and trying to hug and kiss me. I escaped into Penny's house but found she had all our friends round, and they told me I was utterly ridiculous to be so upset. But when I looked out of the window as I prepared to leave, I saw the cowboy on a bench – a menacing grin on his face and a knife in his hand – waiting for me to come out. Luckily, at that point I woke up.

What makes one have such horrible dreams? Like Hamlet, it's the only thing I fear about death – that it might be full of these terrifying images and horrible people.

Anyway, I dropped Gene back in time for a bonfire night party that he was going to, bearing not only the equipment for our two experiments but also some brandy snaps we'd managed to make. (I haven't seen brandy snaps in the shops for ages.) We even managed to make a brandy-snap basket and fill it with Smarties, though there weren't many Smarties left by the time we got back to his house . . .

November 8

Finally had my dinner with Graham. I'd decided to cook him a delicious beef stew but when I tasted it an hour before supper the meat was hideously tough. Frankly, it was inedible. Then I realized that, instead of simmering it slowly, I'd left it for a while on the boil. Honestly, sometimes I think I've simply forgotten how to cook. It's not like riding a bicycle – something you can either do or not – but nothing I make these days seems to work. I think it's because I simply don't do enough of it. Not having anyone to cook for means I'm nearly always out or standing at my fridge, just picking.

Luckily, I found a piece of frozen smoked haddock and some spinach, and rustled up a reasonably delicious supper out of that. I had to throw the stew away, imagining my mother looking down at me with horror on her face as she witnessed my wasteful ways.

Poor old Graham. We started off chatting rather over-politely about various household things like whether he preferred long-life bulbs or incandescent ones and whether he found the ironing board still stuck when he tried to open it, then a bit about his work, and finally, over coffee in the sitting room – I lit the fake coal fire and it was all very relaxed and cosy – we got down to brass tacks.

'Okay. Zac,' I said. 'What's happening? He seems so unhappy!'

Graham immediately went into zombie mode. I've seen this happening with children when they've been accused of doing something wrong, or when they find a subject hard to address. His eyes looked dead as if he were withdrawing into himself, and then he tried to speak – but as he did so, his voice broke into a choking sob.

He was crying so much that eventually I went into the kitchen and got a few paper towels and came back and sat down beside him, with my arm around him, saying, 'Don't worry. It's all right. Don't worry.' Over and over again.

Finally it all came out. It turns out that, even though it was Julie who'd shown him the door, when he had actually packed his suitcase and told his son he was leaving, Zac had burst into tears and reminded him that only the week before he'd solemnly sworn that – though he'd spent a lot of time away – at least this week he'd be around. They'd made lots of plans in the past, and Graham had gone and let him down about all of them. Zac had shouted that he never wanted to see him again, and for some reason this remark struck Graham with such force that he actually took it seriously. A week later, when he started to think it might be the remark of an emotional five-year-old and perhaps not true, Julie had told him that Zac had gone round telling people that his father had died. This had been the final straw.

He explained. 'When I was young, my dad left home, and I hated him. He was a drunk and he used to beat up my mum. Still, Mum forced me to see him every week – and I dreaded these visits. I can't ever forget them. The one thing I couldn't bear is for Zac to go through the same. If he doesn't want to see me, then I think it's the best thing for him if I keep away and respect his wishes.'

At this point he asked if he could smoke and I said of course he could, did he think I was a member of the health police? Couldn't he see the ashtray right in front of his nose? Then I sat back and marshalled my arguments.

'Look, the child's only five! He doesn't know what he wants, you big wally. You're the grown-up. And you're a loving dad, not a monster. Zac loves you! The longer you don't see him, the more he'll think you don't love him, and no doubt feel that this split is all his fault because he's done something wrong. You should see him, Graham! He's completely gone into his shell and never smiles. I beg you to make an effort, risk his fury and see him. He'll probably behave really badly but stick with it. He's only pushing you away because he loves you so much. Can't you see that?'

'That's what Julie says,' said Graham morosely.

'I thought she refused to speak to you,' I said. 'Or was it you who refused to speak to her?'

'Oh, that changes all the time,' said Graham, rather desperately. 'I don't know what's going on.'

'Anyway, she's right about Zac pushing you away because he loves you,' I said. 'And I'm a very experienced old teacher, with a son and a grandson, so you've got to trust me. Just remember this. *Zac is not you.* Can you say that back to me – Zac is not me?'

'Zac is not me,' said Graham. 'Zac is not me.' He thought a bit. 'You think that, though I hated visiting my dad, it doesn't mean that Zac will hate visiting me? Or me visiting him?'

'He won't want to come at first. But if he still doesn't want to come after visiting regularly for six months, then maybe you start to think again. And only then can you *start* to think again. But you can make it work. You love him and he loves you!' I paused. 'Can I suggest something? I'll ask Julie if he could come over here one day and I'll tell her I'll be around all afternoon. Zac and I get on pretty well. And Julie and I seemed to get on reasonably well, too, despite her thinking that I was a fiend in human shape before she actually met me. Let me give it a go.'

Graham looked very uncomfortable. Then he started crying again. 'I love Zac so much, I couldn't bear him to have to suffer like I did!' he burst out. My heart bled for him. There's something really ghastly about seeing grown men in tears and, while Penny, Marion and I cry all the time over anything from computers going wrong to whether the milkman forgot to deliver that morning – men seem to find it so much more difficult. When they cry it's because their whole worlds have collapsed.

Inside I was thinking, 'Stop being so preoccupied with yourself, you selfish chump! Consider your poor little boy!' But I decided that wasn't the right thing to say at that particular time.

Eventually, rather hopelessly, he shrugged and said, in a beaten voice, okay. He'd go along with anything I said. He didn't think it would work, but it was worth a try. Then he said he was going to go upstairs and, if I didn't mind, he was going to have a joint because he needed something to calm him down. Whereupon I said why didn't he have a joint down here and if he'd offer me a drag so much the better. At least then I could fulfil one of my New Year's resolutions about taking drugs. Admittedly when I made that commitment, I was thinking about something a bit harder than dope. But as it was 'hydroponic', according to Graham, I could legitimately say it was new.

November 9

Woke this morning with a horrible post-dope headache. I'd forgotten how rough it always used to make me feel. And I suspect that the stuff Graham smokes is about 500 times the strength of what I used to smoke. Skunk, it transpires, is a different proposition from the friendly little dried leaves that I'd encountered before. And despite my liberal 'smoke wherever you like and whatever you want' approach to life, I have to say I did make pretty free with the lily-of-the-valley room spray, because downstairs smelt like one of those old pubs you used to go into in the Sixties.

As far as Zac goes, I've got no idea if my wheeze will work, but the situation can't be worse than it already is. So, next time I'm in school, I'll try to broach the subject. Not looking forward to it, though, I must say.

Later

Marion rang to tell me that she and Tim are having a wedding anniversary party in a couple of weeks, and would I mind if they asked David because they remembered him with such affection and knew we got on. I said it was fine. Actually, it'll be rather nice. Quite looking forward to it. At the moment. Though when these things actually get closer, who knows?

November 10

I thought Sylvie and Harry should be back from Africa by now, so I gave them a call and explained about Chummy.

'He's a very nice old thing,' I said. 'And I know you must miss Hardy.'

'Well,' said Sylvie, 'we weren't going to get another dog . . .'

'But he's had such a terrible life!' I interrupted. I laid on his miserable existence so far with a trowel. 'When are you next coming up to London? David's coming here for a party soon and could bring him then, and at least you could come and have a look at him! I bet you'll like him. All dog-lovers love him. David would keep him but he feels he comes up to London too much and doesn't want to leave him alone. And Pouncer and I aren't really dog-lovers, sadly.'

She said it would be impossible to take him permanently until just before Christmas because they've got the builders in, but she was coming up for present-shopping next month so if she could have a look at him then she'd let me know if she wanted him or not. Oh God, that means I'll have to get

David to bring him up and then I'll have the wretched animal for God knows how long before she takes him away again. *If she takes him away.* Still, I can't really start niggling about it all. I suppose I'll cope. Just hope that Pouncer comes back when Chummy's gone for good. He pops in now and again, but I hardly see him at all these days.

November 11

After school today I waited with Zac until his mother collected him. She looked diminished, and her thin blue checked coat was far too meagre to combat the biting wind that was rushing through the playground. I suddenly saw that she was just as unhappy as Zac. What a terrible time they must have at home, I thought, each more miserable and rejected than the other. For the first time in my life, 'unhealthy and dysfunctional' seemed to be the *mots justes*.

When she saw me, she looked up. Was it hope I saw in her eyes? I think so. 'I expect you're here to tell me you didn't get anywhere,' she said. 'Oh well.'

'No, it's not that bad,' I said. 'But could I have a word with you alone?' I added, signalling at Zac with my eyes. After a word, Zac went back to the classroom to fetch something – though I couldn't imagine he was fooled for a moment – and in the few minutes before he returned I explained the situation. I found it extremely embarrassing admitting that her husband was actually my lodger but, after looking fairly incredulous, she seemed to accept it.

'This isn't some kind of set-up, is it?' she said. 'You really didn't know about the relationship till last month? It seems too extraordinary.'

'I know,' I said. 'But it actually makes it all a lot easier. Because now Zac can come over and visit Graham at my house which will, I'm sure, make him feel safer.'

'But did you get any explanation from Graham about why he hasn't persisted with wanting to see Zac?' she asked.

'It's all about his childhood,' I said to her, exasperatedly. 'His father was a monster, apparently, he had to visit him and he was miserable, so he imagines Zac is feeling the same.'

'Blah, blah blah . . .' said Julie, wearily. 'That's one thing I don't miss about Graham. Always going on about his wretched childhood. I mean I know it was miserable, but didn't we all have miserable childhoods? Get over it! Anyway, then what?'

'Well, I appear to have convinced Graham that Zac must come over and visit,' I said. 'I can promise Zac I'll be there with him while he meets his dad. And I can *absolutely* promise Zac nothing unpleasant will happen. It's just a matter of your persuading him to come.'

'Easier said than done! Look, I tell you what, why don't you just ask him over, say nothing about his dad, and then Graham can walk in casually. How about that?'

'It's certainly an idea,' I said – but a rotten one, I thought to myself. (If this was how Graham and Mrs Graham organized their lives – full of subterfuge and secrecy – no wonder it had all gone wrong.) 'Look, let me have a go. I'll talk to Zac.'

She agreed, so I'm going to have a try.

November 12

Another hospital appointment. This time I had to spend hours in the waiting room with a whole bunch of people who, by the look of them, had but weeks to live. I felt rather a fraud because, although I'm still worried by this lump, it doesn't seem to be life-threatening – or if it is, it doesn't seem to be having any effect on my energy levels. At least not yet.

Ben was as charming as usual.

'Take a seat,' he said. He stared at his notes and then looked up at me, giving me a dazzling smile. 'That procedure and the sample we took – I can't say if the news is good or bad. I've consulted with Dominic Sheridan and he says it's a bit JDLR.'

'JDLR?' I said, rising to the bait.

'Just Doesn't Look Right,' he said in a positive upbeat way, but not smiling as he did so. 'He suggested we sent your results to a lab in the States where they've got better equipment to check over this kind of thing. I'm afraid that'll take another month but I really think we ought to do it, just to be on the safe side. And let's have another look at it while you're here.'

After he'd examined me, he looked a bit more worried. 'Have you noticed it's got a bit bigger?' he said.

'No,' I said. 'I try not to look at it too much. I get freaked out.'

'Well, it *is* bigger. But we'll get to the bottom of it. I'll be in touch when I've got the results. And in the meantime, *don't fret!*'

Don't fret? How can I not fret when he says it's got bigger

and it's a case of JDLR? I thought I'd managed to put it to the back of my mind and now I'm starting to worry myself sick again.

November 13

'Farewell green and pleasant land! New towns to cover entire green belt!' (*Daily Rant*)

November 18

At the end of the lesson today I finally had a moment for a few words with Zac, so I stopped him on his way out and asked if we could talk. We sat down in the empty classroom and he looked at me suspiciously. 'I don't want to see my dad,' he said, 'if that's what you want to talk about.'

With great difficulty I explained the situation.

'You mean you have my dad living in your *house*?' he said, hardly able to believe his ears. 'Does Mum know? Are you his *girlfriend*?'

'Darling, I'm old enough to be your dad's mother,' I said. 'Don't be silly. No, I have people living in my house as lodgers and your dad arrived one day and I didn't know he was your dad and it was before I started teaching here and got to know you. But anyway, he's living there now, and I wondered if you'd like to come over and have tea with me, and maybe you could see your dad as well. Do say yes. I've got lots of things I'd like to show you.'

'I'd like to come to tea with *you*,' said Zac, tactfully, 'but I don't want to see my dad. He's not my dad. I don't like him.'

'He'd love to see you,' I said. 'When I told him I was teaching you, you know what he did? He burst into tears.'

'My dad? Burst into tears? I've never seen him crying,' said Zac, showing a macabre interest. Then he said, 'That doesn't sound very likely.' I almost jumped. He said it in that peculiarly adult way that children employ sometimes, as if under all that screaming and Batman and Robin and 'ner-ner-ner-*ner*-ner' there lies a sternly moral judge of about 90. Then he returned to being Zac, whiny and sulky and miserable. 'I don't want to see him.'

I went on manipulating, cajoling, trying to be sensitive, but in the end he just turned on me. 'I don't want to see my dad!' he snapped sharply. He didn't exactly say, 'Read my lips' but that's what I imagined he would say if he'd summoned up the internal old judge again. 'I want to go home now.' Then he walked out of the classroom and towards the playground, where his mother was waiting for him.

I left feeling totally cack-handed and horrible, particularly because the way Zac is behaving is hardly endearing. I tell myself it's because he's so unhappy, but it doesn't stop him being rather vile in his misery.

When I got back, I noticed a motorbike parked outside my door. On the black plastic box at the back, the owner had attached a sticker reading, 'Make my day! Run over a paedophile!'

I came in, shaking my head. How could anyone have a

sticker like that on his bike, even as a joke? With any luck, the bike would be gone the following day. I couldn't bear to have to read that every time I left my front door. As I went into the sitting room, the telephone rang. It was Julie, Zac's mother, and I began, apologetically, 'I'm so sorry I wasn't able to persuade him . . .'

But she interrupted. 'Zac's coming over this weekend,' she said, peremptorily.

'This weekend? Oh, er, that's fine,' I said, confused. 'But he said he didn't want to see his dad ever again! How on earth did you get him to change his mind?'

'I'm fed up with all this. He's got to see his father some time. I told him if he didn't go over to you, he wouldn't get any Christmas presents but if he did, I'd buy him an Xbox.'

'Oh, er, ah . . . Jolly good.' I couldn't think of anything else to say. In one way I was terribly disapproving of her, thinking that it would be much better for Zac to make a proper decision by himself. And on the other, I was curiously impressed that she'd fixed the whole thing with a bribe. Sometimes these totally non-liberal and insensitive ways of operating do work magic, I must admit. But crikey, I'd better be sure Graham's here, and we've got a very nice tea. I blithely say, 'Come over and everything will be fine' – but it's quite possible there'll be the most ghastly scene and it'll be All My Fault.

About to pour a large drink when the phone rang again. This time it was David. Thank God. He first asked me about the lump and was extremely sympathetic.

'I'm starting to imagine that I'll become the Incredible Lump. Soon it'll be bigger than me,' I said.

'It's probably going up and down all the time and you don't notice,' he said. 'No reason to imagine it's going to take over.'

Then I asked if he'd got Marion and Tim's invitation to their wedding anniversary party.

'Indeed I have, and that was partly why I was ringing,' he said. 'Now you've got to be absolutely honest with me.'

'Oh please, not that!' I interrupted. 'Whenever anyone asks me to be honest with them, it always involves my having to come up with some ghastly lie on the spur of the moment!'

David laughed and went on. 'Do you think you could face having me to stay that night? I'll quite understand if you say no. I rang Jack and asked if I could stay there, but they've got a pool table in their spare room which they're keeping for a friend till he moves house. Would you mind awfully? I know you might feel funny about it, but . . .'

'That would be lovely!' I said, though of course I felt *terribly* funny about it. I mean, to be together in the same house as my ex for the first time in 15 years. 'I hope you don't mind being put up in the room where I work, though, on a put-you-up bed. It won't be very comfortable.'

'I'd be happy to sleep on the floor,' he said.

I was just sorting out the time he'd arrive so I could be in to give him the key, when he added, 'I hope I haven't put my foot in it, by the way.'

That meant, of course, that he had.

'What have you done?'

'I forgot you hadn't told Jack about this lump of yours so I said something on the lines of "You must be worried about Mum's lump" and he said what lump and that he'd never heard of it. I backtracked quickly and said it was nothing, and not to worry, but I'm afraid he got a bit upset that you hadn't told him. Or that he didn't appear to know, anyway,' he added.

My heart sank. I should have known it would get out sooner or later. I'm so busy being all pious and telling Graham that he should be open and honest and Julie that she should be open and honest and then it turns out that I'm just as secretive as everyone else.

'Oh God, I should have told him!' I said. 'It's not your fault. I should have warned you. What an idiot – me, I mean, not you,' I added hastily. 'By the way, David,' I said, 'Sylvie can come up to have a look at Chummy in a couple of weeks so when you come up, why don't you bring him up too? I can hang on to him until Sylvie visits and hope he can charm the pants off her. Kill two birds with one stone?'

So he'll do that. In a funny way, I'm rather looking forward to seeing the old thing again, bad breath and all. That's Chummy I mean. Or do I mean David, too? Not about the bad breath, obviously. Oh dear, I am in a muddle. I'm starting to depend far too much on David.

Later

Rang Jack who naturally enough sounded rather icy about me not telling him about the lump.

'Look, I'm your son, Mum!' he said. 'I need to know if you're ill. I should be the first person you tell if you're not well. How long has this been going on?'

'First, I didn't want to worry you,' I said, 'And second, there's no reason to think I'm not well. No one seems to know what this thing is. I've only had it for a month' (lying again) 'and David's the only person I've told' (more lies). 'Oh, and,' I added, 'the doctor I'm seeing, who should he turn out to be but Brainy Ben! Your Ben! Ben from school!'

'The one you found with the dope . . .'

'He's a doctor now,' I said.

'He's more than a doctor, he's a consultant. Oh, well, that makes it better. You'll be in good hands there. What an incredible coincidence!'

And somehow the conversation got diverted and Jack calmed down a bit. But he did make me promise that, from now on, I must let him know every doctor I saw and every result I had the moment I received it. Afterwards I felt strangely consoled. It was very comforting that he'd been so concerned about me.

November 20

Went to a concert at the Wigmore Hall last night. By myself, which is unusual, but I couldn't find anyone who wanted the other ticket and so I gave it to a very smelly music student (so he told me) who had been waiting an hour for returns. Honestly, looking round the audience I felt I was in a *morgue*. A quartet played a nice bit of Brahms, but unfortunately it was followed by an entirely new musical work, composed by the viola player. It was called *Rhapsodie 123*, which didn't give a lot away, and by the end of it I wasn't any more enlightened. All plink plonk and long silences and dissonant chords. I suppose a musician would have known what was going on, but to me it was just musical gibberish.

Halfway through the second piece, one half of a couple behind me whispered to the other, 'Well, I suppose it could be worse,' while the man next to me started to slump until his head eventually crashed down onto his chest. If he hadn't emitted small snores from time to time, I would have been certain he'd died of boredom, in his seat.

November 22

The postman delivered the invitation to Marion and Tim's 45th wedding anniversary, next Sunday. Tim had clearly done it on a computer template, and the whole card was covered with pictures of glasses of champagne, party hats and streamers. Printed diagonally across it were the words 'We're having a PARTY!' in fake handwriting, just in case anyone failed to get the message. And 'We're forty-five years old!'

To my great relief, Marion had very kindly written, 'No presents! But we'd be grateful if anyone who feels like it would make a donation to www.farmafricapresents.org.uk so that a goat can be given to a needy farmer.'

Despite my huge reservations about the ethics of giving goats to Africa, I duly went to the computer and bunged another wretched animal across the equator, in the hope that it would bring profit and delight and not be eaten for Christmas dinner the moment it arrived. Still so guilty about Marion's scarf. Almost feel like buying another one exactly the same and wearing it, just to vindicate myself. However, it would confuse her terribly.

November 23

Today was the day that Zac came over to have tea and meet his dad again. It wasn't a total success but at the same time I still feel there's hope.

The situation wasn't helped by Zac and his mother arriving at exactly the same time as Melanie was leaving her house to go off somewhere. (No doubt a Pilates class.)

'Oh, and who are you?' gushed Melanie peering down at him over the wall. 'Zac? That's lovely! Are you a little friend for Gene? Or are you a nephew of Mar's? Perhaps you're Mar's sister?' she added, staring Zac's mother up and down. 'How lovely to meet you! I'm Mel from next door. That's what everyone calls me – Mel-from-next-door – because even if I don't live next door to them, it always feels like I do! What a lovely community spirit this street has, don't you think? You can feel it in the air. Do try to persuade Mar to paint her door greige. A while ago, I tried to twist her arm so she'd fall in with the rest of the street, but no luck. Our Mar knows her own mind, that's for sure! Still, maybe you'll be more successful. You see, all the people in the street are painting their doors greige . . .'

'Come in!' I said, sharply to Zac and his mother, bustling them both into the hall. 'Sorry about that,' I added as I closed the door. 'She's a nightmare.'

I felt myself exuding embarrassed charm as I showed them into the kitchen, where I'd got out some of Gene's toys to make Zac feel welcome. I offered his mother a cup of tea but she said she'd got shopping to do and would come back in an hour. (We thought it best to make it a short visit, the first time.) Zac became a bit tearful as she left, but was willing to be led back inside eventually. I gave him Ribena and biscuits and we started making a farm out of Play-Doh on the kitchen table.

'Is Dad coming?' he suddenly asked in a sullen voice.

'Yes, he'll be down in a minute,' I said. I went to the bottom of the stairs and called up. 'Graham! Zac's here!'

There was the sound of feet coming down. Graham appeared like a guilty schoolboy but Zac didn't even turn round. Graham came over and gave Zac a manly ruffle on the head, and Zac flinched, rather too obviously I thought, as if he'd been touched by something unpleasant. I couldn't help but notice the faint smell of dope emanating from Graham's jacket. Poor chap had no doubt been psyching himself up for the occasion.

'How's things, Zac?' he said. 'I say, you've got a lot bigger since I last saw you! Where's that tooth gone? And how's everything at school?'

Zac said nothing and just stared ahead of him, kneading his Play-Doh.

'Is it okay? You doing well?'

'Fine,' said Zac in a grudging whisper. He started to model a dragon that he insisted would live on our farm. I was busy making a flock of geese and hoping that Zac wouldn't get too keen on the white Play-Doh because, once children get their hands on the white, it isn't white any longer.

'How's Mum?'

Zac didn't reply.

'Well, it's good to see you!' said Graham, rather desperately.

'Why don't you come and join us?' I said, gesturing to a chair.

Graham came over cautiously. 'What shall I make?' he said jovially. 'Shall I make a giraffe?'

'Giraffes don't live on farms, you idiot,' said Zac, displaying a sudden violence.

'Well, nor do dragons, come to that,' said Graham good-naturedly.

But Zac had had enough. He got up pointedly and went over to a far corner of the room where he found some old plastic figures and started playing with them by himself. Meanwhile, Graham and I continued making a farm all by ourselves. Feeling, I might say, like total chumps.

After a short while I said, 'Well, we're finished now, Zac. Would you like to come and see it? Your dragon looks very good! So does Dad's giraffe!'

Zac got up and came over. 'It's stupid!' he said, angrily and, putting out his fist, squashed the giraffe flat. 'It's a stupid farm. There aren't any giraffes on farms. It's a stupid giraffe.'

Then he returned to his corner.

'Go and sit nearby and I'll make some tea,' I whispered to Graham, and he dutifully sat down, keeping an eye on Zac who ignored him completely.

Having given Graham his cup of tea, I sat down further away, pretending to make a list while keeping an eye on the proceedings.

Zac had got Gene's Planet Protectors out. He was muttering to himself, making up their dialogue. 'I'm good!' he said. 'And you're the baddie! Pttch!' The 'baddie' flew into the air and, as it was a character called Doc Tox, it kept saying, 'I'm Doc Tox! I pollute the planet,' over and over again. 'Then there was a big whirlwind,' Zac said to himself, 'and all the people were thrown in the air!' – he hurled the figures around – 'and it destroyed everything!' Next, he started chucking cushions at the walls. 'Everything's dead! Here it comes! Whoosh! Whoosh!' Furnishings seemed to be flying everywhere. I looked with trepidation at some of my ornaments, praying they wouldn't get damaged. 'WHOOSH!!' he said finally, throwing a cushion to the floor and stamping on it angrily.

'You're dead,' he said, with some satisfaction. 'You're all *dead.*'

This entire scene was clearly some kind of enactment that it was important Graham should witness. Zac was, it seemed, very keen on expressing his rage to his father, but indirectly. After this outburst I suggested Graham show Zac his room, and see if they could find Pouncer on the way.

Zac seemed interested in the cat, but wouldn't go with

Graham. 'You come too,' he said, tugging at my hand. So we went around the house looking for Pouncer but, unfortunately, with no luck. Ever since Chummy came to stay, Pouncer's virtually left home. He eats his food, but then he goes out. Often he's not even back at night.

Next we tempted Zac into Graham's room, though when he arrived there, he said, sourly and inaccurately, 'It's very messy.'

Graham looked more and more like a beaten schoolboy, but luckily at that moment the bell rang and it was Julie, come to pick Zac up.

Graham was clearly set on staying in his room, but I insisted he come downstairs with us. He hung about in the shadows of the hallway as I opened the door, but when Zac's mother caught sight of him, I realized this must be the first time they'd seen each other since the split.

'How are you?' Graham asked Julie, nervously.

'Fine,' she said. 'How are you?'

'Fine,' he replied. 'Zac's been great. It's been really good seeing him again. Will you come next weekend, old chap?'

'Mum's giving me an Xbox to come here,' said Zac.

'Yes, and you're coming next weekend,' said his mother. 'That was the deal. Same time?'

'Same time,' I said.

'But I don't want . . .' Zac began, protesting. 'You said only once, Mum . . .'

She pulled him away sharply. 'I didn't say anything of the kind. Say thank you to Mrs Sharp,' she said. Zac grunted out some thanks and I followed them down the front path.

'It's been lovely having you, Zac,' I said. 'I look forward to seeing you next week and we'll make another farm, shall we?'

At this point Melanie arrived at her gate.

'Have you had a lovely time?' she asked, gushingly.

'Mrs Sharp thinks you're a *n* . . .'

'Lovely neighbour!' shouted Julie, obliterating the word 'nightmare'. Then they left.

Later

'I can't go through that again!' said Graham. From the smell I realized he was actually smoking a joint in the kitchen. And I couldn't blame him.

'But it was brilliant!' I said, enthusiastically. 'At least he made a connection with you!'

'He hates my guts!' said Graham. 'And he's right!'

'But I thought that was really good,' I said. 'He did interact with you, even if it was only indirectly.'

'I suppose so,' said Graham, dolefully.

'You sound just like Zac,' I said, and I couldn't help bursting out laughing.

But Graham let out a kind of choking sob. 'I don't know I can go through that again, Marie,' he said. 'It was so painful. My boy. He'll hardly speak to me. What have I done? I'm such a shit. A shit. I'm no use to anyone.'

'Stop wallowing in self-pity,' I said, trying not to snap. 'Of course you can go through it again. Now, shape up. You're his dad. If we keep up these once-a-week visits, we'll have you speaking before Christmas, I'm certain,' I said, decisively. Though I wasn't, of course, at all certain.

November 26

David arrived with a small bag to stay the night. Just before he came in, I pointed out the sticker on the motorbike, which had been re-parked in front of Melanie's house. It looked as if the rider of the bike lived round here, so I'd have to put up with it.

'I wish I dared unpeel it,' I said. 'But I've seen him out of my window and he looks like the sort of Hell's Angel who'd snap my spine in two with one hand if he caught me at it.'

When we got into the house, it was very strange, being together. Suddenly I was very glad that David had brought Chummy with him, because fussing about the dog lessened the tension.

'You remember Marie's house, don't you, old boy?' said David, as he led Chummy in. 'I'll be sorry to see you go, old man, we've had good fun together . . .' In the corner Pouncer, who has only just decided that it's safe to return to his old haunts occasionally, sat motionless in a corner, bristling with hatred and fear.

Oddly, the dog seemed perfectly at home, and, on David putting his bed down in the usual place, snuggled down in it quite happily, as if he'd never left.

David and I sat awkwardly at the kitchen table, staring at

each other. Then David said, 'It's very nice to be here, old thing, though a bit odd, isn't it?' And I agreed and we laughed and the ice seemed to be broken.

We chatted over a cup of tea and, just as I was about to get up to clear away, David said, 'Tell me, what do you think of being on your own?'

'I think,' I said cautiously, 'that I like it. That's not to say there aren't moments when I don't think it would be jolly nice to have someone else around. I mean, you have to work hard at a relationship, but sometimes I think you have to work harder to be on your own – successfully that is. You've got to keep up with all your friends, make sure you're busy and get involved in local affairs. Sometimes I just miss someone to watch telly with – just the humdrum things – and of course to share all the little worries about Gene and Jack and Chrissie. But luckily, you're very good like that,' I added, lest he thought I thought he wasn't sympathetic.

To my amazement, he got up with our two mugs, walked to the sink and started washing them up.

'David, what's going on?' I couldn't help asking. 'You've turned into a new man! A very nice new man, but you'd never wash up in the old days!'

David turned and smiled.

'Well, one thing Sandra did do was teach me quite a lot,' he said. 'She wasn't one to let me get away with not helping round the house. And then there was a point when we had counselling together and I realized what a selfish bastard I'd been – not just to you but to her. And I decided to change. Not that it's difficult.' He reached for the sponge pad and squeezed it under the tap. 'It's all about surfaces, they say.' He started wiping everything down. 'What every woman wants is a man who wipes the surfaces. And as that's the case, the surfaces I shall wipe!'

I could hardly believe it as I watched him. And I must say, it was an extremely nice feeling, sitting here as he cleared every crumb and smear from the beautifully re-varnished wooden worktop.

'Well, while you're doing that, I'll feed Chummy and then bring down the spare bed and put the sheets on,' I said. But again David surprised me.

'I wouldn't dream of it,' he said. 'Tell me where the bed and the sheets are and I'll sort it out. Come on! I'm sure you've got masses to do!'

So, feeling incredibly relieved, because getting out the put-you-up bed is always an incredible chore, I went to my bedroom to sort out what I might wear that evening. Marvelling at my ex-husband's change of personality as I did so.

Decided that the little black number I'd got from Cos was the answer. As it so often is.

Later

Normally I dread events like Marion and Tim's party, when the time actually arrives. They so often feel like *Groundhog Day*. I must have been to at least 20 parties exactly like theirs in my life. A lot of grey-haired old people, a lot of pasta salad and bits of salami, gallons of cheap Prosecco. Not enough chairs to sit on, not enough space and, always, some hot-blooded young person who opens the door to the garden halfway through because they're 'boiling', leaving the rest of us to freeze in our party dresses.

But for some reason this time was different and in any case I couldn't have given a pin if it was exactly the same as every other party I'd been to. I was looking forward – okay, secretly longing – to see the surprise on people's faces when I arrived with David. Also, oddly, I was actually looking forward to going to a party with David myself. It would make a change from skulking in on my own and having to crank up the old social skills the moment I put my foot in the door. Going with David felt – well, it felt cosy. Easy. Natural.

David was certainly looking forward to it, anxious to encounter old faces that he hadn't seen for 15 years or so.

'I probably won't recognize them – they'll all be so *ancient*!' he said.

'And they won't be able to recognize you, either!' I joked.

'Oh, they'll know who I am all right, because I'll be with you.'

'No, they'll just think I've found some presentable older man.'

'Presentable, eh?' said David, preening rather. 'That's a big compliment from you, my darling.'

And he did look very presentable. He's still got a lot of hair, but not too much, which he gets nicely cut. And he's always been very good on clothes, so his suit was extremely sharp, and his silk tie – since he'd bought it from the Royal Academy shop ages ago – still looked stylish and edgy. Indeed, he was looking so cool, I would almost have called him dishy. Rather dreaded some ghastly female latching on to him at Marion's.

As we entered the party, David caught sight of us in a mirror. 'Actually, there's a very presentable pair, I'd say, wouldn't you?' he said, joking.

Much to my surprise there seemed to be a lot of young people at the party, which was a change.

'I always think it's so good to mix old and young,' said Marion, when we said hello. 'Don't you?'

Hmm. Well, I quite like it but I feel sorry for the young people. The last thing I wanted to do when I was young was to talk to anyone over the age of 30.

'It's lovely to see you, David,' she added. 'You haven't changed a bit!'

'And nor have you!' said David. 'You look younger than ever!'

Everyone continued to lie their heads off for a while. Then Melanie, spotting a new man on the scene, came up to us. When she saw who it was, she went into flirtatious mode.

'Is it David?' she said coyly. 'Well, we met in *very* different circumstances last time, didn't we!'

'I don't think we've met before,' said David, not too gallantly, putting out his hand.

That threw her. 'Most people would remember something like the last time *we* met!' she purred, giving him a broad wink and moving on mysteriously, the only thing she could do, really, in the circumstances.

'Most people!' said David. 'Why will people never realize that I'm not "most people"? And nor, my darling, are you. Now, let's a get a drink.'

We pushed through to a table at the back where Tim was serving drinks. He was wearing an apron upon which had been printed the words *The Man, the Myth, the Legend*. As we waited for him to open another bottle, a couple near us were saying, 'Oh, but with *Breaking Bad*, you really can't say you like it or not until you've watched the whole of the first series! We've got all the boxed sets!' On the other side of us a woman said, 'The extraordinary thing is that, when you get down to it, London is just a group of villages.' And behind us someone else was explaining that, despite house prices going up, it didn't make any difference if you were moving because it was all relative. It crossed my mind that the Ancient Romans probably made conversation almost identical to this in Latin when they were meeting for an orgy. Villa prices, obviously, but I wonder if they said things like 'You can't say you like *Antigone* or not until you've watched the whole of the beginning of the Theban cycle, *Oedipus Tyrannus* and *Oedipus at Colonnus*.' Or 'Rome is just a group of hills when you get down to it.' Or 'Once we've put the hypocaust in, it'll be worth twice what we paid for it.'

We managed to stick it out for a couple of hours and then David came up to me. 'I'm ready to roll,' he said. 'How about you?'

Realizing I'd drunk far too much, I agreed. And we left, having given Marion and Tim numerous hugs and kisses and congratulations.

Outside it was absolutely freezing, and there was ice on the ground.

'You'd better take my arm,' said David. 'Don't want you breaking your leg outside your own front door.' And as we walked towards my gate, there, glinting in the street-light, was the motorbike with the horrible paedophile sticker on it.

'Let's hurry past,' I said, under my breath. 'I can't bear to see it.'

'Even better,' said David, 'Let's get rid of it.' And reaching down and picking at the sides with his fingernail, he peeled it off and put it in his pocket.

'You're so darling! I mean daring,' I said and went bright pink in the darkness. Freudian slip or what? Oh gawd. One too many as per . . . 'What if he's been watching us through the window and comes down and tears our heads off?'

'Tough,' said David, pretending to flex his muscles. 'Aye aye! What's going on there?' He pointed, and we saw a dark shape sitting in the shadows on Melanie's downstairs windowsill. Before we'd grasped it was Pouncer, the window opened quietly, and a braceleted hand reached out and helped him into the house. Honestly! I knew he'd absconded to Melanie's but I hadn't realized he'd actually been aided and abetted by the old bat. Charming!

'Melanie!' I said. 'How *dare* she! First she paints my door and now she's stealing my cat! I've half a mind to ring on her doorbell and demand him back!'

David put his arm round me as he guided me up the path. When we got in, Chummy performed his usual Red Indian act of whooping and celebrating, but eventually calmed down and went away to his bed. We stood awkwardly at the bottom of the stairs.

'Are you sure you wouldn't like a hot drink?' I suggested, feeling I sounded like some old nanny. 'Is there anything you need upstairs? Another blanket perhaps? An eyemask if the light gets in through the curtains?'

'Everything's perfect,' he said. 'Or perhaps, come to think of it, there is just one more thing I'd like . . .'

And much to my surprise he put his arms around me and gave me a long and lovely kiss full on the lips. 'Just for old times' sake,' he said, drawing away just as I was getting into it. 'Doesn't mean a thing. But mmm! That was nice! You're just as lovely as you ever were, you know, Marie!'

I was left reeling as he turned to go upstairs. He was right. It *was* nice.

'No, it doesn't mean a thing,' I repeated, in a stunned way. 'Not a thing.'

And he gave me a long warm smile and went upstairs to his creaky put-you-up bed.

But surely it *does* mean a thing, doesn't it, I'm thinking now, as I'm writing my diary rather drunkenly in bed? All very confusing. But very nice, all the same. Oh God! What *am* I getting myself into?

Tried to take my mind off everything by scheming how on earth to lure Pouncer back home once Chummy's gone. A bowl of sashimi in the garden? Roast organic chicken stuffed with catnip? Bowls of cream sprinkled with tasty fish-food?

Arrows leading from the wall of Melanie's house to his cat-flap, which I would smear with liver pâté?

Even later

Marion's Facebook page: 'When life gives you lemons, make lemonade!'
   Christ.

DECEMBER

December 1

Very embarrassing waiting for David at breakfast this morning. Luckily, as I was putting the kettle on, he came downstairs, put his arm round me and gave me a squeeze, saying, 'Sorry. I got rather carried away last night. Jolly nice, I must say, but not what I intended. Oh, God, I mean I meant it but, oh crikey, what *do* I mean? You know what I mean . . .'

I smiled, turned, gave him an affectionate peck on the cheek and somehow it was all carried off without a hitch. He went off pretty soon after breakfast and promised to ring soon, and in a way I was quite relieved to see him go. I've felt pretty flustered all day. It was so strange! He smelt just the same, and kissed just the same and for quite a few moments in the morning I was transported back to those happy days when we were first married. There were occasions since when I'd been so preoccupied with anger about the whole wretched separation that I'd completely forgotten the good bits – and there were some wonderful times. Best of all, lots of laughs.

But as for him saying, 'You know what I mean,' I really don't know *what* he means.

Anyway, I was brought down to earth by turning on my computer to find that Penny has posted a picture of a roller-skating dog with the words 'Isn't this S-W-E-E-E-T!' underneath it. I can't imagine old Chummy getting his skates on. Sylvie's coming up next week to have a look at him and I do hope she wants to take him because by then I'll have become a mixture of dependent on the old wretch, getting really fond of him and being driven completely up the wall by him. Though I know Pouncer will be glad to see the back of him. I fear my lovely cat is seriously considering moving next door for good.

December 2

Woke up feeling unutterably gloomy. As always, I tried to analyse why and wondered if it was because David had kissed me and then said he didn't really mean it – or because, as I suspected, he *had* really meant it. And now he'd gone. Then I thought the gloom might be down to the weather. It does nothing but rain and drizzle and then, when it's finished raining and drizzling, it starts to rain and drizzle again.

When Penny rang to have a post-mortem about Marion's party, she said I sounded down, and I said she was spot on but I couldn't understand it.

'Of course, by rights, we ought to feel down all the time,' she said, 'considering we're single women of a certain age.'

'Quite the reverse!' I said. 'Can you imagine how ghastly it would be to be a *married* woman of a certain age? No hope, with some frightful old partner getting deaf and forgetful and eventually losing his mind . . .'

'. . . losing his looks and getting a paunch . . .'

'. . . drinking too much and still thinking he's one hell of a hit with what I imagine he still considers "the birds" . . .'

'. . . and wearing an apron with the words *The Man, the Myth and the Legend* on it,' said Penny.

'Wasn't that the utter limit?' I said. 'How can Marion bear it? Sweet as he is. No, as for the gloom, I don't know what it is. I just woke with one of those pits of horror in my heart. Baffling.'

There was a pause.

'Didn't your mother – or was it your father – die round about this time of year?' said Penny after a moment. 'I'm sure you felt a bit gloomy last year around this time. Could that be it? They say anniversary deaths keep coming back.'

'What date is it?' I asked. And it turned out that, blow me, today is the very day my dear old dad died, so no wonder I'm feeling low. So weird the way one's body remembers things that one's mind doesn't. Quite creepy actually. Oddly, the moment I knew it, I started feeling better.

Later

During my afternoon nap, I had a very sexy dream about

Graham. Terribly embarrassing. Wondering how on earth I can face him on the stairs.

Read a couple of chapters of a much-acclaimed book by some new young writer called Barnaby Maxim. Marion had thrust it on me at the party, saying she knew I'd love it. It's a science fiction saga but set in the American War of Independence. Gawd. On the back, there's a creepy photograph of the said Barnaby, with curly hair, thinking he's incredibly handsome. Unfortunately, he can't write for toffee. The blurb said that he 'divides his time between Umbria and Norfolk'. I wonder how you divide your time. Does Barnaby M have anything else to do with his time, except, I wonder, to divide it?

Went back to *Phineas Finn*, by Trollope, which I've been dipping into over the last month. What a dreadful time women had in those days, being owned by their husbands, who could take all their money and even force them to return to the marriage if they ran away from any amount of violence and brutality. Odd how very close we are to that time – it was only about 150 years ago. Although I'm by no means a feminist and never have been – I believe in equal rights, pure and simple – I still feel some of that ancient men-mighty-and-clever and women-feeble-and-silly culture clings to me. And that if a man is boring me stiff, I have to listen and nod. And if he wants a cup of tea, I have to make it. I don't believe it rationally, obviously. It's just that I find myself doing these things without even thinking about it. I suppose it's all ingrained through the generations. Thank goodness I didn't have a daughter, because when she was small I might have ingrained a bit of it in her.

Happily, Jack is a completely new man, who used to change the nappies and rock Gene to sleep, and has no problem with doing the weekly shop at Sainsbury's.

December 3

Before I went to sleep I heard a frightful buzzing in my room, but I knew I hadn't left any electrical appliances on. It came and went, and I wondered if it was on Melanie's side of the wall.

Hoping her washing machine hadn't got a 'short', whatever that is, and was about to explode, I nodded off. But this morning I could still hear the buzzing, so after breakfast I looked more thoroughly and found the source was a poor little bee, which had got stuck between the panes of the double-glazing in the bedroom window.

As mine is DIY double-glazing, it should technically be possible to lift the inside frame of glass, but it takes a man with thumbs of steel and muscles of iron to heave it up. The sort of man who can flush loos with buttons in the wall with his little finger. However, with the aid of a couple of screwdrivers and using all my strength, I managed to open the pane about a centimetre. By this time the bee, who was clearly not the brightest bee in the hive, had crawled up to the middle sash and was batting about there, despite the escape route below.

The idea of it spending its last hours beating its fragile wings against two panes of glass tormented me. But in the end I left it, hoping it would crawl down again at some point. Must stop anthropomorphizing. I kept imagining it like a hostage kept by Somali pirates in some dreadful cave, away from its family, full of anguish and misery and spiritual angst.

Later

So much for letting Nature take its course. I checked on the bee's progress every half-hour – to think this is how I spend my day, rescuing bees! – and after lunch discovered that it had fallen to the bottom, no doubt exhausted. However, on being prodded with a screwdriver, it set up a frightful buzzing, sparked back into life and somehow managed to fly into the room. Then of course I imagined that, in its final throes of agony, it would turn on its rescuer and sting me to death. My next move was to trudge down to the kitchen to find a glass, root about for a piece of card and do the old glass-and-card trick, which took another quarter of an hour. And by the time I'd caught it and put it out into the garden, I was worrying whether it would be so shocked by the cold that it would die anyway.

Whatever, I have to say that, as it flew away into the crisp air, I finally felt released from the torment of my ludicrous thoughts.

December 4

Had the unpleasant experience of falling asleep in my bath this morning. Woke to find the luke-warm water lapping around my lump and, for a moment, imagined I'd been swept away by a Thames tsunami. I quickly came to my senses but only just managed to get out and dressed in time to greet Sylvie, who'd come up by train and now wanted to take a look at Chummy.

It was a beastly day – leaves swirling and rain lashing down – and she almost fell through the door, in a flurry of umbrella, drips and stamping of feet. After she'd taken off her coat and given her hair a shake, she said, 'Oh look!' as she spotted Archie's old fishing hat, hanging up in the hall to deter burglars. (Not sure whether the prospect of being faced with an ancient fisherman would really deter the Romanian gangs that the *Daily Rant* assures me are soon to invade our homes, but still.) 'Dad's hat! Oh, isn't that lovely that you've kept it on display!'

'And I still sleep in those sheets of his that you gave me,' I said.

Sylvie was looking really pretty, and just hearing her voice and seeing her after so long reminded me of dear old Archie – his expressions, his gestures. Obviously, since Archie's death I've popped down to their place in Devon now and again, and we've had the odd lunch in London, but naturally we've drifted apart. You can't, sadly, keep every friend you make or they start weighing you down, like old barnacles on a ship. But there's always a real loving connection between Sylvie and me, however long we've been apart.

Luckily, there also seemed to be an instant loving connection between her and Chummy. I didn't like to point out that he's a sucker for anyone who comes into my house, since he clearly feels it's a haven of friends and allies, but I have to say that – even by his standards – the doggy charm was completely over-the-top. Maximum slobbering. Maximum staring at her in silent awe as if she were a goddess. And when not in awe-struck silence, barks of utmost delight at her presence, tail thundering on the carpet like a tom-tom, plus an occasional charming leap into the air with what seemed like pure joy. I felt that, if she didn't fall for him, then nobody could fall for him. But she fell.

'He's absolutely *gorgeous*!' she said, giving him an affectionate pat on the back. Then she leant her head over his and started muttering doggy things in his ear about 'Good boy, beautiful boy'. Pouncer sat in a far corner radiating catty contempt, but even his chilly disdain couldn't dull the love affair that was blooming in front of my eyes.

'But how can you bear to part with him?' she said, kneading Chummy's neck with one hand and trying to drink her coffee with the other.

I lied through my teeth and said it was hard, but I knew he needed country air and lots of love and that I just didn't have time – the usual guff.

As she'd said before, she couldn't take him straight away, but would come up next week with her car. When she got up to go, Chummy, just to perfect the act, dutifully started whining and almost blocked her passage to the door. Sylvie was in tears when she left, as indeed was I. Or nearly.

Phew! I gave Chummy a dog-chew as a reward for his sterling efforts. In fact, I was so relieved that I was tempted to bury my head in his neck while muttering, 'Good boy, beautiful boy!' but I didn't go that far. As far as I'm concerned all dogs, however often their owners brush their teeth, have powerful doggy breath, and I have to hold mine whenever I get too close to Chummy's mouth.

December 5

Woke up to find a complete winter wonderland outside the window – snow had fallen during the night, and there was that eerie stillness about London that makes me wonder if everyone hasn't been captured by aliens except for me. Went out into the garden to fill up the birds' nut cage and noticed the lovely sight of dozens of spiky triangles pressed into the snow, the footprints of sparrows who'd been pecking, rather hopelessly I should imagine, for frozen worms. No paw prints from Pouncer, sadly. I bet Melanie has simply abducted him.

Because I had shopping to do, I drove off incredibly carefully to the Waitrose in Marylebone and, after I'd parked, tiptoed gingerly across the road, in case I slipped. I managed to get back to the car with three bags of shopping, but I'd noticed on the way that there was a farmer's market in a square round the corner. So I dumped all the shopping in the car and again, keeping close to the wall in case I fell and hanging on to every railing in sight, I edged along the street to the market, picked my way through the stalls and managed to buy a few organic bits of nonsense without so much as a wobble.

Felt very pleased with myself when I parked outside my

house but, bearing in mind the icy front path, I took extra special care walking, laden with shopping, to the front door. I finally got inside, strode confidently into the kitchen, breathed a sigh of relief and was about to sit down when Chummy leapt up at me, slavering with joy, and began thrusting his great head between my legs, his huge tail swinging from side to side. For a moment I kept my balance and then I tottered, slithered, fell and sprawled on the floor with my hips twisted, my ankles skewed, my shoulders at an angle and shopping everywhere.

I struggled to get up, cursing poor Chummy who, of course, thought it was a huge game. Seizing a packet of fennel in his jaws he rushed off with it triumphantly, returning occasionally to taunt me with it and then, when I reached for it, rushing off again. Dogs! Gawd!

Now feel absolutely frightful and am covered with bruises. Just hope I haven't got a black eye as I hit the corner of a chair with my face when I went down. What a life.

December 6

No black eye so far, thank God. I can imagine the meal old Melanie would make of that. 'Oh, so you slipped on the kitchen floor, did you?' she would say, with one of those thought bubbles appearing above her head containing the words 'A LIKELY STORY!'

But certainly feeling a bit achey and wobbly.

December 7

Another visit from Zac. Graham agreed it was safe to have Chummy on the premises when Zac came, so long as I was sure to lock him in the garden when Zac was in the house and lock him in the house when we were in the garden. Not that we're likely to go out in this weather. The problem is that I have absolutely no idea how Chummy behaves with kids. He might have been brutally teased by small children with pea-shooters and catapults when he was a puppy and ever since been biding his time, patiently waiting for the moment he can get his own back.

I've noticed that now, if Graham says anything to Zac, he will at least look up, though he still refuses to respond to his father except with insults and grumbles. I'm starting to wonder if this was such a good idea after all. Maybe Graham's right, and these visits are just re-traumatizing the poor boy.

Today Zac sat on the floor with some of Gene's toys and built an airport. Rather an odd airport, full of plastic dinosaurs, but he assured us it really was an airport. And when Graham added anything to it, I was glad to see Zac didn't sweep it away instantly, but somehow incorporated it into his play. I sat by, pretending to chop vegetables, feeling dreadfully self-conscious like one of those psychologists I used to read of the Sixties who did play-therapy with children. The only problem is that I'm *not* a psychologist, and it's no use pretending I am. What I'm doing is organizing a family situation with no idea of how I should guide it, and just hoping it comes out right. I realize it's all rather dangerous and that I'm actually being quite irresponsible. Just because I feel in my gut that this is right, doesn't mean it is.

After a lot of Zac bringing in aeroplanes with a whooshing noise and having them take off, and baggage smashing into other baggage, and planes crashing, he suddenly stopped. He looked up at Graham. 'Can you hear that?' he said.

'No,' said Graham. We all listened. Then Zac started making a big groaning noise which got louder and louder. 'It's a big storm!' he said. 'And it's coming to blow up the airport and it's coming and it's going to *kill* you . . .' and here he picked up a cushion and threw it at Graham saying, 'It's killed you! You're dead!' Graham dutifully slumped in his chair for a few minutes until Zac started to reassemble the airport.

'That was good,' he said, half to himself. 'Let's do it again.'

Graham looked at me helplessly while I made nodding motions and thumbs-up signs. Another storm came, and this time Zac pelted Graham with more cushions, and even got angry when Graham came back to life again rather too quickly. 'You're DEAD!' he shouted. 'You're DEAD!'

I made a pot of tea and gave Zac some Ribena and a biscuit and he seemed very happy to reassemble the airport again. 'This time,' he said to Graham furiously, 'the storm is *really* going to kill you! And you!' he said, viciously, turning to me.

So we had to go through the whole scenario again, and each time Zac got angrier and angrier.

Fortunately, before we could go through a fourth killer-storm, the bell rang and it was Julie.

'Come in,' I said. 'Zac is just playing. You're early.'

She came in, taking her shoes off at the door. I didn't have the heart to tell her it's a shoes-on residence. This was the first time she'd come right into the house, and she perched nervously on the arm of a chair and watched. I gave her a cup of tea, Graham looked distinctly uncomfortable and Zac stared at her.

'I've been killing Daddy,' he said, angrily. But he didn't repeat the performance, and we grown-ups managed to make polite conversation about the weather. I even told them about the bee, in an attempt to get them to focus on something outside of the terrible triangle that was their relationship – and was later surprised to find Zac had been listening intently.

'You're a very kind person,' he said, suddenly, as he lined up the aeroplanes inside their hangars. 'That bee was a very lucky bee.'

Everyone agreed that I was a very kind person, and soon Julie said, 'Well, time for your tea, Mister Zac,' and I accompanied them to the door.

'I enjoyed that,' said Zac, surprisingly, with his serious face on.

'Well, so did I!' I said, lying through my teeth.

'Say goodbye to Daddy,' said his mother.

'Daddy's dead,' said Zac. And off they went.

I poured Graham and myself two huge glasses of wine. We both downed them in one and I refilled our glasses.

'God,' said Graham. 'I *feel* as if I've *really* been killed. Several times over!'

'That's what you're meant to feel,' I said, assuming my cod-psychologist role. 'It's all good stuff. He's expressing his anger.' I felt like a prat. I also felt emotionally drained, just witnessing the intensity of the last hour or so.

'I really don't think we ought to meet again,' said Graham. 'It can't be good for him.'

'Well, I think the complete opposite,' I said firmly. 'I think you ought to ring him up in an hour or so, when he's home, and send him lots of love.'

'Why? He's just said he hates me and wants me dead.'

'I know, but I think it would show that you don't hold any grudges,' I said.

'Oh dear. Do I have to?' said Graham. Then he looked at my determined face. 'All right, if you say so.'

And I was glad I'd suggested it, because when Graham rang he had a chance to talk to his wife, who told him that Zac had been much more himself on the way back in the car. He'd chatted and laughed, apparently, and had even asked to build a snowman with his mum.

She'd persuaded Zac to have a word and Graham had said his stuff and Zac had said nothing except that they were going to build a snowman and call it 'Daddy' and he was going to throw snowballs at it until it fell down.

'Jolly good!' Graham had managed to choke out. 'Hope you don't give him a carrot as a nose. I wouldn't like a carrot as a nose.' Which had apparently elicited a very grudging laugh. And a giggled 'Well, your nose *is* like a carrot, poo-face!'

'He called me "poo-face"!' said Graham, as he put the

phone down. He looked shocked. 'First he wants me dead, then he says my nose looks like a carrot and now he calls me "poo-face"!'

I couldn't help breaking out laughing. 'That's very good!' I said. 'He's made a joke! And he's calling this snowman "Daddy"! I know I'm clutching at straws here, but it's better that he at least acknowledges your existence.'

'Or non-existence,' said Graham gloomily, as he went upstairs.

Later that evening, the strong smell of dope wafted down the stairs. Poor old Graham.

December 11

Just managed to send off all my Christmas cards – I'd made a woodcut and had great fun stamping it out. It was of a large robin on a branch and I was rather pleased with it. After I'd finished a hundred, and painted in a hundred red breasts and glued a hundred little silver circles on as robins' eyes, they looked utterly charming. And I have written, on each one, 'Happy Christmas', in defiance of all those people who insist on saying 'Happy Holidays'. The school, for instance. They had what they called a Winter Festival this year, featuring a dreary musical which was far too long and, though it included Jack Frost, made no reference either to Father Christmas or the crib in a manger (in order, I presume, to pacify all those of Other Faiths). I was forced, reluctantly, to get the class making 'Happy Holidays' cards. No turkeys or Santa Clauses allowed, no stars over Bethlehem and no Christmas trees. We ended up with rather dismal snowmen onto which we glued bits of cotton wool. I broke up some charcoal for the eyes, and each one had a bit of wool round its neck as a scarf.

I have to say the change in Zac has certainly been evident. I even found him larking about in the playground with one of the other children today. He's got more colour in his cheeks and he's put on a bit of weight. He looks more like a child, actually, and less like some poor maltreated chimney-sweep from Dickens. This afternoon he came up to me, slipped his hand in mine, and then rubbed his cheek against the back of my hand. I was so touched I didn't know quite what to say. I gave his hand a sympathetic squeeze and then he mooched back to see his friend.

December 13

Every day I get more cards, and keep remembering people I've forgotten to send them to. At this rate, I'll have to rustle up another batch. And if only next week would arrive and Sylvie would come and get Chummy! I'm fed up with walking him round the block. All these dog-lovers keep coming up to me and starting conversations and I haven't got time to chat – and anyway, I don't speak dog-language. They keep asking if he's a 'cross' and I say deliberately obtuse things like, 'I hope not, he seems very placid to me,' and we don't get anywhere.

And today I got the first of those embarrassing Christmas letters.

'Bob has scored a real hit with the vicar this year! In his role as bursar – a job he's been doing now for the last five years – he has sometimes to check on the fabric of the church and this year he discovered the old door was nearly coming off its hinges! Heaven knows what would have happened if he hadn't seen it! It might have crushed one of our congregation, or it could have collapsed in the night, leaving the door open for who knows what passing villain to spot the "easy pickings". Imagine if someone had stolen the church plate! God has blessed us in other ways, too – Vanessa got a 2.1 at uni. Of course we'd had high hopes for a first, but her tutor said she'd worked hard. We went in the summer to glorious Glyndebourne in deepest Sussex – and I wore an old dress I found that I could fit into again. (One of the few advantages of having had cancer!) We listened to the divine *Così fan Tutte* and were transported by the marvellous Mozart. It really took us out of ourselves and made us forget about the problems with Gerald. (Though thanks be to God, he is much better since coming out of rehab and we have "high hopes" for him in the future.) We mourned the passing of Tiddles, our faithful goldfish who has been with us for the last two years. Godfrey suspected Buster, but "Big" Buster rarely deigns to pay us "mere mortals" a visit and prefers his perch on the curtain rail these days!' I had absolutely no idea who these appalling people were. I looked at the envelope to see if there were any clues and discovered it was addressed to Melanie. (A closet Christian?) I Sellotaped it up and bunged it next door.

Perhaps I should write a Christmas letter myself. 'Dear all, I have discovered I have a strange lump on my tummy this year and have spent nearly every day sick with worry that it might be cancer. Happy Christmas! Love from Marie x'

December 14

Zac came over again, sulky and angry, but at least he came over.

'I think the only reason he comes,' said Graham earlier, when he was downstairs borrowing the iron, 'is because he just wants to kill me again. And again. And again.'

Anyway, round he came. I'd locked poor Chummy in the garden again because, even though it was cold, I thought he must be used to a couple of hours feeling nippy after his horrible treatment by the ghastly woman across the road. And this time Graham, completely off his own bat, because I would never have suggested it so early on, suddenly said to his son, 'What if I come over to see you next time? Would you like that? I could take you out somewhere – we could go to the aquarium – or maybe we could do the London Eye? It would be fun to see London from the air in the snow!'

Zac gave him one of his cold fishy stares. He paused in the marble-run – like a Cresta Run, for marbles – that he was constructing. It had been going wrong and he refused all offers of advice about how to make it work.

'I'm here to see Mrs Sharp, not you,' he said with icy cruelty. 'We don't want you round at our house.'

Even I felt a pang of misery when he said this. I could hardly bear it. Graham, looking white-faced, got up from his chair and came over to the other side of the room, turning to the wall to hide what I could see were his tears.

'Zac!' I said. I couldn't help it. 'That really wasn't nice! You know your daddy loves you and wants to see you!'

Zac rose to his feet and gave me one of his space-boy looks. He was trembling. Like his father, he was about to cry himself. He opened the door to the garden and walked out – and at that very moment Chummy, who'd been barking dismally outside, and had clearly been waiting for the door to open, rushed inside, almost knocking Zac over in his effort to get back into the house.

At which Zac screamed and, bursting into tears, rushed over to his father who was rushing towards him.

'Daddy! Daddy!' he cried, terrified. And he buried his head in his father's shoulder and clung to him, sobbing his heart out.

Graham by now was weeping openly, and I could hardly see to get Chummy under control because I was welling up too.

As for Chummy, in that idiotic way that dogs have, he was happily wagging his tail and shoving his way up to Zac, trying to ingratiate himself by pushing his nose between the boy's legs. Graham carried Zac to the chair, muttering to him as they sat down. 'Don't worry, mate,' he kept saying. 'It's all right. Daddy's here . . . The nasty dog won't hurt you. Nothing's going to hurt you . . .'

Meanwhile, my legs trembling, I tried to inject some normality into the situation.

'What a nasty fright!' I said, in a business-like way that reminded me of my own grandmother. (She always seemed to have great presence of mind in an emergency.) 'Now, let me make you some Ribena, and we'll put Chummy outside again. Naughty Chummy,' I said half-heartedly, as I pulled the poor beast back into the snowy garden – though privately I wanted to give him a prize for his incredibly timely intervention in the whole scene.

Zac was still beside himself. I suppose he wasn't crying for more than about ten minutes but it seemed as if it went on for about an hour. Now I look back on it, I imagine he was pouring out all the unhappiness he'd felt when his father had left home.

And then we all sat around shiftily, not quite knowing what to do next.

Luckily, Graham took the initiative. While Zac was drying his tears, he said, 'Now, this marble-run. I'll tell you where I think you've gone wrong, mate, if you don't mind my interfering . . . you've got this arm going upwards when, if we turn it round, it'll be going downwards . . .'

For the next half hour or so they both played happily and I went upstairs, feeling in need of a good lie-down. When I came back, we all had tea, Graham toasted some crumpets,

Zac and he then discussed whether they were toasted enough, and Zac buttered them.

We ate them and declared them perfect. For a while we were the ideal little family and I was reminded of those occasions when David, Jack and I would sit round a tea table in total harmony.

Eventually the bell went and it was Julie.

'Things are going much better,' I whispered, as I opened the door. 'They're finally playing together.' (I rather hoped Zac wouldn't tell her about being nearly savaged by a wild Alsatian.) And when she came in, I could see her face relax with pleasure as she saw Graham and Zac engaged in their game.

'Look at this, Mum!' said Zac, showing her the marble-run. 'It's brilliant! I did this bit and Dad this bit . . .'

When he was finally persuaded into his coat and out into the corridor, Zac looked up at his mother. 'Dad wants to take me on the London Eye,' he said. 'Can I go?'

'Well, if Graham's sure,' said his mother, hiding her astonishment as well as she could.

'Of course, mate,' said Graham. 'I'd like nothing better. We'll have a great time, just you and I.'

'Just you and I,' said Zac. 'And we won't take Mrs Sharp, will we?'

'No, we won't take Mrs Sharp,' said Graham, smiling slightly. 'Unless she very much wants to come, of course.'

'No, no – I've been up it. I don't want to go again!' I said hastily.

And I left them to say their goodbyes.

Crikey. Not only am I all-in, but I am suffused by a rather despicable feeling of such joy and self-satisfaction I can hardly bear it. Thank God it's all worked out. Or, as my father would have said, more cautiously, so far so good.

Later

Graham came down with a bottle of champagne. He gave me a big hug and said he couldn't believe Zac had actually agreed to go out with him on his own.

'I feel like a young man who has rung up a girl and she's agreed to a first date!' he said. 'I never imagined it could work out like this. Isn't he a great little chap?'

I agreed that he was, indeed, a great little chap.

'And even Julie seemed warmer this time, didn't you think? She actually looked me in the eyes for once. And smiled.'

'Perhaps she feels she's punished you enough for that stupid one-night stand.'

'Don't remind me,' said Graham, wincing. 'Next time, even if it's Jennifer Aniston herself on bended knees begging me, I'm not going to touch her.'

'What do you mean, next time?' I said.

December 15

Went to Waitrose in Marylebone this morning. Wandered about a bit, got a trolley full of stuff and was halfway through checking out when I discovered I'd somehow acquired the wrong trolley during my shop! I'd done my shopping, left my trolley to get something at the cheese counter and then turned back to it and had obviously grabbed someone else's. What was so awful was that all the other person's stuff had been carefully measured from the meat and fish and deli counters. The staff were very nice about it – I suppose they're trained to be – but I felt such a wally.

Later

A call from Sylvie saying she'll pick up Chummy tomorrow. Thank God.

Even later

Suddenly thought: perhaps it was the other shopper who was the Waitrose wally? Perhaps she pinched my trolley first. Why is it that one always thinks it's one's own fault and not the other person's?

Jack rang to make arrangements for Christmas. Brilliant news – they're coming here this year, which means I'll have to get out the ladders and start bunging up the Christmas decorations. Although Penny's going to her daughter's, James is booked in too, and when I rang him, he said he'd be happy to help.

'But what about Mel?' he said.

'I'm sorry, but I just can't face having her round,' I said firmly. 'Year after year I've martyred myself and had horrible people round for Christmas and it's always ruined it, and I'm not doing it again. I've had it.'

'She's not that bad,' he said.

'She's one of those people who always manages to get a

dig in. There's always a little remark she makes that upsets me. No, she can jolly well go to her other friends this year or dump herself on her children. I know that somewhere in her she's got a warm heart but she leaves me cold.'

Later still

Naturally enough, as I gave Chummy his last meal and looked into his wretchedly mournful eyes, I had a dreadful moment of wishing he wasn't going. Now Pouncer's left home, there's only Graham in the house, and I feel a bit lonely.

I gathered up Chummy's lead and the remains of his dog biscuits and tins to put in a bag for Sylvie. Chummy, dogs being what they are, seemed to know what was going on because he whined and came up to me as I was sitting down and put his ridiculously big head in my lap and stared up at me doing that plaintive gawping look that dogs do so well. Just hope he doesn't think he's going back to the ghastly woman across the road. I feel like a murderer, even though I know that actually Chummy will be far happier in the country with Sylvie than in London with resentful old me who doesn't really like dogs anyway.

When the bell rang, Chummy gave a final whimper and slunk back into his corner of the kitchen. But I have to say he perked up when he saw Sylvie. I bet he could smell the scent of the hills and the grass and the wide open spaces that lingered around her.

'Here I am at last, old boy!' she said cheerfully, barely acknowledging me. 'We're looking forward to having you!'

As she said this she snuck him one of those revolting bits of transparent pongy artificial dog 'bones' and he cheered up at once. Never know what they're made of. Reconstituted cartilage? Melted-down horses' hooves? Yuk.

Later, she asked me down for Christmas which was kind of her. Of course I had to refuse, but was so touched to be asked.

'You must come and stay soon,' she said. 'You know you'll always be part of the family, and now we're having Chummy there's even more reason for coming – to see him as well as us!'

We finished our cup of tea and as she got up I felt a lump in my throat.

'I'll be so sorry to lose him,' I said. 'I've grown quite fond of the old thing.'

Later
After I'd thrown away anything Chummy-related that was left behind, I burst into tears. Too much had been happening. I felt I didn't know who I was any more. Everything – Pouncer disappearing, the mysterious lump, Zac's unhappiness, David's kiss – it just overwhelmed me. But then the phone rang and it was James, who came over right away and sat down and gave me a cuddle, and slowly everything seemed to get back to normal. We cracked open a bottle of wine and he told me I was his bestest friend and how, if the lump was truly a worry, they'd have done something about it months ago, and Chummy would be so happy, and I was a marvel, and I could always get another cat, and as for David's kiss . . .

'Well, I have to say,' he said, pouring me another glass, 'that *is* a bit strange.'

December 16

When I woke up this morning I didn't miss Chummy a bit. Sylvie rang to say he was in his element in Devon, that he'd spent the day leaping about the lawn and running for balls and sticks, had curled up in his basket by the Aga at night, and clearly felt completely at home. Harry and he had got on like a house on fire, and Chummy followed him around as if he were his guru – which is just the sort of thing Harry enjoys. If there's one thing about dogs I really don't like, it's their complete dependence on human beings. They always seem to me like wet lovers, who spend their time at your door with wilting bunches of flowers and drippy bits of poetry, trying to spend every waking minute with you. Sometimes, I wish that, like cats, they'd occasionally put on their hats and coats (as it were) and buzz off on special and mysterious assignments. But Harry's quite happy with a grovelling follower, so that's great.

The snow's starting to melt and turn into slush. Curiously warm today, for December, and it's almost like spring. Poor old plants. They're probably feeling a bit like I did yesterday. Confused.

Spotting Pouncer on the wall between my garden and Melanie's, I went up to him and gave him a thorough stroking. I managed to pick him up and bring him inside, to show him the delicious bits of chicken breast I'd been keeping for him.

Looking round warily, he started to eat, though between each mouthful the poor boy kept an eye out for any sign of large dogs.

Afterwards he checked through the whole house, rather like Hercule Poirot searching for clues. But I'm afraid after an hour I heard the cat-flap click and, looking out of the window, spotted him returning to Melanie's garden.

December 17

School's breaking up tomorrow, and it's all a bit sad. The Head has said she'd give anything to take me on as a permanent part-timer, but her budget won't allow it. And though it would be great if I could come and run the odd special art day next term, Angela is now well enough to get back on the case and 'do things her way'.

To be honest, I can't say I'm heartbroken. I've enjoyed my time at the school so much, but I wouldn't mind a bit of a break. It was a long way to travel, south of the river, and it was pretty hard work. I've had a great time, though, and the Head actually asked if I'd go and have dinner with her and her husband one day, which is a huge compliment.

After my chat with the Head, I got back to find Graham gearing himself up for the great London Eye trip. (He's collecting Zac from school tomorrow.) 'I'm looking forward to it so much, I feel like a child again myself,' he said, sweetly. 'And Julie's asked me to stay for a drink when I take Zac back.'

'Do you think there's any hope you might get back together?'

'I don't know. I hope so,' said Graham. 'I did manage to have a long conversation on the phone with her the other evening and she's finally got it into her head that I wasn't having an affair with that woman and it was all some stupid drunken mistake. She's still upset, but I could tell she was starting to feel she might have over-reacted.'

'I so hope things work out for you, darling,' I said, taking both his hands in mine. 'I've grown so fond of you. I'm torn between longing for you to be happy with your wife and longing for you to stay here with me as my lodger for ever and ever. But I know that's not possible'

Graham gave me a hug. 'I don't know what I'd have done without being here,' he said. 'It's been like Shangri-La. A haven of peace.'

Funny so many lodgers say that about this house. To them, it's like some kind of luxury spa hotel. Mysterious.

December 18

Last night I was woken at three in the morning by the phone. I was certain it was going to be Sonny ringing again from India, trying to persuade me that my computer had got another virus, but it was Chrissie.

'Marie . . . I just had to ring you,' she said. 'Jack was taken terribly ill in the night, he's in hospital and he's having an emergency operation to take his appendix out. I didn't want to worry you earlier, but they say it's going to be fine, and I'm so relieved he's finally getting this sorted out. I knew this would happen. I kept telling him but he wouldn't listen.'

'Are you sure he'll be all right?' I said, with a catch in my voice. I fumbled for the light. 'Are you sure they've got him in time?'

'Yes, don't worry. It's all going to be fine, and he'll be out in a couple of days. But what an idiot he is,' she said, her voice a mixture of love, irritation, anxiety and relief (rather an odd mix but I knew exactly how she felt). 'It's been so stressful, Marie,' she added. 'I've wanted to talk to you about this for ages, but Jack made me promise to say nothing because he was certain he was okay and he didn't want to make you anxious. We've had such arguments about it. Thank God it's all over now.' And she started to cry. 'When I heard about your lump I wanted to ring you but I knew that, if I did, I'd start talking about Jack. I hope you didn't think that I didn't care. Oh, it's been such a nightmare. Honestly, men are so weird, aren't they? I know he's your son, but . . .'

When I put down the phone I felt as if a great weight had been lifted from me. I clearly hadn't realized how concerned I'd been about Jack, being selfishly worried sick about my own stupid lump. I felt as if every muscle in my body had been released from some twisted-up position, as if I was flooded with happiness chemicals. It was like taking Ecstasy, I imagine. I was incredibly calm and relaxed, and fell into a deep, dreamless sleep.

Later

Last day of school, which broke up at lunchtime. I'd brought in loads of balloons and the idea was to draw faces on them with felt-tipped pens and glue on decorations, so there was a great deal of popping and releasing them round the room like rockets. It was all a bit chaotic but huge fun.

The only person who refused to join in was Zac. For a moment I thought he'd crawled back in his shell again, but he was doing a picture. It involved lots and lots of tiny circles, each one drawn meticulously. When I checked later, it appeared to be some kind of dish on a plate, placed in the middle of a table. Sitting round it were three figures.

'What's this, Zac?' I said, sitting down beside him, trying to avoid the whizzing balloons.

'It's Dad's special risotto,' said Zac. 'That's my dad, that's my mum and that's me, and this is the special risotto he's going to cook for us tonight. He's coming to tea at home!' he added turning to me, joyfully. 'And he says he's got a special risotto with a special ingredient in it. Can you see it? It's here . . .' As I craned my head down to inspect a tiny speck of red, Zac suddenly put his head close to mine and gave me a very quick peck on the cheek. I could feel his soft little lips on my skin, and was touched and surprised. Then he turned back to the picture. Neither of us said anything. 'I know it's going to be yummy!' he said, getting back to drawing more rice. 'Dad said so.'

On my way back from school, I popped in to see Jack at the hospital. He was looking a little embarrassed. The operation went very well, apparently, and he even said he was relieved to get rid of the appendix at last.

'And it wasn't as bad as you thought, was it?'

'Not bad at all, Mum,' he said. 'I didn't even know it was happening. They just gave me a shot and then I woke up and it was all over. I don't know what I was worried about. I should have listened to you and Chrissie. Anyway, I won't be so silly in future.'

December 19

'The appendix: is it a vital organ after all?' (*Daily Rant*)

Later

It's one o'clock in the morning and Graham's still not back. Probably should double-lock the front door. I imagine that his risotto has gone down pretty well with everyone . . . I hope so anyway. But it does feel lonely here, just me by myself in the house, with no lodger, no Chummy, no Pouncer. When I was young, I had a book called *The Little House That Creaked*. In it, a woodcutter brought everything he could think of back to the house to stop it creaking – first a wife, then a cooker, then a fire – but nothing would stop the place from creaking. Finally he discovered two little children in the forest and it was only when he brought them home to give to his wife that the Little House became a Little House That Creaked No More.

Suddenly, David came into my mind and for some reason I felt terribly tearful. I've got to face it. I do rather miss him.

Appointment with Ben tomorrow. They have the results from America. Oh dear. I really do feel worried sick. And frightened, too. I must concentrate on Christmas. At least the family is coming over here for a change – so for one night, at least, the house won't creak.

December 20

Leaving for the hospital this morning, I met a rather sheepish Graham coming up the stairs, back to change his clothes.

'I think I'll be moving out and going back home,' he said, with a funny look. 'Julie's asked me to move back in before Christmas. Which is fine by me. I can't tell you how happy I am, or what a nightmare it's been.'

I couldn't talk more because I had to dash off, but my mind was whirring by the time I got to see Ben.

He shook his head as he looked through my notes.

'I'm afraid there's still no conclusive verdict, Mrs S,' he said. 'You've managed to baffle America's finest. So I think we'll just have to monitor it, and get you in every three months to check on how it's going. And you'd better come back if you notice any changes. To be honest, it really does seem to be the GOK I suspected to start with.'

I felt very deflated. I was hoping to have some kind of verdict.

'Anyway,' he said. 'Let's have a little look now, and see where we're at.'

We went through all the him-going-out-of-the-room lark,

with the nurse coming and the curtains and the towel to protect my modesty, and then he returned. He put on his white gloves and gave me a prod. Then he gave me another prod.

He looked a bit puzzled. 'It was on the right side, wasn't it?'

'Yes,' I said.

'Tell me,' he said, 'can you feel it? Can you show me where it is?'

My hand flew to the usual place. But I couldn't feel anything. Push as I might, it all felt perfectly normal and squishy and tummyish to me. Not a lump to be found.

'It couldn't be hiding, could it?' I asked. 'Waiting to leap out at twice its usual size?'

Ben smiled. 'No . . . but this is most odd. There's definitely nothing there. I hope it's not a miraculous recovery. You haven't been to see any weird healers, have you? They do seem to pull off the odd coup, rather irritatingly.'

'No,' I said. (I wondered if David's hand on the area might have played a part, but dismissed it.)

After I'd got dressed, I sat down in front of him again. He shook his head.

'Just to make sure, I think we should make another appointment in three months, to monitor you,' he said. 'Even though I can't see much point.'

'Wouldn't I just be wasting your time?' I asked.

'Not at all. BSTS. Better safe than sorry,' he said. 'Make an appointment on your way out. But in the meantime,' he continued, leaning back in his chair and putting his hands behind his head, 'there's been no change in your lifestyle, has there? I'm just grasping at straws here. Everything all right at home?'

'Yes, absolutely!' I thought. 'The cat seems to have disappeared – do you think it could have been an allergy?'

'Possibly,' said Ben, 'But unlikely. Never seen anything like that before.'

'Otherwise, no, everything's fine. I've recently stopped teaching at this school I worked in part-time,' I said racking my brain for any changes. 'The lodger's going. Jack's just had his appendix out . . .'

As I said this, I saw a slow smile spread across Ben's face. He leaned forward. 'I wonder if that's it!' he said. 'A PPS!'

'What's that?'

'A Psychosomatic Sympathy Symptom. Like a phantom pregnancy. When did you first notice the lump?' He looked back in the notes.

'It was . . . well, actually, now I think of it, it was just after Jack had his first grumbling attack, some time at the beginning of this year,' I said. 'But surely that couldn't be it?'

'The swelling was in just the right place,' said Ben. 'I wouldn't be surprised. Well, fancy that. You'll be reading of this case in my memoirs if I'm right. And I bet I am. What a surprise! This is a medical first – in my career, at least – though I have read of such things in the text books.' He shook his head. 'Still, let's not worry too much about the whys and wherefores. Let's just be glad it appears to have gone. It was lovely to see you again, Mrs S. And I look forward to seeing you next year. But I hope you'll be symptom-free for years to come!'

He got up and gave me an affectionate pat on the shoulder. 'Give my love to Jack,' he said. 'And wish him happy Christmas!'

I felt lightheaded as I walked to the car park. Much more stoned than if I'd smoked a whole joint of Graham's skunk. A kind of euphoria gripped me. I even found myself staring at the sky and thinking how amazing it was. I suddenly noticed all the tops of the buildings and realized that for the last year I've just been looking down. A wonderful feeling. And I couldn't wait to get home and tell everyone. But the odd thing is – it's not that I miss the lump, it's more that I've got so used to it being there and upsetting me, I can't quite believe it's gone. They were so uncertain about what it was, I feel it'll be a couple of months before I'm really completely reassured that it's never coming back. And what can I say it was? I can hardly tell people that it might have been some phantom symptom in tune with Jack. I'd look totally potty. I'll have to say it was a temporary benign tumour. A TBT.

Later

When I phoned them, Penny shouted 'Hooray!', Marion burst into tears, and James rushed round eager for a celebratory drink. Even mad old Melanie, who I told over the wall, clapped her hands saying, 'Well, I put it all down to prayer! I hadn't told you, Mar, but every single night and morning I've prayed for you, and every time I visit a church I light a candle. Talk about evidence for the healing power of faith! You see, you don't even have to believe for it to work!' She pressed her hands together and looked upwards as if in thanks. 'You've been amazing this year, Mar,' she said. 'You've battled cancer *and* you've sorted out the dog! Why don't you come in and let me give you a big drink to celebrate?'

And to my surprise I found myself entering Melanie's house and knocking back some bizarre (and rather evil) drink from South America called Pisco. Well-named, if I may say so. To my surprise, I was so overcome with emotion that I found myself asking the old bat for Christmas.

'How sweet of you!' she cried, 'But next year, perhaps? You see, I'm off to India tomorrow, to stay with my daughter and the family.'

Phew!

So I now find myself back at home, slightly pissed and feeling I've not only done my duty by Melanie but escaped by the skin of my teeth. A 'good ask', as my mother used to say, when she felt obliged to invite an old bore to dinner, and the grateful old bore had to decline, due to a prior engagement.

Even later

Although Jack sounded cool and collected when I rang him in hospital, I knew that really he was tremendously relieved about my disappearing lump. 'I never thought it was anything that bad, Mum,' he said. 'Because I know Ben would have done something if there'd been a real problem. But it's great it's gone. That'll make Christmas even nicer, won't it? Oh, by the way, I was just thinking . . . I know we're coming to you for Christmas, but do you think you could ask Dad, too? Otherwise he's going to be very lonely. I'd completely forgotten that, now Sandra's gone, he'll be on his own.'

Of course I've been thinking about David a lot recently. And secretly, I've been longing to ask him for Christmas, but I've been so frightened of being too forward and Aha-now-Sandra's-gone-let-me-take-you-over-ish, that I haven't dared suggest it. So I was incredibly pleased and relieved when Jack did it first.

'And presumably he can stay with you now, can't he?' I said, 'I imagine the pool table's gone?' I wasn't sure, to be honest, whether I wanted the answer to be yes or no.

'No, it's still here but you don't mind, do you? You've had him to stay before,' said Jack.

So when I've collected my thoughts I'll ring David and ask him to stay for Christmas. I hope he doesn't get any funny ideas. I mean, I do love David, but I'm very confused about everything.

December 21

David of course was lovely about the lump. He's the only one I told about it being a sympathetic reaction to Jack's appendix.

'Jack's appendix!' he said. 'I've been unable to sleep with worry about that some nights, and the other nights I've been unable to sleep with worry about you. These things have such a knock-on effect, don't they? Where did we go wrong with that boy that he's such a coward about hospitals? He doesn't get it from me, that's for sure.'

'Nor me,' I added, hastily. 'Anyway, he's very chastened, and another time I think he'll be haring into hospital the moment he gets a symptom. I guess he was scared it would hurt.'

'Now. Christmas,' said David, changing the subject. 'I'd love to come. What about if I turn up on Christmas Eve and then I can help lay the table and peel the potatoes and maybe put up some decorations? I'm sure you don't feel like going up a ladder on your own these days.'

'Not much,' I said. 'And you can stay in Graham's room, because Graham's moving out.'

'That's interesting!' said David. 'So you'll be looking for someone new, eh?'

Wondered why he said that.

December 25

Just had a roller-coaster last few hours. I'm upstairs typing, while David's downstairs putting up paper-chains before everyone comes for lunch.

David insisted on taking me out to supper last night. He'd booked a table at an old-fashioned Greek place in Queensway where we always used to go for celebrations when we were married. To my delight, Mr Michaelides, the owner, was still there and greeted us warmly. He obviously had no idea we'd ever divorced and we didn't disabuse him. Then, over tiramisu, David became rather sentimental and took my hand.

'You've got such a bond with Jack,' he said. 'Fancy you actually getting symptoms which chimed with his! I almost envy that kind of closeness. Not that I don't feel close to Jack. And to you too, sweetie. I had no idea how much you meant to me until you told me about the lump. I'd been feeling all miserable about Sandra, but when you told me, I realized I was actually much more worried about you than her. Funny, isn't it? Time just can't break connections like ours, can it?'

'No, it can't,' I said, tears pricking my eyes. 'And I'm very lucky that you and I still have such a deep friendship.'

We got back home and, apart from a peck on the cheek and a hug, there was nothing more. And to my complete and utter astonishment, I was actually disappointed. I'd felt so close to David over supper and, after what he'd said, I thought we'd at least have a little cuddle. But just as I was settling into bed, there was a knock on my door.

'Marie, I'm so sorry to disturb you,' said David, peering round the door. 'But I can't work the lights up in Graham's room. Is it the switch at the door or the lamp? Or does the light need a new bulb?'

'Oh, there are three switches that can control that lamp,' I said. 'I'll sort it – don't worry.' I went upstairs to Graham's room (which he's left very neat and tidy, I must say) and stood by the door in my nightie, flicking the wall-switch up and down while David played with those on the lamp and the flex, and we finally got the light working.

Just as I was turning to go, David patted a spot on the bed beside him. I sat down. 'I just wanted to ask you something else,' he said. 'What would you say to my taking this room as a pied-à-terre for when I come up to London? I'd never be here more than three nights a week, but it would be lovely to have a guaranteed bed in London. Somewhere without a pool table. Somewhere with you.'

I started back, surprised.

'Well,' I said, 'that would be lovely. But wouldn't you want somewhere where you could be private? I mean it's fine having you to stay, but if you wanted to bring someone back, er, I mean . . .'

'I don't want to bring anyone back, you old silly,' said David, putting his arm round me. 'There's only one person I want to bring back.'

I looked at him, puzzled. 'Who's that? You're not pining for Sandra, are you?'

David shook his head impatiently. 'No, sweetie. Haven't you caught on by now? All that ringing up? All that looking after the dog? I just wanted to be in touch with you. I even went along with your mad idea of trying to find me a wife, for God's sake! How can I put this? Look,' he said, 'are you sure that lump has really gone away? Don't you think I should give you a second opinion? Or perhaps you've got lumps somewhere else? You never know.'

And he drew me to him and kissed me.

This time I couldn't resist him. Christmas was coming, we'd had a lovely supper, and all the old feelings flooded back.

'Just for old times' sake,' whispered David, as he drew back the bedclothes.

'Just because it's Christmas,' I smiled, feeling rather breathless.

And it *was* just like old times.

In the early morning, we lay just chatting. Finally David stroked my forehead. 'Well I think I can declare you completely cured,' he said sweetly, and kissed me. 'And now there's a turkey to put on. I'll go down and bung it in the oven. You stay here.'

But just then there was a creak on the stairs. We both held our breaths. 'Did you hear that?' I said. 'It's certainly not Father Christmas.'

The creaking continued. And then I smelt a faint whiff of patchouli oil.

'It's Melanie!' I whispered to David. 'Come to spy on us!'

Frozen, we watched as the door seemed to open by itself. No one there. And then there was a miaow and a thump on the bed. Clawing the duvet, there was Pouncer, looking very self-satisfied. He slunk up to us, rubbing his patchouli-smelling head on our cheeks, his fur puffed out in pleasure. Then he started purring and kneading.

'Happy Christmas, darling,' said David.

'Happy Christmas, David,' I said.

Later

And it was.